On a Beautiful Day

Lucy Diamond lives in Bath with her husband and their three children. When she isn't slaving away on a new book (ahem) you can find her on Twitter @LDiamondAuthor or Facebook at www.facebook.com/LucyDiamondAuthor.

What Lucy's fans say . . .

'Wonderful characters and the stories are always great, with twists and turns'
Gemma

'Lucy's books are as snuggly as a blanket, as warm as a cup of tea and as welcoming as family'
Cheryl

'Full of friendship, family and how when life throws something at you, you have to fight back!'
Emily

'A skilful writer with the ability to place herself in anyone's shoes'
Sue

'Lucy's books make me smile, cry and give me happiness, a little bit of escapism from everyday life. Page-turners I just can't put down!'
Mandy

BY THE SAME AUTHOR

Novels

Any Way You Want Me

Over You

Hens Reunited

Sweet Temptation

The Beach Café

Summer With My Sister

Me and Mr Jones

One Night in Italy

The Year of Taking Chances

Summer at Shell Cottage

The Secrets of Happiness

The House of New Beginnings

Novellas

A Baby at the Beach Café

Ebook novellas

Christmas at the Beach Café

Christmas Gifts at the Beach Café

Lucy Diamond

On a BEAUTIFUL DAY

PAN BOOKS

First published 2018 by Macmillan

First published in paperback 2018 by Macmillan

This edition first published 2018 by Pan Books
an imprint of Pan Macmillan
20 New Wharf Road, London N1 9RR
Associated companies throughout the world
www.panmacmillan.com

ISBN 978-1-5098-5106-5

1 3 5 7 9 8 6 4 2

A CIP catalogue record for this book is available from the British Library.

Printed and bound by CPI Group (UK) Ltd, Croydon, CRO 4YY

For all my friends, with love

Chapter One

It was May, soft and warm, all apple blossom and sunshine; one of those days that take you by surprise and remind you that summer might actually be around the corner after a long wet spring, even in Manchester. It was the kind of day when a person's thoughts begin to drift towards the pleasing prospect of painted toenails and bare legs, of half-term on the horizon, of Wimbledon and Pimm's. For India Westwood, it was also a day when she'd left her husband and kids back at home and caught the bus into town for a post-birthday lunch with her three best friends. *Hello!*

God, but she loved birthdays and all their accompanying fuss, even as an adult; still waking up with that childlike fizz of excitement in her belly each time, just as she did when it was Christmas morning or had snowed outside. Any excuse to string some bunting about the kitchen and light candles on a cake, any excuse to get family and friends around the table and line the mantelpiece with colourful cards and flowers. Besides, when you had just turned thirty-nine and there was the big Four-Oh looming in the distance, you might as well wring out every last drop of joy you could, right?

Right. Which was why this was actually her third birthday celebration in as many days. Get her, and her impressive Milking It skills! She'd been treated to a takeaway and presents on Thursday, her actual birthday, followed by dinner and drinks with her husband Dan the evening after, and now, Saturday, she was on her way to lunch with Eve, Laura and Jo, as per their tradition. She'd picked Jean-Paul's as the venue, a new French bistro near the Albert Hall, not least because they were running a bargain lunch menu, which, by India's logic, would leave them more money for cocktails and wine. Genius.

The restaurant was just beginning to fill up when she arrived: clusters of people lingering at the pavement tables with morning coffees, other early lunchers descending upon the larger tables at the back of the main room. India plumped for a seat outside, wanting to make the most of the spring sun, enjoying the feeling that she could be on holiday somewhere glamorous – Paris, Rome, Madrid – as she left her shades on and ordered an espresso and a jug of water.

And relax, she thought, leaning back against the curlicued iron chair and breathing in the mingled scents of the air: the waiter's woody aftershave, a twist of cigarette smoke from the next table, a passing plate of hot salty chips. The combination was undoubtedly more exotic than the smells of home: cat food, unwashed children, something burning under the grill. In her imagination, she transformed accordingly; no longer a mere frazzled wife and mum who spent her days shaking maracas in chilly church halls for the benefit of grizzling babies and their sleep-befogged mothers. Today she was carefree. Sophisticated. Perhaps even a little mysterious.

'Here you go, darling,' said the waiter just then in broad Manc, breaking the spell as he set down her drinks.

'Merci,' she said. 'I mean – ta.' Oh well. She might not be in Paris or Rome, but she did have a free pass for the whole afternoon, she consoled herself. Plus she had made an effort and dry-cleaned her favourite black silky blouse with its bold plunging neckline that always made her feel a million dollars; she'd squidged into her nicest and most bum-flattening jeans; and, for once, her flyaway chestnut hair had allowed itself to be tamed into a smooth chin-length bob. Make-up – tick. Perfume – tick. Friends on the way – tick. They'd have a slap-up lunch and an excellent gossip, then she'd suggest a mooch around the shops and go crazy with her credit card, knowing that the other three would all support her wholeheartedly in this decision. To a woman, they were excellent enablers when it came to shopping matters.

Talking of which . . . There was Laura striding across the road right now, regardless of a red Ford Focus that braked sharply, the driver gesturing something rude and cross at the wheel. But Laura, smiling as she saw India, was quite oblivious, her long blonde hair tousling in a breeze, her handbag sliding off one shoulder as she waved. And there too was Eve, coming from the other direction, all high cheekbones and poise with the mix of Ghanaian and Scandinavian in her genes. As ever, she looked neat and crease-free in a white body-con dress, her hair a glossy dark waterfall as she paused to wait at the crossing. Oh, and three out of three – here was Jo as well, stopping to take a call and . . . India pushed up her sunglasses and leaned forward nosily to see better. Whoa. Was down-to-earth, no-nonsense Jo actually giggling and blushing as she chatted into her phone?

Yes, she most certainly was. Jo's round freckled face was suffused with pink and she was putting a hand up to her cheek in a . . . well, there was no other word to describe it – a *flirtatious* way. What was all that about then, eh?

'Hello, hello!' The four of them kissed and embraced, laughing at their simultaneous arrivals, as if they were a well-rehearsed mini-flashmob descending on India.

'Happy birthday!'

'You look gorgeous!'

'What are we drinking?'

Oh, she loved these women with all her heart, India thought fondly, as Eve took charge, asking for menus and the wine list, and Laura flapped around unpeeling a silk scarf and not noticing as it slithered to the floor, and Jo stuffed her phone in her bag, still pink in the cheeks with a – yes, a *secretive* sort of smile, India observed. Curiouser and curiouser.

The four of them had known each other for years now, finding one another through different channels: she and Eve had met at an antenatal yoga group, for instance, forming a bond as they disgraced themselves by sniggering childishly at the woman in front of them, who kept farting through her downward-dog pose. Then Eve had introduced her to Jo, having known her since school, and on another night, Jo had brought along her sister Laura, too. And just like that they became a foursome, an all-conquering group of friends who would drop anything for one another when the chips were down. They'd been a tag-team of support throughout Jo's divorce the previous spring, getting her drunk, helping her find a new flat, dragging her out shopping – whatever it had taken. They had lived through the pain and misery of Laura's miscarriages with her as well, holding her hand, bringing her cake, comforting her as best they could through the agony. And Eve had always been a total rock when it came to scooping up India's kids whenever there was some A&E crisis or other. It was good to know that someone had your back in your hour of need. Three someones, in fact.

But they were there for good times as well as the bad, that was the loveliest thing – for birthdays, of course, but also every month for gossip and wine at someone's house.

And here they were now, making India feel loved and special: ordering champagne, complimenting her on her blouse, pressing beautifully wrapped gifts on her. *Yes*, she thought, feeling a rush of contentment as she decided on the mustard chicken and skinny chips and eyed up the delights of the dessert menu further down the page. Come to Mama. This was more like it. Friends and sunshine and a generously filled bread basket; the smell of chips and perfume; the clink of bracelets at her wrist – oh, it was heavenly, it really was. ('I fully intend to be drunk and incapable of anything later,' she had warned Dan, her husband, prior to leaving the house, to which he'd rolled his eyes and replied, deadpan, 'You surprise me.')

'So,' she said now, helping herself to a chunk of crusty baguette and slathering it with salted butter. 'Down to business. Jo Nicholls – I think you should know that I spotted you giggling coyly into your phone just now. Is there something you want to tell us?'

Jo looked startled, then turned bright red. 'Well . . .' she said sheepishly, at which they all pounced.

'*What?*' cried Laura, choking on a breadcrumb in her surprise.

'I knew it!' exclaimed India, clapping her hands together.

Eve put down her butter knife and leaned forward. 'We're all ears,' she said.

*

Jo hadn't known whether or not she should say anything about Rick to the others yet. It had been such a whirlwind, after all, meeting him in the very last place she'd ever expected to find a new man – in the grubby, damp-smelling waiting area at her local garage, while her car was undergoing its MOT. There he had been, too, wincing as he sipped from a plastic cup, his tall frame folded into one of the uncomfortable red plastic chairs, glancing up at her from his phone. 'If you value your life,' he'd said conspiratorially, 'I advise you not to try the coffee.'

Jo had been in an exuberant sort of mood that day, having just heard from her solicitor that the buyers of the Stretford house were finally ready to exchange contracts. Not just that, but her hair had serendipitously fallen into perfect coppery waves after her morning shower, and she'd squeezed into an old denim skirt that had previously been too small for her for at least four years. She had smiled at the man – Rick! – and sashayed across to the coffee machine regardless, joking, 'Hey, I've always been one to live on the edge.'

Listen to yourself, Nicholls, she'd scoffed inwardly as the machine went about noisily spurting brown liquid into a plastic cup. Living on the edge indeed, when in reality she was far too cautious a person to go *near* the edge usually. But there was something about his face – his open, friendly, extremely good-looking face, with that gorgeous flop of dark hair – that made her want to present a better version of herself in return. Then, of course, she'd tasted the disgusting coffee and promptly spluttered on its bitter, nasty taste. 'Christ,' she'd yelped and they'd both laughed.

'I did say . . .' he reminded her, his brown eyes amused.

'You did,' she agreed, wincing, 'and that'll teach me to ignore perfectly good advice at my peril.'

He'd grinned at her in reply, and then they'd just got chatting about this and that, and it had all been remarkably easy and enjoyable. Added to that, he was so handsome and interesting that she'd soon started to feel a bit breathless. Was it her imagination or was there some kind of . . . spark between them? An undercurrent?

A giddy feeling took hold of her; she was giggling at his funny stories in a seriously un-Jo-like manner, high-pitched and girlish. Was it a bit naff of her to be acting like a teenager with a whopping great crush, when she was forty-two years old, divorced and plucking out her first grey hairs? Oh, who cared, though; this was fun. Knowing her luck, he was probably gay anyway. Plus – real-life klaxon – he was way out of her league!

A few minutes later, a blue-overalled mechanic stuck his balding head around the doorway. 'Mr Silver? Your car's ready.'

Jo had given the handsome stranger a rueful smile as he

got up and went to the door. So that was that, she'd thought, surprised at how disappointed she felt.

But then something extraordinary had happened. The sort of thing that never usually happened to Jo. Instead of walking through the door and vanishing from her life forever, the man had hesitated there, one hand on the jamb, a distant din of clanging and engine noises behind him. Then he turned back. 'Look, no worries if you're with someone or married, or whatever,' he said. 'But . . . er . . . would you like to meet up again some other time?'

There had been the merest hint of vulnerability in his body language, an unexpected shyness all of a sudden, and she'd felt it then, true and clear, deep inside her: I *like* this man. Not only that, but *I like this man and I think he's asking me out. Asking. ME. Out!*

Feeling flustered, absurdly flattered and wildly excited, she had tried very hard to contain herself. 'That would be lovely,' she managed to say, and then her lips twitched. 'Although, to be honest, after such fabulous surroundings – ' she flung out an arm to indicate the dismal little seating area, the rancid coffees, now cold and abandoned in their plastic cups, the scuff marks on the walls – 'anywhere else could be a hard act to follow.'

'This is true,' he said, nodding sagely. 'We've set the bar pretty high today. I'll have to go all out to impress you after this, won't I? Pull out all the stops.'

'Every last one,' she agreed. 'Quite a challenge, frankly.' Check me out, *flirting*, she thought, hysteria bubbling up inside her. Who *is* this bold, brave Jo?

'Mr Silver?' repeated the slack-jawed mechanic impatiently, scratching his neck in the manner of someone who didn't have time to waste indulging waiting-room romances. 'Your car?'

Ignoring the interruption, Rick quirked an eyebrow at her. 'Challenge accepted,' he said, then grinned, his eyes all shiny and soft. Goodness, he was lovely. Surely too lovely for Jo. 'Let's be wildly extravagant,' he said and passed her a business card. 'Coffee sometime next week? A proper one, in an actual mug, that doesn't taste like a small animal has died in it?'

'You know how to treat a girl,' she said, dimpling. *Girl, indeed*, she thought, with an inward snort. She pocketed the card, trying to look cool about the fact that his fingers had just brushed against hers. Mmmm. Nice strong man-fingers. Phwooar. 'Thanks. I'll call you.'

God, but it was *fun*, having a man say *Let's be wildly extravagant,* even if he was joking and only referring to coffee. Greg, Jo's ex-husband, had been the sort of person who would ring up the gas board to enquire about an extra two pounds on the bill; who would sit in a restaurant seething about the over-priced wine list, and drink water all night to prove a point. 'I just like things to be fair,' he would say, as he kept tally of who owed what for rounds in a pub. Being fair was one thing, but being stingy was quite another, in Jo's opinion.

And so she and Rick had met at Moose for coffee that Saturday, and despite being a bag of nerves about seeing him again – would he regret his impulsive suggestion, would he realize how plain and ordinary she was and make excuses to get away, were her jeans too tight and muttony? – the conversation had barely let up for a second. He ran his own PR agency and almost made her cry from laughing at tales of his latest client who designed and produced outfits for dogs, and who sounded both eccentric and a complete pain in the neck. 'That's ruff,' Jo had joked. 'I hope she hasn't been hounding you.'

'Barking up the wrong tree, usually,' he replied, and his smile was so infectious that she'd found herself becoming positively melty inside. Gooey, even. And then he suggested ordering some American pancakes to share, and they bonded over the joys of streaky bacon and maple syrup and . . . Oh, it was all good, basically. It was really, really good. She could feel herself not *falling* for him exactly, but certainly teetering in a hopeful, excited sort of a way.

A week later they'd gone out for dinner (Italian, her favourite – and his too, as it turned out), and then the week after that they'd met for really good cocktails in The Alchemist, followed by quite a lot of X-rated kissing, before reluctantly getting separate cabs home. *I like him*, she kept thinking, smiling in a dreamy sort of way whenever he crossed her mind (approximately nine million times a day). *I really, really like him. But surely there's a catch? There's always a catch. Surely this is all going too well to be true?*

And then, last night, she'd discovered the catch. That catch had come slamming up against her and knocked her sideways.

They'd gone to a Mexican restaurant in Spinningfields with a resident mariachi band that wandered around and singing to the customers, and they were drinking tequilas and having such a good time that, even though Jo kept sternly telling herself, *Remember Greg; don't get carried away*, she was starting to think that this could really be it – Rick might very well be the one, her happy ever after. Daringly she'd also been thinking that yes, if asked, she would go back to his place afterwards and make things official, so to speak. (Full disclosure: she was wearing her nicest satiny knickers especially, *and* a matching bra, and had rubbed scented body lotion all over herself after showering earlier. She was, it had to be said, kind of terrified at the prospect of stripping off in front of a new man, but she had a feeling, given his excellent kissing abilities, that it might just be amazing.) What the hell, she'd thought recklessly, smiling at him over the table as he applauded the mariachi band with gusto, hands above his head. She *would* live on the edge for once, she *would* go with her instincts and throw caution to the wind.

But then . . .

'Jo? Are you deliberately keeping us in suspense, or what? Tell us more!' cried India at that moment. She had never been very patient when it came to important gossip and the speed with which it was forthcoming.

Jo snapped out of her reverie. 'Sorry. Um . . . Yeah. So I've been seeing someone,' she said, her face flaming as the others made high-pitched *Ooh* noises and instantly leaned closer, a circle telescoping in on itself. She pushed away her doubts – don't worry about it, she told herself for the hundredth time, it'll be fine – and gave them the lowdown. 'He's called Rick, he's forty-four, divorced but sane, and . . .' Her cheeks burned even hotter but she couldn't resist a smirk. 'What can I say, he's sexy as hell.'

'Go, Jo!' cheered Eve. 'You dark horse, you.'

'Whoa. Since when?' squealed Laura. 'I can't believe this. Tell us everything! And show us photos!'

'Amen, sister!' cried India, putting a hand up for Jo to high-five. 'This is brilliant news!'

Until then, Jo had been so thrilled by her own good fortune that she'd felt superstitious about confiding in anyone else, for fear of breaking the spell. But now she found herself desperate to share everything with her friends, and the joy came bubbling right on out of her. 'I *know*,' she giggled.

'I am one smitten kitten' – which, even as she said it, she knew was completely ridiculous, because, being awkwardly tall with sturdy thighs and a bushy mane of red hair, she had never remotely thought of herself in kitten terms. Her own mother had once described her as 'solidly built' in the way that you'd speak of a bungalow or a kitchen extension. And yet, with Rick she felt feminine and frivolous and slinky. Remarkably kittenish, now that she thought about it. Me*ow*!

'Just *look* at you,' India said approvingly, eyeing her from head to toe and taking in the French Connection asymmetric black dress (bought for her cocktails date) and the red lipstick (an impulse payday purchase, just because). 'You look *fabulous,* like you've had a ton of sex. You lucky cow.'

'I can hardly remember what that feels like,' Eve sighed, but then she was smiling across the table. 'You do look radiant. So is it serious, do you think? Are we talking the big L here?'

'And when are we going to *meet* him?' Laura put in before Jo could reply. 'God! Talk about secretive. I can't believe you've been keeping this to yourself. How mean!' She was huffing out her lower lip, pretending to be indignant, but Jo could tell Laura was a tiny bit aggrieved for real. It had always been her and her sister against the world while they were growing up, and they were still close.

'I didn't want to jinx anything,' Jo replied. 'Remember Handsome Harry?'

Oh, they all remembered Handsome Harry: Jo's first date since her divorce, courtesy of a matchmaking app, and it had gone so well. So brilliantly well, in fact, that she'd texted all her friends the next morning saying: *Oh my GOD! I'm in love! He's amazing! Think I just met my Mr Right* – only to never hear a single word again from Handsome Harry. Nothing. 'You've been ghosted, my friend,' Jo's colleague Alison had informed her.

The waitress arrived with their starters just then and the memory of Handsome Harry hung around the table with them for a few moments like a bad smell. 'Anyway, it's early days,' Jo said firmly, remembering how the alarm bell had started ringing in her head the night before. How she'd gone home feeling confused and thinking: maybe this isn't going to work out after all. She'd spent the whole night tossing and turning and changing her mind about what to do. Because who, having gone through a divorce, wanted to get hurt again, if they could avoid it? Not her. No, thanks. But then Rick had rung her twenty minutes ago, and had been so charming and apologetic and funny that she'd wavered again. 'I'm . . . I don't know. Maybe it's too soon. Maybe I'm not ready yet.'

'Too soon? It's been – what? – a year since you and Greg split up,' Laura reminded her. 'I think you're allowed to have a bit of fun after a year. You *are* ready, you're just being a wuss.'

'Sometimes you have to take a deep breath and go for it,' India agreed.

'Sounds to me like the pros definitely outweigh any cons,' said Eve, who was an accountant and couldn't help calculating balance accounts, when it came to emotional situations as well as financial ones.

Jo twirled her fork through the rocket leaves on her plate as she listened to them, one after another, being her personal cheerleaders: Team Jo all the way. They were probably right. She was out of practice when it came to dating, that was all, and last night's unexpected ending was . . . well, she'd just have to deal with it. 'Thanks, guys,' she said, then decided to direct the limelight elsewhere. 'Anyway, enough about me. How's everyone else? Eve? What's the latest with you?'

Eve smiled brightly as the attention turned her way. Brightly but not sincerely, because she had been dreading this question. You could fool some people – her husband, her kids, her boss – that you were absolutely fine, by carrying on as normal, being your same old competent, organized self, but her best friends were less easy to beguile. They were the ones who'd look into her eyes and know; who'd see in an instant that, actually, she was not fine at all. Actually she was freaking out and didn't know what to do.

It had been there for three weeks now, a hard lump, the size of a pea in her right breast. Her fingers kept returning to its solid wrongness, prodding and poking, as if her touch might somehow erase it, as if she didn't quite believe it was real. But it was real. And it was still there. And even though she had been telling herself that it was probably nothing, just a lump, some kind of cyst, harmless, loads of people got them, there was also this other voice in her head which kept whispering that she was going to die, and that Grace and Sophie would be left motherless, two small figures in black coats weeping over her grave.

This was not a topic for India's birthday lunch, though. No way would Eve bring down the mood with her secret worries, when India looked so cheerful, and Jo seemed positively dazzled by this new man. Added to which, Eve didn't want to be confronted with their concerned faces staring back at her if she confessed her fears, either. India, an emotional sort, would probably burst into shocked tears. Laura would be upset too and would want to know every detail, her blue eyes shining with anxiety. As for Jo, well, she was a nurse and so would be chivvying Eve to get herself checked out, offering to go with her to an appointment, not letting up until Eve was sitting there opposite a doctor and being given a diagnosis. They would fuss, basically. They would fuss and be on her case, it would be impossible to tuck her secret back in the box again. And Eve just wasn't sure she could handle any of that. Not yet.

Burying her head in the sand, on the other hand – that seemed way simpler an option.

The irony was that normally Eve prided herself on being in control. If one of the girls was falling behind at school, she'd be straight in to talk to a teacher, finding out what could be done. If her casework piled up in the office, she would stay late to tackle the backlog or plough through it on the kitchen table after dinner, methodical and focused. If there was a problem at home – a leaking tap, a missing roof tile, a blown light bulb – she would know about it, and either deal with the matter herself (she was pretty handy with a screwdriver or drill) or call in assistance from a professional. And yet this time, when her own body had done something it shouldn't have, she was holding back in terms of immediate action. She was dithering and prevaricating, pretending the problem wasn't there.

Her friends were looking at her expectantly, she realized with a gulp, anticipating no doubt her usual sort of reply – an amusing story about the kids, or news from work about an annoying client – and she licked her lips, trying to formulate a valid response. She never did get to speak, though. Because all of a sudden there came a tremendous commotion from behind them and then, as she spun round in alarm, it was as if the world had sped up before her eyes.

A blue car seemed to have lost control on the road, veering wildly across its lane, engine roaring. Other cars hooted in alarm, passers-by yelled and leapt out of the way. 'Bloody hell!' cried Laura. In the next second, the blue car came swerving in the direction of the café – straight towards them – and shouts of panic arose, glasses toppling over as people jumped up. 'Shit!' yelped India, scrambling back off her chair.

Eve felt frozen to her seat, unable to move, staring in horror. The car was going to hit them. It was coming right at them. She could see the whites of the driver's eyes, one hand clutching at his chest, his mouth opened in an agonized shout. He couldn't stop. *He couldn't stop!*

Then she blinked and the car lurched back away, zigzagging drunkenly across the road, before mounting the pavement and crashing into the flower shop opposite. The noise was incredible, like something from a film but worse, louder, the air vibrating with the boom-crash of impact, the shatter of glass ripping through the atmosphere.

'Oh my God,' gulped Laura, swaying dazedly on her feet, eyes huge with shock. Jo, meanwhile, was already pelting towards the scene, shoes slapping across the tarmac. 'Ambulance, please,' India gabbled urgently into her phone, the colour draining from her face. 'There's been an accident.'

Across the road, the car's front had crumpled, as if a giant fist had punched it. A man in a City football shirt wrenched at the driver's door to pull him out. 'He's having a heart attack. Somebody help me!' he yelled before two women ran over, arms pumping with urgency. Buckets of flowers lay tipped sideways on the ground in front of the shop, water puddling around them. Traffic was backing up around the crash, there was a woman crying somewhere and high-pitched voices . . .

Eve swallowed, blood throbbing in her ears. She could see Jo crouching beside a woman on the ground, other people hurrying to help. Everyone seemed to have reacted except her. *So much for survival instinct*, she thought shakily, trying to catch her breath. She had sat there in the face of danger, and done . . . absolutely nothing.

I'm alive, her pounding heart told her. I'm okay. But what about the driver and everyone else?

Chapter Two

'Will I be able to walk again, do you think?' the woman asked, her voice so faint that Jo had to lean in to hear. 'Only I can't feel anything below my pelvis, you see, and I've got horses. Two horses, and they're my life. I'll die if I can't ride them again.'

Jo had found herself amidst a scene of carnage. At a first glance, the blue car had hit at least three people before smashing through the shopfront; there were shards of glass and metal strewn about liberally, and the sales assistant from the florist's was sobbing hysterically nearby. Further down the pavement, she could see someone giving chest compressions to the driver, who lay unmoving. *A heart attack rather than a deliberate attack then*, she thought with a shudder, *but horrific nonetheless*.

'Can you tell me your name? I'm Jo, I'm a nurse – the paramedics will be on their way,' she said, taking the woman's hand and finding her pulse. There were flowers scattered around her on the wet pavement, the clashing scents of roses and lilies and hot metal in the air. Blood, too. You could smell the iron tang of blood.

'Star and Chestnut, they're called. They're everything to me,' the woman said desperately. She was wearing a smart fawn-coloured dress and silver earrings, her tights ripped to shreds where her legs had been crushed. There was a nasty graze on her temple and two stray marguerite petals in her hair. 'I'm Miriam,' she added belatedly. 'Miriam Kerwin.' And then her mouth buckled, and tears glistened in her very blue eyes. 'Oh dear. You'd better tell Bill, I suppose. He's going to be so worried. Will you ring him for me? Will you tell Bill?'

'Yes,' Jo promised, holding Miriam's hand as the wail of an ambulance sounded in the distance. 'I'll tell him.'

'Please – on the house,' said the manager of the restaurant, a tray of brandies on one arm, his eyes darting to the scene of the accident, where paramedics were stretchering people into ambulances. 'We are the lucky ones, *non*? Lucky, but a little shocked, I think.'

Lucky? None of them felt at all lucky. India was in tears, Eve was pale and quiet, dazedly asking for the bill, and Jo had returned from the crash site with a smear of blood across her cheek, shaking her head when Laura asked if she was okay. Laura, for her part, felt stunned. For a horrible moment she'd thought the car was going to plough straight into them and she'd been screaming, scrambling to get out of her seat, her adrenalin jagging through the roof. *And I never got to have a baby,* she'd thought, her life flashing before her eyes, before the car had swerved away again and she'd been left swaying there in shock, breath heaving in her lungs. *Oh my God. Oh my God. Oh my God.*

'I just want to go home and hug Dan and the kids,' India said with a sob in her voice, sniffling and dabbing her eyes with a napkin. 'I feel terrible for moaning about that oven glove he bought me for my birthday now. Terrible. When there are people who might be dying – when we just s-s-saw . . .' Her words petered out.

'I know what you mean,' Eve said dully. 'Neil and I had a row this morning about stacking knives in the dishwasher . . .' Her lower lip trembled and she wrapped her arms around herself. 'Seems kind of pointless, all of a sudden.'

Jo had returned from the bathroom, her face clean once more, and Laura fought the urge to rush over and cling to her, as she'd done as a small child whenever their mum had gone off on one. 'You all right?' she asked instead, remembering that Jo probably felt worse than any of them. 'That must have been grim.'

Her sister was holding a small white business card with a bloody fingerprint on the back. 'I've got to make a phone call,' she said miserably. 'And tell some poor bloke that his wife . . . Well, she's almost certainly lost the use of her legs.'

She grabbed a brandy from the manager's tray as he went by. 'Thank you. I'm going to need this.'

Once they'd paid the bill and said goodbye, hugging each other for a second longer than was usual, the four of them went their separate ways, each with a heavy tread. Laura felt wired, her nerves jangled, as if she'd stayed up all night. Again and again the car careered towards them, in her mind's eye; again and again she screamed and leapt to her feet. You thought you were invincible, you thought you had all the time in the world until something like this happened, shaking up your world as if it were a snow-globe.

And I never got to have a baby, the voice kept saying in her head with such devastating clarity. *I never got to have a baby.*

'Is that Bill Kerwin?' Jo had found a quiet shady spot near the town hall and was sitting on a stone wall, brandy and adrenalin still spiking through her. 'My name's Jo Nicholls, I'm a nurse and I've just . . .' She swallowed. 'I'm afraid I've got some bad news for you.'

Christ, Jo found herself thinking as she outlined to Miriam's husband what had happened, she had forgotten how you came up against it with emergency medicine. How brutal it could be, the intensely charged dramas involved – and how safe and straightforward it was for her these days, in comparison, working as a practice nurse: carrying out cervical smears, changing wound dressings, taking blood or giving injections, checking urine samples. You went in and did your job, helping patients in a routine sort of way, but you never had to tell a poor, stunned man down the phone that his wife had been badly injured and that life, as they knew it, was suddenly over.

His voice was thick when he eventually replied; gruff, as if emotion had got the better of him. 'Thank you,' he said. 'I'll go there at once.' And then his voice cracked a little and he added, 'She's the love of my life, you know. It's only ever been her, for me.'

Jo's hand shook on the phone. Despite all her training and experience, sometimes a patient just got to you and it was impossible to remain detached. 'I'm so sorry,' she said, helplessly.

'I forgot to tell her that I love her, before she went out,' he said, sounding upset. 'I forgot to say it.'

'You can tell her at the hospital,' Jo soothed. 'I'm sure she knows you love her, don't worry.'

'I . . . I'd better go,' he said shakily. 'Thanks for letting me know. Do me a favour, will you? Tell your husband you love him today. Tell him. While you have each other. Will you do that for me?'

'I—' Jo felt slightly lost for words. Now was not really the moment to confess that she was divorced and had only recently started dating again. 'I will,' she assured him instead. 'Take care, Bill. And give Miriam my best.'

Right, then, Eve said to herself, walking away after lunch. Deep breath. Let's get on with the rest of the day.

She had always been good at compartmentalizing, at blocking out any troublesome worries in order to concentrate on something more compelling. Whenever she walked through her office door, it was as if Home Eve was put on standby while Work Eve took over. Some of her colleagues had photos of their children on their desks and indulged in long daily conversations with their childminders or even the school-age children themselves – 'Having a nice morning? How was your music lesson?' – but Eve privately found such behaviour faintly pathetic. She loved her children – obviously! – but there was a time and a place for family, and the workplace was neither.

So. She would put the roadside drama into a box too, seal it off, maybe come back to it later on, much later, when she could process how she had felt. When she could ponder at greater length exactly why she had reacted – or, rather, not reacted – in the way that she had. Why her survival instincts had failed to materialize, as if there was some disconnect in her reflexes.

But anyway, onwards! Time to reset the afternoon and

get on with the current list of tasks earmarked for attention today. A new towel for the bathroom. The length of gingham Grace needed for her Textiles project at school. A bunch of flowers for her neighbour's birthday. Lots to do, no time to waste navel-gazing or wallowing. First stop: Debenhams.

She moved briskly through the crowds, swerving to avoid the slow-moving packs of teenage girls, not making eye contact with the buskers, right foot, left foot, keep going, don't think about it. But then, once in the bathroom department at Debenhams, a wave of shock suddenly caught up with her, flooding her system with anxiety so that her knees wobbled violently and she had to clutch onto the shelf of folded Egyptian cotton towels for support. Her heart pounded, adrenalin crashed through her, and then she caught sight of her face in a row of mirrored cabinets nearby, and realized in horror that tears were leaking down her cheeks and that she was weeping soundlessly, her mouth open and red.

Oh my God. Was that really her, Eve Taylor, having a breakdown in public? In the *Debenhams bathroom section*? Common sense immediately snapped back in, like a twang of elastic, propelling her off to the Ladies to dry her eyes and splash her face with cold water. Pull yourself together, Eve. For heaven's sake, *pull yourself together!*

The loos smelled of sickly air freshener and Eve held her wrists under the cold tap, vaguely remembering that it was meant to help with shock. Or was it to bring down a high temperature? She couldn't remember any more. Her brain seemed to have its facts jumbled up, displaced from their usual neatly filed and collated system. All she could hear in her head was that screeching of brakes, the grinding of metal. The driver's face kept flashing up before her eyes, his terrified expression as the vehicle had lunged straight towards them . . .

'Are you okay, love?' asked a woman in a red hijab who was at the next sink along. Her brown eyes were kind as she gazed at Eve's blotchy face. 'Can I help at all?'

'I'm—' Eve's breathing had become tight and strained; she had to grip hold of the basin and stare down at the rushing water for a moment. Was this what a panic attack felt like? Why couldn't she breathe normally? 'I'm fine,' she said eventually and not entirely convincingly. 'Thank you,' she added, so that the other woman wouldn't ask any further questions.

She *was* fine, she told herself savagely. She hadn't been injured, had she? No. So why was she making such a silly fuss, why was she overreacting like this? In bloody Debenhams, of all places?

The woman was still looking at her sideways with an expression of concern and Eve couldn't handle it any more. She turned abruptly, shaking her hands dry, and darted into the nearest cubicle, bolting the door and leaning against the cool tiles, her heart still pounding: boom, boom, boom.

It's okay. You're okay. Keep breathing, she told herself desperately, closing her eyes. Just keep breathing.

Sitting on the bus, India found she was shivering and put her arms around herself. Hurry up, she thought, as the traffic lights ahead changed to red and they wheezed to a halt. Hurry *up*. All she wanted to do was to get home, to throw her arms around Dan and the children, to immerse herself in the comfort of their warm bodies, to smell her kids' necks and count her blessings. Shut out the rest of the world. There was nothing like coming up close and personal to blood and trauma to make a person want to dig down deeper into their own burrow.

When the car had come hurtling towards her and her friends like that, and she'd felt for a terrifying split second that she might actually die, she'd thought, No, not like this. Not on my own, leaving Dan and the kids behind!

Except . . . She shivered again, even though the bus was stuffy. Except that wasn't quite the truth, was it? If she was being strictly honest about the order of things, her family hadn't been her first thought at all. No. Because in that moment when the driver had lost control and the car had roared in their direction, her whole body had trembled as if anticipating retribution, as if this was Judgement Day. As if she'd been waiting for something like this to happen for years. And the first thing that had flashed through her head? *I knew I wouldn't get away with it forever.*

Chapter Three

Walking back to her small rented flat in Hulme, Jo found herself wishing that, like her friends, she had someone waiting for her at home too, someone who would hold her close and exclaim, *Oh God, how awful, are you okay? That must have been shocking.*

Just someone to make her feel less alone. Who would listen while she talked.

She'd been living on her own since her marriage had broken down, first in their old house in Stretford before she and her ex decided to sell up, and more recently in her own place, but she still hadn't quite got used to the silence of an empty flat when you walked through the door. Sure, she'd learned how to fill up her time, she'd come to know the TV listings backwards and burned through many evenings watching what her ex-husband had always scathingly termed 'brainless TV', but there was, most definitely, a whiff of sadness about her new place. The way the sofa sagged at one end where she sat and ate biscuits from the packet every night. The hush of the bedroom when she turned the light out and rolled over in bed. She had been lonely there, far lonelier than she liked to admit.

Until she'd met Rick, of course, and it had been like opening a dark curtain and letting sunshine pour into her life again. Only . . . Well, where did they stand now, after what had happened last night? What was she meant to think?

She frowned, feeling her head sink as she trudged along. There they'd been at the restaurant table, her with her satin knickers and perfumed skin beneath her clothes, and seconds after the waitress had whisked away their starter plates (garlic prawns, delicious, although she was already worrying about her breath and all the snogging she hoped to do), Rick's phone had rung. 'Sorry, I'd better take this, I won't be long,' he promised. But Jo only needed to hear half the conversation – 'What, now? We're in the middle of dinner . . . Well, I'm with a friend . . . No, not Bobby . . . No, it's not Dave, either. Look, that's not the point, have you tried the neighbours?' – to get a sinking feeling. And then, when he hung up and said, 'I'm really sorry about this, but that was my daughter Maisie and – well, to cut a long story short, she's on her way here now because . . .' His expression changed from apology to exasperation. 'Because she's locked out of the house and my ex-wife . . . Oh, you don't want to know.' He sighed, then reached over and took her hand. 'I'm sorry. Maisie's thirteen and she's been a bit all over the place since the divorce. I can't really say no to her at the moment.'

The daughter that he couldn't say no to. The words reverberated in her head warningly and she felt her skin prickle, the first red flag of disquiet. *There's always a catch,* she heard her mum's cynical voice sigh. *Bloody men, they're all the same, and I should know, I've tried enough of them.*

To be fair, when you reached your forties, everyone had baggage, everyone had their past dragging around behind them like a ball and chain. In Jo's case, it was a bad marriage and the fearful conviction that she was destined to be a spinster for evermore. In Rick's case, the baggage was apparently an unreliable ex-wife and a needy teenage daughter. Oh, he'd given them fleeting mentions before now – she knew they were there in the background – but it was quite a gear-change, from them being shadowy abstract concepts to coming face-to-face with the reality. In this case, his thirteen-year-old daughter, who turned up halfway through the main course, all flicky eyeliner and long hair and scowls for Jo; who waited until Rick was trying to catch the waiter's eye, before giving her the finger. All of a sudden, Jo was feeling quite a lot less confident about the situation, especially when Maisie went on to talk repeatedly, and in glowing terms, about her mother, Rick's ex.

Hey, Dad, did Mum tell you about that amazing party she went to? It was after the opening night of Manchester Fashion

Week, and loads of famous people were there. The goody bag was SO cool.

Did you hear Mum on the radio the other day? Yeah, Woman's Hour *– they were interviewing her about her book. She was trending on Twitter for, like, two hours afterwards.*

Did Mum say: she's going to take me and her to New York over the summer? I can't wait!

How to intimidate your dad's new girlfriend in three easy steps; Jo had sat there feeling frumpier and duller by the second, as The Other Woman became real, inked in, a threat. *She'd* never been to New York, or on the radio, or invited to an after-show party, after all. *What's he doing with you?* a mean voice kept asking inside her head, while her jaw ached from maintaining a fixed polite smile. And then, when dinner was over and it was clear that Rick, telegraphing apologies with his eyes, would be going home with Maisie, rather than Jo and her best knickers, she had felt embarrassed and self-conscious about kissing him with his daughter standing there, rolling her eyes and making vomit noises in the background. All in all, it had been a major passion-destroyer. Back in her quiet flat, doubt had pierced her heart for the first time since meeting him, and she'd wondered if her instincts had been wrong all along.

It was tricky stuff, trying to negotiate the dating world in your forties, frankly, especially when you felt you didn't really know the rules any more. Should you hold back and protect your heart, or throw yourself in with abandon and take a chance? She thought of poor shaken-up Bill, rushing across town to see his wife, and how he'd urged Jo, 'Tell your husband you love him'. Life could change in an instant, couldn't it? The world could knock you sideways from out of nowhere. And here she was now, on her own again, heading back to her lonely, empty flat, while all her friends hurried home to their loved ones. Was that really what she wanted?

Twenty minutes later, Jo was just walking rather despondently towards her front door when her phone rang. When she pulled it from her bag and saw Rick's name onscreen, she found herself giving a little sob of relief, her emotions brimming to the surface again. 'Hello,' she said, turning the key in the lock and shouldering the door open.

'Hi – oh, thank God,' he said, and she could hear the breath rushing out of him as if it had been stoppered up until that second. 'I've just seen the news. Are you okay? Wasn't that crash, like, about fifty yards from where you were having lunch?'

A spark flared inside her at once, a warm glow kindling at the concern in his voice. Rick sounded so *worried* for her. He had seen the news and thought immediately about her well-being, and had actually said 'thank God' at the sound of her voice. Hadn't she just been wishing for someone to care about her as well? She *loved* that he'd asked. 'I'm fine,' she said, kicking off her shoes and wandering through to the kitchen, 'but yes, we were just on the other side of the road. It was pretty awful to be honest. Oh no!'

'What?'

Crossing the floor towards the kettle, she'd walked through a large puddle on the chipped laminate floor and now her tights were full of water. 'Shit, there's been some kind of . . .' Water was pooling out from the bottom of the freezer, she noticed, and she yanked open the door to see that her food in there – the sad single-lady stuff of leftover curries in Tupperware containers and massive special-offer tubs of ice cream bought on sod-it days – was all gently thawing, drips of water collecting on the bottoms of the drawers. 'Oh, bollocks. Either the freezer has died or . . .' She flicked at the light switch – on, off, on, off – but nothing happened. 'Damn it, there's been a power cut. Can I call you back?'

'Sure.' He hesitated for a second. 'Or I can come over, if you . . . ?'

'I'm fine,' she said quickly because this was the new Jo, who was resolute in coping without a man and his toolbox and advice. 'I'll ring you back in five. Sorry about this.' She ended the call before she could change her mind and prodded what had once been a frozen chicken breast. From its spongy texture now, though, she estimated that the power had been lost hours ago, certainly too late to save this particular dinner from the dustbin. Great. As if she hadn't had enough drama for one day.

Letting out a groan, she went in search of the fusebox. It was only *groceries,* she reminded herself, thinking back to Miriam's white, anxious face and trying to get some perspective. She could do this.

Because Greg, Jo's ex, had been a handyman – and something of a male throwback in terms of feminism – she had never been trusted with any DIY jobs around the house throughout their marriage. Even when she'd picked up a paint tray and roller one weekend when he'd been off at a stag do, and painted their bedroom as a surprise, he'd come back and immediately gone over her work with a new brush, shaking his head at her wobbly lines and uneven coverage. If she ever went to change a bulb, he'd laugh and say, *Step aside, princess, this is man's work,* and pluck the light bulb from her hands as if her delicate princess brain couldn't possibly cope with the responsibility. It had been a bit of a joke at first – she would roll her eyes and call him a sexist pig – but gradually she came to realize that he actually meant it. He genuinely thought that way. And it hadn't been good for either of them.

Luckily she wasn't married to Greg any more – and was perfectly competent herself, moreover, able to do all those little jobs denied to her for so many years. She had rewired a plug a few weeks ago. She could pump her bike tyres, without him watching beady-eyed and telling her she was doing it wrong – *give it here, let me*. She had changed light bulbs, and set the timer on the cooker, and hung up all her own pictures. So a piddly little power cut – although inconvenient and frozen-curry-destroying – was not about to set her back now.

Unfortunately, when she eventually located the fusebox and googled what to do on her phone, she could see that the fuse hadn't tripped after all. In fact, everything looked as if it should be working just fine. She glanced at her phone, weakening for a second as she thought about calling Rick and asking him to come and help, but then – no – back came her resolve, and instead she called the electricity company to find out if there was a problem in the street that might explain her own power loss.

'Did you not see the red bill? And the final warning? I'm afraid you've been cut off, darling,' the woman from the helpline told her, when she eventually got through.

'Cut off? But . . .' Jo's mouth dropped open before she could finish her sentence. There must be some mistake. Her rent at the flat included the bills – gas, electricity, council tax, water: the lot. The landlord, Dennis, was meant to take care of such services, not allow them to be severed unexpectedly. 'But . . . I'm not the bill-payer. My landlord must have fallen behind . . .' She could hear her own voice petering out in dismay. What did the helpline-woman care?

'I'm sorry, love, but the account's in arrears and we can't switch the electricity back on again until we've received full payment,' came the response. Sorry, but not sorry, in other words – and actually, fair enough, Jo thought wearily, when she was told the amount that was owing, a sum of money that left her feeling faint. 'If you speak to him, get him to contact us urgently about payment, otherwise we'll have to take further steps.'

Oh, great. Did this mean that her gas supply might be in similar peril? she wondered, despair welling as she hung up and searched for her landlord's number. The next thing she knew, someone from the council would be banging on the door because the council tax hadn't been paid, and then the water would be cut off and all, and she'd drop dead from dehydration. Probably.

Surprise, surprise, her landlord wasn't answering his phone and her call went straight through to voicemail. 'Dennis,' she said firmly, 'this is Jo Nicholls, from Harold Street. My electricity has been cut off because the bill hasn't been paid. Please could you settle the account as soon as possible, as this is really inconvenient to me. Thank you.'

She sank into a chair, feeling thoroughly fed up, before remembering the puddle on her floor and getting up again to find the mop. Bloody hell, this was the last thing she needed. She'd have to go and stay with Laura, she supposed, or – last resort – camp out in her mum's spare room. But Jo was really trying not to lean on Laura quite so much these days, and she wasn't sure she had the energy to endure an evening spent listening to the latest lurid instalment of her mum's soap-opera life. Or, worse, being dragged out on the pull with her. *Us single ladies have to stick together!* Not a good idea. Was there anything more demoralizing than going out with your own mum and discovering that she was apparently way more of a catch than you?

Just at that moment, her phone rang again and it was Rick, wondering what had happened to her – at which point she found herself telling him the whole dismal story.

'You could pay the bill yourself, and get the money back off the landlord in lieu of rent,' he pointed out when she'd finished.

'I did wonder about that, but . . . well, it's quite a lot,' she had to say, feeling embarrassed at her own budgetary constraints. Until the sale of her old marital home was completed – a matter of weeks now, she hoped – things were pretty tight on the financial front, a situation that hadn't been helped recently with all the impulse spending she'd done: lipsticks and perfume and that new dress, not to mention their nights out together.

'Okay, so why don't you pack a bag and come and stay at

mine for a few days, just until this landlord of yours pulls his finger out and gets everything sorted?' he suggested next.

Jo shut her eyes, not trusting herself to speak for a moment, because she really did not want to be the sort of woman who always needed to be rescued by a man. Plus there was that whole awkward daughter thing now, too. 'Well . . .' she said, then hesitated because despite all that, she'd had a tough day that had left her feeling vulnerable and she did actually quite want to be with someone tonight, to be held and comforted. Experienced as she was at dealing with a trauma situation, she was not a complete robot.

'Are you still there?' he asked, sounding confused. 'No worries if you've got other plans, it was just a thought.' He laughed. 'You *can* say no, Jo, I'll take it on the chin, honestly. I'll live!'

There – so he didn't think she was incapable, she assured herself. He thought she might have other plans anyway and be too busy to come over. And wasn't this what being a couple was all about, looking after each other when things went wrong? She found herself thinking of Bill Kerwin again, imagining him at his wife's side in an A&E cubicle by now, holding her hand on the crisp white hospital sheets. Not all couples were doomed. 'That would be great, if you're sure,' she said meekly. She had tears in her eyes for some stupid reason; perhaps this was the shock catching up with her at last. 'Thanks, Rick.'

She blew her nose, then went to her bedroom to pack a few things, where she made the mistake of glancing over at an old photograph of her mum. Helen Nicholls in her prime: great legs in a pea-green mini-dress, that huge mane of fox-coloured hair around her face, sharp eyes pinning you to the spot. *Don't say I didn't warn you,* Jo heard her admonish. *Staying for a few days at his place, when you've been having doubts? Talk about out of the frying pan and into the fire!*

Chapter Four

'Aaaaand . . . are we ready? Miiissss Polly had a dolly who was SICK, SICK, SICK . . .'

It was Monday morning and India was leading from the front, a maraca in each hand. This was what she did: chief musician in her very own orchestra. Or, rather, she ran the Mini Music: Happy Tunes for Happy Children franchise for south Manchester, and hosted baby and toddler classes in various draughty church halls four days a week. This, needless to say, had never been part of the career plan. This had not been what teenage India had envisaged all those years ago when she'd had a provisional letter of acceptance from the Royal College of Music. That was life for you, though, wasn't it? Life and its nasty little habit of lobbing you a curve ball just when you weren't expecting it.

'She called for the doctor to come QUICK, QUICK, QUICK!' Beam and sing, beam and sing: that was the mantra that circled around her head sometimes, as she worked through her repertoire. 'Throw yourself into it,'

Lisa had advised when she'd handed over the franchise to India. 'It's all about the energy and enthusiasm. Big smiles and joyful faces mean big cheques and rebooked places!'

'The doctor ca-ame with her BAG and her HAT . . .' Yes, India *had* changed the gender of the doctor, and what of it? Why not start the girl-empowerment right here, when they were eight months old? Sometimes it was only by amusing herself with such small acts of rebellion that she managed to stop herself from stabbing the maracas into her own eye sockets. 'And she kno-ocked on the door with a RAT-A-TAT-TAT!'

Someone in the room had silently filled their nappy. Perhaps it was India's over-enthusiastic knocking on the floor that had startled them into a bowel movement, although, let's face it, dreadful smells and loud farts were invariably an occupational hazard of this line of work. She would open a window just as soon as this song finished, perhaps make a joke about it. A polite sort of joke, obviously. ('Do not, under any circumstances, offend the parents,' Lisa had warned, back in the day. She was blonde and perky, with frosted eyeshadow and energetic hand movements. 'I know you wouldn't, but – we've got to make *them* feel great too, yeah? This is all about enrichment, fun and joy!')

These words had echoed grimly around India's head for the four years she'd been running the classes. It had seemed like a good idea back when Kit, her youngest, was two and

Lisa announced she was going back to her old job in HR, and thus the business was up for grabs. 'India, you're musical,' she'd said, dimpling at her at the end of a session. 'Ever thought about a new career?'

It had been like the universe laughing at her, right there. As if Lisa knew about India's past. Oh, ha-ha. Let's kick a woman while she's down.

Sleep-deprived and – yes, okay, judge her for it – just a tiny bit bored of being a full-time mum, India had been flattered by Lisa's comment, though. An exhausted mother of three, you had to take a compliment whenever you could get it, frankly. And maybe this was a chance to put her crap business degree into practice, the business degree she'd ended up taking when she mucked up her A-levels in spectacular style and didn't make it to her prestigious music college.

Besides, if ever there was a means of atonement for mistakes made, then this was it, she had realized. See how nice I am to the babies, see how hard I smile at them despite their crusty noses and foul-smelling nappies, see how I can get those toddlers doing the actions to 'Wind the Bobbin Up' with such charming exuberance that their parents are all beaming with pride. I'm sorry, Universe, okay? This is me, abasing myself and taking my punishment. Am I forgiven yet?

'I'll be ba-ack in the morning, yes, I WILL, WILL,

WILL!' India clapped her hands and smiled round at her class. 'Well done, everyone, what a lot of super singing! And, just like the dolly's doctor, *I'll* be back too, same time, same place next week. But now it's time to put all our instruments back in the box, please. Thanks for coming!'

Driving home after her last class of the day, tambourines clinking in the boot as she went over each speed bump, India realized that she was humming 'Five Little Ducks' under her breath and rolled her eyes at her own ridiculous self.

I think you've got something special, Miss Nolan, her A-level music teacher, had once said to her. Miss Nolan who had a permanent cold and who crunched blackcurrant-scented cough sweets through every lesson. Her eyes had been so earnest and hopeful that gauche teenage India had felt embarrassed, unsure what to do with the compliment other than shuffle her feet around. *I mean it, India, I think you're the real deal.*

So much for that. If Miss Nolan could see her now, she'd probably have a good old laugh at what had become of her former star pupil, India thought glumly. Either that or give up making doomed predictions for evermore.

She switched on the radio to banish the irritatingly stupid five little ducks from her head, cursing as a bus pulled out in front of her with a stinking belch of exhaust fumes.

'The time is coming up to three o'clock, let's have the local news,' said a young male voice, and India drummed her fingers on the steering wheel, glancing at the clock and hoping she wouldn't be stuck behind the bus for too long. She first had to make it home, find somewhere to park (not one of her skills) and then dash breathlessly along to the school in order to pick up her younger two children. Esme, who was nine and drifted through life in a sparkly day-dream, never seemed to care what time her mother arrived, but Kit, who was six, liked to see her waiting in the play-ground for him the very instant that school was over, taking it as a personal affront if she was even a minute late. (George, her eldest, was eleven and no longer wanted to be seen on the same bit of pavement as her, electing instead to make his own way home. 'You are too embarrassing,' he had informed her, devastatingly.)

'Police have released further details following the crash that took place in the city centre on Saturday,' said the news-reader, and India felt herself stiffen. She'd avoided watching the news all weekend, not wanting to see footage or hear updates, and she was about to turn the radio off again when she saw a chance to overtake the bus, which she did, rashly and too fast.

'Two of the injured pedestrians remain in hospital, as well as the driver of the vehicle, who is thought to have suf-fered a heart attack at the wheel. Police have named the pedestrians as Miriam Kerwin, fifty-seven, from Didsbury, and twenty-year-old Alice Goldsm—'

India gasped out loud, swerving inadvertently towards an oncoming Fiat, before pulling over at the kerb and putting a hand up to her mouth. Oh my God. Her heart was pounding.

'Meanwhile, the driver, sixty-two-year-old Sandy MacAllister, remains in a critical condition,' the newsreader went on, and India jabbed at the button with shaking fingers to silence him. Her blood seemed to be throbbing in her veins. *No,* she told herself. *No, India. Don't be silly.*

The bus sailed past her once more but she barely noticed, one hand up on her chest as her breath came, fast and shallow. It was only when she realized it was five past three, and she really, *really* needed to get a move on, that she started the engine and numbly pulled out once more.

Meanwhile, across town, Laura was not exactly having a productive time at work. In the morning she had stared at a blank screen for a full twenty-five minutes, willing the press release about Glow Wonder Night Serum to write itself. Being the communications manager for a beauty-products company seemed kind of trivial today. What is the point? she kept thinking, swinging to and fro on her swivel chair as she searched fruitlessly for inspiration. What is the point of this?

Ever since Saturday, and the horrific metal-grinding car crash, she had been asking herself this question a lot. Deliberating over which fabric conditioner to buy in the supermarket, putting on mascara in the morning, sitting through interminably long production meetings at work . . . why was she bothering with any of it? Why did anyone care about these ridiculous things, when there were people still in hospital after Saturday's accident, when Death could come at you from out of nowhere? Life was *short*, she kept thinking, it was really, really short, and time could pass you by when you were looking the other way. Look at her working in this place, for instance – five years she'd been at BodyWorks now: five whole years. That had never been part of her life-plan. Sure, it wasn't terrible; the location was great – two minutes from Market Street – and her colleagues were mostly lovely, but sometimes she couldn't help feeling that the beauty industry was all just a tiny bit too . . . well, shallow, basically. Frivolous. Spending her days thinking up campaigns that encouraged people to waste money on products that barely made any difference was hardly the pinnacle of achievement for mankind; not exactly up there with pioneering scientific breakthroughs or saving people's lives. Was this *really* what she wanted to be doing, when there were so many other possibilities out there?

Heaving a sigh, she stared back at her computer. Meanwhile, here in the real world, there was still an empty screen in front of her, a patiently winking cursor and no press release.

Glow Wonder is . . . she typed, then paused, hands on the keyboard, her creativity seemingly having taken an early lunch break. She found herself remembering how, back when she'd originally applied for this job, she'd had to submit a test press release for a new hand cream as part of the selection process. Trying to help, Matt had spent a whole evening brainstorming with her, although his main contribution had been the completely unsexy suggestion 'It's kind of . . . *gooey*?' They had roared with laughter at the sheer crapness of the sentence, at how hilariously inapt it would be within a press release and, since then, it had become one of their in-jokes, frequently wheeled out to describe a dodgy cheese soufflé, an ancient tube of glue, a mawkish Christmas card from his mum.

Kind of gooey, she typed now, for her own amusement, before backspacing through the letters again. It had been a while since she and Matt had laughed like that, admittedly. He'd come back late and steaming drunk from the football on Saturday (happy drunk – United had won in extra time and his throat was hoarse from singing), and then they'd been at his parents' house for Sunday lunch, after which he'd slumped on the sofa and nodded off until it was time to go home.

Staring at the screen again, she felt a wave of boredom

break over her. The thing was, back when she'd accepted this job, she'd secretly assumed she'd only be there a year before getting pregnant and swanning off on maternity leave. But twelve months had slipped by, and then another twelve months, and she'd started to feel trapped, as if she couldn't leave. What if she handed in her notice and *then* got pregnant? What if she started a new job and *then* got pregnant? The timing would be all wrong. The safest thing, she had decided, was to stick it out here, and keep on trying in the bedroom. And trying. And trying. And . . .

Anyway, she said to herself, forcing a stop to her downward spiral of doom as she noticed her boss, Deborah, approaching. Okay, Glow Wonder Night Cream: time to pull some writing out the bag, and fast. Shallow and frivolous or not, it was Glow Wonder and its stablemates who were paying her wages, after all.

So that was the morning. The afternoon saw Deborah calling the entire company to the boardroom to make a big announcement: that BodyWorks would be bringing out a new line of maternity and baby products, and that the whole team was going to be involved 'pretty much from conception onwards, ha-ha'. As the senior management team elaborated about luxury body lotions for mums-to-be, and a delicate organic range for the newest of new babies' sensitive skin, Laura could feel a creeping agitation start up inside her, a prickling dismay. Oh *Lord*. And she was going to have to write gushing press releases for all of this stuff, wasn't she, wanging on about the beauties of a pregnant belly and the gorgeous smell of a newborn baby's head, while inside she felt like screaming and crying and throwing things around the office. Because that was what happened when, month after month, your own reproductive system refused to cooperate with your wishes. That was the sort of maniac spell it cast upon a woman.

Deborah had broken off, mid-spiel, and was giving her a very odd look. Yikes, thought Laura, she hadn't gone and blurted any of that out loud, had she?

'Laura?' her boss was saying. 'Are you with us?'

'Of course, yes, absolutely, just thinking how wonderful it all sounds,' she cried enthusiastically in response. Ground, come and swallow me right on up, she thought, her cheeks becoming fiery as everyone turned to stare.

She and Matt had been unofficially trying for a baby for almost six years now, originally in a casual, laying-off-the-contraception-and-seeing-what-happens manner, and then more recently with an increasingly serious, charting-ovulation, we-need-to-do-it-TODAY approach. So far she had had three pregnancies – joy, joy! – followed by three agonizing miscarriages, and she was starting to despair that her own body had it in for her. *Ooh, look, pregnant, hormonal – this could be it, this could be happening . . . NAH. Changed my mind. Off to hospital, for a scrape and a cry, you go.*

Three tiny babies who never made it past the ten-week stage, a trinity of tiny snuffed-out infants who hadn't reached the finish line of birth. She carried them with her always, that unborn trio – her *failed pregnancies*, as the medical staff spoke of them – ghostly and far away, their pale infant arms reaching imploringly to her across the divide. *My darlings. My angels.* Although she and Matt had tried their hardest not to dwell on the what-might-have-been, those phantom babies had taken up space between them, moving in silently and reproachfully, to create a division of dead air that it was proving more and more difficult to ignore. *I'm sorry,* he had said each time she ended up in hospital, and he'd held her and soothed her, and they'd cried together, tears wet on one another's shoulders. But however kind he was, however supportive and tender, she could see it in his eyes sometimes, a flash of disappointment – with her and her incompetent uterus, her body's inability to hang on to those poor helpless babies quite long enough.

These days they had stopped talking about the subject altogether. He had asked her to desist from telling him when she was ovulating, because he said it made him feel under pressure, like he was some kind of performing bear. She had reached a grudging stand-off with her body, as it dutifully offered up a period every twenty-eight days, and she had learned to squash down her hopes of a small, warm body in her arms, of Moses baskets and baby vests and travel-system pushchairs, just in case it was her wild, desperate yearning that was actually putting the baby off. (Somehow. Maybe. Look, she wasn't a scientist, all right? But she wouldn't be surprised if such a phenomenon was possible. Wouldn't that be just her luck?)

Tuesday afternoon was Jo's sexual-health drop-in clinic and even though she had so far seen a selection of genital warts and quite the most disgusting discharge in one case of gonorrhoea, she found herself singing 'Oh Happy Day' without a single shred of irony as she threw another pair of latex gloves into the bin. Because it *was* a happy day, despite the grey clouds outside, despite the rashes and crusty bits and weeping sores that would be making up her workload for the next hour and forty-five minutes.

Who would have thought, twelve months ago, when she was on her knees with marriage break-up agony, that she would ever feel like this again? That she would have met someone like Rick, who was so funny and sexy and lovely, who kissed her all over, as if he really liked her too, who brought her coffee in the morning and had the most fantastic flat in a fancy new apartment block right in the centre of town? Who? Nobody – that was who. Least of all Jo herself.

Goodness, though, the last few days had been glorious. The passion! The laughs! The cosiness and cuddling, too; the waking up and not being on her own in bed . . . just that closeness of having another person to go back to after work. How she'd missed it. How she loved it.

She had stayed at Rick's place the whole weekend and still hadn't left. Rushing into things? Whatever. Her landlord remained AWOL, the electricity remained off, and so Rick had shrugged and extended the invitation. 'Stay as long as you like' had been his exact words, and a thrill had surged through her, both at his generosity and at the fact that this bubble of bliss could continue. *And* that he hadn't gone off her, either, having now seen every inch of her naked, freckled body.

'Seriously? That is so kind,' she'd said, stunned. They were in the bath at the time, a deep hot bubbly one, with glasses of wine and candles. (The decadence! The luxury! Jo had almost stopped feeling self-conscious about her wobbly bits, it felt so fabulous.) 'Are you sure? Wait, though . . . Aren't you off to Dublin this week?'

That easy shrug again. 'That's all right. You can stay here while I'm away.' He'd raised an eyebrow at her and, for some reason, it made her pulse race. (The man even had sexy *eyebrows,* would you believe.) 'You can go crazy and water my plants for me, if you feel like it.'

'I will shower them with love and care,' she assured him. 'I might even put your post in a neat little pile for you and everything. No extra charge!'

She smiled now, remembering, whilst trying to ignore

the suspicious voice that kept muttering darkly in her head about this all being too good to be true. Three whole nights they'd spent together now, and it was as if her body had been shocked back into life, reawakened after a long lonely slumber by the things he did to her. Whoa. How unlikely and unexpected to feel like this again, at the age of forty-two, when she'd all but written herself off as spinster material for the rest of her life!

Anyway. Enough sighing and dreaming. It was time to call in her next patient, who would no doubt bring her back down to earth. But just then she heard the sound of her phone ringing in her bag. Whoops, she thought guiltily, because she must have forgotten to turn it to silent. In the next second she thought, *I hope it's him.*

It was a local number, but not one that came up as a contact. 'Hello?'

'Hello, love, it's Bill here. Bill Kerwin. I hope you don't mind, I saved your number on my phone.'

Bill Kerwin? It took her a moment to place him – oh gosh, the husband of the woman who'd been hit by the car. 'Bill, hello, are you okay?' she asked in surprise. 'How's Miriam?'

There was a pause. A sort of gulping noise down the line. 'She's . . .' he began, and then stopped. 'She's got to have a double below-the-knee amputation,' he said, his voice cracking.

'Oh, Bill. I'm so sorry. Poor Miriam.'

'I know. She's . . . she's devastated.' The pain in his voice was enough to break your heart, even a hardened old seen-it-all-before nurse like Jo.

'That's really tough. I'm so sorry,' she said again. And then, even though she had a waiting room full of warty, pus-oozing patients outside and shouldn't really be taking private calls in work-time, she found herself asking gently, 'And how about you? I know this sort of thing is hard on the whole family. Do you have support? Do you have people around to help you?'

'Well . . .' His pause said it all. 'I'm struggling a bit, to be honest with you, love. I'm . . . not doing all that well, truth be told.'

Jo guessed this was a massive understatement. She'd met men like Bill before, who relied on their wives for everything and completely fell apart when they had to cope alone. With one eye on the clock – she really had to get a move on – she hesitated before asking, 'Can I help at all? I might be able to put you in touch with some organizations that could be useful, or you could ask the nurses at the hospital for—'

'Well – no, I'll be all right,' he said although his voice lacked conviction. 'I'd better go. I just wanted to tell someone, that's all. I'll be fine. I'll be all right. It's her who needs looking after, not me.'

'Okay, Bill, but if you change your mind . . .'

'I've got to go. Thanks anyway.'

'Give her my best,' she said, just as he hung up. The screen went blank on her phone and she turned down the ringtone, before stuffing it back in her bag. Poor guy. You couldn't look after everyone; there wasn't space in a nurse's head to carry every single patient with you, but there was just something about Bill and his wife that had got to her. It happened sometimes. Maybe she was just going soft in her old age.

Pulling herself together, she went back to the waiting room, professional smile in place. 'Michael Pettifer?'

Chapter Five

Tuesday night was the one evening of the week when India actually peeled herself away from the sofa and TV in order to venture out for some self-improving Pilates with Laura. They'd been going together as a result of a muffin-top-reducing New Year resolution eighteen months ago, although, if she was honest, the bit that India looked forward to most was after the class had actually finished, when they could slope off to the pub and have a drink. It was all about balance, right?

Here she was now, abdominals tight – or as tight as they would ever be, amidst the jelly of her belly, anyway – her right arm pointing up towards the ceiling before moving it out and over to the left, as guided by the calm, slow voice of Jan, the class instructor, who had the tranquil air of a woman at ease with the world. (There was no way Jan would ever sink to the depths of screaming like a harridan at children who were squabbling over whose turn it was to claim the free sticker in the cereal packet, for example.)

'Feel the mermaid stretch,' urged Jan in her soothing Radio 4 tones, and India found herself thinking of the mermaid Barbie, once beloved by her daughter Esme, all pointy boobs and hair, with that dead-behind-the-eyes expression. India had tried her hardest to steer her daughter towards scientific toys, great books, musical instruments – anything vaguely improving, basically – but Esme was resolute. Unicorns, Barbies, make-up and sparkles all the way. Whatever, thought India, tugging surreptitiously at her too-tight waistband in a decidedly un-sirenlike manner now. (She always felt faintly self-conscious throughout Pilates, imagining a race of Martians seeing this room full of prone, heavily breathing women in leisure gear draped in strange positions on mats, and wondering what the hell was going on.)

'Very nice, ladies,' said Jan. 'Well done. Let's go into our relaxation now, before we end the session. Lie flat on your backs and close your eyes, allowing your thoughts to float away. Be aware of your breath filling in your lungs, your chest rising and falling – that's it, gentle and slow, the weight of your body sinking right down into the mat . . .'

I am calm and relaxed, India told herself. My breath is filling my lungs, my thoughts are floating away . . .

Oh, it was no use. Her thoughts were mutinously refusing to float anywhere, and her breath alone was not enough to hold her attention. In fact she was starting to feel guilty about her easy carefree breathing when, following Saturday's horrific crash, poor Alice Goldsmith was still in an induced coma, Miriam Kerwin had lost both her legs, and it had been on the news earlier that Sandy MacAllister, the driver of the car, had died, never having regained consciousness. India had been between classes when she heard this, wiping down the chewed handles of the mini-shakers and squirting a scented plume of Glade around the room, the radio burbling in the background. 'Oh *no,*' she'd sighed, dropping the can of air freshener with a clatter. Sixty-two years old and hoping to retire at Christmas, according to his widow. He'd been working overtime that Saturday, as they'd just celebrated the birth of their first grandchild and he and his wife Patsy had been saving up for the little one. There was a clip of Patsy speaking, after the news was announced, saying, 'We're all in pieces', her voice catching on the words. 'He was the loveliest man. He'd do anything for anyone.'

God, it was awful, it really was. India had been obsessing over the story ever since she'd heard the headlines on the radio the day before, reading everything she could on the local news websites, particularly about Alice Goldsmith. 'Only twenty years old, it's so tragic, isn't it?' she'd sighed to Dan last night when they were getting ready for bed. 'According to *Look North*, she was just home from uni for her parents' anniversary that weekend.' To her embarrassment, she'd found herself sniffing, like one of the kids when they were trying not to cry. 'I can't stop thinking about her.'

'Come on, love,' Dan had said, ever the practical one. He was a plumber and liked being able to fix things, including her, his wife. 'I know it's sad, but it was a one-in-a-million thing, and you've got to put it behind you now. Move on.'

'Yes, but . . .' Move on, he said, like it was that easy. How could she explain in a way that he would understand? She had never told him her darkest secret, and she certainly wasn't about to start hauling it out now. *Well, you see,* she imagined herself saying, *I'm not the person you think I am. Did I not mention what happened when I was eighteen?*

She shuddered, and he patted her arm comfortingly. 'Survivor's guilt, that's what they call it,' he informed her, padding through to the bathroom to brush his teeth. He'd assigned himself the role of Comforter in their relationship, while she was permanently stuck in Worrier mode. Kids ill in the night? India's imagination leapt straight to meningitis, septicaemia, a dash to A&E, while Dan's first thought would be one of cynicism: that they were putting in an early bid for a day off school. When Kit had been the last in his class to read, India had immediately begun exploring the possibilities of dyslexia, learning difficulties, some crucial thing she must have done wrong during the pregnancy – while Dan had put it down to their son being 'a lazy sod'. Even when his job was in jeopardy the year before, and India was doing her best not to panic about them falling behind on mortgage payments and terrifying herself with visions of bailiffs pounding on their door, he'd been able to assure her that 'something would come up'. Nine times out of ten, he was right (irritatingly), and she would have fretted through sleepless nights for nothing.

'It's perfectly natural to take on that kind of guilt when you've witnessed an accident,' Dan told her in his oh-so-rational way as they got into bed. 'But what happened wasn't your fault, was it?'

Lying there in the darkness, he'd pulled her into his arms and she lay listening to the slow, measured tick of his heart, feeling his solid comforting bulk against her. ('He reminds me of that actor,' her mum had said after meeting Dan for the first time all those years ago. 'What, George Clooney?' India had joked. 'No, that podgy one,' her mum had replied, rather less flatteringly. 'I can't think of his name, now. You know, local fella, goggly eyes, always looks confused.' This was not exactly a description anyone wanted to hear about their beloved, but never mind.)

'India!'

Her eyes flicked open in surprise, to see that the rest of the Pilates class were getting to their feet, stretching and rolling up their mats. Laura was standing over her, mat already tucked under one arm. 'Wakey-wakey,' she said, poking her in the ribs with a bare toe.

India blinked before struggling into a sitting position. Usually by the end of the cool-down she was fidgeting and ready to go, with an itch on her ankle or the pressing need for the loo. Today she hadn't even been aware the class had finished. 'I was miles away,' she confessed.

'I could tell.' Laura waited for her to get up, then they walked over to the side of the church hall together where everyone had left their belongings.

India shoved her feet into her trainers and bent to tie the laces, her thoughts already skipping ahead to getting home: George would be back from cricket club and no doubt loftily delivering a ball-by-ball forensic analysis of the entire hour. Esme, meanwhile, had almost certainly seized the chance to sneak up to India's dressing table and rifle through her make-up bag. And Kit would be lying like an adorable starfish, his duvet already dangling half off the bed, rosebud lips sighing out each slumbering breath. Oh, and of course the pots from dinner would still be festering unwashed in the sink, at a guess, and the shamefully high tower of ironing would be looming like a cliff-face, where she hadn't been able to face it over the weekend . . . Compared to women like Eve, who managed to do all of this *and* hold down a proper job *and* never seemed to need anyone else's help with emergency childcare, India sometimes felt as if she wasn't all that good at motherhood. Or life, come to that.

'Fancy a quick half and a bowl of chips?' she asked hopefully.

'Thought you'd never ask,' Laura replied.

Eve's final appointment of the day on Thursday afternoon was with a new client, one Lewis Mulligan. 'Okay, so let's start with your expenses,' she told him, briskly opening up his file onscreen. 'Have you brought your receipts with you?'

The man sitting across from her – scruffy, tracksuited, unshaven – raked a hand through his shaggy red hair before thrusting it into a pocket and pulling out a handful of crumpled pieces of paper. 'Sure did,' he said proudly, leaning down to retrieve the ones that floated off the desk like pale butterflies. She could see scribbled figures on some of them, the ink smudged where they'd become damp.

'Right,' said Eve, struggling to mask her disapproval. This was her very worst kind of client: disorganized and unbothered, running a small business like it was some kind of hobby. *No*, she always wanted to reprimand these ones. *This is serious. These scraps of paper are important. You are answerable to the tax office and you need to be professional. Do you really not see that?*

But of course she never said these things, because untangling other people's untidy paperwork was merely part of an accountant's lot. So she took a deep breath and steepled her fingers together, as he dumped a second fistful of screwed-up papers onto the first.

'And are these in any kind of . . . order?' she asked politely. 'Is there a system?'

He looked blankly down at the heap of paper and then back up at her. He was in his twenties, she guessed – Scottish, affable, easy-going. 'Nope,' he replied, somewhat predictably.

Nope. What a surprise. 'Okay, so why don't we start sorting through them between us,' she suggested. 'We can group them together – say if you have expenses for marketing, or advertising—'

'Nope,' he said again, albeit with good cheer. 'Not a penny. All word-of-mouth, that's me.'

Impressive. Or, rather, it would have been, if the profits for his personal-trainer-cum-boot-camp-instructor-cum-mindfulness business weren't pitifully low. 'Okay, so expenses for travel, then, or if you've had to rent premises, or buy equipment . . . ?'

'What about,' he said, 'if I rented a place for a wee mindfulness retreat for, like, ten people, but then eight of them wanted their money back?'

Oh dear. He was more hopeless than she'd thought. 'Is that what happened?' she asked.

'Aye, because we got there and the woman who was meant to be cooking for us took ill with bronchitis, and so I had a wee bash and made my veggie chilli, but some people were a bit – you know – arsey about it and complained, and . . .'

Eve had heard enough. 'Let's just go through what you've got here, and deal with that when we come to it,' she said firmly.

An hour or so later they had dragged their way through his accounts, an experience that Eve was in no hurry to repeat. Judging by the wan expression on Lewis's face, he hadn't enjoyed it much, either, seeming all too glad to make his escape.

'Hopeless,' sighed Eve to her colleague Allan after the door had swung shut behind her exasperating client. 'Honestly, where do you start? Too busy being mindful to mind his bloody accounts, if you ask me. No idea whatsoever. What is wrong with these people?'

'Er . . .' said Allan awkwardly, and Eve turned to see that Lewis had reappeared in the office behind her, having forgotten his jacket.

'Oh,' she said in embarrassment. Had he heard her being so scathing? Almost certainly yes, judging by the way he held up a stiff hand before leaving once more. Now who was the unprofessional one? she thought, a rictus smile in place.

'Whoops,' said Allan mildly, and Eve's face flamed hot. She never usually messed up like that. In fact, she'd once overheard some of her colleagues describe her as a robot behind her back – 'Calculating! Calculating!' they'd said in mean android voices, although she had tried not to care. What was so wrong with setting yourself high standards anyway? Nothing, that was what.

All the same, her high standards seemed to have faltered a little this week. On Tuesday she'd somehow muddled up two tax returns and sent them to the wrong clients, resulting in furious emails from them both and a concerned intervention from her boss, Frances.

'Everything okay?' Frances had asked, unable to conceal her surprise. Eve didn't make mistakes. Ever.

'Fine, fine,' Eve had replied, unable to meet her eye. 'It won't happen again.'

She meant it too – get a grip, Eve, come on! – but then yesterday it had been her day off, and she'd completely overlooked the fact that she'd promised to go in to Sophie's class and listen to some of the slower readers. Mrs Marlowe from the school office had rung to find out if there was some problem: 'Only it's not like you to let us down, Mrs Taylor!'

Gosh, that brought her up short. It had been a very long time since she'd been accused of letting *anyone* down. Apart from those clients whose tax returns she'd mucked up, she supposed with a swirl of guilt. What was going on with her? Why had she turned into such a flake, all of a sudden?

It was the randomness of the crash on Saturday – that

was what had rattled her, she thought, swinging away from Allan's gaze in order to save her work onscreen and tidy her desk. The fact that, despite a person's best attempts to keep their world in order, sometimes that world refused point-blank to comply with their wishes. Lightning struck at will, storms uprooted mighty trees, earthquakes shook the ground beneath your feet. A lump could appear in your own body, a strange malfunctioning cluster of cells that refused to melt away, no matter how you tried to wish it gone. And a man could have a heart attack at the wheel of his car, inadvertently bringing bloodshed and trauma to a pavement just metres from Eve herself. What was the point of making lists and compiling spreadsheets, she was starting to wonder, when something like that could just *happen* anyway, like it or not?

She switched off her computer, pushed her chair under her desk and buttoned her navy-blue cardigan. Forgetfulness, insulting clients, weeping in department stores: were these symptoms of cancer too, or merely the onset of some dreadful mental degeneration? Maybe she should draw up a new spreadsheet to chart her imminent decline, she thought bitterly.

Allan was still eyeing her in a speculative sort of way. He was a lumbering Liverpudlian whose suits always looked a size too tight, with a deep growly voice like a bear. 'You all right there, Eve?' he asked, raising a bushy dark eyebrow.

God! Why did everyone keep *asking* her that? Eve had always had an excellent poker face, she was good at covering up her feelings, keeping her cool. When you grew up with a father like hers, who would punch the wall or throw his plate across the room for no apparent reason, you learned to put a lid on your emotions and sit tight. And yet recently it was as if everyone else could see the vulnerabilities locked away deep inside her. *Is everything okay? Is there some kind of problem? Are you all right?*

'Yes, absolutely,' she snapped, more curtly than she intended. Then she felt bad at his surprised face, because Allan had always been a kind, calm soul in the office, and she seemed to remember some grapevine rumour about his wife being seriously ill. 'I mean – yes. Thank you,' she added. She slung her bag over her shoulder and turned for the door. 'See you tomorrow.'

Right, then, she said to herself once in the car, clicking her seatbelt into its slot. Now to drive home and pick up the family reins again. To snap back into normal, competent Eve mode. The lamb tagine had been in the slow-cooker all day and should be fragrant, rich and meltingly soft by now. It was a Thursday, so Grace would be late home after band practice, while Sophie needed picking up from gym club. Oh, and she must ask Grace how her history exam had gone, and remind her to get that science homework completed.

The sky was flinty, a light drizzle speckling the windscreen and, as Eve left the office car park and drove past the cemetery, her checklist continued to scroll through her mind. She should give her mum a ring, they hadn't spoken in a couple of days; oh, and she'd promised to sort through some of the girls' old clothes for a charity collection at Sophie's school, hadn't she? And . . .

Wait a minute. She frowned as her thoughts juddered to a halt, then went spooling into reverse. She *had* switched on the slow-cooker that morning, hadn't she? She could remember briskly cutting the lamb into pieces, measuring out the spices and water, chopping the aubergine and . . . Indicating left as she approached the junction, she tried to recall if she'd actually flicked on the switch at the wall, once the ingredients had all been added. She could picture it: the white socket, the plug in place, but when it came to visualizing her finger on the switch, her memory blanked. Oh Christ. Had she really forgotten? Could she have been so stupid? Would she arrive home to find the meat still raw, and starting to taint, no doubt, where it had been left at room temperature all day?

THUMP. *Crunch*. 'What the hell? Jesus!' yelled a voice, and in a single shocked heartbeat, Eve was wrenched away from her kitchen and back to the real world where – oh *shit* – a cyclist was sprawled on the pavement to her left, his bike clattering beside him. Oh my God. She hadn't been concentrating. She hadn't been looking. She had been thinking about lamb tagine and a socket switch and she must have swung round the left turn without noticing the cyclist, who was now . . .

Panting in horror, almost crying with shock, she thumped at her hazard lights and lunged for the handbrake, spilling out of her driver's door and almost being hit by another car in the process, speeding around the turn. BEEEEP. 'Bloody idiot!' the driver yelled at her.

'I'm sorry!' she cried wretchedly, running round to the cyclist, who was gingerly sitting up and unclipping his helmet in order to rub his head. 'Oh God, I am *so* sorry,' she began, and then her heart almost went into arrest as she realized that . . .

'Lewis?' she gulped, and he scowled up at her. Of all the people. *Kill me now*, she thought.

'We meet again,' he said sourly. 'Do you do this to all your clients, or just the really "hopeless" ones, eh?'

Her face flamed. So he *had* heard. 'Are you okay?' she asked, mortified. 'I am really, really sorry. I didn't see you. I just—' She put a hand up to her mouth, trembling all over. 'Should I call an ambulance? I'll pay for your bike. I'm just . . . I can't believe I did that. God. I am so *sorry*.'

'Aye, right,' he said crossly, inspecting his elbow, which had scarlet blood leaking from it, as wet and glossy as paint. 'So you keep saying.' Then he glowered up at her. 'Have you not *heard* of cycle lanes or something? Because the way you were driving, you didn't seem to have seen one before.'

Eve hung her head in shame, her breath tight and painful in her chest, knowing that she deserved every bit of his sarcasm and anger. Blood dripped messily from the ripped skin of his arm, leaving splotches on the pavement; angry red splashes that danced before her eyes when she looked away. *She* had done that to him. She, Eve Taylor, the most careful driver in Manchester, who had never got so much as a parking fine or a speeding ticket before, let alone injured another person, causing them to bleed onto paving stones so vividly. It was a horrible echo of the accident on Saturday, she thought, only she wasn't having a heart attack and losing control at the wheel. What even *was* her excuse? *Oh, I was thinking about a lamb tagine actually.* It was ludicrous. *She* was ludicrous!

Another car blared its horn, bundling around the corner too fast and almost slamming straight into the back of Eve's Golf which she'd left skew-whiff, sticking out in the road.

'You should probably move that,' Lewis commented. He was still sitting down on the pavement and tentatively shook one leg out, then the other. There was a hole in one knee of his jogging bottoms, and Eve had to suppress a mad accountancy instinct to remind him that he could put a new pair on expenses. *Not the time, Eve.* Besides which, if anyone should be buying new trousers for him, it was her. 'Your wee car,' he prompted when she didn't reply. There was a sneer in his voice as he looked up at her. 'Don't want to cause any more accidents now, do we?'

She swallowed hard, trying to get a grip on herself. *More accidents,* like this was a habit of hers. 'Yes,' she said faintly, but didn't seem able to move. *I have just been involved in an accident,* she thought, in a daze. *I have knocked this man off his bike. I could have killed him. And I didn't even notice he was there.* The front wheel of his bike was bent and buckled where she'd driven right over it, and bile rose in her throat as she realized it could have been his arm or leg, breaking beneath the weight of the vehicle, his bones snapping like twigs.

'Are you . . . Are you all right? Should I take you to A&E?' she asked tentatively. 'Do you think anything's broken?' She tried to summon up the first-aid training she'd done when Grace was tiny, back when she still thought she could protect her family from everything. Head injuries – that was what she should be worrying about. 'Um, did you hit your head?'

'I'm okay,' he said, grimacing as he pulled a lump of gravel from his elbow. 'Few bumps and bruises, but nothing broken. Well, apart from the bike.' He bent over to inspect it.

'I'll pay for another one,' she said at once. 'And let me give you a lift to wherever you were going. Please. It's the least I can do. I can probably fit your bike in the back of my car, if I fold the seats down.' She rubbed her arms, feeling shivery even though it was early evening and still warm, despite the drizzle. 'And we should swap numbers and all that – sort out how much I owe you. Will you . . .' A terrible new thought struck her and she bowed her head in penitence. 'Will you want to report this to the police? I guess we probably should.'

'To the police? Don't be daft. There's no need for that. They've got better things to do and . . .' He softened a little, seemingly noticing her distress. 'Look, there's no real harm done, eh? It was an accident. You don't seem like the sort of person who goes round shoving cyclists off the road out of some – I dunno – mad vendetta or grudge.'

'I'm not,' she agreed gladly. 'I don't. I really don't.' She twisted her fingers together, feeling utterly wretched. 'Thank you,' she added. 'You're being very kind. I'm not sure I deserve—'

Yet another car beeped them and flashed its lights as it came round the corner, and Lewis put up his hand in apology. 'Sorry, mate,' he called. 'We're just going.' Then, with a certain amount of stiffness – was he more hurt than he was letting on? she wondered – he took hold of the bike. 'Come on,' he said. 'We should get out of the way at least.'

Her hands trembled as she opened the boot and they manoeuvred the bike inside the car. Then they both clambered into the front seats and she took a deep breath as she slid the key back in the ignition. Right, then. Try again – and this time, *focus*. Concentrate. Do not think about lamb tagines or how you nearly just killed someone.

Breathing hard, she indicated to move back into the road, checking her mirrors several times over before setting off. 'Where am I taking you then?' she asked.

'I was on my way to my girlfriend's house near Gorse Hill,' he replied. 'If that's okay.' His legs looked long and lanky, crunched up as they were in the small front seats, and there were blood spatters on his mustard-coloured T-shirt.

'Of course,' she said humbly.

They drove the rest of the way in silence. He was simultaneously texting someone and giving her intermittent directions, and Eve felt too wrung out to think up any other kind of conversation, the moment of impact still looping ceaselessly in her head. This was the sort of thing that happened to other people, not her. India, for example, a self-confessed terrible driver, who thought nothing of jumping out of her car in a supermarket car park and asking a complete stranger to reverse it into a space for her. (Eve had felt an appalled sort of awe when this story had been cheerfully related over lunch the other day. You had to applaud India for her shamelessness sometimes.) Or Janie, one of the PAs at work, who was so ditzy that she was permanently losing things – files, data, her phone. *She* was the sort of person who knocked into innocent cyclists. Not Eve.

As they arrived at the house, thankfully with no further mishaps, Eve killed the engine and dug out a business card. 'My phone number and email address are on there,' she said shakily, passing it to Lewis once they'd clambered out of the car. 'I can cover the cost of repairing your bike, or get a new one if it's a write-off. And if your T-shirt needs dry-cleaning, I can pay for that too. And some new jogging bottoms.'

He was already heaving his bike out of the back, grunting a little with the exertion. 'Okay, thanks, I'll be in touch,' he said, slotting the card in his back pocket.

She could see a woman with raven-black hair peering out of the window expectantly – his girlfriend, presumably – and felt a prickle of embarrassment that she'd ended up in this predicament, with a client, no less. All of a sudden she felt the burning need to explain herself, to make him understand that this – this behaviour – was not her. Not at all. 'Listen, I'm really sorry about . . . about everything,' she blurted out. 'It's because . . . well, I found a lump,' she heard herself say. 'I'm just scared. And a bit all over the place. And . . .' She cringed, wanting to stop, but the words kept on tumbling out. 'And nobody else knows, not even my husband.'

It was written all over his face then, a new wariness – oh Christ, mad emotional woman: run away, run away – and she wished she'd kept her mouth shut. 'Right,' he said uncertainly, hesitating on the pavement.

'But anyway,' she went on in an over-bright sort of way,

shutting the boot with a too-loud slam. 'I'm really sorry, is what I'm trying to say. Have a good evening. And let me know about the bike, won't you?' She scuttled round to her door and got inside the car before he felt obliged to reply. Poor bloody sod. First she insulted him behind his back, then she nearly drove over him, then she started burdening him with her problems. *Get a grip, Eve. You are behaving like a total basket case.*

Mortified, she drove away, just remembering to pick up Sophie en route, before returning home, where an aromatic and perfectly cooked lamb tagine awaited their return. Of course it did.

Chapter Six

'Is this yours: "Miriam Kerwin"?'

Rick was kneeling on the bedroom floor, packing for his Dublin trip, and Jo looked across to see him holding up a small white business card that she must have dropped.

'Miriam – oh yes,' she said, before returning to the business of make-up removal at the mirror. Rick had such beautifully crisp white bed linen that she felt obliged to be absolutely scrupulous when it came to this job, for fear of smearing mascara all over his pillowcases. (Needless to say, she was much sluttier when it came to her own ancient bedding.) 'She's the woman who was hurt in the crash – she asked me to ring her husband.'

'Ash Grove,' Rick said, reading the address on the card and quirking an eyebrow. 'That's a coincidence; it's where I used to live, in Didsbury.' He corrected himself quickly. 'Well, they're still there, of course. Polly and Maisie. Anyway – here.'

'Thanks,' said Jo, tucking it in her make-up bag. 'Small

world,' she added, trying to sound nonchalant, although really she was imagining the big Didsbury family house he'd once called home and the quiet leafy avenues of his former neighbourhood. Did he miss that sense of community and belonging, now that he lived up here in the luxurious hush of his executive apartment block? she wondered. Did he think back to that suburban way of life – the generously sized garden, the dinner parties with posh neighbours – with a pang of regret? Sure, he might have this lovely new flat, all clean lines and sleekness, but in some ways it was more like staying in a fancy hotel than an actual *home*.

'Have you, um, heard from Maisie at all since the other night?' she dared ask with faux casualness. Although he'd apologized about his daughter turning up mid-date like that, saying that he'd had a word with his ex-wife Polly and that it wouldn't happen again, he hadn't really said much else about either of them since.

He glanced up at her quizzically for a moment, then resumed folding a shirt. 'This and that. A few texts, nothing major.' His face was guarded, wary. Warning! Proceed with caution!

'And . . . Polly?' Jo went on bravely. It was the first time she'd ever dared say the other woman's name aloud. She had googled her, of course, after Maisie had sat there trumpeting her mother's many achievements the other evening, and had discovered, with dismay, that the girl's claims appeared to be largely true. Yes, Polly Silver *was* a fashion journalist who seemed to be friends with umpteen beautiful people. She *had* co-authored a glossy coffee-table sort of book about shoes, the sort of thing Jo would never read. Not to mention the fact that she appeared intimidatingly beautiful in all the online photos, toned and tanned with a shoulder-length blonde bob and come-to-bed blue eyes. Jo swallowed, trying to banish the now-familiar stab of jealousy. 'How are things with her? Are you two amicable or . . . ?'

He gave a short barking sort of laugh, one she'd never heard him make before, not a proper laugh at all in fact. 'We're not exactly amicable, no,' came his sardonic reply, with accompanying grimace.

Okay. Enough said. More than enough, judging by the tension in his shoulders. No further questions, Your Honour. 'Er, by the way, is there anything I should know about this place while you're away?' she asked, changing the subject. 'Things I should be locking, or checking, or cleaning . . . ?'

He zipped up the case and shook his head. 'Nope,' he said, and then at last he was smiling at her. 'It's all yours. Just make yourself at home.'

'Make yourself at home, he said,' Jo sighed down the phone to her sister when they next spoke, two days later. She'd popped out on her lunch break and caught herself reflected in a shop window, hardly recognizing her own face with its big, silly smile. 'Honestly, Laura, it's like being on holiday. It's dead glam. He's going to have to drag me bodily out of there, if he ever wants the place to himself again, I'm telling you.' She found herself imagining him grappling with her in the hall, the two of them laughing breathlessly, her grabbing Rick's tie and pulling him down to kiss her, as if they were starring in a cheesy romcom. (All of a sudden she quite fancied herself in that role.)

'You lucky cow,' Laura said in her ear, interrupting the reverie.

'I know,' Jo agreed, thinking about the thick, pale carpet that felt so soft and luxurious when you took your shoes off. The chrome light fittings, the granite worktops in the kitchen, the monsoon shower in the bathroom. Rick's PR firm was clearly doing pretty well, if these were the accompanying fruits of his labours.

'And have we been respecting his boundaries and privacy while he's away?' Laura asked sweetly. 'Or have we been poking through his stuff, trying to find some dirt about his ex-wife?'

'Laura!' cried Jo, trying to sound indignant, but she could feel her cheeks turning red with guilt at the same time. Trust her sister to go asking the one thing she'd been feeling bad about all morning.

'Come *on*. I know you too well. What did you find? Wait, let me guess. Was there loads of kinky sex stuff in his bottom drawer? A secret door leading to a bondage dungeon? His ex-wife, dead in the attic?'

'Bondage dungeon?' Jo yelped, perhaps louder than intended, because a woman walking a Westie nearby gave her a very odd look. 'What sort of films have you been watching lately?' she hissed. Then she sighed. 'Although . . . Oh, Laura, I've done something awful. I've kind of blown my cover.'

'What? What have you *done*?'

'Well . . .' Jo still felt sick when she thought about what had happened. She'd honestly been quite restrained initially, when first alone in the flat, confining herself to a brief skim through the bathroom cabinet (it was the nurse in her), a leafing-through of books and clothes and then a nosy at what he had on his TV planner (some dull history documentaries, a Scandi detective series, a BBC Four programme on punk). Then she'd noticed that at the top of the floating white bookshelves in the living room there appeared to be a set of photo albums. Evidence, she'd thought, of his life pre-her, when he lived in that fancy house in Ash Grove with Polly and Maisie, his suburban family existence. And all of a sudden she was desperate to pore over them, to see the at-home side of the woman who'd gone before, the woman he'd been so cagey about.

'Uh-oh,' said Laura, as Jo related all of this. 'Now I'm worried.'

'So I'm up on this footstool, on my tiptoes, stretching to reach them down, just for a tiny little flick-through, just to check precisely how happy he really looked in all those old pictures, and then . . .'

Thump. Something had gone whistling past her, landing on the floor. Shit, she thought, peering down to see a painted clay trophy, presumably made by Rick's daughter when she was younger. *BEST DAD!!!* was lovingly carved into the front in childish writing and there were two rather lopsided handles, one on either side, so that the whole could be thrust into the air, in the manner of a triumphant Wimbledon winner (or indeed a champion parent). Except that it now sported a large crack down the middle, with one handle broken clean off.

'Nooo,' wailed Laura when she heard. 'You're kidding me.'

'I wish I was. Of all the things to go and break, it had to be the irreplaceable one.' Jo groaned, remembering the cold, panicked sensation that had flooded her system. 'I felt *so* bad,' she went on. 'And I must pick up some superglue in a minute, actually, so that I can mend it before he gets back on Friday. He must never find out what a terrible girlfriend I am.' She gave a little laugh, but it sounded hollow to her own ears. Thank goodness for thick carpets, was all she'd been able to think, guiltily lifting the broken pieces onto the coffee table. If the floor had been slate tiles or even varnished boards, she'd be looking at a whole new jigsaw.

'Want me to come over and help?' Laura asked. 'After work, I mean. I'm a dab hand at gluing, it's one of my skills.'

Despite the awfulness of her predicament, Jo laughed. Gluing skills, indeed. Her sister was so blindingly obvious at times. 'You mean you want to have a nose around, too? I get it,' she translated, although she didn't really mind. In fact, she felt quite excited to be able to show her the place, just to see the expression on Laura's face. There'd be no more 'poor divorced Jo', that was for sure, no more sorrow and sympathy. 'Sure. Why don't I meet you outside Deansgate station at six, then we can walk up together? You can demonstrate your superior gluing talents, then I'll give you the full guided tour.'

Shortly after six that evening the two of them were cruising vertically in the noiseless lift that ran up through Rick's apartment block. 'We are now . . . in the very epicentre . . . of the habitat for the Manchester metropolitan elite,' Laura intoned in a breathy, David Attenborough-style voice. 'Notice the chrome fittings in the elevator. Observe the smooth mechanism. Listen to the sound of wealth.'

'I know, right?' Jo laughed. 'Check me out, and my fancy new life. I told you it was flash here.' The doors slid open and they stepped out into the plush carpeted corridor. 'If you'd like to follow me, madam,' she went on, adopting a silly voice and thoroughly enjoying herself as she led the way. 'Ta-dah!' she cried, unlocking the door and pushing it open with a flourish. But no sooner had they crossed the threshold, sniggering like a pair of naughty schoolgirls, than a voice was heard from further within: female and most definitely not friendly.

'Who the fuck is *that*?'

Jo stopped dead in the hall, flashing a look of panic to her sister as all glee instantly evaporated. What the—? 'Um . . . hello?' she called in reply, shrugging blankly at Laura's questioning expression. Could it be the cleaner? she wondered doubtfully. A burglar?

'You'd better not be some psychopath, because I've got a knife here and I'm dialling 999 right now,' came the voice. A not very old-sounding voice, now that Jo thought about it, despite the tough words. Which meant . . . oh hell. *No*. Say it wasn't so.

'Maisie? Is that you?' she called, hurrying into the living room with a lurching sensation inside. Ding. Right third time. Because Maisie it was indeed, still in her school uniform, hands on her hips and a scowl on her face. 'Um . . . hi,' Jo said, stopping short and trying not to squirm. 'This is my sister, Laura. Laura, this is Maisie, Rick's daughter.'

'Oh, *hi*,' said Laura interestedly, trotting in behind Jo and not seeming to notice that the girl in front of them was radiating full-on hostility. 'Wow,' she added, taking in the gorgeous surroundings and gazing around. 'Cool room. Very posh. Look at that view!'

Maisie's lips were thin and bloodless, her nose tilted in a sneer as she stared Jo out. She was tall and willowy with long tawny-blonde hair in a side-plait and copious make-up, her school skirt hitched up to show off her coltish legs. Without saying a word, her gaze dropped pointedly to the coffee table, on which lay – oh *God* – the broken remains of the trophy. 'I take it you did this?' she demanded, one eyebrow arched accusingly.

'Ah,' mumbled Jo, wringing her hands with a dreadful churn of guilt. 'You see, the thing is—'

'Don't tell me,' Maisie interrupted sarcastically. 'It just jumped off the shelf, all by itself.'

'It was an *accident*.' Jo felt awful. This was the girl she was hoping to get onside, after all: Rick's beloved daughter, the shining light of his life. And here she was – Jo, the undeserving and nosy girlfriend – with a smashed trophy to show for herself, having invited Laura round to ogle his flat while he was away. The situation did not exactly cast her in a favourable light. 'I was going to mend it. I've been out to buy superglue in fact and—'

'Really,' said Maisie, those cat-like green eyes of hers shining pure disbelief. 'Remind me again what you're even *doing* in my dad's place, while he's out of the country? Does he *know* you're skulking around here?'

How was it, thought Jo, reddening, that a thirteen-year-old could achieve such impressive self-possession? She'd been all blushes and stammers herself at that age, awkwardness personified. 'Of course he knows!' she cried. 'I'm just house-sitting while he's away. He didn't say you'd be coming round.'

'It's not like I need to ask permission,' Maisie replied haughtily. 'I've got my own keys; I've got my own *bedroom* – it's my home too.' Then she tossed her hair, snatching up a bag of clothes. 'Well, good luck telling Dad that you broke his favourite thing, anyway. I'm off.'

Jo opened her mouth to reply, but then closed it again as Maisie stalked stiffly past. 'Bye,' she croaked after a moment, then they heard the front door slam.

'Jesus H,' said Laura, pretending to wipe sweat from her brow. 'Well, she's a charmer.'

'Yeah,' said Jo, feeling defeated. Then she pulled a face, attempting a joke. 'I'm pretty sure she likes me, though.'

Laura snorted. 'I could tell. You'll wake up in the night, and she'll be standing over you with a bread knife,' she predicted, clasping her hands together as if wielding a blade. 'This is for the trophy . . . stab.'

'Laura!'

'Well, she had the look about her, didn't she? Daddy's precious girl doesn't want to share him.' She lowered her voice in imitation of a melodramatic film-trailer voiceover.

'He was the first man she'd ever loved – and she would kill to keep him all to herself . . .'

'Will you shut up?' Despite everything, Jo found herself bursting into nervy laughter. Great. There was something to keep her awake at night now. She'd definitely put the chain on the front door before going to bed. 'Rick is nicer than his daughter anyway, I swear. Quite a lot friendlier. Better sense of humour, too.'

'Thank God for that,' said Laura. 'She's enough to put anyone off having a kid. Although—' She broke off with a strange expression, and Jo had the strong sense that her sister was about to offload something personal. But then she gave a bright smile and the moment had gone. 'So! Where's this superglue, then? Let's fix this wretched trophy, then you can show me these photo albums.'

Chapter Seven

Alice Goldsmith, India had learned, had been a straight-A student at Altrincham Grammar School, playing clarinet in the orchestra as well as being a member of the hockey and athletics teams. A keen theatre-goer, she'd almost completed her second year of an English degree at Liverpool University and was gorgeous and smiley, with long brown hair, freckles and ever-so-slightly goofy teeth that gave her an endearingly earnest expression. And yet now, following her injuries the previous Saturday, she had a collapsed lung and a broken femur and remained in an induced coma. Her friends were completely devastated, according to her Facebook page (yes, India had scoured it). Her parents and brother were praying for her, according to the *Manchester Evening News* website (ditto).

In another world, Alice would shortly be taking her exams and then gallivanting off to Glastonbury or V Festival with her mates, she might be saving up to go travelling or getting some crummy job over the holidays, or falling madly in love. But not this summer, by the look of things. *Oh, Alice*, India sighed, combing through the latest news pieces about her, seeking out updates at every opportunity.

Dan was starting to get exasperated with India's new obsession. He hadn't shown so much as a flicker of sympathy when she'd told him the sad news about Sandy MacAllister's death. 'Oh well,' he'd said, irritatingly prosaic as ever. 'Looking on the bright side, at least you won't get called in for any witness statements, or whatever now.'

'*Dan!*' India had felt quite shocked at his heartlessness. 'There *is* no bright side. A man has *died*. At the crash where I was *present*. It happened right—'

'In front of you, yes,' he'd interrupted, taking the wind out of her sails. He was washing up at the time, and so didn't get to witness the full indignation of her expression. 'But you didn't know him, Ind. It wasn't like you had more than the most tenuous of connections. And you're alive, and so are your friends, and none of you will have to relive the whole thing by going through a gruelling court case, that's all I'm saying. *That's* the bright side. There's always one if you look.'

She had stared at him in speechless outrage for a long five seconds, until he glanced round at her. 'Oh, come on,' he said mildly, rinsing suds off the frying pan. 'You can't take every lost soul to your heart, love. I know it's awful, and sad for the families, but . . . Just leave it be now. Get on with your own life.' He'd chucked a tea-towel at her. 'Make yourself useful and dry this lot, for starters.'

She snorted, remembering this, and refreshed the page on her laptop where it had gone to sleep. 'Muuuum?' came a voice just then, and India jumped back into the moment, spinning round to find her youngest child, Kit, mere inches from her, his Haribo-scented breath warm against her face. He had the disarming habit of moving very quietly when he wanted to remain undetected. 'When will it be tea?'

'Er.' She blinked, having been lost in her own world for . . . gosh, quite a long time, she realized, seeing the clock on the wall. She'd only intended to reply quickly to some work emails, but had become immersed in Alice Goldsmith's Facebook page – greedily, like some kind of creepy voyeur who couldn't look away. 'Soon,' she assured her son, who liked to know exactly when things were happening, particularly where food was concerned. 'Very soon. And it's going to beee . . .' She paused for dramatic effect, although really she was casting about vaguely in her memory for what might be in the cupboards or fridge. 'It's going to be Pasta Surprise!' she cried with fake enthusiasm. The surprise being, of course, that she didn't have a clue what would be dished up with said pasta. She'd fully intended to stop at the Tesco Express after her last class that day, but there had been a bumped head to deal with after a jostle to get the bongo drums, which meant they ran over time; and then one of the mums had cornered her afterwards, frowning with solemnity, saying she felt that her little Mia-Rose needed more of a challenge in future lessons, because she was very gifted, musically, and needed to be 'stretched'. This was Mia-Rose who was eleven months old, by the way, the still-bald, pink-faced chubster who'd just spent the entire lesson gumming her slobbery wet lips around one of India's plastic shakers. What could India say, other than a smiling 'Of course'? *Then* the traffic had been abysmal, and so that had been that. Time up.

'She means pasta with a blob of dried-up old pesto and some hard mouldy cheese grated over the top,' George translated crushingly, from where he was sprawled on the sofa, killing zombies on some computer game or other. He let out a groan, the poor malnourished child that he was; clearly on the verge of starving to death. 'Can't we go to Eve's house for tea tonight?'

'No!' cried India, stung. George had had this downer on her culinary abilities compared to Eve's ever since he'd been there a few weeks ago, when Eve had conjured up a chocolate fondant for dessert, with a proper melting middle. India had found a similar pudding in Morrisons, but, according to her critical son, it hadn't been 'as good as Eve's'. Nothing was, apparently. This was probably why Eve never took up India's offers to have Grace and Sophie round, because standards were abysmally lower in the Westwood household.

(It was lucky that Eve, as well as being perfect, was also kind, witty and thoughtful, otherwise their friendship could have been over long ago, quite honestly.)

'We've got chips,' Kit advised her, and India forced a smile, but her thoughts were already sliding back to Alice Goldsmith's parents, wondering what they were like, and if they'd brought up Alice in messy chaos like India's house, or if they'd been proper grown-up parents, who never had to resort to 'Pasta Surprise' for dinner. Then she found herself wondering idly if they might have posted some of Alice's baby pictures online because – well, it was silly of her, it was nosy too, but she did really want to look at them, now that she thought about it, and . . .

'Muuuum!' Kit shouted crossly just then, right in her face. 'You're not listening to me!'

'I *am*,' she protested. 'Chips, that's what you were saying. I'm not sure if we *have* any chips, but . . .'

'We have,' he assured her. 'Me and Esme had a look in the freezer. And we HAVE.'

'Right,' she said distractedly, tuning out once more as she followed him out of the room. Thinking of the Goldsmiths reminded her how Dan had scoffed when India had mentioned her idea of popping into the hospital to take some flowers to the crash victims, but she could still go, couldn't she? Maybe with a couple of presents for Alice, too. Things she would have liked herself at that age – treats that she'd have liked to buy for her own twenty-year-old daughter if . . . you know. If she had one. She could choose some nice pyjamas and toiletries for her, maybe some books – *The Color Purple*, *The Edible Woman*, all her favourites from when she'd been twenty herself. Just as a gesture. Would that be weird? Dan would think so, obviously. Dan would tell her: Absolutely not, don't be daft. But then Dan didn't know the half of it, did he?

'See – I told you we had chips. Look!'

Finding herself in the kitchen, India looked. She looked and saw that the freezer contents must have been investigated quite some time ago, back when she was online and oblivious. The door was still open, small drips gently plopping from the ice at the top as it thawed, and several items – a packet of sausages, a tub of ice cream and, yes, the bag of frozen oven-chips – had been carefully arranged on the floor.

Esme was sitting at the kitchen table and colouring in a poster, her blonde curls glowing in a streak of afternoon sun that splashed in across her. She had the sort of angelic prettiness that older women clucked at approvingly. 'Isn't she bonny?' went the general consensus, and Esme was a terrible one for playing up to them, tilting her head winsomely and lisping, 'Fank you' in an affected sort of way that set India's teeth on edge. She turned and beamed a pink-lipsticked smile at her mother's arrival now. 'I got them all ready,' she said proudly.

'Oh, Esme! On the *floor*? What a silly thing to do,' India scolded, as the drips went on trickling. 'You left the door open as well, and now everything's melting!' She bent down to pick up the chips – soggy with water – and the ice cream, no doubt already liquefying, and groaned. 'And have you been helping yourself to my make-up bag again? For heaven's sake, Ez, you're nine, not nineteen. You don't need make-up at your age.'

'I like it,' Esme said mutinously. 'And anyway I did *tell* you,' she said, leaning over her poster and colouring even harder. 'I came and said I got tea ready, and you said, Lovely darling, well done. You were on the *computer*.'

The words sounded plausible enough to stop India short before she could launch into a full ticking-off. *Had* she actually said that? Sometimes she did find herself zoning out when the kids pestered her about things or argued, as if her brain simply refused to take in any more of this nonsense. Enough, already.

'She's in big trouble now, isn't she, Mum?' Kit asked gleefully. 'Are you really, really angry?'

'I am quite cross,' India conceded through gritted teeth, chucking everything back into the freezer, defrosted or not. Whatever. She'd worry about food-poisoning possibilities some other time. 'And it's pasta for tea anyway.'

'WHAT?' Kit yelped. 'But, MUM!'

'You did SAY!' Esme cried, looking close to tears now. 'You can't just *not* say now!'

'Tough,' India said shortly, banging around to find the big saucepan and filling it with water. 'There are children out there . . .' She could feel herself coming over all sanctimonious, her default defence mechanism. 'There are children out there who have *nothing*,' she reminded them. 'And people who are ill and in hospital. Do you think they—?'

'I wish *you* were ill and in hospital,' Esme interrupted savagely, throwing one of her crayons at the wall. 'Then we could have *chips*.'

'Hey!' cried India, wounded, but Esme had already snatched up her poster and flounced out. Kit, meanwhile, had collapsed on the floor, weak from the bitter disappointment of a no-chips dinner. 'SO unfair,' he moaned to the lino, banging a small fist and kicking his feet up and down.

'Mum, you've got to control them better,' George called patronizingly from the other room. 'They don't respect you, that's the problem.'

Oh, for heaven's sake, India thought, growling under her breath. Sometimes her children – condescending, maddening and melodramatic by turns – were enough to send any mother demented. Control them better, indeed. That would be the day.

Stepping over her prostate, still-writhing smallest son to

put the pan on the hob, she lit the burner, vowing not to lose her temper even though she could feel herself perilously close. Annoyingly, she did even quite fancy chips, too, now that she thought about it, and bunging a tray of them into the oven would have been a damn sight more straightforward than faffing around trying to conjure up a pasta sauce and salad from the meagre and possibly mouldering contents of her fridge. Sometimes a woman just could not win at life.

'Roll on bedtime,' she muttered under her breath as she ripped open a bag of fusilli, only to send spirals clattering and bouncing all over the floor.

Chapter Eight

One of the women in Laura's office, Gayle, had a thing about Friday nights being 'date night' for her and her husband. Kids, work, pets, life in general – they all took a back seat on a Friday night, 'for the sake of my marriage and sanity', as Gayle put it.

Laura had always been not scathing exactly, but faintly dismissive of the concept. Wasn't it a bit cheesy, a bit naff to schedule a date with your other half into the diary like that? Besides, when there was just the two of you, and no kids or pets to factor into the equation, every night of the week could be 'date night' if you felt so inclined. Saying that, though, she was taken aback to realize that she and Matt hadn't actually been out together as a couple for quite some time. Weeks, possibly. She couldn't remember when they'd last booked a table for two in a restaurant, or met for a cinema trip or spontaneously arranged to go to the pub together after work. And so, seeing as it was Friday, she decided to take the initiative for once. Not least because she had a proposition to put to him.

Talk to Matt, Jo had urged the other night, when Laura's feelings came spilling out of her unexpectedly in a big messy rush. *Tell him how you feel.*

Jo was always right about these things. As the elder sister, she'd acted as protector-in-chief for Laura's entire life. Bully at school? Jo was on it, squaring her shoulders and threatening retribution. Mum being flaky? Jo had thrown on a pinny and assumed responsibility for the cooking and shopping, commandeering the laundry basket too, to ensure they had enough clean school blouses and tights for the week. Disastrous A-levels? Jo was there with news of a temping job where her friend worked, just to tide things over until Laura made up her mind about what to do next. Basically, when her sister issued an order, Laura took notice. *Talk to Matt*, Jo had decreed, and Laura had nodded. Yes. She would.

Fancy dinner after work tonight? she texted him that lunchtime. *We could go on a date! Lois from the office has vouchers for Dough Pizza Kitchen . . . x*

Nice one, he replied a short while later. *Meet in The Lamb around six?*

Great. See you then xx, she typed, a funny little shiver down her back. Lure him in with a pint and his favourite pizza – what better way was there to launch a high-stakes conversation with her husband?

Matt, I've been thinking, she imagined herself saying, leaning over to take his hand. *We're not getting any younger, are we?*

She swallowed, already apprehensive. Before then, though, she needed to be prepared, to have done her research and be word-perfect. Casting a wary glance over her shoulder – the perils of working in an open-plan office, when your colleagues were all such nosy parkers – she called up Google and typed in *Fertility clinic Manchester.* Just so that she knew there even *was* one, before she took a deep breath and made any suggestions.

There wasn't just one clinic, though, judging by the list of results that flashed up in the next second – there appeared to be at least ten based in the area. *Clinical excellence. No waiting lists! Highest-quality IVF treatment. Tailored treatment. Success rates . . .* The phrases leapt out at her temptingly, bedazzling her for a moment so that she didn't know where to begin. She could almost feel her womb ache with yearning.

Clicking randomly on one of the sites, she began devouring its promises. There were bright pictures of cute chubby babies on one page, a shot of reassuring-looking medical staff with non-scary body language on another, and – best of all – a photo of a rapturously smiling couple holding hands over a Moses basket. *Be Our Next Success Story*, she read, a lump in her throat. Yes, please. She wanted very badly to be that couple in the photo, to have what they had, to be a success story for the clinic. Maybe she and Matt might even appear in a future version of the company website, beaming over their own perfect, beautiful child. *Look what we made!*

They hadn't discussed IVF before, or undergoing any tests. As a sales manager for a medium-sized insurance firm, Matt could talk for Britain about claims and premiums; as a lifelong United fan, he could bore on for hours with his mates about managerial tactics or the pros and cons of the 4-4-2 formation; but ask him to go into detail about his baby-making skills and he would fall uncharacteristically silent. *Nobody else's business,* he would rail to Laura in private, if they'd suffered an intrusive line of questioning from an insensitive aunt, say, at a family gathering (christenings were the worst, everyone falling over themselves to ask, *And when will it be your turn then?*).

It would take a serious amount of persuasion and cajolement, in other words, maybe even some begging on bended knees, to coax her husband through the doors of a clinic to discuss their situation, let alone undergo the embarrassment of tests. And following the miscarriages, the two of them had stopped talking about parenthood, full stop, both feeling defeated and despondent. She'd thrown herself into Pilates classes and doing up the living room, he'd busied himself joining a local five-a-side football team. Sex had returned, eventually, to being love-making rather than baby-making, but maybe the time had come to step things up a gear again. Try a different tack. Because – hello! – just look at the babies on the website. Witness the adorable tiny fingers and toes, the soft rounded tummies. She zoomed in on one particular toothless cherub and sighed. Surely she could convince her husband that a gorgeous babe-in-arms – *their* gorgeous babe-in-arms! – would be worth a few quick tests and procedures?

'Oh, I see, teacher's pet: swotting up, are we?' came a teasing voice just then, and Laura's breath seized in her throat, fingers fumbling to close the site, as real life came crashing back in, in the form of Jim, one of the designers. Young, cocky and good-looking, he was something of a heartbreaker along Canal Street, by all accounts, and the prime source of most office gossip stories. 'Won't our Deborah be pleased with you then, eh, kid?'

He meant the new maternity range, Laura realized after an agonizing few seconds of confusion, and relief promptly cascaded through her. Oh, thank goodness. He thought she was researching cute babies for an ad campaign, even though there wasn't even a single product out of development yet. She flashed him a smile, despite her nervous panic at almost being caught out by the office loudmouth. 'You know me, Jim, one step ahead as usual,' she replied with a little laugh. She'd always been a terrible poker player; never able to disguise the emotions that flickered across her face. 'Try to keep up.'

The Lamb had been gentrified since Laura was last there for a drink. Formerly a scruffy old boozer with sticky carpets and a broken jukebox that favoured Meat Loaf's *Greatest Hits*, like it or not, it had now been tarted up practically beyond recognition and was all moody charcoal walls and dim lighting, big, craacked brown leather sofas and artistic black-and-white prints. As she waited at the bar that evening, she could hear the soulful tones of Adele from the speakers, so presumably Meat Loaf had been banished too, into a skip along with the old carpets.

Matt was already at the bar, shirt-sleeves rolled up and his tie loosened. He'd be forty next year, but there was still something of the inky schoolboy about him, with his gangly physique and that cowlick of brown hair, which he had to smooth down every morning with gel. By the end of the day it was always rebelliously springing up again, too wayward to be tamed for long.

They kissed hello, ordered a drink each (red wine for her, Boddingtons for him) and found a quiet corner, easing into one of the creaking leather sofas together. 'So, how was your day?' she asked, thinking how nice this was, how cosy. Maybe Gayle had a point after all.

'Well,' he began, and there was something about his

voice that made her turn in surprise. He never usually replied with anything other than a perfunctory 'Fine'. 'Actually, it was kind of interesting.'

He seemed pleased with himself, Laura noticed, intrigued. Had he pulled off some mega-deal or other? Received an unexpected bonus? 'What?' she asked, nudging his knee with hers. 'What's happened?'

'There's a job that's come up, it sounds really good,' he replied. 'Better pay, more senior. I could do it, Laura.'

'Oh, wow! Cool,' she said, taken aback. Matt had worked for the same company since they'd met, his position every bit as steady and reliable as his personality. He'd always been a contented sort of soul, never bothered about pushing ahead and seeking glory, just clocking in and out every day, doing his job, getting paid – end of story. It was one of the things she loved about him, that unchanging solidity. And yet here he was now, looking excited about some new career prospect. She hadn't seen that one coming. 'Tell me more,' she said.

'Well, it was Elaine, really, who got me thinking,' he began. His eyes were actually sparkling, Laura realized. 'She was like: Matt, you could do your job standing on your head. You're too good to stay in this position forever, you do know that, don't you?'

'Elaine?' Laura echoed. She'd been dragged along to the

company Christmas do enough times to have met a number of his colleagues by now, but had no memory of an Elaine.

'Yeah, the new department head. Only been here since February,' he replied. 'Wants to shake things up a bit, she said.'

'Right,' said Laura, feeling wary all of a sudden. Matt was normally averse to being shaken up about anything, after all. A picture was forming of this new boss as matronly and interfering, one of those people who thought they knew best for everyone and couldn't help poking their noses in, for the sake of it.

'So she's been going through our records: targets and yearly averages, that sort of thing. And she wants us – me and a couple of others – to be brand ambassadors for the firm.' His eyes met hers, but she couldn't tell if he was amused by the naff phrase or chuffed.

'Brand ambassadors!' spluttered Laura. 'Will I have to start calling you that? I feel like I'm in a Ferrero Rocher advert. "Good evening, Ambassador." "Hello, have you met my husband, the ambassador?"' She elbowed him teasingly. 'I hope they're going to give you some military stripes to wear on your suit jacket. A special badge.'

'Well, it's not definite or anything,' he said, with just a hint of defensiveness that made her think she'd overstepped the mark. 'We've got to apply for the jobs, and go for interviews – it's not in the bag.'

'Right.' Her laughter subsided. 'Exciting, though. Could be good.'

'Yeah.' He hesitated, and then she realized there was something else. He swirled the beer around in his pint glass before adding, 'Because they're opening a new branch up in Newcastle, see, so . . .'

Clunk. The penny dropped. 'And that's where the job is? In Newcastle?'

'Um – well, yeah,' he replied, not meeting her eye. 'I'm just thinking about it,' he rushed on, as she let out a startled squawk. 'It's not definite, like I said. It's only an idea. But . . .' He reached out and took her hand. 'It might be an adventure, you know. It might do us good, moving away, making a change.'

'Shaking things up a bit,' she said faintly, but he didn't seem to notice she was mimicking his boss and not being serious.

'Exactly!' He beamed. 'I mean, it's early days, nothing confirmed, but . . . I feel positive about it. I think it could be . . . exciting.'

Exciting? From the man who liked routine and order, whose week ran like clockwork with everything just the same – work, football, pub? Laura could hardly believe what she was hearing. This was Matt, who'd had a pension since he was twenty-two, who actually wrote an email of complaint when Marmite brought out squeezy bottles because 'it was wrong'. 'God,' she said, swallowing hard. Well, that had taken her by surprise all right. Was this some kind of midlife crisis, maybe, now that he was almost forty? More to the point, how was she supposed to launch into *her* proposition of fertility clinics and gummy-smiling babies after that?

'So, let me get this straight,' she said, trying to recover herself. 'If you got this job in Newcastle . . . you'd want to move? It's – what, three hours' drive from here? You couldn't do it as a commute.'

'Well, no,' he conceded after a moment. 'I mean . . . I figured we'd talk about that, once I knew a bit more about the job.'

Her mind was spinning. It was like having a different person sitting next to her. She'd woken up this morning with her ordinary, amiable husband, who was looking forward to the long bank-holiday weekend, with the *Britain's Got Talent* final, a Sunday roast and an extra lie-in in the offing, and somehow between then and now he'd transformed into this go-getter who wanted to leave everything behind, to become a so-called 'ambassador' in sodding Newcastle. Talk about *Invasion of the Body Snatchers*. 'You'd really want us to go?' she pressed him, incredulous. 'Leave everyone we know – our families and friends? I'd have to quit my job,' she realized aloud, trying to get her head round this whole sea-change. It was crazy. He wasn't serious, surely?

Then the killer question occurred to her. 'You'd want to move away from *United*?'

There, gauntlet thrown down. Forget their little semi, forget his parents down the road; it would be the prospect of moving 150 miles from his precious Old Trafford that would surely signal the death-knell of this whole startling Newcastle business.

'Well . . .' he said, grimacing slightly. Ouch, yes. United. Witness the abject torment in his eyes. 'Look, I don't know. Not really. But Elaine reckons our own management team aren't going anywhere. She thinks a promotion in the regions is the best way to advance my career.' He shrugged. 'I could give it a few years there, and come back. That's what people did in her last company.'

'This Elaine of yours seems to have it all worked out,' Laura commented, feeling her voice tighten at the woman's name. Who even *was* this Elaine, anyway, to take such an interest in Matt's so-called career advancement, putting wild ideas in his head? When now, of all times, Laura wanted him to simply walk hand in hand to the nearest clinic with her, so that they could have their own beautiful baby!

'It's just a thought,' he said, his eyes reproachful, and then she felt bad for giving him the third degree. Chances were he'd change his mind when next season's fixture list came out anyway. 'Seemed like a good opportunity, that was all. The chance for a new start. Worth thinking about.'

She saw her chance. *Do it, Laura*. 'I was kind of wanting to talk about a new start for us as well, actually,' she said slowly, picking her words. She took a slug of wine for Dutch courage; *here goes*. 'Because . . . Well, it was the crash, really. Seeing the crash the other weekend, it made me think about life and death – and what's important.'

Now it was his turn to look surprised. 'Right,' he said uncertainly. Then his face changed. 'Don't tell me: this is all about getting a new car. Because—'

'No,' she cut in. 'It's not about a new car.' She took another gulp of wine. 'It's like you were saying – sometimes you need to try something different in order to get what you want,' she went on. 'And it made me realize what *I* really want . . . which is a baby.'

He seemed to deflate there and then, sinking back into the sofa as if undergoing a slow puncture. Undeterred, she continued, quickly before he could stop her. 'We've tried and tried and it hasn't worked out for us,' she said, battling to keep her voice steady. 'It's been disappointing and upsetting. But I don't think we should give up.'

Oh God, his body language was definitely not good right now, she noticed. Had he actually shrunk away from her in the last minute?

'I've been doing some research,' she went on valiantly, 'and there are loads of clinics that can help. I bet there would be some in Newcastle as well,' she threw in for good measure. *You humour me*, the subtext was, *and I'll humour you*. He could go off to his swanky new job while she went to pregnancy yoga and pushed a pram around unfamiliar streets. It wouldn't be so bad, would it? Her hands now all thumbs with sudden eagerness, she pulled a printout from her bag, details from one of the websites, having sneakily copied and pasted them while the rest of her colleagues were in a meeting. 'Here. This one, for example, has no waiting list, apparently, and I'm pretty sure we could afford it. I haven't made an appointment yet, but maybe next week we could . . .'

He didn't seem to be listening any more. In fact, he was frowning in a baffled sort of way. She'd lost him, Laura thought with a pang. She'd blown it, gone in too fast, too soon. At long last he spoke. 'But I thought . . .' he began, staring down at the printout. Then he raised his eyes, looking awkward. 'I thought we'd stopped all that.'

His words were like hammer blows to her head. *What?*

'You thought we'd . . . *stopped*?' she repeated.

'Yeah. I thought we'd—' He stalled, his gaze sliding sideways, avoiding her face. 'I thought we'd given up,' he finished gruffly. 'Accepted that it wasn't gonna happen.'

'But . . .' The revelation took her breath away. Her fingernails dug into her palms under the table and she didn't know whether she was closer to screaming, crying or laughing hysterically in shocked disbelief. This was worse than the Newcastle conversation. This was devastating. 'You – you want to . . . give *up*?'

'Well.' He shifted on the sofa. 'I thought we already had. Hadn't we?'

Tears stung her eyes. 'No!' Give up, on her dream? On her dearest wish? Her throat tightened. '*I* hadn't given up.'

'Oh.' He stared at his glass, his face rigid. An excruciating moment of silence passed. 'The thing is . . .'

A tear plopped onto her lap. No, she thought. Don't say it. Don't tell me. I don't want to hear. 'Wait,' she pleaded, but he was talking over her.

'It's too much, Laura,' he said sadly, and for a foolish moment she thought he meant financially.

'We can afford it!' she cried, clutching desperately at a solution. 'I can take out a loan, I'll get another job—'

'No,' he said unhappily. 'It's not the money. I mean, it's too much to go through again, too painful.' He sighed. 'After last time, with you in the hospital, losing another baby . . . I couldn't bear it again, Laur. It nearly broke us. It was awful. I just . . . don't want to any more.'

She had to wrench her gaze away from those sorrowful hangdog eyes of his. '*I* don't mind going through it,' she persisted. 'I can cope. I can do it for both of us.'

'But *I* can't! That's what I'm trying to say. *I* can't cope, Laura. Seeing you like that – I couldn't handle it.' He pushed the printout away from him. 'I'm sorry, but . . .'

'We could adopt, then. We could foster! We could find a sweet orphaned baby and . . .'

But he was shaking his head with such awful finality that her voice trailed away. 'I don't . . . Where has all this *come* from? I had no idea. I thought we'd moved on.'

Laura flinched. Moved *on*? 'You can't just *move on* from wanting a baby,' she cried, louder than she'd intended. The power chords of an Adele ballad chose that moment to end, and the pub fell uncomfortably quiet. She leaned forward, lowering her voice. 'You can't just switch it off, like it was never there!'

'No, but . . . You went quiet on the subject. I thought we'd both agreed.'

'*No!* When did we agree? I went quiet because I didn't want you to feel under pressure. I was hoping it would just happen for us, without making a big fuss, getting all stressed again.' Tears were rolling down her face; she felt frantic for him to understand, to change his mind. He couldn't mean it, surely? 'I thought you wanted us to have a family!'

'I did! But if it's not going to happen, then—'

'It could still happen, Matt, that's the thing. If we go to the clinic, it could still happen.'

They had reached deadlock. She could feel the argument starting to loop around, to close in on them like a strangle-hold. And he was shaking his head again, apologetic but firm. 'I don't think so,' he said.

Her lips trembled. She had to gulp for air because it was as if she had forgotten to breathe. *I don't think so.* He was saying no. He didn't want to have a child. All her hopes and wishes and plans and . . . and he had somehow moved onto a different side; he was off with Elaine, getting excited about a job in *Newcastle*. A small sob escaped her throat and she put up a hand to shield her eyes, no longer wanting to look at him.

'You're upset,' he said calmly. 'And I'm sorry. We should have had the conversation, we should have talked about this sooner, rather than making assumptions about what the other one wanted.'

She still couldn't speak. Upset, he said. *Upset?* He'd just stamped all over her heart and ripped up her dreams, and he had the brass neck to sit there and comment on her being *upset*? She wrenched herself up from the table, just wanting to get away from him, and stumbled unseeingly towards the pub door.

'Laura!' he called after her. 'Come on, we can talk about this—'

Her legs felt wooden and strange, as if they didn't belong to her, as she staggered past the bar, ignoring the barmaid's concerned expression, past all the other couples and workmates enjoying their Friday-night drinks. Oh God, oh God, she thought, I can't bear it, I can't bear it. Misery propelled her through the door into the warm evening air, and then, once outside the pub, her energy drained away and she found herself leaning against the wall, sliding down onto her haunches. There was rough brick against her back, the scent of diesel and drains, but all she could think of was Matt's face, his sad apologetic face as he shook his head. *I don't think so. No.*

Now what? she thought despairingly, as the conversation whirled around her mind like a ride on the waltzers. *Now what?*

Chapter Nine

'Right! Can we have those PE bags emptied, please, and dirty things put straight into the washing machine? Both of you get changed, and find a book to read on the journey. Dad wants us to be ready for six-thirty.'

'Ungggghhh.' Grace, Eve's thirteen-year-old daughter, was rolling her thickly eyelinered eyes up to the ceiling and pretending to hang herself there in the smart, magnolia-painted hallway. 'Do we *have* to go? I can't believe you booked somewhere with no Wi-Fi. That's like going back to the Dark Ages. Can't I just stay with Flo for half-term?'

'No! We've been through this,' Eve replied, bending down to take off her shoes. They were meant to be going to the Peak District for a half-term holiday in approximately two hours, there was no time to waste rehashing an already well-worn argument. 'It'll do you good to have a break from your phone. We're going to have lots of fun doing other things. Family things.' Long energetic walks and bike rides in the great outdoors, a trip to Chatsworth House. Card games in the evenings, a log fire if it was chilly, her and Neil managing to unwind for once. Maybe, just maybe, she'd pluck up the courage to tell him about the lump . . .

'But I hate family things!' Grace was groaning, meanwhile.

Eve could feel the stress-twitch of a tic under her eye. She always got one before they went away. Plus they'd been a person down in the office that day and she'd been flat out with work. *And* Frances, her boss, had tasked her with sorting out the office team-building away-day for September, which was exactly the sort of forced jollity she loathed. 'Look—'

'Mum, she's just moaning because she won't be able to Snapchat her *boyfriend,*' jeered Sophie, who was ten years old and thought she knew everything. (To be fair, in this instance she apparently knew more than Eve. Like the fact that Grace had her first boyfriend. Since *when*?) 'And he'll probably go off with someone else who doesn't have spots and fat legs. Ow!'

Grace had launched herself at her younger sister, fists flying. 'Shut up, stupid bitch! What do you know about anything?'

'Girls! GIRLS!' Eve cried in horror. 'Grace! Do not use that word about your sister. Or about anyone! And Sophie, don't you—'

But her words of motherly wisdom were soundly ignored,

as Sophie lunged to grab Grace's hair, and Grace kicked out in retaliation. '*Ow!* Mum, tell her!'

'Get off me!'

'I hate you!'

Goodness, her daughters were so loudly emotional about everything! They wore every feeling on their faces, they voiced their opinions with wholehearted passion, they screamed, laughed, yelled. It always made Eve flinch because she, by contrast, had learned at an early age to shut down these feelings, to keep them in check. 'What's so funny?' she remembered her dad snapping once, whirling round at her when she and her sister Rosalind had been giggling about something silly. Eve had been so afraid she'd wet her knickers and then he'd shouted at her for that, too.

'Girls, *please*,' she cried now, trying to pull them off each other. 'Stop it! This minute!' Firm and in control, that was what the parenting guides advised. Calm and clear; no need to ever raise one's voice. But when your offspring were actually *brawling* on the hall carpet, it turned out that a calm, clear voice had zero effect. Then, of course, her phone picked that moment to start ringing. Neil, probably, telling her he was going to be late again. Or some annoying cold caller, just to really tip her over the edge. 'Will you BE *QUIET*?' she screeched at her still-wrestling daughters, snatching up her phone.

Both girls stared at her in surprise and Eve turned away, shaken by her own outburst. For a second she'd sounded like a crazed harpy, a mad old fishwife. For a moment she'd been tempted to wade in and dish out a few slaps herself. What was happening to her? She had never screamed at them like that before, never. There went that tic again.

Belatedly remembering the phone in her hand, she tried to compose herself. 'Hello?'

'Is that Eve? It's Lewis. The guy on the bike?'

Lewis. Oh God, *him*. Ever since their unexpected encounter she'd been driving like someone who only recently passed their test: nervy and hesitant, hands clamped at ten to two on the wheel, braking down through the gears with exaggerated care each time she slowed. 'Hello,' she said again. 'How . . . How are you?'

Behind her, Sophie was hissing something defiant to Grace, but Eve swung round with a look of such fury that both girls quailed and fell silent. 'I'm not so bad,' Lewis was saying in her ear. He was Scottish, that's right, with that shaggy coppery hair and the low musical voice. 'I was just calling to—' He broke off, and she cut in quickly.

'Yes,' she said, sensing his awkwardness. 'I owe you some money.' And then, not wanting her daughters to get wind of what had happened – she hadn't even told Neil about the accident, too ashamed – she hurried into the kitchen and shut the door behind her. Let the girls rip each other's hair out while she wasn't looking, she no longer cared. 'Was the bike a write-off? What's the damage?'

He hesitated again and she immediately feared the worst. Oh no. The Taylors' boiler had given up the ghost back in February and then the tumble drier had died shortly afterwards; it wasn't as if they were swimming in cash right now. 'I did ask about getting it repaired,' he began, apologetically. 'But because the frame has been bent, the guy in the shop reckoned that having it sorted will cost more than the actual bike did in the first place.'

'Ah,' she said, grimacing as she leaned against the worktop. So it was going to be a whole new bike then, in other words, which would be what: five hundred pounds? A thousand? After one small slip of concentration: ouch. Meanwhile, where was she supposed to find that sort of money?

'But the better news – for you – is that my bike was shite anyway,' he went on, 'so we're talking a couple of hundred quid, rather than a couple of grand.' He gave a cough, sounding uncomfortable about the situation. Not as uncomfortable as Eve was, though.

'Okay,' she said, trying not to sigh. It wasn't his fault, after all. 'And . . . how about your T-shirt? Can I pay for it to be cleaned or . . . ?'

'Naw, you're all right,' he said. 'Bit of Vanish and a cold-water wash, it came out okay.' He laughed. 'I sound like my granny.'

'Very resourceful,' she said, managing a shaky laugh herself. Okay, a few hundred pounds. It wasn't the end of the world, she supposed. She could put in some overtime between now and the summer holidays. 'And your arm's okay? It's healing up? I did wonder if we should have gone to A&E so that you could have it stitched.'

'It's fine,' he said. 'No bother.' There was another strained moment of silence and then he rushed in with a question. 'How about you? I mean, what you said to me, at the end. Have you been to see anyone?'

'Have I been . . . ? Oh.' She cringed, having forgotten that she'd told him about her lump like that, blurting it out in some misguided attempt to explain herself. 'No,' she confessed stiffly after a moment. 'Not yet.'

He cleared his throat. 'I think you should.'

'I beg your pardon?' Surprise had sent her all Victorian and formal. This had better not turn into a lecture about mindfulness, she thought, hackles rising. If he dared start giving her some sales pitch for one of his crummy wellness retreats . . .

'Look, I know it's none of my business but . . . it's important. These things can accelerate quickly, if they're aggressive. You need to get it checked out.'

Her jaw dropped in shock, that in a matter of moments he'd cut straight to the personal. Personal, verging on intrusive. None of her other clients knew a thing about her, other than that she could transform a messy set of accounts into something acceptable to the tax office – and she liked it that way. Just because she'd knocked him off his wretched bike, *by accident*, it didn't give him the right to ask difficult questions or lecture her on her health! 'Well,' she began, but then in burst Grace, looking aggrieved.

'Mum, will you please TELL HER that—'

'I'm on the phone,' Eve snapped, making shooing motions. 'Go and pack your things!' Thankfully Grace merely pulled a face and stamped out again, and Eve was able to close the door, feeling frazzled. She hadn't even started on her own packing yet. Hadn't she said to Neil that trying to get away on the Friday night was a bad idea? It wasn't him who had to organize everything, to corral their daughters and remember to pack towels and swimming costumes and the first-aid kit. She would be packing gallons of wine too, that was for sure. Maybe she'd start on a bottle after this phone call, in fact. Or maybe she would lie on her bed and scream into the pillow.

She took a deep breath. No, she wouldn't. Eve was not the sort of person who screamed into pillows, who lost her temper with her children. Usually. 'Sorry about that,' she said, switching to a more businesslike tone, just as he asked, 'You've got kids?'

She sighed. There were a million things to do before Neil got back, and he'd expect everything to be ready. 'Er . . .

yes,' she replied through gritted teeth. *Not that it's any of your business.* She opened the cupboard and pulled out baked beans, coffee, tea, porridge oats ready to pack. 'So you've got my email address,' she went on, wanting to get shot of him now. 'And if you send me your bank details, I can transfer—'

'Yeah, sure,' he interrupted. 'But, Eve . . .'

It felt oddly intimate, him saying her name like that. It caught her off-guard, slicing through her brisk facade. 'Yes?'

'I'll go with you, if you want – to the doctor, I mean. If you're scared. I don't mind.'

'*What?*' Her hand froze around the packet of chocolate digestives.

'To the appointment. I'll go with you.'

'I'm not *scared*,' she retorted hotly, snatching a bag and stuffing the groceries into it. Pasta sauce. Spaghetti. A tin of olives. Honestly, to think that this guy – this *lad* – with whom she'd exchanged barely two minutes' worth of conversation, had the nerve to think he knew anything about her . . .

'Great, so make the appointment, and give us a shout if you change your mind. Just a thought. I know my mum didn't want anyone to know at first. Took her three months before she told anyone else in the family.'

'Your mum?' Oh God. Don't say his mum had died of breast cancer or something. Was that why he was being such a vigilante, getting on her case? On second thoughts, she didn't want to know. 'I'd . . . I'd better go,' she said in clipped tones. 'Have a good weekend.'

Then she hung up before he could say anything else, and sank into a chair, arms around herself, feeling vulnerable. This was what happened when you revealed a chink in your armour, when you showed yourself to be weak. This was why she shouldn't have said anything – not a word – to anyone!

Eve lowered her head so that it rested against the cool oak of the table, feeling very tired and very un-holidayish. Her tic twitched like a warning light and she sighed. Scared, indeed, she thought in the next moment – what a nerve. 'Go and sort out someone else's chakras,' she said rudely to her silent phone. Then she got up, took a deep breath and carried on packing.

Chapter Ten

'Ms Nicholls?'

Jo was just heading out on her lunch break when her phone rang with a local number. 'Yes, that's me,' she said, stepping out of the surgery into warm sunshine. Ahh, that was better, she thought, turning her face up appreciatively. She'd had back-to-back appointments all morning – the baby vaccination clinic (always a bit distressing, especially seeing the mums' traumatized faces) and then a steady stream of minor ailments, including one infected horsefly bite, which was like something from a horror film.

'Ms Nicholls, this is Mr Hedgethorne's assistant at Nash, White and Beaumont. I'm calling about the sale of the Barkway Road house?'

'Oh, yes, hello,' Jo replied. The house in Stretford, where she and Greg had lived, bought for a song when they were newly-weds. 'Is it today?' she realized, with a start. 'The completion?'

This was a sign, if ever she needed one, of just how

distracted she'd become by Rick in recent weeks. The full extent of how utterly away with the fairies she obviously now was. Because today – 'Yes, that's right,' the woman was saying – today was when the new people were moving in, when the sale was finalized, money transferred. 'I'm happy to let you know that we've received full payment, and that everything's completed without a problem.'

Jo stopped dead in the street, a huge smile breaking on her face as this glorious news percolated through her mind. The house was sold, finally – third time lucky, after two other prospective purchasers had let them down at the last minute. She had *money* again. 'Thank you,' she breathed, grinning at random passers-by like an idiot. 'Thank you very much.'

Could this day get any better? Not only was Rick back from Ireland later that evening but now a large lump sum – more money than she'd ever had at one time – had just gone walloping into her bank account. Admittedly she couldn't help feeling a bit weird at the thought of a new family moving their belongings into her former address, organizing furniture and repainting the place, maybe hacking back the dense privet hedge that had loomed so darkly over the house, almost certainly ripping out the hideous pink bathroom suite that she and Greg had never quite got round to changing . . . Even so, it drew a line under the split with Greg – it marked the end of things, proper closure. Plus she could enjoy financial independence at last, after so many tight, penny-pinching months of having to pay for two places at once. Yes, that was a *really* good thing. A weight off her shoulders. A new beginning, as well as an ending.

In fact, thought Jo, arms swinging a little as she strode towards the nearby shopping parade, a celebration was due. Tonight, in fact. Let the celebrations begin tonight!

Six hours later and still in a great mood, Jo was just backing into a space at the airport car park when her phone made a triumphant little fanfare sound. Yanking on the handbrake, she pulled it out of her bag to see a new message onscreen: *Dublin to Manchester flight has now LANDED.*

'Hooray,' she said out loud, turning off the engine.

Yes, okay, so she *had* downloaded a flight-tracking app for the express purpose of checking to the exact second when her boyfriend returned to Mancunian soil. What of it? She couldn't wait to see Rick again. Had it really only been a matter of days since he'd left town? Perhaps it was staying at his lovely flat all week that had made her miss him so much. She'd spent every evening surrounded by his possessions, sleeping in his bed (hugging the pillows that smelled so deliciously of him), lounging on his extremely comfortable sofa, admiring the impressive assortment of condiments in his big fridge whenever she made dinner . . . Was it any wonder that she'd been thinking of him round the clock?

All right, so there had been the small problem of Maisie's unexpected appearance and the broken clay trophy, but she'd mended it now at least, and was sure Rick would be cool about the whole thing. What was more, the flat looked pristine, in readiness for his return. She had put a vase of sunflowers on the mantelpiece, tidied everything away and put a fresh sheet on the bed. That entire day she'd found herself feeling almost light-headed whenever she thought about his return. Giddy, even. ('Sure it's not an inner-ear infection?' her colleague Alison had asked sceptically when Jo had voiced such dazed feelings. 'I could have a look for you, if you want.')

It was not an inner-ear infection, needless to say. It was happiness. New-found wealth and independence. The fact that she'd loaded up a basket in the Little Waitrose that lunchtime and bought steaks and champagne and a fabulously calorific banoffee pie for afters, and that she was here now, at the airport, all set to give her boyfriend a joyful surprise when he walked through Arrivals was proof of that.

Fancy seeing you here, she was going to say, all coquettish and pretend-nonchalant. She'd put lipstick on and everything, and planned to dash into the Boots in the main building just as soon as she got there, in order to squirt on some free perfume. *I don't suppose you fancy a lift into town, do you?* she would ask, raising an eyebrow. *Thought I could treat you to dinner later – my way of thanking you for having me stay all week . . .*

'Slick,' Alison had pronounced approvingly when Jo had run this past her during a brief chat at the filing cabinet at the end of their working day. Then she'd wrinkled her nose, teasing, 'Look at you, going all pink in the cheeks because your boyfriend's coming home. Jo Nicholls, I never thought I would see the day.'

Nor me, Jo had thought. Nor me, Alison. But here I am, pink-cheeked and enjoying life, no longer saddled with a house I don't want, no longer scrimpingly skint and, best of all, ready for some fabulous reunion sex with my gorgeous new boyfriend. She was going to stop worrying about rushing into things with him too, because . . . Well, because so what if she *was*, basically, when it made her feel this good?

Hurrying through the car park, she could feel cheerfulness sparking inside her. He'd be off the plane by now, heading for the Baggage Claim area, and then . . .

Her phone rang and her heart skipped a fluttering beat to see his name on the screen, as if she'd summoned the call with her own joyful thoughts. 'Hi,' she said. 'How are you?'

'Good,' he replied. 'Just landed.'

She resisted the urge to tell him that she knew, she had an app – perhaps that was a shade too keen – and said, 'Welcome back' instead, a big smile on her face. Oh, she could not wait to throw her arms around him again!

'So, about tonight,' he went on, and she almost wanted to giggle, fighting the urge to tell him that she'd already planned it all out.

'Yes?' she said instead.

But then he sighed. 'Listen, I know we said we'd see each other tonight, but I've just picked up a voicemail message from Maisie and she sounded really upset. Something about a broken . . . To be honest, I couldn't hear very well. A broken trophy or something. Must have happened at school, I guess, but she seemed pretty tearful.'

An icy chill spiralled down Jo's spine as the words sank in, and a vision flashed through her mind of Maisie's smug, triumphant smirk. *Gotcha*. 'Um . . .' she stuttered, but nothing else came from her mouth.

'She said she'd tell me the whole story later, whatever it is, but she really wanted a dad-and-daughter night. Would you mind if . . . ?'

'Oh.' Jo stopped dead in the car park, about one hundred metres from the airport entrance. Tanned people in big sunhats were wheeling out trolleys laden with suitcases, a group of blokes in City football tops sang beerily as they headed the other way. 'No,' she managed to say. Maisie had got there first, she thought ruefully. Crying down the phone to Daddy, no less, pulling rank, stirring things up. *Choose me, Dad, choose me!* And how could he not? 'Of course I don't mind,' she said woodenly, visualizing the girl gleefully pouring out the trophy saga, embellishing it, no doubt, to make Jo look like some kind of hooligan who smashed up kids' artistic creations for kicks. She should probably get her side of the story in quickly, she realized. 'Actually, I think I—' she began, but he was already speaking.

'I mean, I don't want to leave you in the lurch. What's the latest with your flat – has it all been sorted? You're not going to be stuck for somewhere to stay, are you?'

Jo cringed at the question. This was not how she wanted him to see her – 'stuck' and unable to cope without him; that kind of relationship would be veering straight back into marriage-with-Greg territory. 'Of course not!' she cried gaily, trying not to think about the steaks in the boot of her car, the champagne, the banoffee pie, which was probably starting to melt. Then she imagined him walking out of Arrivals and seeing her there outside the building – *Jo? What are you doing here?* – and she wheeled around on the spot, scurrying back towards the car. 'Just let me know when you're around, then. Okay, better go,' she said before he could hear how defeated she sounded. 'Bye!'

It was only when she'd hung up that she realized she hadn't told him about the broken Best Dad trophy. Bollocks. Should she ring him back now, fill him in on the details? Send a quick text? *Oh btw – the thing Maisie was crying about into your voicemail? It's not a big deal, honestly, just an accident. All mended! Nothing to get mad about!*

Oh God. She should have fessed up earlier, when it happened, shouldn't she? She should have apologized in advance for being a clumsy house-guest, just got it out there in the open. Whoops, my mistake, sorry! Because now it looked really bad, him hearing it first from his daughter, rather than from the culprit herself. Like she was trying to hide it and get away with the breakage, like she was dishonest or something. Damn it.

She got back into her car, trying to talk herself round. Breathe, Jo. Chill! She was turning a small accident into a huge overblown saga. Let Maisie have her moment of melodrama, Rick would understand that these things happened. He wasn't the sort of person who would turn against a girlfriend for a small pottery breakage. Was he?

Oh, shut up, brain, she said, as she searched around for the exit signs and began driving away. Just shut up, okay?

'Joanna! I thought you must have dropped dead or something! No phone calls. No texts. I thought: either she's in a huff with me for some crime or other I've supposedly committed, or she can't be bothered with her poor old mother any longer. Just let me die in my galaxy of loneliness – you carry on without me, I was thinking. And here you are now, on my doorstep, when I've got Peter coming over in twenty minutes and I haven't done my nails yet . . . Oh well, never mind, I suppose you'd better come in. Come on then, if you're coming!'

If it needed saying, Jo and Laura's mum, Helen, was not your average mother fodder. Opinionated and acerbic, with an enviable mane of red hair and even better legs, she had never been the cuddly sort of mum who would 'there-there' a person and assure them that everything would be all right. Helen was more likely to pour you a massive gin and assure you that the world was going to hell in a handcart, so sod it, you might as well get drunk together and go out in a blaze of kebabs and dancing.

'Hi, Mum,' Jo said wearily, holding up the carrier bag of slightly sweaty dinner-for-two shopping as she stepped across the threshold. 'Um . . . I brought food?'

Following her airport rebuff, she'd driven dolefully to her flat in Hulme, thinking that maybe by some miracle Dennis, her landlord, had paid the electricity bill and that the power would be back on, but unfortunately this was not the case. Not only was there no electricity, but the fridge and freezer smelled heinous where the contents had thawed and gone off, the kitchen floor was a sea of dirty water, and she saw what looked very much like a rat's tail flicking behind the dustbin – the combination of which was enough to send her straight back out again. All the way round the ring road to the small terrace off Moseley Road where she'd grown up, in fact. Crawling back home to Mum, who was wearing a bright-orange mini-dress and fawn over-the-knee boots, an armful of bangles and half a ton of spiky black mascara.

'Waitrose? Very posh,' sniffed Helen, peering into the bag. 'Oooh, fizzy wine, nice. Peter's expecting a casserole, but never mind, I suppose there'll be enough for three. Or I can send him to the chippy.'

What casserole? Jo wanted to ask, following her into the kitchen and seeing that the oven was off and there were no signs whatsoever of any food preparation. 'Who's Peter?' she enquired instead, leaning against the worktop. 'Can I stay tonight, by the way?'

'Who's Peter? Who's Peter, she says,' Helen scoffed, puffing on an electronic cigarette and rolling her eyes. 'If you'd bothered ringing me, you might know. He's my new boyfriend.'

'Oh God.' Now it was Jo's turn to roll her eyes. She had lost track of her mother's tumultuous love-life; it didn't take a psychoanalyst to work out why she and Laura had both been attracted to safe, dependable men, when they'd grown up with a backdrop of ever-changing boyfriends falling for their mother like lemmings over a cliff.

'Less of that, thank you,' Helen tutted. 'And yes, you can stay, but you'll have to put up with the sounds of our love-making through the wall – just warning you now, so like it or lump it. He gets quite animalistic after a few tequilas, does Peter, so—'

'Mum! Please. I don't want to know!'

Helen cackled. 'It's not too late to pop round to the all-night chemist and pick up some earplugs,' she said, elbowing Jo. 'I'm kidding. We're taking things slowly. No need to look like that! We're only on our second date. I do have some standards, thank you very much.'

'It's your second date and you've promised him a casserole, which is . . . where?' Jo asked, gazing around the room, as if a casserole dish might present itself with a little fanfare from behind a cupboard door.

Helen pulled the steaks out of the carrier bag and dumped them on the side. 'Looks like we're having steak, after all. I must have known you would turn up. A mother's intuition is a wonderful thing.' She cackled again. 'Now quick, before he gets here: what's up with you, and why have you knocked on my door with the ingredients for a romantic dinner and a face like a slapped arse? And don't try and tell me otherwise, because I'm not a complete idiot.'

'Well,' Jo began and then sighed. Her mum had a way of getting straight to the heart of an issue, even when you'd rather not discuss it with her. She heaved herself up onto the worktop, legs dangling, just as she'd done when a teenager all those years before. 'I've met this bloke . . .'

Helen put a hand up. 'Stop! We need alcohol.' She pulled the foil off the champagne and held it aloft. 'Shall we?'

'Mum, it's lukewarm, it'll be – oh, whatever,' Jo said, as

Helen twisted the cork regardless. The genie, like the cork, was well and truly out of the bottle now, and there would be no stopping her mother until every detail had been heard. 'Yes. Okay, then. Fine. Thanks.'

Chapter Eleven

Half-term began with the punishment of an overnight trip to stay with India's brother Nicholas and his Swedish wife Petra over in Southport, who thought they were it, just because they had a big house in Birkdale, the posh end of town. 'I don't know why you always get so uptight about going – he *is* your brother,' Dan reminded India in an irritatingly mild-mannered way, while she was trying to get ready that morning. (This involved an emergency attempt to lose an immediate half-stone by wearing her one and only pair of Spanx, for which she practically needed haulage equipment to winch up her thighs. Oof. There.)

'But you *like* your family, remember,' she replied sourly, sucking in her stomach and turning sideways to inspect herself in the mirror. Nope. Not working. Not likely to fool anyone, either, least of all her eagle-eyed sister-in-law, who would spot the trembling rolls of fat forced up above the control pants and would give India pitying looks the whole time, as a result. She breathed out crossly and began peeling off the rubbery torture-wear again with a mixture of relief and resignation. Sod it, she'd just look porky then. She'd let her stomach hang out and be done with it. There was no point anyway trying to compete, belly-wise, with a woman who went for a five-mile run at six every morning, come rain, come shine, come hangover. ('It makes me feel so alive,' Petra had once sighed beatifically. Alive, indeed, India had scoffed in private. Personally she'd rather be alive and in bed at that time of day.)

'And I like your family, too,' Dan was saying, still with that same Mr Reasonable expression. He stuffed a jumper into his weekend bag, followed by – optimistically – a pair of shorts. Despite it being almost June, this was a bank-holiday weekend and therefore they could expect freezing temperatures and gale-force winds, if previous years were anything to go by. Perhaps some light blizzards to top things off.

'Yeah, but . . .' India sighed, tiring of the conversation. 'That's because you're nice to everyone, while I'm just a horrible, bitter old shrew.'

Dan zipped up the bag and headed for the door. 'Come on, Misery Guts,' he said. 'It's only one night. And they're not that bad. Let's just get them hammered on their expensive booze and they might even lighten up for once.'

The last time they'd gone to visit India's brother and his family had been for New Year, and on the way home, quiet and fragile, they'd been halfway back along the M62 when Kit had piped up from the back seat, 'Mum, what's a chav?'

Despite the queasiness of India's hangover, her senses had flicked to red alert. 'It's a horrible, nasty word that snobs use when they're looking down on someone who has less money than them,' she found herself saying, with extra ferocity.

'Why do you ask, Kit?' Dan wanted to know, although India already had a pretty good idea.

'Oscar said I was one,' Kit had replied with shattering honesty, shrugging his skinny shoulders.

'Well, you are,' George told him, in the brutal sort of way that only an older brother can.

'No, he is *not*,' India had growled. 'None of us are.' Bloody Oscar, she thought, fuming. Nick and Petra's son was eight, blond and pretty, the sort of kid you might see in a Gap catalogue, looking adorable. He was also, and India didn't say this lightly about her own nephew, a complete and utter little shit. Every time the two families spent any significant time together, Oscar would always thug it up around Kit – pinching, punching, pushing. ('Boys!' Petra would sigh affectionately, not seeming to notice the way Kit grew quieter and quieter, pressing himself against India. Then, invariably, would come the bad dreams and wet bed, which was exactly what had happened at two o'clock in the morning on New Year's Day, just as India and Dan had sunk into a drunken slumber. Hooray. Have some wet pyjama bottoms in a plastic bag. 'Don't tell Oscar, will you?' Kit had begged fearfully, anticipating further misery ahead.)

A chav, indeed, she'd fumed at the time. Was that what they all thought? Her own parents, certainly, always made a tremendous fuss whenever they came to stay with her, fretting that there was nowhere to park on her street; and, goodness, would the car be all right round the corner like that; and really, when was she going to move out of this grungy end of Sale and get a proper house with a drive, and a nice back garden?

Maybe when a pig flies across the moon, Mum, India had had to resist saying through gritted teeth.

And here she went again, she thought now, as they turned onto the quiet leafy avenue where her brother lived: falling straight back into the same old well-trodden paths of inferiority, slipping into her part as Nick's contrary little sister, or her parents' wayward daughter, the one who . . . *Yes, her. We don't like to talk about that, though.*

It was ridiculous, really. She was thirty-nine years old – she was nearly *forty*! – and still couldn't escape the dictates of the role set down for her in childhood. Who even was she, these days? The wife of Dan, sure; the mother of George, Esme and Kit, yes. She had her place in the world in their noisy, messy home, and throughout her music classes. But then yesterday she'd stepped right out of her usual confines, rocking up at the Intensive Care unit at the hospital with a bag of nice new pyjamas and shortbread and some classic feminist novels in a carrier bag for Alice Goldsmith. 'A friend of the family,' she'd told the nurse, handing over the goodies, before walking back down the echoing corridor to her car, resisting the urge to run, fast, before anyone could start asking questions.

No, she hadn't told Dan about it, nor Eve when she saw her at the school pick-up later, nor any of her other friends. It had been a secret sideways step out of her ordinary life. Was it wrong that she had experienced a prickling sort of frisson whenever she'd thought about it since?

Realizing that her brother's smart modern house was looming up before them, she banished the thought hurriedly. Okay, right, best face on, she vowed. Today she would be sweetness and light, gracious and friendly; she would rise above absolutely everything and refuse to be riled. As Dan parked their old Volvo on Nick and Petra's crunching gravel drive, India took a deep calming Pilates breath and reminded herself that she was relaxed. Really.

The Burrells all rushed out to greet them, Nick with a laughing Meg on his shoulders, Petra looking cool and stylish in a maxi-dress and bare feet, Oscar sporting a grudging expression, as if he'd rather not be mingling with the proles, thanks. Despite having packed jumpers and waterproofs, the air felt benevolently warm and India breathed in the sweet scent of the wisteria that dripped its luxuriant lilac blooms above the front door.

'Hello!'

'Welcome!'

'Lovely to see you!'

The adults' voices rang out through the drowsy suburban air. The children hung back, apparently struck by shyness at the sight of their cousins, apart from Oscar, who folded his arms across his chest. 'Your car is *very* dirty,' he commented.

'And so it begins,' India muttered under her breath to Dan, her smile as bright and shiny as the miniature chrome jaguar, poised mid-leap on the bonnet of her brother's (spotless) car.

'Do you ever wonder,' mused India over dinner that night, 'if you are in the right life? If somewhere along the way you took a turn you shouldn't have and, if you'd just made another choice instead, your whole world would be completely different?'

She was asking the wrong people, she realized, as soon as the words were out of her mouth. Because here they were, in Nick and Petra's beautiful airy kitchen, with its big windows letting in the last of the day's honeyed light, drinking delicious and no doubt cripplingly pricey wine, while all five children shrieked and laughed in the garden. What was more, they had just put away an exceedingly good meal consisting of two roast chickens, tossed green salad and a couple of trays of fragrantly herbed diced potatoes, all of which Petra had knocked up with Zen-like serenity. Of *course* these two didn't feel they were in the wrong lives! They probably didn't know what it meant to make a bad decision. Meanwhile, her own husband was looking hurt and defensive, as if he was wondering whether he had been included as one of India's mistaken turns.

'I mean,' she went on hastily, 'I'm not saying anything's terrible about my life as it is right now – so you can get that worried look off your face, Dan – but take my work, for example. I can't even remember why I took on the business now. Sleep-deprivation madness, it must have been. I thought I'd give it a whirl until I had a better idea . . . but I'm still there, shaking my bloody maracas. The better idea never happened. Not in this universe, anyway.'

'So you think that, in another universe, you'd be doing something you enjoyed more?' Petra ventured, a small frown creasing her forehead. Even when she was frowning, she appeared beautiful, with her angular cheekbones and long elegant neck. (*In another universe I'd look more like you, Petra*, India managed to stop herself from blurting out with an envious sigh.)

'You could see it the other way round – in another universe, you might be on the dole,' Nick pointed out, ever the pragmatist. 'A terrorist bomb could have wiped out your street.'

'Thank you, Captain Optimism,' India said, rolling her eyes.

'Nick!' Petra remonstrated.

'England could have been knocked out of the last World Cup in the first round,' Dan put in glumly. 'Oh no, wait – that did happen, didn't it?'

'I'm just saying, you can get bogged down with all these "what-ifs",' Nick said. He'd been tipping back the booze all afternoon and his face was a mottled brick-red as he filled their glasses once more. 'And what for? You're in this life – and from what I can see, it looks a pretty decent one – so what's the problem?'

'There's not a *problem*, I just meant – oh, never mind.' Now India felt churlish, as if she'd been ticked off for moaning about her 'pretty decent' life. (Pretty decent, indeed. She wondered how he'd class his own golf-playing executive lifestyle, and reckoned it would be quite a lot more generous than 'pretty decent'.) 'I just find it interesting, that's all, to wonder. What other versions of me might be doing. Petra – you must have thought the same, haven't you? If you hadn't saddled yourself with my brother, you could be . . . I don't know. Shacked up with someone good-looking and clever, for instance. Joking!'

Petra looked confused. For all her general Scandi perfection and wholesomeness, she didn't have much of a sense of humour, India remembered too late. 'But I want to be with Nick!' she cried, reaching across the table for his hand. 'He *is* good-looking and clever. And I don't want to be doing anything else.'

Oh dear. The conversation was sliding away from her, and now India's last comment sounded bitchy when that had really not been her intention. 'I was *joking*,' she repeated, noticing that her brother wasn't smiling, either. 'It was more that . . . Look, I saw this horrific crash just after my birthday, all right? A car smashing into a shop, right in front of me. People seriously injured, everyone screaming. And since then—'

'Here we go,' muttered Dan.

'And since then, I've been thinking: what if the car had hit *me*, rather than the other people? How come I was spared like that, unhurt, when—'

'Hardly *spared*,' her husband pointed out. 'This wine is excellent, by the way, Nick.'

It was no good, they weren't playing along, and India finally ran out of steam. 'Oh, never mind,' she said, defeated, and feeling as if everyone was annoyed by her. She glanced out of the window, to where Oscar appeared to be dragging Kit around by his ankles, and wondered if she should intervene. As the youngest of three, Kit was able to put up with a certain amount of rough and tumble, but there inevitably came a point where he couldn't cope and would crumple into tears. Added to which, his older siblings, heartless to the core, would not be dashing to his rescue any time soon, she predicted.

'It's a Garrus Rosé, Château d'Esclans,' Nick replied. 'More like a white Burgundy really – it's widely regarded as the best rosé these days. It's one I got from our wine club a few months ago, and we liked it so much, I ended up ordering a case. Are you in a wine club, Dan? I can recommend ours, if not.'

'No,' said Dan, carefully avoiding looking at his wife, who refused to buy any wine that cost more than six pounds, on principle. 'We're not in a wine club.'

Petra at least took pity on India. 'Well, I think *I'm* going to make the decision to find the cheesecake,' she said jovially. 'I hope that will not be a wrong turn.'

India smiled back. 'That definitely sounds like a right turn.'

'A right turn and a good decision,' Dan told Petra, twinkling.

'Good decisions, bad decisions, everyone makes them,' said Nick. Of course he had to have the final word. 'Everyone's life is constructed by their own set of decisions. For example, I could have decided not to attend a particular client dinner one night – but I did attend, and I met Petra.

Likewise, Petra had the chance to study in the States or in the UK – but she made the decision to come here, luckily for me.' He glanced fondly over at her, where she was getting bowls from a cupboard. Then he turned back to India and his eyes narrowed slightly, making her wonder if he was remembering her comment about Petra choosing a better-looking husband (which had been a *joke*!). Nick was nice enough, as brothers went, but if there was one thing he hated, it was people laughing at him. When they were much younger he had sometimes been cruel to her, if she'd dared tease him. 'As for you—' he began, and India had a sudden premonition of doom.

'*Exactly*,' she interrupted, not liking the way he was looking at her. 'And Dan and I might not have got chatting at a dodgy house-party that time, and all the rest of it. This is what I've been trying to say.'

'Or you might not have gone to university,' he went on, his voice alarmingly silky, his eyes hooded. 'You could have stayed at home and—'

'Well, yes, quite,' India said loudly, fearful of where this was leading. There was a dangerous glint in his eye and she jumped to her feet, desperate to head him off, fast, before he went any further. *I know you*, that glint said. *Don't forget that*. 'I'll just check on the kids,' she said, walking briskly towards the back door. 'Kit, are you okay?' she called for good measure as she went out. 'Gently with him, Oscar!'

The air was starting to cool outside, with shadows silently gathering in the corners of the garden. India shivered as she stood there for a moment, her back to the house, not wanting to return inside until she'd regained her equilibrium. What had Nick been about to *say* just then, before she'd interrupted him? Was he seriously about to dredge up the darkest moments of her past at his middle-class dinner table, detonate her marriage on a whim, when he'd been sworn to secrecy all those years ago? Oh my God, she thought, feeling the alcohol buzzing around her, as she imagined her husband's face. The Burrells had never since spoken of that summer, when she'd been a heartbroken teenager and her parents had seethed with barely suppressed disapproval. Nick had been at university by then anyway, so he had missed the worst of it, and she'd hoped – foolishly, admittedly – that he might even have forgotten about the saga. But if her instincts had been right – if he'd been on the brink of hauling the whole sorry tale back up, in order to make some kind of point (*Don't you dare insinuate I'm not clever and good-looking, in front of my wife!*) – then she would have to tread very carefully around him.

'What are you doing, Mum?' asked Esme just then and India jumped, realizing she was still standing there in the darkening garden, staring anxiously into space.

Act normal. Give it your best shot. She forced herself to smile, even though she could see that her daughter must have furtively applied several coats of mascara behind her back – Petra's expensive Estée Lauder stuff, as well, she bet – and now her perfect sister-in-law would probably judge India on that, too. 'I just came out to say that it's time for pudding. Did you all hear? *Pudding!* Come and wash your hands.'

Her announcement was greeted by exuberant cheers and then a charge for the kitchen, with India hurrying to keep up with them. Safety in numbers, and all that.

She woke in the night with a start, having dreamed about Robin for the first time in ages. He still appeared to her like this every now and then – fixed, as if in amber, at eighteen with his tousled brown hair, his rockstar white jeans and clumsy eyeliner, his body as wiry as ever. The disturbing thing about these dreams, as far as India was concerned, was that she was always kissing him, and they would always rip off each other's clothes in a very X-rated way. Occasionally she had woken up panting, convinced she'd just had an orgasm in her sleep, and would glance across at her husband, sleeping beside her in the bed, and feel a stab of guilt at her own treachery.

Robin Fielding. They'd met in sixth form, where people had just about stopped calling her 'Barrel', thank goodness (she had been a bit chubby throughout school; no, it wasn't a particularly witty nickname). They had sat next to each other for English Lit and bonded over their shared feelings for Ted Hughes (good), David Bowie (a genius) and overbearing parents (his were religious, hers just strict). Robin could be caustic and liked to argue – rumour had it he'd been expelled from his last school for fighting. He introduced her to smoking dope and obscure psychedelic bands, and sometimes wore black nail varnish, just to wind up his dad. Oh, how India had loved him. How hard and breathlessly she had fallen. She would have done anything for Robin; she would have thrown herself off a motorway bridge if he'd asked her to, set herself aflame with lighter fuel, tattooed his name across her body, anything at all. It had been mutual, too – a furnace of passion, heady and all-consuming. He would break out of his house in the middle of the night, pick flowers from random people's gardens and leave them on her doorstep. He had once punched a boy for calling her fat, and had to go and see the head of sixth form because the other boy's nose was broken. He had written her love-poems, even, his soul laid bare on lined paper torn from an exercise book; she had kept them under her pillow at night, reading them so many times that the paper became soft.

Nobody had ever written a love-poem for her since, obviously, apart from her children, occasionally, under duress for Mother's Day, but that wasn't the same. Dan was a good man, sure, a lovely husband, and she wasn't knocking him at all really, but he was the sort of bloke who, if pushed to express his feelings for her with pen and paper, would come up with a dirty limerick and expect her to think herself lucky. 'Look, I'm a plumber, not frigging Shakespeare,' she imagined him saying in exasperation.

Anyway. Whatever. Here she was in bed with *Dan*, who might be crap on the poetry front, but who was safe, solid and dependable nonetheless, who had given her three beautiful children and put up with her whims and moods. Robin was ancient history and had never been settling-down material – there was no way the relationship would have survived the grown-up years of living together and paying bills, all the boring stuff that was the real test of a partnership. The past was the past, and it should stay there.

She rolled over in the dark, feeling uncertain and, for some reason, unhappy, wishing they were at home instead of here. Wishing, too, that she could feel a bit more secure, more content with her lot these days, instead of glancing sideways at the what-ifs all the time. She needed to start counting her blessings, making gratitude lists and remembering that she was lucky, actually, and had a perfectly good life, so there.

Just then she heard soft footsteps along the corridor outside. The slow, wary creak of the door. 'Mum?' It was Kit, clutching his old bear, light from the landing spilling around him as he hovered on the threshold in his Chewbacca pyjamas.

India propped herself up in bed, guessing already the cause of this night-time visitation. 'Are you all right, love? Was it a bad dream?'

He stepped towards her, still muddled with sleep, his dark hair sticking up on his head. A whiff of ammonia came leaking through the darkness and she tried not to sigh. Oh no. Here we go again. When she'd made a point of reminding him about having a last wee, as well. *'Is Kit still not dry at night?'* Petra would cluck in the morning, all sympathy, and India hated herself for knowing that she'd feel ashamed.

'Never mind, pet,' she said, heaving her legs out of bed and reaching to put her arms around him. *This* was her real life, she reminded herself, not teenage sweethearts and other people's families; it was time to stop all the nonsense and come back down to earth. 'Come on, let's get you sorted out.'

Chapter Twelve

Back when they were schoolgirls – Jo sixteen and Laura twelve or thereabouts – Laura had once overheard a conversation that had stayed with her ever since. She'd been in the girls' loos at the upper school, fluffing up her blonde hair in the mirror and almost certainly adding another ozone-killing blast of hairspray, when her attention was caught by the sound of her own surname. There'd been a high window slanted open in the bathroom, she seemed to remember, one of those uselessly small windows designed to prevent students from escaping, and the voices – male, teenage – had come floating through.

'Yeah, what's-her-name – that Nicholls girl – she's pretty fit.'

Laura had frozen, hairbrush in hand, as she caught her own eye in the mirror. Who, me?

'What, *Jo Nicholls*? Are you kidding? I saw her playing netball the other day, legs like tree trunks. The ground was practically shaking.'

'No! Not her. The fun one. The blonde. Can't remember what her name is.'

'Oh yeah, I know. Laura.'

'Yeah, Laura. She's well fit.'

The fun one. It had stuck in her mind, that phrase; she had felt it settling around her shoulders like an attractive sort of cape, and she liked the way it fitted. Who wouldn't want to be the fun one? she'd thought, preening, unable to help exchanging a knowing smirk of satisfaction with her reflection. She could afford to be the fun one, too, being the younger, dafter sister who didn't have to worry about stuff. Especially because she knew it would all get taken care of by sensible, responsible Jo, who was, as a result, far too busy to care about trivial things like her own thighs and what boys might say about them.

Even as an adult, the phrase had remained key to how Laura viewed herself. I'm the fun one, mucking up my exams because I'm going to house-parties and snogging boys. I'm the fun one, giggling in interviews, playing up to the dizzy blonde stereotype, always up for a night out. I'm the fun one, never taking life too seriously, making people laugh. 'She walks through life on the bright side of the road,' Matt had said in his wedding speech and Laura's eyes had welled up at his unexpectedly poetic turn of phrase.

But suddenly, almost imperceptibly, she had stopped being the fun one. Somehow or other, she had become a person whose side of the road was now darkened by clouds, whose own husband had given up on her. How could you be fun when you felt like the weight of the world was pressing down on your shoulders, like your emotions were constantly in danger of erupting?

And now look at her, knocking meekly at her mother's front door on a Saturday morning because she couldn't stand being at home any more, when Matt had said he thought they should give up on the baby plan. Frankly, this was all very far from her definition of 'fun'.

The night before, after he'd said those terrible things, she'd reeled out of the pub and walked blindly through town, barely stopping to check for traffic as she crossed each road, just stumbling forward, dazed with shock. She'd ended up in some awful bar, drinking whisky on an empty stomach (she didn't even *like* whisky) and then, on the way home, some guy had tried to chat her up – yeah, because she was such a catch, obviously, pissed and on her own, eating a bag of chips in a bus shelter. She'd ended up bursting into tears on him, clinging to his arm and telling him she only wanted a *baby*, that was *all*, why wasn't anyone letting her have a *baby*? – which proved to be a very effective way of getting rid of an unwanted admirer, at least.

Once she'd finally made it home, she'd found Matt pacing about, desperately worried about her ('Why was your phone off, Laura? For goodness' sake!') and she'd thought for a brief, bright moment that this might be the turning point, that she'd be able to talk him round. He loved her, didn't he? He'd been worried about her! But no. Still no. The more she tried to persuade him that IVF or another fertility treatment was the best way forward, the more he dug his heels in. He was a Pisces and she knew full well that you couldn't tell a fish which way to swim.

Knocking again at her mum's front door – please let her be in, please – a memory flashed into Laura's head of being in the loos at work last year, leaning against the cubicle wall and sobbing soundlessly at the arrival of her period, punctual as ever. Of screaming out loud in her car as she drove home one night because it was so unfair, because she was so sick of the disappointment, because she just couldn't bear it any more. Of the maniacal joy and fear she'd felt last November when the pregnancy test had said positive, and how she'd taken to using hand-sanitizer every ten minutes (you couldn't be too careful), walking everywhere with great care, with no sudden moves so as not to somehow jolt the baby out of her (was that a thing? Probably not, but she wasn't taking any chances); how she'd dutifully swallowed her folic-acid tablets and forced herself to eat kale and blueberries and spinach, for optimum nutrition . . . only to have her hopes snatched away yet again.

Was that all over for her now, then? The closing of a chapter? The drawing of a line?

She couldn't stand it, if so. Okay, so those times had been hellish, but while there was still a possibility, still a chance, surely they should keep on trying?

'All right, all right, no need to bang the door down!' At last – there was her mother on the doorstep, in a hideous paisley dressing gown and fluffy slippers, bed-hair and no make-up. She frowned in surprise to see Laura there, tear-streaked and wan. 'What the . . . ? What *is* this, my bank-holiday weekend surprise? First one turns up, then the other: what's going on with you girls, for goodness' sake?' She narrowed her eyes suspiciously. 'And why have you got that face on, like you've just found out about the tooth fairy?'

'Mum, I . . .' Laura said, and then the grief, combined with the whisky hangover, hit her with a wallop and she found herself hiccupping and stumbling forward into her mum's bony embrace. 'I'm really, really sad.'

'Oh, chick, come here.' Helen smelled of talcum powder and stale Southern Comfort and unwashed bed-sheets, but her arms were strong and tight, and for a second it was as if Laura was eight years old and one of the big boys had pushed her over on the way home from school. All too soon, though, the hug was over – her mum had never been the touchy-feely type – and Helen was bellowing up the stairs. 'Jo? JoANNA! Your sister's here. Yes, on the doorstep!' She rolled her eyes, hauling Laura inside the house and shutting the front door again. 'It's like bloody Piccadilly around here, I can tell you. Is it too early for a drink?'

Then Jo was stumbling downstairs, her hair a massive orange fuzz-ball where she'd just got up, pulling on a dressing gown with a startled expression. 'What are you doing here?' she asked.

'What are *you* doing here?' countered Laura, staring.

'Why don't I make us all a nice Martini?' suggested Helen.

It was like old times at first – the three of them on the sofa together, taking it in turns to fetch provisions from the kitchen every now and then: biscuits, coffee, toast, a second box of tissues when Laura started crying again. Theirs had been a relationship of three for many years, after all, since Laura and Jo's dad had walked out, never to be seen or heard from again, two weeks before Laura's fourth birthday. He was a flickering sort of figure to her now, barely remembered, and after his departure, her childhood had centred around this tight little three-way knot. And here they were again: same living room, same wallpaper, same sofa – only this time it wasn't some teenage crush her mum and sister were advising her on, it was her *husband*, her *marriage*, her feelings of utter doom.

'He'll come round. You two are the golden couple!' Helen and Jo kept telling her. 'He'll see sense eventually, he always does. Remember when you fell out over what colour to paint the bathroom?'

'And what about when you couldn't decide where to go on holiday last year? You got your way in the end, didn't you?'

Laura knew they were only trying to be helpful, but really – the colour of a bathroom and a holiday destination were pretty insignificant, compared to whether or not she and Matt should keep trying for a baby. 'I guess,' was all she mumbled, though, worn down by the drama.

'You wait, he'll be back, on bended knee. Mark my words! I know I'm always saying that all men are bastards, but your Matt – he's different. He's one of the good guys, and take it from me, there aren't many of *them* around.' Helen gave one of her long-suffering sniffs. 'I should know, I've been looking for one for the last thirty-five years.'

Laura and Jo eye-rolled each other, because this topic of conversation was never all that far away where their mother was concerned. 'So this new guy – Pete, was it? Where does he stand?' Jo asked, before adding, for the benefit of Laura, 'I met him last night, by the way. I'm not sure we'll be getting a new stepdad any time soon, to be honest.'

'Oi! He's all right.'

'Mum! Come on. He's got really bad BO, for one thing – and he was wearing this horrible stained tracksuit.'

'He's got kind eyes!'

'He's not exactly the next Mr Parkins, though, is he?'

The three of them fell silent for a moment, reflecting. Mr Parkins had been Laura's English teacher on whom they'd all had a massive unanimous crush, leading to several excruciating parents' evenings in days gone by. Laura still tingled with embarrassment to remember her mum leaning forward across the desk, all perfume and cleavage, batting her eyelashes and cooing, while poor Mr Parkins fiddled with his wedding ring and tried to steer the conversation back to a recent essay on *Macbeth*.

'I thought I'd married *my* Mr Parkins,' Laura said dolefully, misery seeping back in like rain through a cheap tent. She sighed. 'Why are you here, anyway, Jo? I thought you'd be cosied up with *your* Mr Parkins. Isn't he back from Dublin yet?'

Jo launched into a saga about an aborted airport reunion, the manipulative daughter ('who *hates* me') and her doubts about whether she'd fallen for Rick too quickly and should have held back before rushing in. Just as she was drawing to a despairing close, her phone rang and Laura noticed her face soften as she glanced at the screen, before standing up and walking away from them to answer it.

'Hi,' Jo said happily, and Laura arched an eyebrow at her mum. Talk of the devil . . .

'Ask him round,' Helen hissed excitedly, already patting

her hair into a tidier shape. 'Come round!' she called. 'The mother wants to look you over!'

'What?' Jo asked. 'Oh. Sorry. That's just my mum. Yeah, I stayed at hers last night.'

'You're welcome any time!' Helen went on, louder still. 'I won't bite! Well, not unless you— Ow!' She broke off as Laura elbowed her. 'What was that for?' she grumbled, rubbing her side.

'Um . . .' Jo was saying awkwardly, 'because . . . Yeah. It's not a big deal, though! He must be on holiday. I'm sure it'll all be fixed soon.' She was doing her best to sound upbeat and breezy – despite the fact that she was presumably talking about her manky rat-infested flat and her useless landlord – but pulled a face at Laura as she said the words, acknowledging the lie. Then she gave a surprised sort of laugh. 'Oh! Oh, there's no need – I'm sure it'll—'

Helen pursed her lips and Laura, too, felt herself wondering what was going on. 'Another cup of tea, Mum?' she asked, not wanting to eavesdrop too blatantly.

'God!' Jo was saying, her cheeks turning pink. 'Are you sure? I mean – it can just be a temporary thing, obviously, we don't have to . . . Okay. Thanks! All right, I'll be over later on. Couple of hours?'

She hung up, looking dazed, then her eyes sparkled as she turned to Laura, loitering in the doorway. 'Whoa,' she breathed. 'So that was unexpected.'

'What? What did he say?' asked Laura and Helen simultaneously.

Jo blinked and tucked a loose curl behind her ear, still with that stunned, dazzled expression. 'Um. Well. He just asked me to move in with him.'

Chapter Thirteen

'You're moving *in* with him?' Her mother frowned with obvious disapproval. 'What, for good? Oh dear. Oh no. No, no, no, Jo, what are you *thinking*?'

'Mum!' Jo laughed. 'Of all the people to be advising me on this, I'm afraid you're about the last person I'm going to take any notice of.'

'Are you sure that's what you want?' Laura hazarded. 'I mean . . . You do have options, you know; you can totally stay with us. If you don't mind a stony silence across the breakfast table, that is, and tension you could cut with a chainsaw.'

Jo had considered this offer for approximately half a second – hmm, let me think: stony silences versus round-the-clock hot new man-love – and had thanked her sister, but said it was fine; and yes, she was quite sure. (And then she blushed cringingly red at the workings of her own brain – hot new man-love indeed – and sent up a grateful little prayer that neither her mother nor her sister could read minds.) She had left shortly afterwards, because she could see Laura's face becoming all tight and teary again, and didn't want to rub her sister's nose in her own wild happiness. Talk about romantic. And exciting. And unexpected! *Why don't you . . . move in with me?* he'd asked, in his sexy, drawly phone voice. How could any heterosexual woman refuse?

It was only after she'd dumped the majority of her possessions at the nearest Big Yellow and was driving over a car-load of essentials to his flat that the Voice of Reason suddenly dialled in, for a one-to-one. *And you've been with this guy for – what, a couple of weeks?* the Voice asked pointedly.

Well, it's been a month now, so . . . replied her heart.

And you're willing to give up your independence just like that, when he clicks his fingers? Even after he binned you off for his kid last night?

Um, I don't think it's quite as sinister as that. I'm *staying* with him, really, not actually moving in. I think.

Says you, with your car crammed full of stuff. Right. So what happened to that new Jo – the strong, not-to-be-pushed-around Jo – who was going to take things slowly, who wasn't about to rush into anything rash, just for the sake of it?

It's not 'just for the sake of it', though, it's . . . Look, it's complicated. And it's only temporary anyway. I'll sort out another flat for myself in a week or so. It's not a big deal.

Really.

'Yes, really!' snapped Jo, before realizing that she'd said

that out loud, with the car window down, and that the driver alongside her at the traffic lights was giving her nervous, mad-woman-alert glances. 'You're breaking up,' she said, pretending she was taking a call and twiddled with an imaginary earpiece for good measure. Then, as she pulled away, she dropped the act, switching on the radio and turning it up loud, so that the dreary, nagging Voice of Reason could no longer be heard. Sod off, Voice of Reason. I'm just having a bit of fun, that's all. Okay?

Having arrived at the flat, sweaty and red-faced from hauling up three cardboard boxes in the lift, she belatedly remembered the third wheel on this vehicle: Maisie, who was also staying at her dad's place, and who, somewhat predictably, turned out to be less than thrilled about the new living arrangements. 'You have got to be kidding me,' the girl cried, hand on hip, not even bothering to hide her scandalized expression as Jo heaved the boxes into the hall. 'Dad – no. This is crazy. What are you thinking? Does *Mum* know about this?'

Rick stiffened at the mention of his ex, while Jo felt her good cheer popping like soap bubbles. 'It's none of your mum's business,' Rick replied curtly. 'And it's not really yours either, might I remind you.'

'Um, it's only temporary . . .' Jo put in meekly, a trickle of nervous sweat running between her shoulderblades.

Maisie ignored her, though, squaring up to her dad.

'Well, it *is* my business when I'm coming to stay with you every other weekend,' she retaliated. 'Ugh! I don't want to be lying awake listening to the disgusting sounds of you two having *sex,* it's—'

'Maisie!' Rick thundered. 'That's quite enough. I mean it. Stop trying to show off, you're just making yourself look immature and crass.'

Ouch. Jo had never seen him so severe. But far from silencing his daughter, his words had the effect of prodding a hornets' nest. Her eyes glittered, her lip curled, her face became positively stony. 'If that's what you think of me,' she began with impressive aplomb, 'then I might as well pack my things and go. It's obvious you've made your choice! One in, one out, would that suit you, Dad?'

And off she whirled, tawny hair swinging round behind her, shoulders rigid. Rick, of course, was powerless to resist and hurried after her. 'Maze – come on. Don't be like that,' Jo heard him wheedling, before there came the slam of Maisie's bedroom door.

Goodness. Maybe this hadn't been such a great idea after all, Jo thought, standing there like a spare part for a moment, before trudging back downstairs to bring up her suitcases full of clothes. But on her return, the lift doors parted to reveal Rick standing there waiting for her, reaching out a hand for one of the cases.

'Are you sure this is okay?' Jo asked in a low voice as they walked along the corridor together. 'I mean, I can go back to Laura's or Mum's if—'

'It's fine,' he told her firmly. 'It's all fine. This is my flat, and Maisie will just have to get used to it.' Which was not exactly the most reassuring line in the world, thought Jo as she tentatively followed him through the front door again, but never mind, here she was. You've made your bed, now lie in it, as her mum would have said. Which, if Maisie hadn't been there, might literally have been the case – the bedroom reunion she'd imagined, the giddy, joyful confirmation of their relationship, and yet . . . Having a stroppy teenager the other side of the wall was most definitely a passion-killer.

I never wanted kids, I don't want to be a stepmother, Jo thought, flinching as loud music started belting out from the girl's bedroom. It was one thing that she and Greg had had in common at least, that shared certainty, so different from her sister's broodiness – and yet here she was, falling in love with a new man whose daughter very much came as part of the package. Dumping her case alongside the rest of her possessions, Jo tried not to give in to despair. Rick was worth it, she reminded herself staunchly. He was worth all of this aggro. And surely Maisie would drop the petulancy and bad attitude soon, wouldn't she?

'Morning, Maisie. Did you sleep well?' It was the following day and Jo had emerged from Rick's bedroom to make coffees. The flat had two bedrooms, a stylish bathroom and an open-plan space consisting of a kitchen area, demarcated by a grey-tiled breakfast bar, and a comfortable living-room area. Maisie, dressed in a zebra-print onesie with the hood up, was sitting on one of the sofas eating a bowl of cereal and watching some YouTube video or other on a laptop.

The girl didn't reply immediately and Jo was just resigning herself to being ignored – whatever, it suited her fine – when a contemptuous reply finally came. 'I'm just wondering,' said Maisie, eyes remaining on the screen, 'what all this shit is, in here.'

Jo's smile faltered. 'What . . . what do you mean?' she asked apprehensively. What was it about this girl that made her feel so uncomfortable? she wondered, peering at Rick's expensive coffee machine and trying to remember how to work it.

'I *mean*,' Maisie said, with exaggerated impatience, 'the shit that has appeared in my dad's living room. Like that weird bird. And that tacky-looking vase. And all those crappy paperbacks.'

The weird bird, tacky-looking vase and crappy paperbacks were, of course, Jo's, as well Maisie knew. Rick had encouraged her to unpack and mingle them with his admittedly more stylish possessions around the room – the sleek grey clock, the pedestal globe, the carved marble book-ends – and it had been a nice moment, the night before, as she'd explained the significance of each item to him. That the pretty glass bird was one of the few gifts she'd ever received from her dad before he vanished; that the glossy red vase had been the first thing she'd bought herself post-divorce, because it looked so cheerful and bright; and that the books – well, it was like bringing a bunch of friends with her, having her favourite novels in a room. But now, seeing them through Maisie's disparaging eyes, she felt defensive and hurt. 'They're my things,' she said, trying not to rise to the jibe. 'Your dad said it was—'

'Well, they're shit,' Maisie pronounced, seemingly not interested in what her dad had said. 'They're fucking shit and you've got fucking awful taste.' All this had been said while staring at the laptop, as if she couldn't even be bothered to look at Jo, but then she swung round, lip curling, and sneered at Jo standing there in her ratty old dressing gown, still trying to make the coffee machine come to life. 'Me and Mum have had a right laugh about them, I sent her photos. She reckons you're Dad's midlife crisis.'

The girl's words, delivered with such casual scorn, were enough to leave Jo feeling winded. They were like knives to the heart: stab, stab, stab, spite upon spite. Jo had worked with difficult patients, she knew how to react in a trauma situation, but right now, when a teenage girl was savaging her so brutally, she had no idea how to respond. Part of her wanted to fight back, to retaliate, but how could she, when this was Rick's daughter and he was sure to take her side? Instead she said nothing, trying to keep her cool, although that was tested even further when the coffee machine abruptly let out a plume of steam and spurted hot liquid from its tap, splashing Jo's hand and making her yelp.

Maisie sniggered, then swivelled back to whatever she was watching, turning up the volume until it was unbearably loud. Presumably this was so that Jo would try and tell her off, resulting in Maisie retorting 'You're not my mum, you can't tell me what to do' and making a battle of it. God! This was why she'd never wanted children, Jo thought, running her scalded hand under the cold tap, just as Rick came out, bleary-eyed, in T-shirt and boxers.

'What the . . . ? Turn that down!' he yelled at Maisie.

'Yes, Dad,' she piped, meek and docile, Daddy's little bunny rabbit. Then, as Rick went over to the coffee machine and swiftly made them each a latte, Maisie raised her hand, middle finger aloft, a private message for Jo.

Message received, thought Jo, turning away and trying to concentrate on what Rick was saying about breakfast. Loud and bloody clear.

Chapter Fourteen

Back in her late twenties, Eve had been one of the last of her group of friends to marry and settle down, always having shied away from serious relationships until then. 'Let's face it, it's because of Dad,' said Rosalind, her sister, who was similarly unattached, although she, at least, had had plenty of boyfriends, however fleeting. Rosalind had a point: having grown up with a dad like theirs – unpredictable, aggressive, volatile – Eve had never felt particularly confident around men. It wasn't as if she was scared of them, nothing so clear-cut as that. It was more a sense of mistrust, a reluctance to reveal her inner vulnerabilities, for fear that she was opening herself up to be crushed. Men with loud voices made her particularly uneasy.

Then she'd met Neil. Earnest, bespectacled Neil, who was quiet and cerebral and a little bit awkward, just like Eve. Their paths had crossed at the Whitworth Gallery, at a pop-art exhibition, when they'd both simultaneously burst out laughing in front of a Roy Lichtenstein piece. *Drowning Girl*, it was called, featuring a close-up of the eponymous drowning girl with a thought bubble above her tearful face, claiming that she didn't care, she'd rather sink below the water than call Brad for help, and Eve had found it funny because it reminded her so much of her own self.

If she had been the superstitious sort (she wasn't) or at all inclined to believe in Fate (she didn't), she might have called this chance encounter with Neil pre-destined, seeing as both of them were there spontaneously alone – Eve killing time before meeting a friend, and Neil having wandered in out of the rain. As it was, they fell into shy conversation following their mutual laughter, and then wandered around the rest of the exhibition together until, eventually, when she looked at her watch and realized with a start that she was going to be late, he had blushingly asked for her number. And so it began.

Goodness knows why that particular memory had drifted through her mind today, she thought, washing up the lunch things in the Peak District cottage where they'd come for a few days over half-term. Perhaps because it felt as if light years had passed since she and Neil had done anything romantic together. That initial fluttery flush of attraction had given way to the predictability of married life, of jobs and children and responsibilities. They barely even went out together any more, because there always seemed to be other things to do – PTA meetings, laundry, taxiing the girls around to gymnastics clubs and the school orchestra, and all the rest of it. Somehow, a night out with her husband seemed to have been relegated right to the bottom of Eve's To-Do list. (Although, to be fair, he could take it upon himself to suggest a date just as well, couldn't he? Why should it be *her* responsibility to organize everything anyway?)

She rinsed the suds from the last plate and stacked it neatly in the draining rack, emptied the water and wiped round the sink. Then she dried everything and put it away. Now what? she wondered, peering through the small window at the leaden skies and the horizontal rain. Having discovered with great joy that the owners of the cottage had in fact recently installed a Wi-Fi router – 'Welcome to the twenty-first century,' Grace had sighed in relief – the girls had flatly refused her suggestions of family card games or a jigsaw, preferring the company of their own phones. Neil, similarly, was glued to his, repeatedly taking business calls, even though this was technically a holiday. It was too wet to go for a run, and Eve had already finished the thriller she'd brought with her. It seemed embarrassing to admit it, but without her usual To-Do list, she felt ever so slightly cut adrift.

'Does anyone want to . . . do anything?' she called up the stairs to the rest of the family. No reply came.

This wasn't how holidays used to be, she thought padding back to the kitchen and making coffee, even though she'd only just finished one. She was used to noise and laughter, family activities and games, racing up hills together and charging about on bikes, not this morgue-like silence. Was this a sign of how things would be in the future? The girls peeling away into their own worlds of independence, she and Neil busying themselves with work, kidding themselves that they still had a purpose, were still useful in the world? She hadn't yet managed to get to the bottom of this apparent boyfriend of Grace's, despite her best attempts at a cosy mum-and-daughter chat. Was she becoming redundant, irrelevant to her own family? For so long she had felt at the centre of things, a crucial cog in the works, keeping the family machine spinning smoothly with all her lists and tasks. Admittedly, a holiday task sheet boiled down to just: Have fun with Neil and the girls – but you couldn't force someone to have fun with you if they didn't want to, could you?

'A walk? A game? Anyone?' she called again, desperate to try and drag them from their screens. Still no reply. Maybe this would be a good moment to sit down with Neil while the girls were busy, and the downpour so biblical, she thought: start a proper conversation. Who wanted to be like Lichtenstein's *Drowning Girl*, anyway, prepared to die from stubbornness rather than ask for help? She opened and closed her fingers reflexively as she pictured herself sitting down on the small double bed with its soft floral coverings and clearing her throat. 'Have you got a minute?' she would say.

But then she heard his voice floating down the stairs to her, mid-phone-call, sounding tense and urgent. 'If the files aren't with the council by the end of play today, then the whole build's in jeopardy. If we're to get this signed off, then . . .'

Eve sighed, wandering into the small living room and sinking onto the sofa there. The financial director of a leisure company, Neil had been distracted for weeks by the current takeover of a small chain of health clubs, and it wasn't a huge surprise that he couldn't switch off. Sod it, she thought. She'd fully intended to have a screen-free break while here, so that she could enjoy her family's company, but they didn't seem to feel the same way. So she plugged in her laptop, feeling guilty about what a relief it was: the thought of catching up on a few emails, keeping on top of things. Maybe she could start looking at possible team-building activities for the company away-day in September too, as a sop to her boss, just so that she could reply, 'It's all in hand!' next time Frances asked about it. *Here's an idea – we could all go to a rainy cottage with nothing to do and try not to kill each other!* Maybe not.

The screen blinked into life and the notifications totted up in one corner. New emails. New Facebook messages. New system updates. Diary reminders. Sometimes her laptop was like one more member of the family, pestering her for attention. She opened her emails and scanned down the in-box. Waitrose vouchers, the library, various newsletters, a Marks & Spencer sale, a bank statement . . . Lewis Mulligan . . . Her finger must have inadvertently jerked while scrolling down the list, because in the next moment his email was opening itself up in a new box on the screen. There were his bank details, as promised, plus the total she owed him (ouch). And there underneath was the question: *How are you, Eve?*

She stared at it for a moment, biting her lip. It was ridiculous, really, that he – her hopeless fuckwit client – was the only other person in the world who knew her secret. Bizarre to have him asking solicitously after her, like she wasn't just his accountant and the distracted driver who'd knocked him off his bike. Like he actually gave a toss.

He was probably only being polite. Probably just wanted her to hurry up and hand over the money she owed him, too. But then again, when was the last time another person had asked that question? Neil was in his own world. The girls, too, were in their private bubbles these days. She'd waved to India a couple of times, fleetingly, at the school gates, and had had a text from Jo about meeting up, but nobody had asked about her, specifically, for quite some days. *How are you, Eve?*

Kind of a mess, actually. Fraying at the edges. Having some dark moments. You?

Thanks, she typed quickly in reply, rejecting all her previous answers. *I'm okay.*

But the words seemed to mock her and she found herself backspacing through them again. *I'm a bit scared*, she typed next, which was more truthful at least, but horribly needy. Delete, delete, delete.

I'm still burying my head in the sand, to be honest, she typed next, and then pressed Send before she could change her mind.

Seconds later, his reply appeared. *Aw, Eve, come on*, it said. *See the doctor. Do the right thing.*

She could almost hear his Scottish accent as she read the words. Her fingers hovered over the keyboard and she felt a weird pang at the sound of Neil's voice drifting through the ceiling. This was wrong, surely, chatting secretly to this guy she barely knew, in whom she'd confided. Then another reply came.

I've got half an hour between classes. Want me to ring and book you an appointment? It's no bother.

God, he didn't let up, did he? For such an airhead when it came to a business model, he was proving surprisingly tenacious in terms of Eve's health. *It's fine, I'll do it*, she replied after a moment. Then, before she could stop them, her fingers seemed to be typing of their own accord. *But what if it's bad news? What if they say I'm going to die?*

His reply came back, swift and pertinent again. *Then you*

need to get on with living, he'd written. *Crack on with all the fun stuff. How about a new career in rally driving?*

'Well, I *am* annoyed, yes, because this should have been done last week, and we both know that,' she heard Neil saying crossly upstairs, and Eve grimaced, Lewis's words resounding around her head. Fun stuff, yeah, right. Was this really the best the Taylor family could manage, sitting in separate rooms, all plugged into different devices? On their *holiday*?

Be careful what you wish for, she typed and was just about to add a winking emoji when she stopped herself hurriedly. This was a client, after all – a pretty irritating one at that, and the last thing she wanted was to encourage him. Still, she thought, her finger hovering over the Send button, at least he cared. *Thanks*, she added after a moment.

Email sent, laptop closed down, she looked out of the window to see that the rain seemed to be ceasing and that the sun had broken through the clouds to cast a gleam on the stone walls. The leaves dripped, wet and lush, the mud glittered, the sky had streaks of white and blue amidst the grey. Enough, she decided. Enough silence and stillness. There would be plenty of that when they were all dead. She went to the bottom of the stairs and yelled, 'We're going out. Screens off. Chop-chop!'

Five minutes later, clad in macs and wellies, the Taylor family were all tramping up the puddle-sodden lane towards spongy moorland, and Neil was pointing out a pair of lapwings above them. Rally driving indeed, Eve thought to herself, with a snort of amusement. But Lewis had been right about one thing, at least. *Crack on with all the fun stuff*, his voice urged in her head, and it was just the kick she'd been waiting for.

'Who's going to race me to the stile?' she yelled impulsively, galumphing away in her wellies, coat flying behind her. 'Catch me if you can!'

For a moment, she thought the girls were going to ignore her, that Neil too would refrain from chasing after her – or, worse, find her behaviour immature. But then came the thudding of footsteps, the squeals of her daughters as they jostled one another, trying to catch her up, and then all four of them were racing along together in pursuit of victory.

I choose living, she thought, accelerating into a sprint, elbows like pistons, almost losing her footing in a particularly craterous puddle and yelping with laughter at the look on Neil's face as Grace outpaced him. See, Lewis? I *am* living. I am.

Tick. Tick. Tick. It was the following Wednesday and Eve was in the waiting room of her local surgery, eyes flicking up impatiently to the clock on the wall. Eight-thirty, her appointment had been set for, and it was already eight thirty-three. If there was one thing that particularly riled her, it was other people's disregard for punctuality – especially when that meant having to sit around for ages in an over-heated waiting room as a result. She shifted restlessly on the hard plastic chair. If I'm still here at eight-forty, she vowed, then I will go, regardless of any so-called deal with Lewis Mulligan. The lump was probably only a cyst anyway, she was almost certainly wasting the doctor's time and—

But then Dr Pathak put her head around the door – 'Eve Taylor? If you'd like to follow me' – and her escape was thwarted after all.

Eve followed the doctor down the corridor, heart skittering up the gears as they went into the consulting room. This is it, she thought with a lurch. No more avoidance, no more head in the sand. Judgement Day.

Dr Pathak was about the same age as Eve, with a pierced nose and businesslike manner. 'How can I help you today?' she asked.

'Well,' Eve began, 'I really hope I'm not wasting your time here, but . . .' The words, so long buried, were difficult to unearth, now that the time had come. 'I . . . I found a lump. In my breast. And maybe it's just nothing – I mean, chances are it *is* nothing, and I've made a fuss for no reason, but—' She swallowed. *Stop babbling.* 'But it's there. And it's not going away.'

'I see. Have you noticed any pain, or a change in your

breast's size or shape?' asked the doctor, who was obviously well versed in dealing with gabbling fools.

'Not really,' Eve replied.

'Any redness or swelling of the skin? Any inflammation, would you say?'

Eve shook her head. 'Not that I've noticed.'

'Okay. And otherwise do you feel well? When did you notice the lump?'

'I'm fine. I'm really healthy. I eat properly, I exercise, I don't smoke,' Eve said. Then she hesitated, the good girl becoming unstuck. 'I first noticed the lump about . . .' She dropped her gaze. 'About a month ago.'

'Right. It's probably best if I take a look, if you don't have any objections,' the doctor went on in a matter-of-fact sort of way. 'If you'd rather, I can ask one of the practice nurses to be in the room as well or . . .' Eve shook her head again. 'Okay, so why don't you pop your top and bra off, and we can take it from there.'

Even though she knew the doctor must see other people's bodies every day, and had presumably witnessed all manner of shapes and sizes before, Eve couldn't help feeling self-conscious as she undressed. Her breasts had never really recovered from feeding her daughters; they were small and deflated-looking, and appeared rather pathetic in the bright light of the consulting room. *They're just bags of flesh – get over it*, she reminded herself, as the doctor approached to inspect the lump. All the same, it felt embarrassingly intimate, having this woman leaning over her, pressing around the skin of her breast with cool, exploratory fingers. Sitting there, naked from the waist upwards, Eve could smell her own deodorant and shower gel from earlier, and prayed that a cheery window cleaner wasn't about to appear at the window and cop an eyeful.

'Okay,' said the doctor, returning to her own chair. 'Thanks. You can put your things back on now.'

Eve's fingers were sweaty and clumsy as she hooked her bra back up and pulled on her silky cream blouse. 'So . . .' she began questioningly, wanting to get this over with. *Tell me. Just tell me.*

'Well, you're right, there's definitely a lump,' the doctor said, 'and the good news is, you've come in while it's small, so we can get straight on and investigate. I'm going to refer you to the breast clinic for some tests, and they'll be able to give you a full diagnosis. Because you're over forty, it'll probably mean a mammogram and possibly an ultrasound initially and then, if they can't determine the cause of the lump, they'll carry out a biopsy.'

Eve swallowed, trying to take it all in. 'So . . . you don't think it's just a cyst?'

'I'm not ruling anything out,' the doctor replied. 'It could well be a cyst, or an abscess even. A lump in the breast is more common than you think, and nine out of ten times they're benign. But let's find out for sure.' She typed on her keyboard quickly, then turned back to Eve. 'I'll get a letter sent out today and you should receive an appointment to be seen within two weeks. In the meantime, I know it's easier said than done, but try not to worry. You did the right thing coming in, and now we'll get to the bottom of the problem. Okay?'

'Okay,' said Eve, her voice barely a whisper. She just about had the wherewithal to thank the doctor for her time before leaving the room, legs shaking.

Chapter Fifteen

'It really is the most precious time. It's *magical*. It actually feels like a miracle.'

'I know! I've never felt so important in my life. People offer me a seat on the tram. Strangers come up and talk to me, and ask me how long I've got to go, and do I know if it's a boy or a girl . . .'

'I've had that, too. Always the older women, who seem so sure about how you're carrying. Load of rubbish, if you ask me.'

'And some of the comments can be quite personal, can't they? I walked into a shop the other day, and the woman behind the counter actually gasped and said, "My God, look at the state of your ankles, love!" – I mean, *I* can't help it if they're swollen, can I? I thought she was quite rude.'

'It's the ones who want to touch you that give me the creeps. Who, like, *hover* with their hand out, doing that weird smile. "Do you mind if I have a feel?" Well, yes, I bloody well do, actually, thank you very much – I'm not public property. Do you know what I mean?'

'It *is* a special time, though.'

'Oh yes, it's delicious. I do feel very blessed. We'd only been trying a month as well. My husband's been swaggering about ever since, believe me. Mr Turbo-Sperm, he thinks he is!'

The three women rocked with laughter and Laura felt the smile on her face become clenched. Thanks, Life, for this particular slap-down, she thought, pretending to consult her list of questions. As if it wasn't enough that she was never going to become a mother herself, due to the ongoing Husband Says No stalemate; now her boss, Deborah, had thought it a good idea to set up a panel of pregnant women to collect feedback for the new product range. And guess who'd been asked to coordinate this? Lucky, lucky Laura!

She stared down at her notes, feeling like crying at the words she'd written so far. *Precious cargo. Treasured. Blossoming. Miracle.* Talk about rubbing a woman's nose in it.

'Moving on,' she said, keen to get through the session as quickly as possible, 'in terms of toiletries, what are you looking for at this time, ladies? Is there anything in particular you appreciate more, now that you're pregnant? Anything you don't like?'

'I feel so tired all the time,' the first woman said. This was the one who didn't like to be touched. She was seven months pregnant, apparently, and had a high rounded bump on which she was balancing a biscuit between mouthfuls, as if it were a useful shelf. 'Really exhausted by the end of the day. So anything that feels luxurious is welcome. Anything where I feel like I'm treating myself, and not just squirting – you know – bog-standard Superdrug own-brand bubble bath into the water, or whatever.'

'Yes, absolutely,' the second woman agreed. This was Mrs Turbo-Sperm, who was younger and more giggly, with long blonde hair in two plaits around her head, as if she were some kind of fecund milkmaid. 'And you feel kind of . . . Well, I don't want to sound up myself here, but you do feel this sense of importance, like I said earlier, about carrying a baby. And you do really want to look after yourself. So, for me, I'm like "Only the best". Does that sound awful? But I'm thinking of the baby, too. I don't want to slather cheap chemical crap all over myself when I'm pregnant.'

'Not least because of the parabens that some companies use, which can cross straight into the bloodstream,' added the third woman. She was the oldest and most earnest of the three, Laura guessed, and had been the most rapturous about the miracles of nature. Perhaps, like for Laura, conception had not been quite so easy for her. 'For that reason, I've been looking for very pure toiletries. Organic ingredients, not too highly perfumed, you know.'

'Okay,' Laura said, scribbling these comments down.

Luxurious – a treat. High-quality – only the best! Pure, natural, organic. The campaign was practically writing itself. 'And in terms of packaging, if I could just show you a couple of different styles . . . ?'

Maybe the universe wasn't completely against her, she thought, returning to her desk later on, because a text had come in from Matt while she'd been away. A text that said: *I'll cook us dinner tonight*, and which felt as if it might just be the olive branch Laura had been waiting for. Goodness knows how she'd slogged through to Thursday this week, when things had been so awkward between the two of them, after his ultimatum; but maybe . . . just maybe he was going to back down at last.

She sent back a cheerful reply and felt the clouds lifting a fraction from where they'd hung damply around her mood for so long. Every relationship had its bumps in the road, its difficult times, right? That was what you signed up to – for better, for worse, for richer, for poorer – and now they'd find a way back again, she and Matt. Together.

'This is a lovely surprise,' Laura said as she walked into the kitchen later on with a bottle of wine and a box of chocolate mints. It was a novel experience, opening her front door and being greeted by the smell of browning meat and roast garlic, and even more unusual to see her husband wearing a striped pinny amidst a faint air of panic. He had set the table for them, with wine glasses and their wedding-present cutlery (so posh you weren't supposed to put it in the dishwasher) and there was an impressive sizzling as he flipped one steak in the pan, then the other. 'Anything I can do to help?'

He didn't answer immediately, pulling the oven door open to check something inside, and then straightening up hurriedly as a foaming pan of carrots threatened to boil over on the hob. 'Um . . . it's all fine, I think,' he said, remembering to give her a kiss in a flustered sort of way. 'It's a dinner-for-two thing from Marks & Spencer,' he added distractedly, as an alarm on his phone started beeping. It was a good fifteen-minute schlep across town from Matt's office to the nearest M&S, so clearly this was him Making An Effort, Laura realized. This was Big. 'Hmm. I think that means the potatoes are done,' he said, frowning. 'Or was it the veg?'

By the time Matt had served up their food, Laura was starting to feel a bit trembly with anticipation. *Please let him have changed his mind*, she thought, nibbling at a lukewarm forkful of potato dauphinoise. *Please let this be the night when things turn around again.* 'Delicious,' she remembered to say. 'Thank you so much.'

'My pleasure,' he said, sawing gamely at his steak. Then he cleared his throat, like a nervous groom about to launch into a wedding speech, and Laura felt her heart accelerate.

'So I was talking to Elaine today at work,' he began, at which she promptly deflated again.

False alarm. Still, small talk was okay. They would chat, take the edge off things for a while, and then get down to the real matter of importance: their baby. She hoped.

'And she's been in touch with the guys at Head Office again, who made all the right noises, she reckons,' Matt was saying. 'So I need to go and meet them, chat things through, but basically, yeah: the job's mine.'

Whoa, whoa, whoa. Rewind a second. *Job?* What had happened to the small talk?

'What?' she asked in confusion. He was looking at her warily, his shoulders hunched as if he was braced for having to fend off an attack. Perhaps with their best cutlery. 'But I thought . . .' She'd thought they'd put this whole Newcastle business to bed last week, that was what she thought.

'I really want to do it,' he said quietly. 'And . . .' He put his fork down and looked at her, his expression anxious and apologetic. 'I'm really sorry, Laura, but I think we should make a clean break. When it comes to us, I mean.'

The potato turned to paste in her mouth, the room seemed to lurch around her. '*What?*' she repeated, her voice rising. Her hands started to shake and she swigged back the rest of her wine. Bugger it, this was an emergency. 'What are you saying?'

'I'm saying . . .' He paused, anguish in his eyes. 'I'm

saying I think we've reached the end of the road, Laura. Don't you? Deep down?'

Oh my God. The end of the *road*? Never in a million years had she expected him to tell her this. This was not steady, safe Matt, the man who'd been her ally and best friend for eighteen years, the man who always let her choose the furniture because he just wanted her to be happy. 'You want us to . . . split *up*?' she ventured in shock. It was like a bad dream, the very worst kind. He couldn't seriously be saying these words, could he? 'You really think that?' She felt a sob in her throat. 'And you . . . you cooked us dinner to tell me that?'

'I'm sorry,' he said wretchedly. 'I'm truly, truly sorry. But after Friday – what we both said . . . Look, we want different things, don't we? Such different things. And this job: I mean, I love it here in Manchester, I'll always love it, but I think that Newcastle could offer—'

'I don't care about your stupid job!' she shouted. 'Stop talking about your *job*!' Then she buried her face in her hands, weeping as if she'd never stop.

'I'm sorry,' he said again, but there was a new determination in his voice, and she knew she wouldn't be able to change his mind, that this fish had already decided which way to swim.

'I could come with you,' she said, tear-streaked and feeling increasingly desperate. 'I don't mind. We could go together.'

His mouth twisted. 'The thing is, I feel as if we hit a wall last week. And I know the baby thing was a deal-breaker for you, so . . .'

She had never felt so far apart from a person, even though they were facing one another across their small kitchen table. *The baby thing.* The fact that he'd referred so glibly to all her fervent hopes and yearning as 'the baby thing' spoke volumes. It said everything, in fact. But yes. He was right about it being a deal-breaker for her, unarguably. Unfortunately it seemed that 'the baby thing' had become a deal-breaker for him, too.

They sat without speaking for a moment, the air thick with misery. Laura's heart was thudding inside her, so loud she half-expected him to comment on it. She couldn't believe this was happening. They had never had such a dramatic, high-stakes exchange about their relationship, never. India and Dan were always joking about not being able to stand each other, bickering and teasing one another so publicly that Laura had at times felt uncomfortable. 'Right – that's it. DIVORCE!' India would declare whenever Dan did something she didn't like: accidentally breaking one of her possessions, buying the wrong kind of cheese, failing to top up her glass over dinner. Jo and Greg too had often rowed, followed by Greg plunging into an almighty sulk. 'He drives me mad!' Jo would groan, clutching the sides of her head. But Laura and Matt had never been like that. They barely disagreed about anything. Until now, this evening, over dried-out steak and undercooked potato dauphinoise.

She pushed her plate away, unable to contemplate another bite. 'So . . . that's it?' she asked. 'You're leaving me, just like that? Don't you love me any more?'

He bit his lip; he felt terrible about this, she could see it on his face. 'It's not so much me leaving you,' he said, 'as us going our separate ways. And of course I love you. But . . . But it's different now. We were so young, Laura. We rushed into getting married. Don't you think?'

'But it worked out!' she felt compelled to remind him. 'For years and years, it worked out.'

'It did,' he agreed, with almost unbearable gentleness. He'd always been a kind person. Even now, when he was breaking up with her, he was looking at her with such concern she could hardly bear it. 'For years and years, it worked out.'

'And it still could!' she cried, but she could tell from his expression that she'd already lost him, that he was halfway to Newcastle, that he was thinking, *No. No, it couldn't. We're done.* She felt hot and cold all over suddenly, she was trembling uncontrollably with the shock. 'Oh God,' she sobbed, not knowing what else to say. *We're over. We're splitting up. This is actually happening, right now, and there's nothing I can do. He wants to have a clean break. We're never going to have a baby. I'll never be a mum.*

Matt rose to his feet, still apparently unable to resist trying to look after and comfort her, even though he no longer wanted to be married to her. 'Come on,' he said, putting his arms around her and holding her close. He smelled of steak and aftershave, of the end of a long day. 'It's okay,' he said, stroking her hair. 'It'll be okay.'

How? Laura wanted to scream, feeling like pounding her fists against his chest. *How will any of this be okay?* But instead she let him hold her for several long minutes while she cried herself out. And then, once her breathing was slightly less ragged, and her tears were shuddering to a halt, he released her and mumbled something about going to stay with a mate.

She heard him tramp heavily upstairs and into their bedroom, presumably to pack a bag of clothes. So he couldn't even stand to stay another night with her, she thought, numb with despair. He was moving out of their house and out of the marriage in one fell swoop, no time to waste: you're on your own now, love. He hadn't even finished this unappetizing meal he'd cooked, so keen was he to go.

Wait! she wanted to yell. *Not yet!* There was still so much left to talk about, there were still so many things they hadn't said. He couldn't just *leave!*

But leave he did, minutes later, coming into the kitchen where she was still frozen in her chair to tell her that he'd ring her in a few days, that they both needed a bit of space to think things through. They could do this like grown-ups, he said, sounding increasingly apprehensive when she didn't respond. 'Well,' he said eventually. 'I'll be off then.'

She was staring at the wall, not wanting to look at him, a tear rolling down her cheek.

'Laura,' he said helplessly. 'I'm sorry. I know this has come as a shock, but . . .'

She clenched her jaw. 'Just go,' she said without turning her head.

Chapter Sixteen

India had just walked into Sainsbury's when she saw the news. It was Saturday morning, and she'd woken up with an absolute belter of a hangover, following the emergency wine-and-more-wine night at Laura's, called due to the shocking news that Matt had left her. (India still couldn't believe it. She'd actually had a tear in her eye two minutes ago, wrestling to unclip a shopping trolley, because a man with the same brown hair and bouncy gait as Matt had walked past, and she'd immediately thought of her friend last night, sobbing to them that she would be a dried-up old spinster for the rest of her life, that she'd never have a baby now, never. India had vowed there and then not to whinge about her own children again, a vow that had promptly been broken at six-thirty that morning, when Kit woke her up by tunelessly playing a recorder in her face.)

But all thoughts of Laura's blotchy, broken-hearted face vanished from India's eyes as she entered the supermarket and her eye fell on the blaring headline of the local newspaper: CRASH GIRL DIES.

It was as if the world had telescoped down to her, one stricken woman and one single news story, detailing how poor, young, beautiful Alice Goldsmith had passed away the day before, following the horrific injuries she'd received at the city-centre crash, three weeks earlier. She'd been just twenty years old. 'No,' gulped India, staring and staring at the photo of her, as if there might have been some mistake. 'Oh *no*.'

'Tragic, isn't it?' an older woman with a mauve rinse clucked, overhearing her. 'Very sad.'

India made a choking noise in her throat, abandoned her trolley and whirled back out through the doors, where she leaned over, hands on her thighs, trying to breathe in and out. Alice had died, she thought numbly. She had *died*. And then, before she knew it, she was scrabbling for her phone and clicking through to Facebook, to Alice's page, where the sorrowful comments were flooding in thick and fast. There were photos – lots of photos – of Alice as a child, pigtails and school uniform; Alice as a teenager, black eyeliner and studiedly cool expression; Alice as a student, dressed up as a chicken; in a nightclub, at a festival, on some foreign beach . . . There were messages, too, from friends and family, people she'd been to school with, neighbours, former teachers and holiday employers – it was as if half of Manchester knew her, as if they'd all been touched by the tragedy. As had India herself, of course.

Chloe Conway: RIP. You were a brilliant friend – so funny, kind and clever. I'll never forget our nights out together – Glastonbury – Madrid!! – the gigs, parties, mornings after, the gossip, the laughs. Love you forever, Alice.

Tess Sweeney: We've been praying for you, darling. Uncle Bri and I are just devastated to hear the news. A light has gone out in our world. Sleep tight, angel.

Amy Fraser: All the hockey girls are in bits, hon. Can't believe you've gone. Love to your family and everyone affected by your passing. You will be so so missed.

India found herself blinking back tears. Stupidly, she'd always believed that Alice would get better, that there would be a happy ending to this story: the happy ending that she herself had been denied all those years ago. What an idiot she was. What a fool, to hope so naively, to keep telling herself that no news was good news; to have gone to the hospital herself like that – her selfish, lunatic pilgrimage, with Sylvia Plath and Margaret Atwood in a crisp Waterstones bag – as if that would change anything. And now the worst possible kind of update had come, and the girl was dead. So much for redemption. So much for second chances.

Standing there beside the snaking metal row of trolleys, she found herself typing her own message:

India Westwood: So very sorry you've gone, Alice. You were loved. More than you know.

She could hear Dan in her head, ordering her to pack it in, to stay away, to stop interfering in other people's lives. *But you don't even know her*, she heard him cry, exasperated.

But I sort of did, she thought to herself, pressing Post. And this Alice had come to symbolize so much for India, had become so real to her, so alive, that . . . Oh, but Dan wouldn't understand. If she tried to explain it to him, he would give her that blank look of his, that scrunched-up face that said, *Is my wife really this nuts?*

She blew her nose, gearing herself up to go back into the supermarket and hoping that someone hadn't pinched the trolley she'd left abandoned by the newspaper stand. But just as she was about to put her phone back in her bag, she saw that a new post had been added at the top of Alice's page:

David Goldsmith: Thank you so much for your kind messages. We are finding comfort in them, on such a dark and terrible day. Alice's funeral will be held on Friday, at Middleton Crematorium. Details TBC.

Oh goodness. Alice's dad. The funeral. Should she go? Say a final private goodbye?

Don't even think about it, Ind, said Dan at once, shaking his head forbiddingly in her imagination. *Not your place, not your business.*

India blinked him away and gave one last sniffle. That was what *he* thought.

'The Lord is righteous in all his ways and kind in all his deeds. The Lord is near to all who call upon him, to all who call upon him in truth. He will fulfil the desires of those who fear him; he will also hear their cry and will save them . . .'

A stout black woman was intoning a psalm at the front of the room and the atmosphere in the crematorium's hall was solemn and subdued. Alice's parents were in the front pew, their body language that of those who had struggled across a bloody battlefield, only to find they'd lost the war anyway: heads bowed, shoulders heavy, expressions of shell-shocked grief.

India, squeezed into a row near the back, felt beads of sweat pop on her forehead as the speaker – the family's neighbour and friend, according to the order of service – went on. Dampness pooled at her armpits. Her long-sleeved boiled-wool dress was too hot for a muggy June day, it was a winter dress really, but had been the only suitable thing in her wardrobe. The situation wasn't helped by the fact that there must be more than two hundred people gathered in there, mourners packed elbow to elbow, the air thick and warm with the fug of breathing. The woman at the front pushed up her glasses with a stern expression as she finished her reading and pressed her lips together in a tight, straight line. Her hands were trembling, India noticed, as she took her Bible and returned to her seat, with a little nod towards the Goldsmiths. 'Christ, it's roasting in here,' somebody whispered in the row behind.

Now Alice's father was approaching the lectern, tall and stooping in his dark suit, his face carved deep with anguish. He told the room that his daughter had been the light of his life, affectionate and good-humoured, willing to do anything for anyone. As a girl, he said, she was the sort of daughter you looked forward to seeing after a day in the office, because she'd always have a funny story, a new joke, an impression of one of her teachers that would have him and his wife in stitches. It's what people had loved about her, he said: her humour, her willingness to see the funny side. Whatever life threw at her, Alice would bounce back, undefeated, undiminished. 'Which is why . . .' His voice began to quaver. 'Which is why it's so very hard for all of us who knew her to come to terms with the fact that . . .' He mopped his brow, seemingly unable to continue. 'That . . .'

India's heart felt as if it were being wrung inside-out; his pain was almost unbearable to witness.

'That she's gone from us. I'm sorry,' he said, gripping the lectern and bowing his head for a moment. 'I'm not finding this easy.'

Sorrow was rising through the whole room like a tide, people were reaching for handkerchiefs, tears trickling down their faces. Just look at the man before them, broken by the loss of his daughter, his voice cracking as he tried to continue. For the first time since her arrival, a feeling stole in on India that perhaps she shouldn't have come here after all. Who was she to intrude on this poor family's grief anyway, piggybacking on these people's despair, when she had no right? She had muscled in on the drama like the worst kind of voyeur, sitting here in her uncomfortably tight dress and sweaty black tights, having been compelled to attend the ceremony in the name of some guilt fetish. Maybe Dan had been right all along, she thought, and suddenly felt ashamed of herself, as if she'd only just noticed her own cheapness in a reflection. This was not her world. She did not belong.

Alice's tired, ashen-faced father had finished his eulogy and was limping away again, and India decided to make a move, squeezing her way through the sniffling ranks. 'Excuse me. I'm so sorry. Could I just . . . ? Excuse me. Sorry. Thank you.'

Out she slunk, relieved to have escaped, shame stinging through her. Let that be the end of it, she told herself severely, gulping in the fresh air as she recovered herself. She seemed to have forgotten how to behave normally these days. Ever since her birthday, she had gone off at one wild tangent after another. It stopped right here.

'Never did get on with funerals myself,' said a voice just then, and she turned to see a wiry man leaning over a railing nearby, smoking a cigarette. She had been so caught up in her own thoughts she hadn't even noticed him there.

'No,' she said quietly, not really in the mood for polite chat. She should get back in the car and go home, try to pull herself together. Try to remember how to be Dan's wife and her children's mother, and be satisfied with that for a change.

'You okay?' He'd turned to look at her and she squirmed a little under his gaze. He was about her age, she guessed, with sandy brown hair and a pierced ear, golden-brown eyes, a lean and athletic build. There was something vaguely familiar about him, but she was still so churned up that she couldn't put her finger on it. 'Knew her well, did you?'

'Um . . .' She was just about to fudge an explanation when his expression changed.

'*India?* That's never you, is it? India Burrell?'

She gaped, and then his features suddenly swam into sharper focus. '*Robin?*' she asked, almost stumbling on his name. It had been so long since she'd said it aloud. 'No way.'

They stared at each other. 'Bloody hell. India Bur*rell*. Look at you, all grown-up.' He sucked hard on his cigarette, then stubbed it out on the wall, a shower of orange sparks cascading to the ground. Then he gave a short, dry laugh. 'And all of a sudden the day just got more interesting.'

India's breath was shallow in her lungs. *Robin.* He'd been on her mind so much lately, and now here he was in person – her first love, her first heartbreak, and at Alice's funeral, of all places. It was as if the last few weeks had been building up in a crescendo to this single astonishing moment. 'Oh my God.' She couldn't stop looking at him. 'Robin bloody Fielding.'

'To use my full name,' he quipped, smiling that funny crooked smile of his, the smile that, once upon a time, had turned her knees to marshmallow. 'History repeats itself.'

'Doesn't it just?' she agreed in a daze. Putting a hand up to her mouth, she wished – moronically, vainly – that she had taken better care of her appearance before dashing out of the house, late as ever, that morning. Wished too that she was wearing something slightly more flattering than this years-old dress, the seams of which were straining on her hips, and that she'd thought to put on some lipstick and . . . *Stop it, India. You're at a funeral, not a Paris catwalk.* 'God. Um. How are you?' Her voice was shaky, her emotions in freefall. Robin Fielding was right here in front of her. She had imagined this moment so very many times.

'I'd always wondered if we'd meet again,' he said, ignoring her question. His eyes were drinking her in, his expression hard to read. (Bemused, perhaps? Was he bemused that she'd turned into a middle-aged frump?)

'Me too,' she heard herself confessing. A multitude of questions brimmed within her, and she wanted to ask them all greedily, to hear the minutiae of everything he'd done in her absence, to know him again. Instead she kept her face neutral and said, 'You know the family then?', gesturing towards the memorial hall.

'Not really,' he replied, shrugging. 'I play five-a-side football with Big Dave on a Monday night. Just wanted to pay my respects, like.'

Of course, he'd always been mad on football. Fast and skilful, although skinny enough back then to be shouldered off the ball by more thuggish players – it was all coming back to her. How well they had known each other once upon a time, and how carefully the details had been salted away in her memory during the intervening years. 'India Burrell,' he said softly again, his voice low and husky, and she found herself blushing.

'India Westwood,' she corrected him, feeling obliged to lay out her stall. *Married, okay? Husband. Kids. Very respectable these days. Just so we know where we stand.*

He raised an eyebrow and grinned. 'Sounds posh,' he commented. 'Is he posh, then, your fella? Is it all wining and dining for the two of youse?'

She laughed at the idea. 'No. He's a plumber. He's not

posh.' There was another pause and then she said, 'How about you, are you married?' just as he asked, 'Is he good to you, though? Is he worthy of you?'

Was he taking the piss? His eyes were glittering and she wasn't sure if he was having a dig or being genuine. 'He's all right,' she replied, shifting from one foot to another in her uncomfortable court shoes. The sound of people singing floated out from inside the crematorium, chords of an organ rose and fell with due pomp. 'Abide with Me' – they'd sung it at her Welsh grandma's funeral two years ago; one of those songs that always made her feel melancholy. She looked at the ground, dirty white splodges of trodden-down chewing gum, a few stray petals from a bouquet, his cigarette end; and then, when she gazed up at his face, it was as if she'd hurtled back through time and they were picking up right where they'd so painfully left off. The past was all around her, drumming through her veins, pounding in her ears and, before she knew it, she had opened her mouth, the words rushing helplessly from her lips. 'Listen, I'm so sorry about—'

'No need,' he interrupted gruffly. Had his face darkened a shade, or was it her guilty conscience?

She wrung her hands, suddenly wanting his absolution, to get this over with, lay some ghosts to rest. It seemed an appropriate place for such an act, after all. 'Robin, I can't tell you how many times I regretted how we ended things, how—'

He cut her off again. 'I know. Me, too.' They looked at each other and then away again. Too much to say. 'Still, we both survived to tell the tale, evidently.'

She looked up warily, but his expression was hard to read. God, *Robin Fielding*, she marvelled again. It was almost as if she'd conjured him up from her imagination – all her wondering about parallel lives, and the different turns she could have taken. And now here was one of those very same untaken turns, standing in front of her, back from the past. 'We did,' she agreed meekly. 'We both made it this far anyway. Twenty or so years, or however long it's been.'

'Twenty-one,' he said, and then surprised her with a loud laugh. 'Jesus, now I feel old. What do you say, kid: shall we have a pint and find out what's been happening in those missing twenty-one years, or what?'

The question seemed to press an accelerator pedal inside her heart. 'What . . . now?' she asked dumbly, thinking about the messy house she'd left behind, the laundry pile that was particularly mountain-like that week, the hoovering that was yet to be tackled. *Your real life, India, remember?* 'Um . . . Don't you want to go on with David and the others, for the wake?' she asked.

'Not really,' he replied, glancing sidelong at her. 'I'd rather talk to you.'

Oh God. And there it was, that look of his, that cheeky, flirty smirk that had only ever led to trouble. How could it be that twenty-one years had passed and he still had this effect on her? Because before she knew it, despite everything, she was dimpling up at him and saying, 'Go on, then. You're on.'

'I should only have a half,' she said, two minutes later, when they were waiting to be served in a pub round the corner. 'I've got the car, so . . .'

'I can't imagine you driving,' he said, sounding amused. 'You were always getting lost around college, do you remember? No sense of direction.' His eyes rested upon her. Dragon eyes, she'd once termed them, because they were brown and flecked with gold. She'd never seen eyes like his, before or since their relationship. 'There's just so much I don't know about you, Adult India. Wait, no, that sounds dodgy.'

'I'm pretty crap at driving,' she confessed, trying to keep the mood light. 'Still get my left and right muddled up.' Just the other day George had crouched low in the passenger seat with his head in his hands as she attempted to parallel-park in their street, because it was 'embarrassing' apparently to be seen in the same car as somebody so rubbish at manoeuvres. Not that she was about to start discussing her kids with Robin. Even being here together, just the two of them, she was already wondering if she'd been too bold, too ready to accept his invitation. *We're old friends*, she told herself. *Two old friends catching up. No harm in that.* 'Half a Foster's, please,' she said to the hovering barmaid, then turned back to Robin. 'What can I get you?'

'Are you buying then? A pint of Boddingtons, please, love,' he said.

Boddingtons, she thought, registering the fact as if adding it to a newly revised Robin Fielding file. He'd drunk vodka or Newkie Brown back when they'd been an item. She'd been a fan of snakebite-and-black herself, resulting in the most lurid purple puke, nine times out of ten. Mmmm. She checked her watch as they waited for the drinks and her skin tingled with the strangeness of the twist today had taken. Half-past one already, and just look at her: having gate-crashed a stranger's funeral, she was now loitering at the bar of a pub alongside Robin Fielding, with this very strange tension crackling between them. All the unsaid words, all those intimate moments, all those years of silence. Maybe this was a bad idea. Maybe she should try apologizing again and leave.

He'd noticed her looking at her watch. 'In a hurry, are we?'

'Not really, but I can only stay for one. I've got to get back for the kids.' *I'm driving, I've got kids to pick up* – oh, she was getting her excuses in early all right, she was setting down those boundaries. Although, as soon as the words were out, she could have bitten her tongue clean through at her own mistake.

He noticed her grimace. 'You've got kids?' His voice was as smooth as silk, but she wasn't fooled.

'Yeah. Three of them. You?' she parried, keen to move on. 'You didn't even tell me if you were with anyone, by the way. Not avoiding the question, are you?'

'I wouldn't dream of avoiding your questions, India Burrell,' he replied, although he didn't choose to elaborate with any kind of answer. She opened her mouth to correct him on her surname again, but then changed her mind, not wanting to labour the point. She had the feeling he had said her maiden name deliberately, anyway.

India paid for the drinks – guilt-money, she thought to herself, handing over a tenner – and they sat down at a corner table.

'So—' he began.

'Do you—' she said at the same time, unnaturally polite. Then they caught one another's eyes and laughed, the momentary tension dissolving again. 'This is weird,' she said, sipping her drink and hoping it wouldn't go straight to her head. Now, of all times, she needed to keep her wits about her.

'Really weird,' he agreed. His face was pale and rather pinched; he was still as slight and angular as ever, India thought, with none of Dan's comforting bulk, which anchored him so securely in the world. There'd always been something fragile about Robin, something kind of brittle. Had life been kind to him in her absence? she wondered, noticing the first grey hairs coming in at his temples, the grizzled five-o'clock-shadow around his jaw, the redness of his knuckles as he lifted his pint. Was he happy?

'Go on, tell me about yourself, then,' she said, taking another sip and feeling the alcohol spread through her body. 'What do you do these days? And where did you go to, after – you know. When you left.'

He shot her a look she couldn't decipher, but proceeded with stories of dodgy squats and time on the dole in Camberwell, before taking her through his jigsaw-like career, a spell as an accounts clerk ('Bunch of number-crunching tosspots'), followed by a few years in social care ('Working with people even more fucked-up than me') and then his most recent job, rehabilitating young offenders and running drug-addiction clinics ('I'm on nodding terms with every criminal and junkie in the north-west,' he told her with that odd mix of swagger and self-defence).

His brittleness gave way to a warmer humour after a few minutes as he teased her about how middle-class she was these days, with her mortgage and family and her job teaching music ('Last of the renegades, you, eh?'). She hadn't let on that her 'teaching music' was to squalling babies and their earnest parents, unable to bear the paroxysms of mick-taking that particular confession would have sent him into. Somehow they were onto a second drink by now – a Diet Coke for her this time – and then they were deep into reminiscences of their old haunts, their old crowd, and all the daft teenage things they'd been so passionate about at the time. (Each other, mainly, India thought to herself, although they were both carefully avoiding getting into that, at least.)

Eventually it was half-past two and she couldn't put off leaving any longer, not if she didn't want to get caught up in a school-run cross-town traffic nightmare, anyway. 'Listen, I've got to go,' she said, reluctantly.

'Back to the plumber and kiddies?' he said, and there it was again, that dangerous glint resurfacing, just when she'd been hoping they might have got past all that.

She refused to rise to his bait. 'Back to the kids,' she said steadily, getting up from the table. 'Well, it's been good to see you.'

'We should do this again,' he said. 'Catch up properly – make a night of it.' She could see his incisors when he smiled, sharp and fox-like, and felt uneasy all of a sudden.

'We could sort out a bit of a reunion,' she countered, feeling the need for safety in numbers. 'See what the rest of the old gang are up to.'

'I didn't mean that,' he said. 'I don't give a shit about the rest of the gang. I meant us two. Me and you. Robindia.'

Robindia. God, she'd forgotten that stupid hybrid of their names. They'd joked about calling their first home that, she seemed to remember. 'Ah,' she replied, trying to formulate the correct response.

'What's up? Worried what your husband would say? Everyone's favourite plumber might go for me with his biggest spanner?'

She didn't like the mocking tone of his voice, the fact that he could turn vicious in a single second. He'd always been sarcastic, rallying against the rest of the world, but she'd never experienced the sharp edge of it personally before. 'Well . . .' she began uncertainly.

'I'm kidding. Sorry. I just like your company, that's all. You're a gorgeous, interesting woman, I could talk to you all night. I'm not being funny with you, honest.'

Her hand closed around the strap of her bag under the table, every instinct she had telling her to leave well alone. Then he leaned forward and she made the mistake of looking into those bewitching, unearthly dragon eyes, as he smiled his most charming smile and said, 'Go on. You know you want to. You know you're curious.'

The problem was he was right. Of course she was curious. 'Er . . .'

'He does let you out, doesn't he, old Mario? You're not physically attached to a ball and chain?'

Robin was peering under the table to check and grinning

at her, and that was when her resolve faltered: because he looked so happy when he grinned like that, and because going out with him again would be like trying on that parallel life for size, and because – damn it – he was still as good-looking and quirky and tantalizing as ever. And so, after just a single heartbeat of deliberation, India heard herself saying, 'Okay. Sure. Why don't you give me your number?'

Chapter Seventeen

The death and funeral of poor Alice Goldsmith had been all over the local news – a tragedy that seemed to have saddened the whole city. There was something about having been there in person, at the scene of the crash, that made even non-superstitious Jo feel like crossing herself and thanking her lucky stars. It also prompted her to text Bill Kerwin, whose wife Miriam she'd tended to on the street that day. Poor Miriam who'd been such a horsewoman, by all accounts, who'd lost both her legs due to her injuries. *Hope the two of you are bearing up okay*, she texted, remembering the tremor in Bill's voice when she'd spoken to him each time, how desperate he'd sounded. *Sending love and best wishes to you both.*

Thanks, pet, came his reply, some hours later. *We're getting there. She should be home in a fortnight, which we're looking forward to.*

Meanwhile, Jo had been tentatively unpacking more of her things around Rick's place, at his insistence. She'd arranged some pillar candles on the mantelpiece, plumped her berry-coloured velvet cushions on the sofa, and unpacked her collection of striped mugs into a kitchen cupboard. *Mi casa es su casa*, Rick had said to her expansively – 'Make yourself at home!' – but it was definitely going to take her a while to get over the thrill of luxury every time she glided up in that lift, unlocked the front door and stepped through onto the dense soft carpet. They even had a *cleaner*, who appeared like magic twice a week and left the place spotless while they were at work. Clothes that had been left crumpled on the end of the bed were neatly folded. The surfaces in the kitchen gleamed. The bathroom sparkled. It was, quite simply, heavenly. She was so lucky. And yet . . .

Oh, she was being silly. Ungrateful. There was a stereo system wired into the *bathroom*, for goodness' sake, and those amazing views out over the city from the balcony. She should be jumping up and down for joy, laughing at her own good fortune to have found herself in such a life! But . . . well. It *was* all a bit fast. This was the warp-speed with which her *mother* usually conducted relationships, and not sensible, cautious Jo. (Oh God, was she turning into Helen now? Please, no.) And much as she enjoyed Rick's company, there had been the occasional moment when Jo had really craved vegging out in a face-mask with a bag of popcorn in front of her favourite trashy TV programmes. On her own, without worrying what anyone else thought of her.

Still, that was the least of her worries really. Because with Rick came his daughter. And with Maisie came the not-so-accidental breakage of one of her mugs. And the surreptitious snipping of the wicks of her candles, rendering them impossible to light. And a hundred other tiny, petty acts of war, which Jo knew she should ignore. *She'll get over it*, she kept telling herself, determined to turn the other cheek. *She'll come round to the idea.* But until then, Jo was beginning to dread the days Maisie was with them. It was hard not to flinch when the girl curled her lip at her behind her dad's back or made some derogatory comment under her breath. Because how could Jo challenge Maisie, when she was Rick's daughter and this was Rick's territory?

'I remember girls like her from school,' she said to Laura one evening after work, perched on the worktop in her sister's small kitchen. Laura had apparently thrown herself into baking as a displacement activity, a means of distracting herself from her newly raw separation, because there was a veritable tower of cake tins in one corner, and the house smelled amazing: of caramel and vanilla and apple. 'Do you? Those mean girls who could, like, kill another person with a single glare. Who would tell other girls' secrets to the boys, just to put them down; who'd steal your homework and kiss someone else's boyfriend without a second thought.'

Laura had taken a tray of fragrant fairy cakes from the oven and was prodding them to check the rise. 'Yeah, I remember,' she said, glancing around for room to put the tray down. 'Budge up,' she told Jo.

Jo jumped off and leaned against the fridge. 'I mean, the other day I overheard Maisie talking to a mate on the phone and she said –' She could feel herself flushing at the memory – 'She was talking about me, and made this scathing comment: "God, this new woman Dad's seeing, she's the sort of person who buys her jeans at Asda" – like that made me the lowest of the low.'

'Nothing wrong with jeans from Asda,' Laura said, her voice muffled from where she was sorting through a cupboard of baking trays.

'Exactly! I bloody love mine. But, to Maisie, it's like *the* worst thing you can say about someone. I mean, she's so shallow like that. Judging me on what I wear, what I look like, my supermarket clothes – just because *Polly*, her beautiful model-esque mother, is into *fashion* and probably buys all that second-mortgage couture stuff . . .'

'Mmm,' Laura said, emerging with a wire cooling rack. 'And what does Rick say about this?'

'Rick? Well . . .' Jo hesitated. 'He says to ignore her. But then again, he doesn't see or hear half the things she does, anyway; it's all sneaky and furtive, behind his back.' She sighed. 'In his mind, she's this golden child, the perfect daughter. If it came down to me versus her, then . . .' She wrinkled her nose. 'I know he'd choose her.'

Laura didn't say anything for a moment, busily scooping the hot cakes from the moulded tray onto the wire rack, and Jo remembered with a lurch that she was supposed to be cheering her sister up, not burdening her with more problems. 'Sorry,' she said guiltily. 'You don't want to hear me moaning on, do you? How are you getting on? Have you heard anything from Matt?'

Laura's face tensed and there was a clatter as she threw the empty baking tray into the sink with rather more force than was necessary. 'I just think,' she said, 'that maybe you should make more of an effort with her. Isn't it worth it – trying to bond with Maisie – for the sake of your relationship? Instead of seeing her as the enemy, can't you try and make a friend of her?'

Jo gave a hollow laugh at the idea of Maisie ever wanting to be her friend. 'Ha,' she replied. 'Not sure that's possible. You met her, remember? She's not exactly overflowing with love for me. And vice versa, might I add.'

'But have you tried? I mean, really tried? She's only thirteen, she's just a *girl*. A girl whose parents have split up and who probably feels a bit lost and confused. She might end up being your stepdaughter one day, after all.' Laura's brow had tightened and suddenly Jo realized just how crass she'd been in complaining, when her sister would probably have given her last possession to have any kind of daughter right now.

'You're right,' she said humbly. 'I *will* try. I'll make the effort.'

'Just do something with her,' Laura said. 'Baking, for instance. Or have a rootle through my stash of freebies from work, help yourself – you could have a pamper session, if she likes that kind of thing. Find out what she's into, what makes her happy. It can't be that hard. Ask Eve for ideas. Grace is that age, isn't she? She'll be able to help.'

Jo swallowed, knowing that her sister would have done a far better job with Maisie than her. Knowing too that to say as much might very well bring tears to Laura's eyes again. 'Good thinking,' she replied instead. 'I'll get on the case.'

Project 'Bonding' starts here! she thought the following Friday evening, as she finished work and set off for the flat, mentally rolling up her shirt-sleeves and trying to be positive. Polly was away in London for a few days apparently, so they had the pleasure of Maisie's company for the duration. And Laura was right in this instance, Jo told herself: it was high time she remembered who was the adult, and worked on the relationship. Act charming and friendly – win the girl over. Somehow. She remembered that narrowed-eye glare that Maisie seemed so quick to give her, that raised middle finger, the scorn that seemed to pulse from her whenever Jo voiced an opinion, and flinched inwardly at the prospect. But faint heart never won fair boyfriend's daughter, or however the saying went. And Jo had never been one to shy away from a challenge.

Eve, unfortunately, hadn't been much help when Jo had called to ask for advice. 'What's Grace into?' she repeated. 'Er . . . selfies; arguing with me; having a secret boyfriend apparently; stealing my perfume and tights.'

She'd sounded so uncharacteristically downbeat that Jo was taken aback. 'Eve, is everything all right?'

'Sorry. Yeah. Just feeling a bit . . . I don't know. Like everything's getting on top of me. You know?'

Jo did know, full well – but Eve was never usually one to admit to a vulnerability. 'Can I help at all?' she asked worriedly, but it was as if the admission had never happened, because then Eve was talking again, in her more usual, brisk way.

'Let me think, though – well, they spend ages on their phones, gossiping, social media, pouting into the camera. Not that you probably want to go there, mind. There are certain series on Netflix they all watch avidly – I'll text you a list; you could find out what she's into and maybe watch something together? Oh, and anime. Lots of them are into that. Shopping. Hanging out in great packs around town. Also younger stuff too, when they're not trying to be cool – pets, baking, books if you're lucky. Sorry if that's vague, there's no real generic "thing"; it's finding out what Maisie herself is really passionate about. Apart from being mean to you, obviously.'

'Thanks,' Jo said, trying to assimilate all of this. 'And if I can ever help with anything in return—'

'It's fine, I'd better go. Give my love to Laura. And good luck!'

Good luck – well, she was going to need that, Jo thought now, letting herself into the apartment block and taking the lift up to Rick's floor. *You're the adult,* she reminded herself. *She's a sad, confused girl and she just needs some boundaries and friendship. Don't let her see your fear.*

'Hi,' she cried with deliberate cheer, pushing open the front door a few minutes later and walking into the flat.

'It's the most gorgeous woman in Manchester!' cried Rick in reply, as he came out from the kitchen area to greet her. He always gave himself an early finish on Friday – perks of being the boss, he reckoned. 'Hello.'

She smiled at him, feeling more confident already as they kissed and embraced, and she breathed in his lovely smell: ironed shirt and the last faint notes of aftershave. Maisie, meanwhile, was sprawled on the sofa, pretending to retch onto the carpet, but Jo chose to ignore that little display.

'Hi, Maisie, good day at school?' she called breezily. *You will not defeat me with your fake sick noises.*

'Er . . . no,' came the deadpan reply.

'Oh dear. What's up? Was there a drama?' She pulled a

box of cream cakes from her bag and set it on the breakfast bar with a flourish. 'Ta-dah! Will a cake help?'

'No, because I'm not pathetic enough to rely on comfort-eating as a *crutch,*' Maisie said witheringly. 'Also because Mum says they're like a million calories and really bad for you?' She then muttered something that might have been 'Some nurse, you are', but it was under her breath and not wholly distinguishable.

Ah – there was the first mention of Polly, in today's round of Maisie-bingo: tick. Jo, however, was not going to be drawn in to comparisons or to beat herself up today. 'Oh well, all the more for me and your dad,' she said airily. 'Isn't that right, Rick?'

Rick was frowning at something on his phone. 'Sounds good to me,' he said distractedly, thus earning him a glower from his daughter. *Ha*, thought Jo with perhaps more triumph than was strictly necessary. 'Listen, I'm just going to have a shower, then maybe the three of us could go out for dinner somewhere?' he went on.

'Lovely,' said Jo, determinedly upbeat. 'Cool.'

Maisie wrinkled her nose as Rick left the room '*Cool,*' she mimicked. 'Only old people say that.'

'What do young people say, then?' Jo asked conversationally, perching on one of the stools at the breakfast bar and spinning round to face her. 'What are the in-phrases these days?'

Maisie gave a snort and didn't respond.

'So my friend's daughter – Grace, she's your age – she's really into this new series on Netflix apparently,' Jo burbled, trying and failing to remember any of the names Eve had told her. 'And . . . er . . . animation.'

'Ani*mation*?' Maisie snorted again. 'Do you mean *anime*?' She started typing something into her phone. 'Animation, oh my God. How lame.'

Jo felt as if her armour of friendliness had just taken a blow. What even *was* anime? Perhaps she should have done more research. She busied herself unpacking the rest of the groceries she'd bought – eggs and bacon for the morning fry-up that she was planning (everyone loved a fry-up, surely); popcorn and ice cream, just in case they got stuck into a film or TV programme together (now looking less likely, granted); oh, and baking ingredients too, in the vain hope that Maisie might deign to spend a bit of time with her in the kitchen. Jo wasn't about to bet her life savings on it, but she had to keep trying.

'So I was wondering,' she began, casual and light, as if it had only just occurred to her, 'maybe you and I could do stuff together this weekend – get to know each other a bit?'

'Er . . . no?'

'Maybe we could bake something, or watch a movie, or . . .'

'I'm busy.'

'Or . . . I don't know, whatever you fancy. Don't tell your dad, but I love a bit of trashy telly myself. All those modelling shows. Dieting shows. Really cheesy American sitcoms – how about you? What sort of thing are you into?'

Sneering, no doubt at Jo's schlocky lowbrow taste, Maisie lifted one shoulder in a limp, can't-be-bothered shrug and went back to her phone.

One last try, Jo told herself. 'Because I was thinking, it would be really nice, while I'm staying here, if we could—'

'Look, I said, *no*,' Maisie snapped, getting to her feet. 'I'm not interested, okay? I don't give a shit what you think.'

Slam! went the bedroom door as she hurled herself inside, and Jo felt her spirits sink all the way down to the ground floor of the building. So that had gone about as badly as possible, she thought, grimacing.

She's just a sad, confused girl, Laura recited again in her head, but the memory only made Jo roll her eyes in derision. Sad and confused – what, Maisie? Spoiled, rude and unpleasant were more fitting adjectives, where she was concerned.

Jo took a deep breath, tried to put the exchange behind her, and resisted the urge to pour herself a large glass of something alcoholic to knock back in a single gulp. If the last few minutes were anything to go by, this could turn out to be a very long weekend indeed.

*

The three of them went out to dinner in a bar down the road, a grungy place, with a high ceiling and old LP covers stuck all over the walls, big rustic oak benches and about twenty different craft ales, by the look of things. Rick knew the manager – he seemed to know everyone, Jo was discovering – so they were seated at one of the best tables, in the window, with a perfect view out onto the city's Friday-night goings-on. Thankfully, Maisie had turned on the charm for her father's benefit, dimpling and giggling at all his stories, even if she also did her best to keep steering the conversation round to old family jokes and memories that Jo was resolutely not a part of. Rise above, rise above, Jo told herself, smiling with gritted teeth, as Maisie came to the end of a very long reminiscence about a holiday they'd been on, which involved a bikini-clad Polly getting swept out to sea before being rescued by Rick, the hero.

'So how did your meeting go today?' Jo asked, changing the subject as their starters arrived at the table and Maisie fell mercifully silent, for a change. 'Was it that coffee guy you were seeing again?' She always enjoyed hearing what Rick had to say about his work; it was so varied, for one thing, the clients he dealt with ranging from prestigious types like the Opera House or the Whitworth, to tiny new start-ups – cafés, retailers, specialist service providers, anyone who needed a PR refresh.

'Yeah, Mr Gourmet Blend,' Rick replied, tucking into the

sharing plate of nachos. 'We were talking over names for the company; he's keen on "Beans".' He licked a blob of guacamole from his thumb then looked at them both expectantly. 'Beans, with a picture of coffee beans underneath?' He fiddled with his phone and brought up an image. 'We've been through several rounds of designs, back and forth from the drawing board, and this is what we've come up with. What do you think?'

'Um . . .' Jo hesitated. To her eyes, the brown, oval-shaped coffee beans brought to mind something completely different at first glance, but Rick was looking so boyishly excited and pleased that she wasn't sure how to break it to him.

'We discussed having the name above the picture,' Rick went on, swiping the screen to show her the image, 'or in the middle . . .' Another image.

Maisie was shrugging, uninterested. 'Dad, aren't there, like, a million coffee shops already in Manchester?'

'Well, yeah, but they're all doing good business,' her dad replied. 'Jo, what do you think?'

She pursed her lips. 'Meet you at Beans. See you at Beans – I'm not loving it,' she said, apologetically. 'It just makes me think of Mr Bean, for one thing. Or baked beans.'

'Hmm, good point,' Rick said, scooping up more nachos.

'Plus, if I'm honest, those coffee beans in your image look more like . . . turds,' she added. 'Sorry.'

Rick spluttered on his mouthful. 'Oh God,' he laughed,

peering at the picture and then clapping a hand to his head. 'You are absolutely right. This is why we need fresh eyes!' He looked at the image again, and laughed even more. 'Hey, let's go to Turds!'

'For that freshly brewed taste!' Jo sniggered.

'You'll love our distinctive aroma . . .' Rick put in and shook his head, half-amused, half in disbelief. 'Do you know, five different people were working on this, and not one of us spotted the unfortunate resemblance. You go through so many different permutations of styles that you stop looking after a while. You stop noticing these things.'

Jo grinned at him. 'I like to be useful,' she said.

'Well, you just saved my client a shit-load of embarrassment, so to speak,' Rick replied, twinkling at her. 'So cheers to you. Fancy a job?'

'Any time,' Jo said, feeling happy as they clinked glasses with each other.

Maisie was looking a bit miffed to have been left out of the moment. 'Yay, good at spotting turds – woo, what an achievement,' she put in sarcastically.

'Hey, it's good enough for me,' Rick said, pushing his foot against Jo's under the table.

'It's totally going on my CV,' she agreed.

If their pleasant, non-combative night out had raised Jo's hopes about bonding with Maisie over the weekend, the following day saw a crash and burn of her optimism. *In your dreams*, Maisie's body language said as, again and again, she rejected Jo's offers of a breakfast fry-up (gross), a shopping trip ('What, with *you*?'), a movie ('I'm busy') and . . . oh, everything, basically. Any nice gesture was rebuffed.

'I get the feeling your daughter's not my greatest fan,' she confessed to Rick with a sigh as they walked along the canal together, Maisie having slunk off to meet friends in town for the afternoon.

'Maze? She'll come round. She's just prickly,' he replied, slipping a hand into hers. The sun was out, sparkling in golden streaks along the water, and he was wearing a grey T-shirt and jeans. Jo could tell, just by looking at his bare arms, that he was the sort of person who tanned a deep olive within five minutes, unlike Jo herself, who went from milk-bottle white to burnt-flesh lobster, with very little in between. 'But she's great, really, when you get to know her.'

'Oh, I'm sure,' Jo said, trying to sound sincere. Then she bit her lip, wanting to confide in him how inferior Maisie made her feel, compared to his ex-wife, but she held back, knowing it would sound needy and wet. There were still so many things they didn't know about each other, she thought; whole uncharted regions of his life where she'd never travelled, and to which she hadn't been invited. The married years. The other women. First loves and greatest disappointments, wildest hopes, biggest mistakes – the cornerstones, in fact, of what made a person who they were: the past that had defined them.

It wasn't as if they didn't talk – they did, all the time; anecdotes about work and friends, what to do each weekend, news and gossip. But not the big stuff. Not the exes. He hadn't even met her sister yet, let alone her friends. They were still in their small private bubble, their romantic, nice, teasing bubble, laughing at each other's bad puns and enjoying lots of passion, and yet . . . Surely there had to be more? She knew, for instance, that she was still on her best behaviour around the flat, wearing only her nicest underwear, watching his favourite programmes without complaint, even though she'd far rather be watching *Don't Tell the Bride*. He was seeing this carefully constructed version of her, her best side. Was that the only side of *him* that she was allowed to see, also?

Rick was frowning at her. 'You okay? You look very far away. Not thinking of chucking yourself in, are you?'

'In the canal? With all the old shopping trolleys and dead bodies? Maybe later,' she replied, then gave a little laugh. 'Um . . . Changing the subject,' she said, 'I was thinking earlier that we've never really talked much to each other about our exes. Have we?'

'Our exes? No,' he agreed, with a snort. 'With good reason, from my point of view, and all. Why? Is there something you want to say about yours?' His eyes narrowed just a fraction, suddenly wary. 'Has something happened?'

'With Greg? God, no. I've no idea what he's doing. Nothing's happened. But . . . wouldn't you like to know about him? About the relationship? Just out of interest?'

He looked blank. 'No. Not really. Should I? I mean, did something hugely significant happen that's impinged on your life now? Because if not, then – no. Zero interest.' He held up his hands. 'Sorry if that makes me sound arrogant or . . . or up myself. It's you I'm interested in, not him.'

'Okay.' So this wasn't going anywhere. Was it a man-thing, that he wasn't bothered about her ex, or was he instead so supremely confident in himself that the idea of being jealous simply didn't occur to him? She tried again. 'It's just that . . . I don't know much about your previous relationship and . . .' *Spit it out, Jo.* 'Maisie mentions her – Polly – a lot, and I just wondered . . . Well. About everything, really.'

'Er . . .' He was taken aback, she could tell. 'It's a bit of a horror story, really,' he said, not meeting her eye. He kicked at a stone on the path and shrugged. 'I don't want to give either of us nightmares, talking about it, put it that way.'

His body language had become wooden, and she could feel him winching up the drawbridge, not wanting to let her in. Not your business, his face was saying. Proceed with caution. 'It's just . . . I don't want to make the same mistakes, I guess,' she blustered, inventing reasons on the spot. 'I mean, whatever went wrong between you two, I would hate that to happen with us.'

He gave a short laugh that contained zero mirth. 'Given that the two of you are completely different in every way, I can't see that being a problem,' he said. Then he pointed ahead to where they were crossing the pretty Bridgewater Canal basin. 'See up there, that was a Roman fort,' he told her, with an abrupt change of subject. 'Mamucium. Used to guard the road that went from Chester to York.'

'He's clever as well as handsome, bloody hell,' Jo said in reply, realizing that the drawbridge was now closed and she shouldn't try knocking again. For the time being anyway, she thought, smiling uncertainly across at him as he dredged up some other facts from his History GCSE days, interspersed with nonsense about the Emperor Squeezer, complete with demonstrations, right there on the tow-path.

It was obvious he was holding back on her, though, not telling her everything. Not *wanting* to tell her everything, more like. But why?

Chapter Eighteen

'Come along then, everyone, remember to wipe your feet as we— Oh.' Eve, with a rabble of children behind her, stopped dead as she reached her front door.

'What is it?' asked George, craning to see.

'Is it a *cake* tin?' asked Kit, who had a very sweet tooth.

'It certainly looks like one,' Eve agreed, tucking it under one arm, before letting them all in. 'Feet, remember! Then shoes off! Kit – go and have a wee, and remember to wash your hands. Then, and only then, will we find out what's in the mysterious tin.'

In barrelled the children – Sophie, plus India's three today, as India had got stuck in traffic, coming back from a music class in Altrincham. This happened quite frequently, truth be told, but Eve never minded. She adored India's children with all their funny little quirks. George liked regaling her with whichever obscure facts he'd learned that day. Esme would act shy for approximately five minutes, before she'd be found rifling through Eve's dressing table in search of stray nail varnish, 'just to try it'. As for Kit, he would want to share every single detail of his day, including what he'd had for lunch, who he'd sat next to, who the teacher had told off (never him, in these accounts) and all the rest of it. She knew, too, that India would arrive flustered and apologetic, blaming traffic, the weather, a meltdown at Mini Music, or whatever else had caused her lateness that day. 'You must let me return the favour – any time!' she would cry, but they both knew that would not be necessary. Eve was too organized to need favours and, besides, she had a thing about not wanting to be in other people's debt. Even for babysitting. No, it was easier to manage things herself than add in complications.

'Everyone ready?' she asked. 'Hands clean, Kit? Let's see what's in this tin then. Somebody give us a drum roll!' She felt curious herself as she stood there, the children clustered around, eagerly thumping at the kitchen table as she pulled the lid off. A cheer went up. 'BROWNIES!'

They were not wrong. Curiouser and curiouser, thought Eve, unfolding a note that had been tucked inside, and recognizing Laura's handwriting:

> *Have gone baking-mad to fill the hours. Hope you and yours can find a home for these – spare me from my greed!*
>
> *Love Laura x*

'What's going on?' called Grace, who'd just come home. 'Hi, Mum. Ooh!'

'You can all have one each – Sophie, could you sort out drinks for everyone? George, you know where the plates are, don't you? What a nice surprise.' Poor Laura, thought Eve, making a mental note to ring her that evening to see how she was doing. It was impressive that she was even getting out of bed in the morning and functioning, let alone baking tray-loads of gooey brownies for her friends, when her marriage had collapsed so shockingly fast. Eve would have been the same though: fill the hours, the minutes, the moments. Don't give yourself time to think.

A contented munching sound soon filled the air, chocolatey lips licked in satisfaction. 'Yum,' pronounced Esme, nibbling her brownie like a little mouse. Eve took advantage of the temporary calm to pick up the pile of post that had arrived, running a finger under the seal of the topmost envelope and sliding out the letter from within.

Sophie and George, both in the same Year 6 class, launched into a story about a younger boy who'd been told off for making rude noises in assembly that afternoon. 'It was *so* funny, Mum, honestly, he just kept *doing* it—'

'PARP,' put in George obligingly, making the younger two fall about giggling.

'And everyone was really laughing, and the teachers were getting crosser and crosser—'

'PARP,' went George for a second time, as Eve shook open the letter and glanced briefly at the contents. Then she let out a gasp and looked again.

'And we were like . . .' But Sophie had run out of steam, sensing her mother's attention was elsewhere. 'Mum! I'm talking to you,' she said reprovingly.

'Sorry, I . . .' Eve swallowed, her eyes glued to the words. An appointment at the hospital. Directions on how to find the breast clinic, and a leaflet about the screening services. Something else about parking, and how to change the appointment, if necessary. Oh gosh, this was it. A date and time. The mechanics of the health system cranking ever forward, with her a spinning cog.

Grace, dabbing brownie crumbs off her plate with a wet finger, dragged her attention away from her phone in order to stare quizzically at Eve. 'Why did you make that noise, Mum?'

'Mum!' Sophie had her arms folded across her chest. 'Are you listening to me or not?'

'Sorry, I . . .' Eve struggled to return her attention to the room. 'What noise?'

'That sort of gasping. You went—' Grace demonstrated a sharp intake of breath, exaggerated for effect. 'Like that. You sounded like Ollie, when Mrs Patterson is walking too fast.'

Ollie was the wheezing, asthmatic pug that lived next

door; it was not a flattering comparison. Eve shoved the letter back into its envelope and shook her head. 'Did I?' she said vaguely. All the children were eyeing her now, until George made a very small 'PARP' noise under his breath and the tension dissolved once more.

'Why don't you . . . um . . .' Usually after snacks and a drink Eve would find something educational and fun for the children to do: a board game, or Lego, or she'd get out the craft box and supervise the construction of various artistic endeavours, in the hope of glitter minimization. Today, though, her mind was elsewhere. '. . . Watch something on TV together? Although no chocolatey fingers on the sofa!' she remembered to yell, as they all went stampeding off to the other room.

Grace was the only one who lingered. 'Mum,' she began, frowning a little, and Eve felt an upsurge of emotion at what she thought might be an impromptu display of daughterly empathy, a concerned *Are you okay, Mum? Because, well, I've noticed you haven't seemed yourself lately.*

'Yes, love?' she replied.

'Um . . . You know I've got all that revision to do, and I'm going to work really, really hard,' Grace began in a wheedling tone. Oh. Okay. False alarm – zero empathy after all, thought Eve, deflating. 'Can I, like, go to the shop and get some sweets, just to help me revise?'

Eve was usually strict about too much sugar, especially

when an enormous rich chocolate brownie had just that minute been scoffed, but she didn't have the energy for a battle right now – an observation clearly already made by her canny daughter. 'Sure,' she mumbled, and went to peel potatoes for dinner on automatic pilot, her mind still on the letter she'd just opened. It was only a while later when the doorbell rang and George shouted, 'It's Mum!' that she stopped, hands wet and raw, and realized she'd gone through the entire two-kilogram bag without thinking, with fifteen or so newly peeled spuds sitting pale and damp on the chopping board. Oh bloody hell, she thought, staring at them in surprise. One stupid letter and she'd lost her marbles.

The paper crinkled in her skirt pocket as she wiped her hands on a tea-towel and went to answer the door.

'I am *SO* sorry,' India garbled as her children threw themselves bodily at her.

'Mum, you are *hopeless*,' George scolded as she ruffled his hair.

'I am, I know, I'm the worst: it's all true,' she replied, rolling her eyes at Eve. 'Thank you – again. Please tell me when I can return the favour. You know I will. Any time. Maybe one day next week the girls could come to me, if you need to work late, or . . . Or I could babysit, or . . . Well, anything. You will ask, won't you?'

'Of course I will.' Of course I won't. 'And it's no bother at all. Especially as Laura dropped off a load of chocolate brownies for us today – you've probably got some waiting on your doorstep at home.'

'Quick, Mum! Before Dad gets back and eats them all!'

Never had children put shoes on so speedily to get out and back home. Moments later, off they all went up the path, George's trousers flapping around his ankles where they had become too short; Esme trailing a dreamy hand along the privet hedge; Kit crouching down for a swift final peer at the place where next-door's cat sometimes hid behind the wall, before he went hurrying on after the others.

Closing the door, Eve leaned against the wall for a moment and read the letter all over again, the words flashing through her mind. An appointment for next Wednesday, eleven o'clock, Dr Jones. Further tests. A matter of precaution.

She was in the system: a number, a patient. Wheels were turning. No more prevaricating, she ordered herself. She really must tell Neil about this now. Tonight.

'Sorry I'm so late,' came the weary tones of her husband, as he shouldered the door open later that evening. Quite a lot later that evening, actually. Two whole hours after Eve had served up the food – a potato-heavy vegetarian cottage pie – and washed the dishes, and tested Grace on her biology revision and . . . oh, the list went tediously on, with all the other domestic stuff that needed attention. 'Don't suppose there's any dinner left, is there? I'm starving.'

'Where have you been?' Eve asked crossly, slapping her book down on the arm of the sofa and coming through to the hall. Oh great, she thought, as she saw his stumbling gait. He was drunk – she could smell it coming off him in waves. 'Did you not get my texts? It's nearly nine o'clock.'

'Sorry,' he said again, clumsily kicking off his shoes. 'Bill's lost his job. Needed a drink and a chat. And my phone was out of charge. Sorry, love.'

'Oh, right.' Her exasperation gave way to concern. 'Bill, as in your colleague?'

'Yep. A management restructure – there have been some redundancies. Bit of a shit day, all in all, everyone panicking.' He rubbed an eye wearily, then lurched through to the kitchen, before stopping dead. She guessed he was staring at the now-tepid remains of dinner, the pie dish sitting there on the hob, complete with the leftovers she knew the girls had scraped back into it when they thought she wasn't looking. 'What *is* that?'

'Extravaganza du Spud,' she replied, rolling her eyes. Admittedly it wasn't the most appealing or successful concoction she'd ever come up with.

'*What?*'

'*Pie,*' she snapped, feeling tired herself, and wondering when it was that her husband had stopped asking her how her day had been, how the girls were, how was her life, by the way? Tonight was definitely not the night to tell him about her hospital appointment, that was for sure. 'Knock yourself out, it's all yours,' she said, gesturing to the left-overs. 'I'm going to have a bath.'

Unfortunately, the following night turned out to be the wrong time to broach the subject of her health, as well. Grace came down with a tummy bug and was throwing up every thirty minutes, and Eve spent the whole evening with one ear tuned to the upstairs loo and miserable shouts of 'Muuuum!', at which she'd race back up there with Dettol and sympathy. The following night she and Neil were out at the school PTA quiz, on a team with India and Dan, which swiftly descended into a rowdy, rivalrous affair with far too much wine – absolutely not the occasion to launch into a heart-to-heart. Then it was the weekend, and they had Neil's difficult aunt visiting and didn't seem to have a moment to themselves.

On Monday the conversation simmered inside her all day, waiting to be released. *Neil, I've got something to tell you*, she mouthed to herself periodically, practising in her head the lines that would follow. *It's probably nothing, but I thought I should let you know*, she murmured in front of her bedroom mirror, once the girls had gone to bed that night. *I've got a hospital appointment on Wednesday because . . .* God, did her eyes always look that round and frightened when she was saying something serious? Her whole face was stiff and taut, like some kind of . . . She grimaced. Like some kind of death-mask. Bad choice of words.

She looked down at the beige carpet for a moment, then lifted her head and tried again. 'Oh yeah, by the way, I've been meaning to tell you,' she said, in more of a breezy, don't-worry sort of way, but there was nothing convincing about her expression, nothing at all. Her lips trembled momentarily. This was *hard*, and that was before she was even properly saying it to anyone. 'I'm scared,' she found herself confessing to the mirror, and then jerked her head away, unable to bear her own vulnerability.

No. Don't, Eve. Don't start feeling sorry for yourself. She gripped the edges of the wooden chest of drawers for a moment, trying to buoy herself up, then let out a sigh. Maybe this was a bad idea anyway. She thought of how she'd left her husband downstairs, hunched over his laptop on the kitchen table, the birds still chirruping in the trees outside. They were almost at the point of midsummer, when the evenings were so long and light, the last vestiges of yellowy sunshine falling like syrup through the window. Neil was already under so much pressure at work. Could she really add to that? Was there any point?

It was just a check-up, after all, she told herself bracingly. Just a few tests and a chat with the doctor. Why have both of them stressing out about it, when he was currently overwhelmed with office politics? She would go to the appointment on her own, she decided, find out the facts and then, once she knew the score, she'd be able to tell him what was happening. She'd fix it, like she always did.

Eve was tough, she didn't need a chaperone for anything, least of all a clinic appointment. And if Neil came, he'd probably only be taking phone calls and having to type important emails, and it would totally get on her nerves. No. She was better off alone. It would be fine.

If Eve was the sort of person who went in for self-psychoanalysis, she'd probably have listed one of her most formative experiences as the day she'd opened her GCSE results as a teenager. She'd worked bloody hard for those exams, put everything she had into them, and had been rewarded by receiving A grades for every single one. Her dad, the person she'd always slavishly tried to please, was proud of her, hugging her and trying to take her to the pub, until her mum had pointed out that, at sixteen, Eve was still too young. Nonetheless, she had glowed. All she'd ever wanted was for him to be proud and say well done, and now he had done both.

But then a strange thing had happened. Within minutes of his praise, she realized the words had made absolutely no difference to her. She didn't even really like him by then; she thought he was volatile and a bully, with no boundaries when it came to self-control. So what if he was proud? She was proud of *herself*. Did her dad's opinion change anything, or matter? No, actually, not a single bit.

Pretty much from that moment on, she had made the liberating decision that she was not going to pass exams – or do anything! – in an attempt to please another person. It was all about *her*, how *she* felt, and she didn't need anybody else's approval to make her feel good. It was a startling, incredible turning point. She could practically feel her butterfly wings emerging, shimmering and bright and beautiful, helping her fly away from the family home eventually and leave it far behind. It was what she tried to teach her daughters: that hard work was its own reward, and independence the winner's prize.

Despite this noble motto, which had always served her so well, the following day at work Eve found it hard to concentrate. As she stared blankly at the unpaid invoices of Maggie Doherty, her ditzy make-up-artist client, a voice in her head kept asking questions. Questions she did not want to dwell upon. What if, the voice persisted, the doctor sits you down tomorrow and announces, *You've got cancer, it's very aggressive – you're going to die within the year*? What then? She pictured herself stumbling through the clinic doors all on her own, crying and shaking, trying to drive herself home with tears rolling down her face . . . It was a terrible image. Even for her, I-can-manage Eve, it felt a step too far all of a sudden.

On impulse, she texted Jo: *Don't suppose you are around tomorrow, are you? Sort of mid-morning-ish?*

As a nurse, but also as Eve's oldest friend, Jo was kind and competent and would know all the right things to say if . . . Well, just 'if'. She was discreet, too, she could keep a secret and wouldn't go blabbing to the others. But then again . . . Eve bit her lip, feeling treacherous. It would be wrong of her to tell Jo and not Neil. What would that say about her marriage, if she went to a friend before her husband? Nothing very positive, that was for sure.

She wished she hadn't started imagining being at the clinic on her own now. Talk about self-sabotage. Because it was all she could think about suddenly – the trawl around the long identical corridors, the sound of her own shoes slapping on the floor as she walked, sitting quiet and frightened in a waiting room with nobody to take her mind off things. Nobody to look up expectantly with an *Are you okay?* face as she came out of the consultation room, to put an arm round her and steer her along to the nearest coffee place afterwards. Oh, help. Why had she ever thought she could tough this one out alone?

There was still no word from Jo, but she was probably busily administering vaccinations to squalling infants, or dressing wounds, or rubber-gloved and in the middle of a smear test, her phone on silent. Fair enough. Perhaps she should just bite the bullet and ask Neil after all, Eve thought. Because he was her *husband*. Her partner and ally against the rest of the world.

Her computer screen had switched itself off through lack of action and she clicked the mouse absent-mindedly, only for a notification to flash up telling her of a new email from Neil. Talk of the devil. Maybe he'd sensed there was something on her mind, she thought in a rush of gratitude, clicking through to the in-box. Perhaps he would have emailed providing a convenient intro – *You all right? We haven't managed to chat properly lately* – and she'd be able to reply, *Actually, now that you mention it . . .* and just tell him. It might even be easier in an email. If kind of unorthodox.

His email, when she opened it, was succinct to the point of being brusque, though: *Don't suppose you've had time to iron my blue shirt, have you? Need it for Sales Conference tomorrow.*

And that was it, the entire message. No 'Dear Eve', no 'Love Neil'. Certainly no please and thank you, and I realize this is a bit cheeky, but . . .

God! She read it again, feeling aggrieved. It was so impersonal, so offish, he might have been addressing some poor lowly skivvy, not asking a favour of his so-called beloved wife. 'You can iron your own bloody shirt,' she muttered to the screen, deleting the message before she sent a rude reply after it. Then the words percolated through. Wait, though. If he was going to the company Sales Conference tomorrow, there was no way he'd be able to sneak out and meet her, whatever the reason. So that was that decision made for her. Damn it.

The phone on her desk rang just then: reception. 'A young man's here to see you – Lewis Mulligan? Says he's found some more receipts, and should he bring them up?' asked Pam, the receptionist.

Lewis Mulligan again, popping up like her guilty conscience. *I'll go with you*, he'd told her without invitation. *I don't mind.*

It would be ridiculous to take him up on his offer, though, wouldn't it? Unprofessional and unconventional, and definitely weird. She bit her lip and noticed that a text had come through from Jo: *Really sorry, manic at work right now. Some other time? xxx*

'Eve?' prompted Pam from the handset.

'Sorry, yes. Um . . . Thanks, Pam. Could you send him up?'

Chapter Nineteen

When Laura was a kid, the man who lived next door to them, Mr MacLeish, had owned a brindled Staffie called Pearl, which completely idolized him. What there was to idolize about Mr MacLeish – bad-tempered and prone to hectoring her mum, Helen, for sundry neighbourly misdemeanours – Laura could not compute, but that dog just doted on him. Whenever her owner went out, Pearl would perch in the window, soulful brown eyes patiently scanning the horizon for his return. With every approaching passer-by, she would stiffen expectantly, chest taut, ears pricked – is it? Could it be? – only to deflate once she'd realized the answer was no. Sometimes they heard Pearl howling and whining through the wall, if he was late home from work. 'That dog can't stand its own company,' Helen would sniff, rolling her eyes in irritation.

Laura thought she understood how Pearl felt, these days. It was over a fortnight now since Matt had walked out, and she still wasn't used to coming back to an empty house at night to find everything exactly as she'd left it, or waking up alone in the bed, feeling marooned in its lonely expanse. Sometimes she would pace restlessly through the silent rooms like a caged animal, her gaze occasionally alighting on some object or other of Matt's – a pair of his old trainers, an ancient football scarf, his beloved Alex Ferguson book – and she'd have to snatch her eyes away, as if the sight was too painful to be endured. All those ordinary, everyday things – things she'd never thought twice about before – had become suffused with heartbreak and melancholy since his departure, symbols of the tragedy that had befallen her. Why hadn't she appreciated the normality of her old life at the time? Why had she taken their easy domesticity for granted?

Just get through each day, Jo had advised, but each day was as unremittingly bleak as the last. Laura found herself swinging chaotically between wild hopes that this would all have been a terrible mistake and that he'd return, begging her forgiveness, followed by a plunging relapse into the depths of pessimism. Then she'd feel crushed by the weight of despair that this was all her life totted up to now: a too-quiet house and the lonely sinking of a bottle of wine at night in front of inane TV programmes, because she couldn't concentrate on anything more profound. Not to mention more cake than any sane person knew what to do with.

'Not going for the heartbreak diet then?' Gayle at work had said unthinkingly, seeing Laura chow miserably down on a large slice of coffee-and-walnut sponge. She'd brought in three full tins of baked goods so far that week, adorned with Post-its saying 'Help Yourself', and some of her colleagues were starting to call her Patisserie Valerie. 'I was always the same – ate my way through the pain. You want to watch it, though; you don't want to pile on the pounds and bump into your ex looking like a blimp!'

Thanks a lot, Gayle, Laura thought, tipping the contents of her plate into the bin when the other woman had returned to her desk. As for bumping into him – that wasn't going to happen, seeing as Matt had already left for Newcastle, promising to come back and sort through the rest of his possessions just as soon as he'd found a flat. Off he'd gone, striking out in his own direction without a backward glance her way. How had he managed to create all this momentum for himself, this impressive forward drive, she kept wondering, when she, meanwhile, had been left to flounder in the choppy waters of his wake, and it was all she could do to keep from going under?

Still, there was work to keep her busy at least – endless expectant mothers to interview, in the name of product feedback; endless meetings about keywords and brand values; endless pictures of smiling fertile women to choose from;

and . . . oh God. Aversion therapy, they called it, didn't they, where you were forced to confront your fears head-on, to look them in the eye, as a means of speeding up the healing process, but Laura wasn't convinced it was working all that well for her. She'd never been one for ripping off a plaster in one swift wrench, after all, preferring to approach it slowly, cautiously, one tiny corner peeled away at a time.

And then one afternoon she was faced with working through the questionnaires that the panel members had filled in for her, uploading every last pertinent detail onto a database so that the company could build a solid bank of potential product-testers who could be called upon for future case-studies. This was a task she'd been putting off for ages, because it was dreary and menial, but a virus had swept through the department recently and unfortunately there was nobody else to whom she could conceivably delegate it.

She began with the very first trio she'd interviewed: the young blonde woman with the milkmaid plaits, the rather grumpy one who didn't like people touching her bump, and the older woman who'd seemed delighted with every aspect of her pregnancy. A mixed bunch, to say the least.

The milkmaid's form was full of exclamation marks, her writing rounded and childish, the content fulsome but essentially bland. The bad-tempered one had been terser in her replies, focusing on quite negative aspects of her pregnancy:

how tired she was, the aches and pains, the indigestion and heartburn. (Ungrateful cow, Laura thought.) And the third one, the older woman, had beautiful cursive handwriting and was measured and thoughtful in her responses, expressing her hopes and joy. Except . . . Ah. This woman – Catherine, her name was – hadn't completed all the sections of the form, Laura noticed. In particular, the details of any partner. Perhaps she was gay. Had she mentioned a significant other? The other two had been very keen to witter on about their husbands – Mr Turbo-Sperm and Mr Rich – but this lady had been rather more circumspect about divulging such information.

Laura dialled her number. 'Hi. Catherine? This is Laura Bassett from BodyWorks Beauty Products,' she said. 'Thanks so much for coming in as part of our panel, it was lovely to meet you and get your feedback.'

'Not at all, my pleasure. I've been enjoying trying out the samples,' Catherine replied.

'Great! Glad to hear it,' Laura said. 'I was just ringing today because I was adding your details to our database and saw you hadn't filled in any partner's details. Was there anyone you wanted me to add to the system? We can send them things to try as well, you see or—'

'No, it's fine. There's no partner. Just me,' came the reply.

'Oh,' said Laura, feeling as if she might have put her foot

in it. Perhaps there was some very sad story in Catherine's background that was none of her business, and she'd accidentally just poked the wound. 'Sorry. That's fine, then. Er . . .'

'No need to be sorry! It was my choice. Got sick of waiting around for Mr Right, took matters into my own hands. So to speak.' She giggled like a naughty schoolgirl. 'I went with Mr Sperm Donor instead,' she explained, just in case Laura hadn't understood. 'Between you and me, it was the best decision of my life.'

'Oh!' said Laura again, taken aback at such frankness. She hadn't been expecting *that*. 'Right! Well . . . Good for you.' Was that an appropriate thing to say? 'So . . . um . . . thanks again for your time earlier. Sorry to have bothered you. And – well, all the best.'

N/A she typed into the 'partner's details' section of Catherine's database entry, once they'd said goodbye and ended the call. So Catherine was going it alone – whoa. That was a brave thing to do, she thought, moving onto the next section and typing busily. To say: no husband, no problem, and just get on with it anyway. To say: I choose a baby, regardless of being single. But was that fair on the baby? Wasn't it, at the end of the day, a tiny bit selfish?

I went with Mr Sperm Donor, she'd said, with as little drama in her voice as if she was describing how she liked her coffee. Did she even *know* the sperm donor, or was it just some random test-tube's worth she'd been assigned in a clinic? And how did you break that sort of news to a child, anyway, years down the line? All of a sudden Laura felt like calling back and asking her these questions. *Aren't you scared?* she wanted to ask. *Aren't you worried about having to do everything on your own?*

She remembered Catherine's happiness from when they'd met before, and had to admit she hadn't noticed a single flash of fear across the other woman's face. Out of all of the panel, she'd been the one who seemed most delighted with her condition in fact, the most relaxed and optimistic. *Best decision of my life!* she'd cried just now, sounding positively jubilant about it.

Interesting, Laura thought to herself, as she typed. Very interesting indeed.

Chapter Twenty

'Bring your arms overhead as you inhale . . . and, as they continue past your ears, nod your head and deepen your abdominal muscles, your upper body rolling up and off the mat . . .'

Here they were again in the dusty church hall for Pilates, the smell of wood polish and cheesy feet lingering in the air. India was barely listening to the soothing Mogadon tones of Jan, the teacher, distracted as she was by thoughts of Robin. Since their initial startling encounter outside Alice's funeral, he certainly hadn't wasted any time. He'd tracked India down on Facebook that same evening and had sent her a friend request and message, to which she was yet to reply, slightly unnerved by how keen he seemed to be to reconnect.

Not only that, but he'd also followed a link to her Mini Music page and had left a comment: *Mini Music: Happy Tunes for Happy Children sounds exactly the charming sort of class my five children, Xavier, Cosmo, Tallulah, Pretentious and Loadawank, would love to attend. Please tell us more!*

She could practically hear the mocking laughter through the computer screen; she could all but see his thin top lip curled in derision. *Music teacher, my arse*, he must have scoffed.

Deleting his comment with shaking fingers, she'd felt exposed somehow, as if she had laid bare her life with all its shortcomings, for him to sneer at. And now here he was, the wolf at the door, knocking and knocking. *Little pig, little pig, let me come in . . .*

'And exhale as you continue curling up, feeling the spine supported by the abdominal muscles. Reach for your toes without losing the curve of your spine . . .'

Okay, so that was a rubbish analogy, India thought: Robin was not the big bad wolf, and she was most certainly not a hapless little pig, thank you very much. But all the same, she'd experienced an odd mix of emotions upon seeing his name there on her laptop screen – a nervous sort of excitement, coupled with the instinct that she was playing with fire, that she should delete everything he'd written to her and hope that he'd go away.

'Well done. And let's now move into our cool-down. Lie flat on your backs, arms by your sides,' said Jan comfortingly from across the room.

There was a shuffling as everyone obeyed, during which time India glanced over at Laura and mouthed 'Drink?', along with a pint-swilling gesture for good measure. Laura nodded, her long blonde hair rustling against the mat, before the teacher walked around in their direction and they both lay still. Good, India thought to herself, trying to concentrate on her breathing. First of all it was excellent progress Laura venturing out at all – this was her first Pilates session since Matt had left, so total thumbs up on that account. Also, more shallowly, India was glad of the chance to go to the pub and pour her heart out. She'd been tying herself in knots all weekend, wondering what on earth she should do about Robin (if anything), and was desperate by now to talk to someone non-judgey about it.

Good to see you, India. Let's do it again soon, he'd put in his message. *What are you up to next Friday?*

Hmm, next Friday, let's see. Well, Robin, I'll probably be cooking fish fingers or Pasta Surprise for my family's tea again, and then watching *Gogglebox* and having a glass of wine with my plumber husband. Because I'm so boringly suburban and domestic these days. How about you?

If he was anything like the Robin of old, his spare time was probably spent in far cooler ways – going to see some edgy band in a club, or out to a mate's house-party, where there would be loads of drugs. She sincerely doubted that he filled his evenings by slumping on a sofa in front of the telly, having nagged three children into pyjamas and bed. Did he even have a partner? she wondered, stifling a yawn as she stretched along with the instructor's commands. Probably not, if he was asking her out on a Friday night.

'And we're done. Thank you very much. Good work, everyone. See you next week!'

India and Laura both sat up and rolled their shoulders, before catching each other's eyes. 'Wine,' they said as one.

'So Matt moved out of town last week,' Laura announced without preamble, once they were seated at their usual table, a bottle of house plonk in a cooler between them.

'Oh, Laura,' said India, feeling bad for not knowing this. There she'd been, all set to unleash her Robin dilemma, and her friend was going through so much worse. 'Ouch. I'm sorry. It all seems to have happened so suddenly. How are you feeling about him now?'

'Sad,' Laura sighed. 'Excruciatingly, monumentally sad.' There were dark hollows below her eyes and a crack in her voice as she spoke, but then her jaw clenched just a fraction, a glint of iron showing through. 'Although I think I might just have come out the other side of the "Numb" stage now at least – that was horrible, like I'd had a lobotomy, in a permanent daze. I reckon I'm dealing with "Angry" at the moment, which seems to mean gallons of wine – cheers, by the way – followed by drunk phone calls to him in the middle of the night. Plus a shocking amount of comfort-eating. Which reminds me.' She reached into a bag. 'Here,' she said, passing over a square tin. 'Flapjacks for you and the kids. I've been baking like I'm . . . I dunno, the long-lost twin of Monica Geller. My freezer is begging me to stop. So is my stomach, come to that.'

'Whatever it takes, darling,' said India, squeezing her hand. 'Whatever gets you through. And thanks. We all love flapjacks. I'm more than happy to be of assistance on that front.'

'That's lucky,' Laura said with a small smile. 'But yeah, I'm still sad. Lonely. Missing him.' She rolled her eyes and grimaced, before squaring her shoulders and attempting to look more resolute. Laura had always been a glass-half-full sort of person. 'Still. I'm trying not to keep wallowing all the time. I'm doing my best to face forward again.'

'Attagirl,' said India with a little fist pump.

'Fearfully, mind you, and between my fingers – like I'm not sure I want to actually *look* at my miserable spinstery future too closely, but all the same . . .' She fiddled with a beer mat. 'Well, I've been thinking.'

'About?' India prompted after a moment.

Laura blushed. 'You're going to think I'm mad – don't laugh at me, will you? But I've been considering having a baby anyway. On my own.'

India didn't follow. 'Er . . . According to my Biology GCSE, it takes more than one person to—'

'Yes, I've heard that. Slight hitch.' Laura pulled a face. 'But you know how much I've always wanted to be a mum. And . . . Well, I met this woman through work last week.

Catherine. She got sick of waiting for a bloke, she told me, and so she went for a sperm donor instead. Just thought: bugger it, and did it! Honestly, India, you should have seen her, she was so happy about being pregnant. She was *radiant*. Which got my brain whirring.' She gave a nervous smile. 'And now I'm wondering about doing the same thing, basically. Weighing up the idea. Is that bonkers?' Seeming flustered by her own honesty, she rushed on before India could reply. 'You're the first person I've mentioned it to. Go on, tell me you think it's a crazy idea, I know you want to.'

India sipped her wine to give herself time to come up with the right answer, her head spinning. *Please*, Laura's face was saying, eyes round and beseeching. *Please don't trash my hopes.* 'I don't think you're mad,' she replied slowly. 'I mean, it's a big, massive decision to have to make on your own, but I do understand that longing. That biological need to become a mother. When it's there, it's not something you can ignore. It's all-consuming.' She remembered, with a guilty flush, how agonizingly superstitious she'd been when pregnant with George. How desperate she'd been to carry him to term, how convinced she'd been that if there was something wrong with this baby, it would be divine retribution, her own damn fault. Then he'd been born and he was perfect, and she'd promised the universe she'd never do a bad thing again.

'Yes,' Laura said, pleating the fabric of her top between her fingers.

'There's a lot to weigh up,' India went on. 'But you'd be a lovely mum, Laura. You really would. And you've got us – your friends – around you who would help out, and your own mum, too.' The more India thought about it, the less outlandish an idea it seemed, actually. Dan was a great dad, sure, but she had plenty of friends whose partners had barely played any part in the parenting of their children, short of their actual conception. 'So how would it work? Do you know anyone who would donate the sperm, or would you go through an agency, or . . . ?'

Laura shook her head. 'I don't know,' she confessed. 'I haven't got as far as looking into that sort of thing yet, but . . . you know. It's there. An option floating around in my head. I guess I should pluck up the courage to go and talk to someone at a fertility clinic, find out a bit more.' She shrugged. 'I know it's not ideal – I always wanted to have a baby with Matt. But I'm thirty-eight, and time's running out. I'm not sure I can afford to wait until I meet somebody else. Her chin jutted. 'And I think I could do it. Go it alone. I think I would love a baby enough for two people.'

'In which case, why not?' India said cheeringly. 'I think it's dead exciting. Good for you! And at least you won't spend the rest of your life wondering and regretting, and thinking "what if?"—' She broke off. There had been one too many 'what-if's flying around her own life recently, and that certainly hadn't been a good thing.

Laura must have caught the strange look in her eye because she asked, 'How about you anyway? Are you okay? Jo said when she spoke to you last, you were upset about that poor girl dying after the crash. It's awful, isn't it? Really tragic.'

'Yeah, I know.' India hesitated, wondering just how much to say. Then she took a deep breath. She had to tell *someone* what had been going on in her head. 'Laura,' she began, 'have I ever mentioned Robin to you?'

Robin, Robin, Robin. She could have talked all night about Robin; about the good stuff anyway: the passion, the love-letters, the laughter. How being with him made her feel as dazzling as a string of fairy lights. How the million joyful moments they'd spent together still sparkled so brightly in her memory.

'God, he sounds wonderful,' Laura sighed, leaning back against the sofa. 'The stuff of teenage dreams.'

'He *was*,' India agreed, not wanting this part of the story to come to an end. 'But . . .' She twiddled a tendril of hair around her forefinger and felt herself clam up.

'Oh no, I was dreading the "but",' said Laura. 'But what? Did he turn out to be a wanker?'

'No,' India replied. 'It was me.' And then, no sooner had

the words left her mouth than she remembered, belatedly, exactly who she was talking to. *Idiot*, India. As if she could tell the rest of the story to Laura, when she'd just been privy to her friend's secret fragile hopes two minutes earlier. Time for a swift fudge. 'Well, let's just say it ended pretty badly,' she said, swerving around the details. 'And we parted ways fairly brutally. We haven't seen each other for over twenty years, and yet I've always carried this tiny little torch for him, always wondered what might have been if . . . if things had been different.' Moving swiftly on. She glugged more of her drink. 'Anyway. I bumped into him last week.'

'You didn't!' Laura's voice was a squeak. She actually clapped her hands, as if this was a good thing and India wasn't already married to somebody else. 'Oh my God. Where?'

Again, India hesitated. That was perhaps another tale she didn't need to tell. 'Out near Rochdale – long story,' she said, waving her hand. 'But, yeah. There he was. The one who got away. And . . .'

'And was he still gorgeous? Had he changed? What *happened*?'

'We went for a drink,' India replied. 'I mean, we've both aged, we're not teenagers any more. He's still . . . attractive.' She felt herself blush. 'And there was still this sort of electricity there, too. This unresolved tension.' That was one way of putting it, anyway. She paused, remembering sitting beside Robin in the pub, how in some ways it seemed only a matter of days since they'd last been in touch, yet equally there was this huge gulf of time stretching between them. Not to mention the floodplains of guilt and recrimination. 'He wants to see me again,' she went on. 'But obviously I'm with Dan now – things are different. I can't just go out with Robin, as if we're picking up where we left off.'

Laura was looking less excited. 'No,' she agreed after a moment. 'You probably shouldn't. But then again . . .'

'But then again, I kind of need some closure,' India finished. Did she ever.

'You totally need closure,' Laura corroborated, ever the enabler. 'Even if it's just to reassure you that you made the right choices. And it's not like you're going to be *unfaithful* to Dan, is it? You can just have a *drink* with this guy.'

India nodded. 'Exactly,' she said, knocking back her wine. 'One single drink isn't going to hurt.'

'Of course it isn't! Not at all.'

There you go: permission. Approval, even. Wasn't that what she'd been hoping for? Even though, deep down, she had the feeling that it might be the start of something very wrong? *Oh, shut up, subconscious. Who asked you anyway?* 'Talking of which . . .' She waggled the bottle. 'Top-up?'

'You bet.'

*

What India hadn't told Laura – and probably never would now, either – was how disastrously things had unravelled for her and Robin, how unhappily the relationship had hit the buffers. Mere weeks away from their A-levels, they had been spending every day together, deep in revision-cramming. Hours would drift by, spent lolling against one another in a companionable silence, broken only by the muttering of French verb conjugations, historical dates and quotes from *Paradise Lost* or *Hamlet*. And practice, endless practice, on her violin: scales and pieces and sight-reading, in preparation for her music exam.

Then one morning, she'd woken up and only just had time to sprint to the loo before she was retching and throwing up. A stomach bug, her mum said, telling her to go back to bed. It would be one of those twenty-four-hour things. Except it wasn't. Not a twenty-four-hour thing, or, as it turned out, a stomach bug. She was pregnant.

Her parents were scandalized. Her mum actually burst into tears with horror, while her dad had to be talked out of going straight round to the Fieldings' house and punching Robin's lights out. India, for her part, was similarly consumed by horror. Fear, too. She didn't want a *baby*. She was only just eighteen, with her whole life ahead of her, and all sorts of plans for music college, festivals, gigs, an exciting career. With that dreaded pregnancy test, it was as if doors were already slamming closed on her, all her dreams being snatched away – for this, a baby she didn't even want. It pained her now to remember it, but in her despair she'd thrown herself down the stairs at home, trying to bring on a miscarriage, in a desperate attempt to rid herself of the interloper. It hadn't worked. In fact, she'd twisted her ankle so badly that her mum had dragged her to the doctor's and told him, mealy-mouthed, 'And when you've finished strapping that up, you can give us some advice about an abortion. Only this one's gone and got herself in the family way, can you believe. The shame of it!'

India had not been allowed to phone Robin, or go out to see him. He'd come round to hers instead, confused by her silence, only to be confronted by India's still-raging dad. 'You've caused this family enough trouble already; go on, get out of it,' he'd thundered. 'Before you feel the end of my boot up your backside.'

India had eventually made contact by smuggling out a letter via a friend, in which she confessed the whole sorry story. She'd been grounded and wasn't allowed to see him until they'd 'sorted this thing out', to use her mum's euphemism. He'd written back telling her not to worry, that he would look after her and the baby, that they could run away together, away from their parents, forever.

Caught in a dilemma over what to do, India had pondered and agonized. She loved Robin with all her heart, and she loved that he wanted to stand by her, that he was unafraid.

But then again, if she went along with his suggestion, she knew there would be consequences, a chain of events like dominoes toppling, and she couldn't ignore her instinct deep down that running away was a bad idea. It was all very well being caught up by romantic notions of elopement, but India was a practical person and foresaw all manner of tricky questions raising their heads. Where would they go? How would they live? And what about their exams, due to start in a fortnight; her hopes for a college place?

There was not a happy ending to this story, oh no. She had let Robin down, she knew full well, and it had haunted her ever since. Because in a weak, vulnerable moment she'd replied 'yes' to him – yes, she would run away; yes, she'd forsake her exams; yes, she'd slip out of the house on Tuesday night and meet him at the bus station with a suitcase. Except . . . in the cold light of reality, she had changed her mind and hadn't done any of those things. She'd stayed in bed that night, barely sleeping for wondering if he was there, waiting for her at the station in the darkness, checking his watch, moving from foot to foot to keep warm. And then she'd sat her A-levels (distractedly, admittedly, playing her violin so badly, so woodenly, that she knew there and then she'd failed) and sniffled her way through the appointment at the Marie Stopes clinic, feeling utterly alone. *Sorry, little baby. I'm really, really sorry. I'm a bad person. It was a mistake.*

Meanwhile, Robin had completely vanished – not turning up for a single one of his exams and not giving word to anyone for six long weeks. Six weeks when India felt racked with terrible, decimating guilt every hour of the day. Was he even alive? He must despise her and her cowardice, if he was. She kept imagining the moment that night in the bus station when he must finally have realized she wasn't going to show, picturing his face hardening in bitterness, the mental two fingers he must have sent her. She'd never even got to say sorry for letting him down.

Eventually a postcard had arrived for his parents, saying Robin was in London. So he had done it then: he'd got away, he'd struck out on his own, head held high. No exams to show for himself, presumably very little money; she dreaded to think how he was surviving in the capital, all alone. And that had been the last she'd heard of him. No wonder there had been an edge to his voice when they next saw one another, twenty-one years later, practically to the day.

You totally need closure, Laura had said with such fervency. *Even if it's just to reassure you that you made the right choices.*

Yeah, quite. But what if . . . Well, what if she hadn't?

India's thoughts see-sawed one way, then the other, as she went home that evening. She should stay away. She should see him. She should stay away. She should see him. She should forget him. She should absolve herself. Oh, how was a person supposed to make a call on such a tough decision, without completely tearing their hair out over it?

He's just an old friend, she reminded herself, stepping down from the bus, but the words sounded hollow even to her own mind as she hurried along the darkening street towards her house. If he was merely an old friend, why did her subconscious keep unhelpfully throwing up memories of what it had felt like to kiss him, how madly and passionately she had loved him? Wouldn't it be the safest option to simply let bygones be bygones and keep him safely stowed away in the Ex-files?

Then again, though, she had never had the chance to properly explain or apologize until now. To say her piece, to tell him: I was young and scared, and I'm sorry I let you down, but I didn't know what else to do. Will you forgive me?

And if he did – if he looked at her and nodded and said, 'Of course I forgive you. We were kids! I was a romantic idiot who shouldn't have put so much pressure on you, it never would have worked out' – oh gosh, the relief she would feel, the lifting of the burden that had weighed down on her for so long. It would be worth seeing him for that alone, surely?

The cat wound, purring, around her legs as she entered the house, taking care to close the door quietly so as not to disturb her slumbering children. Dan was in the living room, his head tilted to the side with a scrunched-up tissue stuffed in one ear, his expression mournful as she sat down next to him. He suffered from waxy ears that sometimes needed drops in them to clear the blockages, and India knew she should try to be more sympathetic, but the thought of the gooey, sticky wax secretly revolted her. Plus, he was the world's worst invalid, feeling sorry for himself whenever he had to deal with the slightest ailment. It was a total turn-off, in India's eyes.

'I don't suppose you could bring me a glass of water, could you, love?' he asked plaintively, gesturing at his ear. That was the other thing – the minute he felt remotely off-colour, he seemed incapable of doing anything for himself, if she could do it for him instead. Presumably having a tissue stuffed in his ear rendered him incapable of getting up and walking to the kitchen, she found herself thinking darkly as she went to do his bidding. (Catch Robin acting like such a big baby? Never, was her next disloyal thought.)

Filling the glass at the kitchen tap, she remembered how, when the children were tiny and she and Dan were struggling through broken night after broken night, they would sometimes murmur to each other, 'I suspect Wild Sexual Shenanigans might be off the agenda tonight', when one of their offspring was teething or throwing up or had a hacking cough. It was a rueful sort of joke between them, shorthand to let the other one know they were still valued, still loved, still fancied, only . . . well. Sometimes parenthood got in the way of a couple's sex life, and sleep became a more yearned-for commodity. 'Do you remember the golden years of WSS?' Dan had sighed sorrowfully on occasion, when they'd woken up with a child or two in bed with them after a particularly dreadful night.

'What's that, Daddy?' Esme had asked in reply one time. (Toddler Esme had never stopped asking questions. What THAT? What HE called? What THIS do?)

'Ah, it's a magical place your mother and I used to visit, far, far away,' he'd replied, winking at India.

'Can *we* go there?' George had piped up.

'Um . . . maybe not with me and Dad,' India had said, trying not to laugh as she caught Dan's eye.

God, she'd forgotten all about that. The kids were growing up so fast, it was rare that one of them even wanted to pile into the big bed any more. Nights were mostly silent now as the family slumbered peacefully till morning. And yet the Wild Sexual Shenanigans had never really cranked up again, not to the lusty, dizzying heights she and Dan had enjoyed pre-babies. It had become something that nagged away at her periodically, another thing on her never-ending list of Things To Do: must initiate sex tonight. Must make a move on him. Which wasn't exactly sexy in itself, was it?

She turned off the tap, tired and befuddled after half a

bottle of wine. Chances were she was not in for any WSS tonight anyway, she thought. Was it very wrong that she felt relieved at the prospect?

Chapter Twenty-One

Eve reversed neatly into a space at the hospital car park, turned off the engine and then sat behind the wheel for a few moments, eyes closed. Okay. Here she was. Ready to face the music. Ready to find out the truth. Ready – sort of – to meet Lewis Mulligan, after some kind of mania had descended on her and she'd asked him to come along with her today. (What had she been *thinking*? The minute the words had left her mouth, she'd regretted them – but before she could go snatching them back, there he was nodding and saying, *Cool, yeah, no problem*.)

Deep breath. Don't forget to lock the car. Got your handbag and appointment letter? Right. And off she went, trudging reluctantly towards the main entrance, where she'd agreed to meet her unlikely companion. Please God let Lewis not seize this opportunity of her being a captive audience to start lecturing her about mindfulness or to tell her that positive thinking could beat cancer, she thought grimly, when everyone knew that it was only cold, hard science that could change anything. What if he tried to get her to meditate with him in the corridor, or started tootling ruddy pan-pipes at her, or whatever other new-age crap he was into? That was if he turned up at all, of course. Knowing how bloody disorganized he was, he would be late or would have got the times muddled up, and then she'd end up flustered and really cross that she'd been so stupid as to ask him along and . . .

Oh. Wait. Was that him, already there by the main doors, checking out a map of the hospital? 'Hi,' he called, seeing her approach. 'You okay? Right, according to this, we need to go along here.' This with an authoritative gesture towards one of the corridors.

Okay, so perhaps she had been a bit hasty to write him off, Eve thought, managing a weak smile. 'Hi,' she said, falling into step beside him as he headed off. 'Thanks,' she remembered to say.

In fact, she realized, as he guided them through the maze of corridors, it was oddly nice having someone else take charge like this, for a change, to steer her in the direction she needed to go. Just once in a while anyway.

'Eve Taylor? If you'd like to follow me, please.'

A pretty Asian woman in a uniform had appeared in the doorway and Eve rose from the slippery vinyl chair, bars of doom-laden music crashing in her head. On the next seat along, rather more hesitantly, a man she barely knew was unfolding his gangly body and turning his head towards hers. 'Um, should I . . . ?' he asked. 'Do you want me to . . . ?'

His unfinished question hung in the air. Did Eve want Lewis Mulligan to come into the room with her while she stripped off and allowed a radiographer to X-ray her boob? Er . . . no. She did not. 'Could you wait here for me?' she asked. 'Hopefully I won't be long.'

The look of sheer relief on his face as she replied in the negative was almost laughable. Bless him, he was only young and had probably never seen a middle-aged woman's naked bits and pieces before; he could have been scarred for life, at the sight of so much sagging and dangling. And yet how sweet of him to have asked in the first place, to have been so considerate, she conceded in the next moment.

'Sure,' he said, sinking back down into his seat, pale bony knees sticking out of his ripped jeans. 'I'll be right out here.'

Feeling rather as if she were walking to her own execution, Eve followed the radiographer down a corridor and into a small room, where she was asked to undress to the waist, before being guided, semi-naked, across to the machine. She had never been particularly comfortable about stripping off casually in front of strangers; not for her the indignity of a communal changing room in a leisure centre or gym; give her a cubicle any day.

'That's it, if I could just ask you to position your breast on the plate here,' the radiographer said calmly, seemingly immune to Eve's embarrassment. 'And your arm like this . . . smashing. It's so we can see the muscle at the back of the breast as well.'

'Right,' mumbled Eve.

'Now I'll be doing four X-rays in all, two of each breast at different angles, so we can have a really good look at what's going on in there, okay? The breast will be compressed during this, which is the uncomfortable part, I'm afraid. Try and relax. I know it's a bit strange, but it won't take long, I promise.'

Try and relax. Eve looked down at her small brown breast, sitting there on the Perspex plate, goose-pimples prickling up all over the flesh, and a lump rose in her throat. You stripped away all the outer trappings of life – clothing, work, family – and this was what you were reduced to: a scared, vulnerable creature, your future swinging perilously in the balance. What was relaxing about that?

The radiographer, satisfied with Eve's position, moved behind a screen in order to start the X-rays, and Eve's heart-rate accelerated into a Derby-winning gallop. Everything about the room swam into sharp focus as adrenalin flooded her system: the squeezing sensation of the machine as her poor little breast was squashed painfully flat, the hum of the fluorescent lights overhead, the clean floral scent of the woman's shampoo as she came back to help Eve switch sides.

Deep breaths, Eve. Keep it together. You will get through this. For comfort, she thought of her children at school, their dark heads bent over exercise books in their classrooms. They were such good girls. Did she tell them she loved them often enough? Grace still hadn't confided in her about this boyfriend. How could she earn her daughter's trust on the matter?

'That's it, and the arm just . . . here. Perfect,' said the radiographer, repositioning her.

Eve's thoughts turned to Neil as a means of distraction, picturing him clearing his throat and clutching his cue cards in preparation for his presentation at the conference. She remembered how he'd been grinding his teeth in his sleep recently, and hoped he wasn't too stressed. The two of them badly needed to talk, to carve out proper time together again, rather than shielding themselves with their laptops and phones evening after evening. And then her mind drifted to her friends, who were going about their days elsewhere in the city, and to Lewis outside in the corridor, jiggling a leg to some unheard beat as he waited. *I don't want to die*, she thought desperately, as the radiographer pressed a few buttons behind her screen again and then came back to tell her it was all over, that she could get dressed and return to her seat.

'You all right? How was it?' asked Lewis when she emerged a few minutes later.

She swallowed, feeling tired and emotional. Guilty, too, that she'd involved him in this at all, poor random stranger that he was. This was why she never usually went to anyone else for help: because you ended up feeling bad for putting them out, and were obliged to reciprocate and . . .

'Listen, I'm sorry,' she blurted out. 'I should never have asked you to come along today. It was . . . stupid of me. Selfish. You've probably got far better things to be doing with yourself.' She sat down next to him and plucked up the last dregs of her courage and dignity to say, rather shakily, 'I'll be fine, you know, if you'd sooner go. I won't mind.'

She didn't wholly mean it, of course. Part of her was desperate for him not to leave her on her own, when she felt so uncertain and scared. But she had to give him the choice at least, if only for the sake of her pride.

He looked at her warily, trying to read between her words. 'If you want to be on your own, that's cool,' he told her after a moment had elapsed. 'But I don't have to be anywhere else, so if you'd rather I stayed, then . . .' He spread his hands wide in front of him. 'I'm totally fine with that, too. It's your call.'

She had to press her lips together hard then, because she wanted very much to cry with relief. How she hated feeling like this, so weak, so needy! It was awful what this wretched lump was doing to her, just awful. 'You are very kind,' she said eventually, feeling so overcome with emotion that her voice wobbled again. 'First I nearly run you over, and now I'm asking this massive favour – I owe you one, okay? Actually, I owe you twice now.' Three times, really, if you counted him overhearing her insult him in the office, she realized, cringing.

'Really, it's fine. My mum went through this, I know it's grim,' he said. He bowed his shaggy head a little, his red hair unnaturally bright beneath the strip-lighting. 'And I wasn't able to sit with her while she waited like this in the clinic. So I'm sort of glad to be able to help. If that doesn't sound too weird.'

'It doesn't sound weird,' she assured him. 'You're probably thinking *I'm* the weird one, asking you, rather than my husband or a friend, but—'

'Mrs Taylor? If I could just have a word?'

And then Eve's adrenalin surged, because it was the radiographer again, looking poker-faced as she beckoned her over.

The mammogram had shown a density in the tissue, which meant that Eve needed to have an ultrasound as well, in order to determine whether it was solid or cystic. So that was another stressful experience, lying there, naked to the waist once more, an arm above her head, as a sonographer anointed her breast with cold gel and then slowly moved a transducer around it while peering at a screen. The sonographer, Irish, young and chatty, explained that she was looking for fluid in the lump, which would indicate a cyst, but then stopped talking and frowned at the screen, confessing that – hmm, it was quite hard to tell, to be honest; she was going to have to take some pictures and get a radiologist's opinion. Which was not exactly the reassuring and cheery response Eve had been hoping for.

They'd had to wait again, in a different corridor, before a doctor called them in to say that the sonogram had proved inconclusive, and that Eve would now have to endure what was called a core biopsy. This apparently involved a massive needle being plunged into her poor soft breast in order to suck out some tissue, which would then be sent on to a laboratory to be tested.

It had been the weirdest thing: Eve had been listening to the doctor and seeing her mouth move – open, close, open, close – but for some reason she couldn't concentrate on what she was being told. Instead she was thinking about how vile it would feel to have a needle stabbing into her breast, how intrusive and unpleasant, how actually she wasn't sure she wanted to know any more about the wretched lump; she just wanted to go home and lie in bed, with the covers over her head. Maybe it was better to remain in the dark as far as some things were concerned; take back control by refusing to find out.

'We'll give you a local anaesthetic and provide you with painkillers before you go, as it can be a bit sore – and there may be some bruising afterwards,' the doctor was saying now.

A tear had worked its way from Eve's eye and was rolling busily down her face. She hadn't even been aware she was crying until it plopped wetly onto her skirt.

'I know it's not a nice thing to have to go through,' the doctor said kindly, passing her a box of tissues. 'We're just erring on the side of caution, but nine times out of ten . . .'

Oh, but Eve was sick of that statistic. Nine times out of ten, it's something benign: yes, she knew, it was on every breast-cancer messageboard and web page in every leaflet. Which was great for those nine people, yes, lovely. But it still meant one person was given the big head-shaking diagnosis, the big 'You're Screwed'. Eve dealt with numbers every day, she understood percentages and calculations, it was what she did. And however good 'nine times out of ten' sounded, there was no escaping the fact that she could quite easily be that one person in ten. The unlucky one.

The doctor had finished speaking and was looking at her with professional concern.

'Any questions?' Lewis prompted when Eve made no comment.

'Sorry. Um . . .' *Am I about to die? Will I be leaving my children without their mother? How will Neil cope, when he doesn't even know how to work the washing machine?* 'Yes,' she said eventually, when a less hysterical question occurred to her. 'Will you be able to give me the result of the biopsy today?'

'I'm afraid not. We have to send the tissue samples off to our laboratory.'

Eve cringed because she remembered then that the doctor had already mentioned this. 'Oh right, yes, sorry. You did say. I'm finding it a bit hard to . . . I'm not concentrating very well.'

'That's quite all right,' the doctor replied. 'And I'm happy to repeat myself as many times as you like.' She was broad and tall, in her fifties at a guess, with cropped fair hair and a calm, no-nonsense air about her. 'Once at the laboratory, the tissues will be examined under a microscope. We can usually let you know the result in a week.'

A whole week, Eve thought, trying not to groan. Seven long days of tearing herself apart with worry. 'Right,' she managed to say. She could feel Lewis giving her an anxious look from her left and with good reason, because she was scared; she was really scared – she had no idea how this was going to pan out. But then she pulled herself together, took a short quick breath and nodded. 'Okay,' she said. 'Let's do it.'

*

Afterwards, when the biopsy was over, when she had a small dressing taped across her breast and dull pain thudding through the skin, despite the painkillers, Eve was free to leave. It was over. And yet she couldn't face returning immediately out into the real world, with its people, traffic and noisy normality. She felt wounded and battered, wrung out from the morning's events. Lewis suggested that they go for a cup of tea in the hospital coffee shop, just until she felt better, and she accepted gratefully. 'Thank you,' she said in such a small voice it didn't sound like her any more. 'For all of this. I don't really feel like going straight back to work.'

'Of course you don't,' he agreed, patting her arm clumsily. 'Christ, you've just been through an incredibly stressful ordeal, there's no way anyone could carry on as if nothing had happened.' He narrowed his eyes a fraction. 'You're allowed to feel overwhelmed, you know. It's completely understandable.'

She stirred milk into her tea, the spoon clinking against the mug. Understandable? He was only saying that because he was a stranger and didn't understand *her*. He had seen her at her worst and weakest; he didn't realize that she was normally the poster girl for self-sufficiency. 'Well, I'm usually pretty good at that,' she found herself replying. 'Carrying on, I mean. I'm usually the sort of person who keeps going, who doesn't just give up when the going gets tough.'

He choked on a biscuit crumb in his haste to reply.

'Giving up? I wouldn't call this giving up!' he spluttered. 'Cutting yourself a bit of slack after three different rounds of tests is absolutely fair enough. Do you hear me? Giving up, indeed. You should give yourself a break.' Then he shot her a shrewd look. 'Is that why I'm here, then?'

'What? To tell me off for being defeatist?'

'No, because you're used to pretending everything's fine,' he replied. 'Is that why you haven't told your husband?'

Talk about putting her on the spot. 'He's busy today, he couldn't have come anyway,' she protested, but felt herself squirming beneath his gaze. 'Oh, look, I don't know,' she added, feeling flustered. 'Hopefully it'll be fine – he'll never have to know.'

Lewis eyed her over the rim of his mug. 'Wouldn't you want to know, if it was the other way round?' he asked. 'If he was worried he had – I dunno – prostate cancer or something? You'd want to be there at the hospital with him, wouldn't you?'

'Yes, but—' She broke off, colour flooding her face. Of *course* she'd have been there for Neil, of course she'd want to know every single development, if he was ill or worried or fearful. She'd have organized every appointment, every stage, with military precision, taken charge. Why had she not given Neil the chance to do the same for her?

She sipped her tea – pretty disgusting – and changed tack. 'Look, I know this sounds mad, and I'm really not a superstitious sort of person, but lately I've just felt as if Death is hard on my heels, out to get me,' she confessed in a low voice. 'There's been one thing after another: lucky escapes, missed chances, other people being struck down, and not me.' She shivered. 'I just can't help feeling . . . it's my turn next. And I want to spare my family the details for as long as possible. Nothing wrong with that, is there?'

He raised an eyebrow. 'You're right,' he said, and she was surprised at how gratified she felt at his agreement – for two whole seconds at least. Then he added, 'About sounding mad, that is. Aye, it does sound mad. It sounds absolutely bloody ridiculous. Death out to get you, indeed. Like we all take turns. The world doesn't work that way, Eve.'

She blushed an even hotter red, feeling stupid, and was about to stammer out something defensive when he put down his mug and stood up. 'Come on. Much as I love over-brewed tea and UHT milk, I'm sure we can find something more uplifting to do instead – take your mind off what's just happened. Fancy it?'

'Well . . . Where? What do you mean?'

He tapped his nose. 'I've got an idea,' he assured her. 'Trust me.'

Trust him, he'd said, which apparently involved them both getting in her car – he'd taken the bus to the hospital – and then allowing him to dictate where they were going, road by road, junction by junction, without providing any further information. For someone like Eve who aspired to precision and control, it was practically a form of torture. 'If you just *tell* me where we're going, I could put the destination into my satnav,' she'd tried saying, but he'd shaken his head, with a laugh.

'You can't bear it, can you? Not knowing. The suspense, eh? Where is he taking me? Why did I ever agree to this? Oh – left turn coming up, by the way.'

'Here? Are you sure?' They had left the city behind by now and the landscape was increasingly rural, the horizon widening out to encompass fields and farmland. The turning he was pointing to looked insignificant, as if they might be venturing down a dead-end, and her inner warning system started to flash with alarm. He didn't strike her as the type of person who'd lure a possibly cancer-riddled woman down a cul-de-sac and finish her off, but you never could tell. If Eve was going to die, then she'd prefer to do it her way, with dignity, rather than ending up as a tabloid story with a lurid headline.

'I'm sure,' he replied, and she indicated left, turned into the narrow road and then, with her warning system still on high alert, abruptly pulled over in a lay-by. There was a farmer with a sheepdog within sight; she could lean on the horn if there was a problem and get attention, she thought, strategizing quickly.

'What are you doing?' he asked in surprise.

'I'm . . .' She sighed. He wasn't going to kill her; she was overreacting, no doubt, but all the same. 'I can't cope with a mystery tour right now,' she told him. 'I'm really tired. I'm not in the mood. Thanks and all that, but I think this was a bad idea.'

He softened immediately. 'You're right. I thought it might be relaxing if I took charge, but . . .' Now it was his turn to colour. 'But I misjudged it. Sorry. Och, I was only going to suggest a walk – the cats' and dogs' home is just another mile down here, and I often walk the dogs for them. There's a great stretch of woodland, and a good wee pub – we could have lunch even or . . .' He was shrugging, looking embarrassed. 'It always makes me feel better, that's all, being out in the woods. And look, the sun's even trying to shine a bit. But if you'd rather not, then that's cool, too . . .'

His voice petered out while she did her best to process all of this. Walking a dog? She'd never really been a pet person. The girls had pleaded with her now and then for some fluffy companion or other, and Eve had refused each time, citing bad smells, fur, mess and the fact that she knew damn well it would be her who ended up looking after the creature, however passionately they might argue to the contrary. But he might be right about being out in the countryside lifting the spirits, she supposed, and it was sure to be an improvement on sitting alone in her living room, listening to her own panicked thoughts.

Her alarm system reset itself again, drama over. 'Okay. That sounds good. Thanks.' And she started the car and set off down the road.

Once at the centre, they were partnered with a black-and-white cross-breed – part whippet, part collie, part something else – which greeted Lewis with huge tail-wagging joy and much prancing about, as if his lean wiry body couldn't quite contain so much excitement. 'This is Huxley,' Lewis told Eve, as he clipped on a lead and signed them out. 'Came in here with a cigarette burn on his head and a broken leg; he'd been dumped in the street and was found dragging himself along, like the most pathetic specimen you've ever seen, apparently.'

'Oh my God,' Eve said, aghast, unable to equate this story with the bright-eyed hound before them that kept jumping up delightedly, trying to lick Lewis's face.

'I know, it breaks your heart, doesn't it? How anyone could do that to an animal? Talk about an underdog. But two months' rehab and loads of love in this place and he's a changed wee laddie. Aren't you, eh? All mended and handsome again?' He crouched down to make a fuss of the excited creature, then called goodbye to the manager. 'Shall we?' he asked Eve.

Beyond the walled car park there was a footpath that led

into a stretch of verdant meadow, long grass speckled with scarlet poppies, buttercups and cornflowers. There was a mass of tall leafy trees at one end, with rolling farmland in the distance, and a lone bird of prey skimming above their heads, a silent silhouette against the clouds. Once the gate had clanged shut behind them, Lewis bent to let Huxley off his lead and the dog bounded ahead down the path, long legs covering the ground with ease. 'That's better,' said Lewis, watching him go. Then he turned to Eve. 'Okay?'

She nodded. 'Better. Thanks.' Being here and feeling the sun unexpectedly warm on her arms as it broke through the clouds was definitely preferable to trudging back to the office. She could smell the earth beneath her feet, sweet and ripe, and felt anchored to it once again; the hospital and its echoing corridors shimmering far behind already like a mirage. 'Tell me about you,' she said, letting her fingertips rustle through the long grasses to her left. She gave a small laugh. 'We've gone through such a weird few hours together and I really don't know anything about you. How did you get into your line of work?'

They walked on companionably together while Lewis told her more about himself: how his mum had died a few years ago up in Fife and he'd gone off the rails afterwards, drinking too much and 'getting into a wee bit of bother with the police'. His voice dropped to a mumble. 'Did a few things I regret.' He'd drifted for a while, before coming to

Manchester for a change of scene, picking up some bar work and labouring jobs, before realizing that being outdoors always made him feel good, and deciding to take a personal-trainer course. 'Running and exercising outside – it's common sense, really. We're animals, like Huxley, it's good for us to get out of our air-conditioned buildings and cars and be in the real world, the living world. I know you think it's all hippy crap, but . . .' He wrinkled his nose and grinned. 'It works for me.'

'No, I get it,' she replied. 'There's something about being outside like this that makes me feel better, too. More relaxed.' She rolled her shoulders. 'I guess I could do with relaxing more.'

He elbowed her teasingly. 'You don't say!'

'Hey!' she laughed, trying to sound indignant.

'You should come along to one of my fitness classes,' he went on. 'Be spontaneous and bunk off work one day, try the afternoon class in Platt Fields. There's a really great mix of people who come.'

'Maybe,' she said, even though she knew already that she wouldn't dream of 'bunking off', not ever. 'Although . . .' She gave another laugh, this one self-deprecating. 'I must confess, I'm not really the most spontaneous person, to be honest.'

He pantomimed shock. 'No! Seriously? Aw, but spontaneity is when all the best stuff happens. You should try it.'

The dog bounded back to them and Lewis bent to fondle

his head while Eve found herself thinking of her own life, so rigidly controlled, so tightly bound by its structures and deadlines that there wasn't much room left for spontaneity nowadays. 'We are so completely different,' she said with a little laugh.

'That's all right, though. That's good! Who'd want a world where everyone was the same?'

'I know, but . . .' She was starting to think she had judged Lewis unfairly, that was what she wanted to say. That she had written him off prematurely as a bit of a loser, only for him to keep confounding her with his real, sincere self. 'Listen, I know you overheard me that time you came back into the office,' she went on awkwardly. 'When I was saying you were disorganized or something . . .'

He waved a hand. 'Och, it doesn't matter. It's true anyway – although you didn't need to run me over for it.'

She snorted despite herself. 'You're never going to let me live that down, are you?'

'I shouldn't think so. But that's okay. We make mistakes – and we keep on going, right? We don't have to let what happens to us define us for the rest of our lives.'

She lifted a hand to shield her eyes from the sun as she turned to look at him. 'Very philosophical,' she commented wryly. 'Life Lessons from Lewis Mulligan – there's a radio phone-in show there somewhere, I swear.'

'It's true, though, isn't it? I mean, look at Huxley, so

trusting and full of love, after everything he's been through. Aren't you, boy, eh?' They watched as the dog galloped away in pursuit of a magpie that he was never going to catch. 'Ach, I'm not trying to get all serious on you, Eve, but . . . well, it's life-affirming, isn't it? He's a good role model for us humans. That life can knock you down, but you've got to—' He caught her eye and then broke off mid-sentence, looking embarrassed. 'Am I laying it on a bit thick, do you think?'

'A bit,' she replied, elbowing him. 'But I appreciate what you're trying to say. I hear you. And thanks.'

Later that night, her breast throbbing like a pulse beneath her nightie where the pre-biopsy anaesthetic had worn off, Eve lay in bed staring up through the darkness and tried to get her head in order. Today had been a very unusual day. She had been through three gruelling rounds of tests at the hospital that had left her emotionally depleted. She had walked a dog for miles through fields and trees, and drunk ice-clinking lemonade in a beer garden with a man who said 'Trust me' and had been unremittingly kind to her. And for the rest of the day she'd put in a bravura acting performance as Eve Taylor, competent superwoman, normal mother and wife, which had apparently fooled everyone.

Tomorrow she would have to get up and go to the office as usual, chat to her colleagues and return to her desk as if her mind wasn't one gigantic ticking clock, counting down the hours and minutes until the results of her biopsy came back. The day after that, she and Neil were supposed to be going out with Jo and her new boyfriend Rick; they would have to be witty and entertaining, make clever comments about politics, books and TV, recount old stories that portrayed Jo in a golden light, and she would have to do that subtle sisterhood thing of catching Rick's eye in a way that said: Hurt my friend and I'll kill you. And all the while not let on, not breathe a word of what was really happening in her life, in her body. How on earth would she be able to pull it off?

Try and put the whole thing out of your mind, the doctor had advised, but Eve felt like laughing with sheer incredulity that anyone could think this was remotely possible.

It almost felt as if she was having an affair – all this secrecy, the double life that she was leading. Not that she thought of Lewis in that way or he, her; he had a girlfriend, Katie, who was into kick-boxing and grungy music and they were very happy together apparently. Still, if Eve *had* been having an affair, she could totally have got away with it right now, she reckoned. Nobody had noticed that anything was wrong with her. Neil, having been preoccupied by the conference all evening, was now making that annoying snuffling sound on the other side of the bed that meant he was already asleep, his face naked and vulnerable without his glasses. Maybe Eve's acting had been more convincing than she'd imagined, after all. Or maybe he just wasn't that interested.

Moving stealthily so as not to disturb him, Eve moved her hand under her nightie and gently touched the dressing still taped to her skin. She had peered at it earlier in the bathroom mirror, furtively and hurriedly, because there was no lock on the door, and had seen for herself thc bruised tenderness there. Her hand closed protectively around her breast and she held onto herself like that for some time, finding comfort from her own touch. She thought of the girls fast asleep in their own beds, dark hair fanning across the pillows: Grace on her back with her arms across her chest, Sophie curled up like a little hedgehog. The images were enough to make her breath catch in her throat again, because she wanted more than anything to stay in their lives long enough to see them grow up, fall in love, navigate their way into careers they each loved, build satisfying and wonderful lives for themselves . . . How could anyone deem it fair to deny Eve the pleasures of admiring their wedding photos on her mantelpiece, or holding warm tiny grandchildren with reverential care, or hearing the latest details of her daughters' success and fulfilment in their professions? What good would she be dead and cold, her ashes scattered to the winds?

A tear spilled from her eye and rolled down into her ear.

Nine out of ten, she reminded herself, trying to hold back from plunging fully into despair. Nine out of ten patients had luck on their side. Who was to say she wouldn't be one of them?

Chapter Twenty-Two

'Oh my GOD, Jo – he's lovely,' Laura pronounced, the minute they were through the door of the Ladies.

'He's so nice and funny and friendly,' agreed Eve.

'He's even listening to Dan's boring plumbing stories and actually looking *interested*.' India put a hand up for Jo to high-five. 'Full marks to you, lady. He's a keeper.'

Jo flushed at this collective display of enthusiasm. The four of them were in the loos at Cane and Grain, where they'd come for a Thursday-night get-together, along with their other halves – or not, in Laura's case. 'Just a drink, no big deal,' Jo had said on the phone, but Laura knew that she had been nervous of them all meeting Rick, and rightly so. Having seen Jo suffer through her divorce, she, Eve and India were extra-protective of her and wanted this new man to be the real deal. And he did seem pretty great, Laura thought, having personally given him her full forensic once-over. He was friendly. Confident. Complimentary about Jo. Generous on the drink-buying front – lots of ticks, in all.

Although . . . not that she would ever dream of saying this, obviously, but he wasn't exactly what Laura had been expecting, especially after all Jo's gushing and cooing. He was kind of . . . well, *chubbier* than she'd imagined, for one thing: round in the face, with the beginnings of a belly on him and just a hint of double chin in the offing. And, goodness, those big juicy lips of his, too – they seemed very fleshy, didn't they, almost womanly in fact. Laura, for one, would not like to kiss those lips.

Not that *that* had ever been on the agenda anyway, obviously – and not that she was exactly in a great position to be critical about other people's new boyfriends, either, right now when, chances were, she was destined for a long old lonely lifetime on the shelf from here on in. *Jealous, are we?* carped a mean little voice in her head.

No! she thought defensively, rummaging in her bag for mascara. It was just something of a surprise, that was all. Greg, Jo's ex-husband, had been tall, athletic and handsome; Laura had assumed Rick would be a similar type. Not a fat fish-face. Oh God, that was mean of her, wasn't it? Very unsisterly. Maybe she *was* a bit jealous after all. Jealous that Jo was so damn radiant with joy. 'Yeah, he's *brilliant*,' she said quickly, trying to atone for her inner witch.

'I'm so glad you like him,' Jo was saying, high colour in her cheeks. She fanned herself jokingly. 'The triple seal of approval – phew!'

'And it's going well, the two of you?' asked India, touching up her red lipstick in the mirror. 'You're still madly happy and in love?'

'Well . . .' And then Jo's face did a strange twisty thing, the exact same one it had done on the day when Laura had been four and Jo eight, when Jo had sat her down and said they had to be very, very brave because Dad had gone, and now it was just them and Mum left, okay? 'Um. Ye-e-es.'

'Do I sense a "but" lingering in the air like a wet fart?' asked India.

'What's up?' Laura asked, pausing in her mascara application to stare at her sister and taking in for the first time the fact that Jo was wearing this silky sort of blouse with a pussy bow at the neck, teamed with a linen skirt and high-heeled sandals, plus quite a lot of make-up. 'It's not this bloody daughter again, is it?' she guessed, eyes hardening. 'The evil stepdaughter,' she informed the other two. 'A little madam who's been running rings around Jo.'

'Oh no,' said Eve sympathetically. 'That's all you need.'

'It's his ex, too,' Jo said in a low voice. 'I haven't met her, it's just . . .' She shrugged unhappily. 'Maisie's always going on about how amazing she is, compared to me. I've seen photos and she's like super-glam and super-beautiful, worst luck. I can't help feeling intimidated. What with that, and Maisie playing up – there's all this *baggage*. I keep wondering if I'm . . . good enough.'

Laura should have known. Jo had always had a bit of a downer on herself about the way she looked. There had been some girls who'd called her Ginger Biscuit for the entire five years of secondary school, even when Jo dyed her hair black in an attempt to shut them up. (A terrible mistake; not only did the shade leave her skin looking positively vampiric, but the girls had switched to calling her Ginger Pubes instead, which wasn't exactly something she could disprove.) Maybe this was the reason behind all the posh new clothes and make-up, Laura thought now with a pang. 'Yeah, but so what? He's binned his ex, she's in the past. She can't have been *that* great,' she said hotly. 'And you're lovely. You're fabulous.'

'You are loyal and funny and kind and gorgeous,' India added without pausing for breath.

'And he wants to be with you,' Eve put in. 'That's got to count for something.'

'You can always stay at mine, if you need space,' Laura reminded her, wondering if Jo was regretting having moved in with Rick so quickly. It had been so out of character for her sister to make such a blind, reckless leap in the first place. *I just want to be with someone though*, she had confessed to Laura in a moment of self-doubt. *Is it wrong, that I just want to be with someone?*

'I'm being silly, it's fine,' Jo said, smiling brightly at them all just then. 'I'm glad you like him, anyway. Who wants another drink?'

It was only later on, when Laura was back home and in her pyjamas, spooning mint-choc-chip ice cream from the tub in front of the telly that she realized she'd forgotten to ask her sister about the dizzy spells. Being related to a nurse came in very handy if you ever had a funny little health quirk, especially when Jo was usually so solidly reassuring about everything.

The weird dizziness had happened twice now: once on the tram home from work, where Laura was standing in the usual crush of people, and once – bizarrely – in her own shower. On the tram, the sensation had come over her with terrifying speed: this strong, frightening certainty that she was about to faint, right there amidst the crowd. Her knees had buckled. Her vision kept going in and out of focus, with black spots flickering before her eyes. She'd broken out into a sweat, her mouth dry, her brain flooded with panic, and had had to get off a stop early, hoping that fresh air would make her feel better. She'd sat down on a bench for about fifteen minutes, scared that she was about to pass out or vomit or both, wishing she could just call Matt to come and get her, until at last the feeling started to fade and she was able to walk slowly home. Then, in the shower the other morning, it had happened again, and she must have blacked out for a second that time, because suddenly she was crumpled at the bottom of the cubicle in a pool of water with no memory of getting there, the showerhead still spraying down on her like rain, her coccyx one painful ache where she'd jarred it in the fall.

It was unnerving, having your body flake out on you like that. Alarming. Was it just the stress of her husband leaving her, or was something badly wrong? You heard such awful stories about people walking around with undiagnosed brain tumours like ticking time-bombs, who then collapsed and died, completely out of the blue. She couldn't stop thinking about what would have happened if she'd banged her head and fallen unconscious in the shower – or even died, with that massive brain tumour she was now obsessing about – and just how long her body would have lain there, naked and numb, the water gently pattering down. Of all the ways to go, it would be typical Laura to have such an embarrassing end to her life. As it was, she'd crawled out of the cubicle onto the bathmat and had curled up there for a moment or two, feeling shaken and scared. *Oh, Matt,* she'd thought, her heart pounding, feeling the sadness grip her all over again. He'd always looked after her when she felt ill; he'd have sent her back to bed and brought her a cup of tea if she'd told him she'd just fainted, he'd have worn that concerned expression that always made her feel so cosily cared for. Curled foetally on a bathmat, shivering alone and wondering what the hell just happened, was really not the same.

She spooned another lump of ice cream onto her tongue, cool and minty, wondering what he was doing tonight, all those miles north in his new start. Was it pathetic of her that she missed him more than ever at this sort of moment, when she was worried about herself and feeling a bit needy? She'd phoned him to tell him about the tram incident, just wanting to talk through the experience as much as anything because it had been so peculiar, but he'd been quite short with her. Uninterested, in fact. He'd actually said, 'Laura . . . you can't keep doing this' as if she was constantly badgering him about trivial things, when she'd only rung him a few times since he'd moved. (Well, all right. Maybe slightly more than a few times. Drunk, occasionally. Also, quite late at night. But she was trying not to, okay? She was trying her hardest. He didn't have to sound quite so offhand with her, just because she was a human being and had feelings!) 'I think we need to move on with our own lives,' he had said at the end, all curt and – yes! – even quite exasperated too, and she'd felt so hurt, so told-off by him, that she'd hung up and burst into tears.

She hadn't rung him once since then. Not even a text when she couldn't remember where he'd put the house-insurance details, when the account came up for renewal. She had deleted his mobile number from her phone so that she wouldn't be tempted, in a weak moment. If silence was what he wanted, then fine, she'd give him silence. If all those years of marriage meant nothing to him, then he could jog on. All the same, it wasn't easy.

Still, apart from the fainting and the over-eating – she put the lid on the ice cream and moved it away from her, along the coffee table – Laura was just about keeping her head above water in this new single way of life, all things considered. The key seemed to be setting her own expectations very, very low, as if she were an invalid, weak and feeble, who could barely do a thing for herself. *Well done, Me*, she praised herself as she made it into work on time each morning, rewarding herself with a frothy latte from the coffee bar downstairs for her effort. *Good going, Me*, she thought as she forced herself out to Pilates with India, rather than sloping off straight home to her sofa. *Great work, Me*, she congratulated herself as she dredged up her most professional, smiling face in order to endure another focus-group session, this time with a bunch of exhausted new mums, even though the jealousy she felt was enough to make her want to double over and howl.

She was coping, hauling herself grimly through every hour, every day, despite the occasional blip. It had been a nightmare trying to cancel the summer holiday she and Matt had booked, way back in the new year, for example, and Laura had ended up actually swearing at the poor travel agent over the phone, before bursting into tears and sobbing out the whole story of their split. There had also been a couple of occasions when she'd got very drunk, all alone, and had felt the need for some angry revenge. She'd smashed one of their big framed wedding photos by hurling it against the wall, watching in furious satisfaction as the glass shattered like crystal raindrops. Another time she'd found a favourite shirt of Matt's that he'd accidentally left behind, and had taken to it with a pair of pinking shears, hacking off the arms and collar as if she were taking part in some kind of crazed sewing-bee challenge. Catching a glimpse of herself in the mirror, red-faced and completely deranged-looking, had not been a proud moment.

But still. Whatever gets you through, as the magazine articles on break-ups advised. Find small things that give you comfort, they said, although admittedly going on a rampage with the pinking shears was not in the list of recommendations. Try to look to the future, rather than the past. You *will* find happiness again, they kept assuring her. You *will*, Laura, we promise.

God, she really hoped so. She really, really, desperately hoped so. Because otherwise how long could she go on like this, feeling so dead inside, so devastated?

The next time she had a dizzy spell was the most embarrassing of all. It was Gayle from the office's fortieth birthday and she'd press-ganged everyone – even reluctant, I-vant-to-be-alone Laura – to come along for drinks at The Turtle after work. The bar was crowded and noisy; it was hot in there as well – too hot – and maybe it was just having been on her feet all afternoon, giving a presentation to some of their retailers, or maybe it was the fact that she'd had a really quick lunch and nothing to eat since, but Laura suddenly felt the weirdness descending all over again, causing her to sway on her heels like a sapling in the wind. Oh no, not here, she thought in desperation. Not in front of all her colleagues.

Gayle was holding court to the group, recounting a funny story, her little bird-like head bobbing as she spoke, but Laura could no longer focus on the anecdote because her legs were starting to go from under her and she had to clutch at the nearest table for support. She wanted to say something, make an excuse and get away, but her mouth felt weird, as if she could no longer move it properly. Gayle had become very distant, as if Laura was looking at her through a telescope and – oh help, those black dots were clouding in front of her eyes again, she had to get out of here, she had to go outside . . .

'Are you okay?' Perhaps she'd let out some kind of despairing sound or perhaps he was just super-observant, because Jim, standing next to her, had taken her by the elbow and was looking concerned. 'Laura?'

'I'm just . . .' Oh, Christ, now Mel and Julie were staring at her too, and still her voice wouldn't work. Gayle had even stopped talking, head on one side, eyes beady. Laura licked her lips and made a valiant attempt to keep it together. 'I . . . I need some air,' she managed to say weakly. 'I . . .'

'I'll come with you,' said Jim, still holding on to her – thank goodness, because otherwise she might well have crumpled and folded in on herself, all the way down to the sticky tiled floor – and he forged a way for them through the crush. 'Excuse me. Could we just . . . ? Excuse me. Cheers.'

'State of her already,' she dimly registered somebody sniggering as Jim steered her towards the exit.

'I think I'm going to faint,' she managed to say to him, feeing limp and wobbly. Her shirt was sticking to her back, her head was heavy and the floor seemed to be lurching vertiginously towards her, like a bad fairground ride.

'You're very pale. Let's just get outside for a minute – it's boiling in here,' he said, supporting her with an arm around her back. She leaned against it, never gladder to feel daylight on her face as they made it through the door.

Outside the bar there was a knot of people with cigarettes and drinks, but Jim guided her past them and to an empty stretch of pavement. Leaning against the wall, Laura tried to catch her breath, but she was no longer able to support her own weight and sank down into a squatting position. *Don't faint. Don't faint.* 'I'm so sorry about this,' she mumbled, her tongue feeling thick in her mouth as she closed her eyes, balancing her head on her knees.

'You're okay. Just keep breathing, that's it. Excuse me, mate, you couldn't get this lady a glass of water, could you, please? Cheers. Thanks.' Jim crouched next to her companionably. 'Now, come on,' he said reprovingly. 'Gayle's stories aren't that boring that you need to go all dramatic on us.'

Despite still feeling fuzzy and strange, Laura snorted a small laugh through her nose.

'I'm not sure you'll be invited to the forty-first birthday drinks now, you and your diva-like attitude,' he went on, 'but we all have our crosses to bear, I suppose . . .' He peered at her. 'How are you doing? Do you feel sick? Because I would like to take this opportunity to point out I've got my favourite shirt on here *and* some expensive new shoes. So if you could try to aim in the other direction . . . Oh, brilliant, that was quick – thanks, mate. Nice one.' Laura registered him standing up briefly and then he was crouching beside her again, passing her a plastic glass of iced water. 'Here. Get this down you.'

'Thank you,' she said, sipping from it gratefully. Her head was starting to clear ever so slightly, the feeling of nausea beginning to subside. She took another sip, leaned back against the brick wall and breathed slowly, in and out. 'God. Sorry. That was completely embarrassing,' she said, rubbing a hand across her face. 'What a dick.'

'Maybe you're coming down with something,' he said, eyeing her. Then he nudged her. 'Or maybe you just really, really don't like Gayle,' he teased, 'and this is all a massive act because you don't want to be dragged on to a karaoke bar to see her murdering Alanis Morissette songs later. Am I right?'

'No!' she protested, although having experienced Gayle's karaoke benders in the past, this was, in truth, not a part of the evening she'd been particularly looking forward to. 'Well,' she managed to joke, 'now that I think about it, you've got a point.'

He laughed. 'Whichever it is, I'd better order you a cab,' he said. 'Because these shoes were, like, eighty quid, and you're still looking a bit queasy. I'm not saying I don't trust you, but . . . Yeah. Cab. Doing it now.'

'Thank you,' she said meekly, shutting her eyes again. It was probably some weird virus, she told herself as the taxi roared her home. Nothing to worry about. Right?

Chapter Twenty-Three

A text message had appeared on Jo's phone from Bill Kerwin. *Hello, love, hope you're okay. Thought you might like to know that Miriam is back at home and we're all adjusting. Bill.*

A nice bit of news for a Friday afternoon, Jo thought as she stood in the entrance to Rick's apartment block, waiting for the lift to descend. *So pleased for you both*, she typed in reply. *Give Miriam my love. x*

Bill and Miriam – what an inspiration for anyone stressing about their relationship, she thought, watching the numbers change in the electronic panel as the lift approached: 9, 8, 7. Her own parents might not have been a shining example of a partnership, but the Kerwins were holding together through thick and thin, life-changing events and all. Surely she herself could see off some doubt and envy, in comparison?

When she'd gone out for drinks with them the night before, her friends had assured her, as one, that she was worrying too much about Polly and Maisie. 'Chill!' India had instructed. 'He's great, you're great – just forget everyone else!'

It was good advice, thought Jo to herself now, as the whirring of the lift became louder; 3, 2, 1, the panel counted down. Because she was going out with *Rick*, not the rest of his family, and it was high time she stopped measuring herself against them so critically. 'Doors opening,' announced the electronic voice in the next moment.

The doors *were* opening: and out came Maisie in her school uniform, all dramatic make-up and hitched-up skirt. 'Oh!' said Jo, trying not to show her dismay. 'Hello. I wasn't expecting . . . Aren't you at your mum's this weekend?'

Maisie snorted. 'In other words: fuck off, Maisie, you're not welcome here. That's nice. When it's my dad's flat.'

'I didn't say—'

'Yeah, anyway I'm going, so whatever.' And with a whip of her long hair, she was off, nose in the air, and out through the main doors of the building into the street.

Jo sighed, feeling her optimism leaking away. *Forget everyone else*, she recited to herself like a mantra, stepping into the lift and letting it sweep her away. If only it were that easy.

Jo didn't usually dare set foot in Maisie's bedroom – knowing her, the girl would have rigged up a tripwire or some security camera in order to catch trespassers on film – but today she braved a peep, curious to know why Maisie had made a detour to the flat that afternoon. The bed was a tangle of clothes, some still with price tags on, and the small white dressing table was cluttered with a vast assortment of cosmetics and toiletries. Jo raised an eyebrow as she took in the Chanel perfume, the Space NK eyeshadow palettes, the Jo Malone body cream. Blimey, this girl had expensive tastes, all right. Back in her own day, she and her friends had only been able to afford Rimmel or Superdrug own-brand stuff, with a liberal spraying of Body Shop White Musk, if you were really pushing the boat out. It was hardly surprising that Maisie looked down on her, with her Nivea moisturizer and Poundland shower gel. Not that Jo could care less, frankly.

She closed the door again, frowning to herself. Something seemed odd, she thought, although she wasn't able to put her finger on exactly what. And was it her imagination or had Maisie seemed kind of manic, bristling with a wild sort of energy as she emerged from the lift? Maybe she was just being her usual unpleasant self, though. Oh, Jo had her work cut out for her with this one, and no mistake.

'Hello?'

Her spirits lifted at once at Rick's voice. 'Hi!' she called, turning and heading for the living room, where he was just walking in with a bag of groceries.

'Hello! Come here.'

They kissed each other, and he folded her into his arms

in that lovely crushing way he had, where she felt truly enveloped.

'Good day?' he asked, nuzzling at her hair.

'All the better for seeing you again,' she replied happily. 'How about you?'

'Excellent in every way,' he replied. She loved that about him, his unremitting optimism and that ability of his to sweep you up in his enthusiasm until you felt the same way. He released her, indicating the bag he'd dumped on the worktop. 'And now I'm going to cook us both an amazing dinner. I hope that's all right with you.'

'Oh, I should think I'd be able to squeeze that into my schedule,' Jo replied, twinkling at him.

'*I'd* like to squeeze into your schedule,' he said in a husky, mock-sexy voice, with an elaborate wink. 'If you know what I mean.'

'I'm sure that can be arranged,' Jo said demurely, trying to keep a straight face.

She perched on a stool at the breakfast bar with a glass of wine, enjoying watching him chopping tomatoes, a tea-towel flipped over one shoulder as he waved away her offers of help. It was all very nice, in other words. All very cosy. *Forget everyone else.* Yes. And right now, she could. It seemed easy. Until she made the mistake of spinning round a little on her stool and saw that, across the room, a murder had been committed.

'Oh *no*,' she cried, leaping off and rushing over to the shelving unit where the broken shards of her precious blue glass bird lay glinting under the spotlights. Hurt and shock stabbed through her as she cradled the glinting fragments in her palm. *No*, she kept thinking, staring in disbelief. The little glass bird was pretty much the only thing she had left that had been given to her by her dad before he'd walked out on them, never to be seen again. She remembered as a child lying on her bed and holding the bird up in the air, making it fly, and watching the shiny blue reflections dance across the wall. And now look at it, the dainty head snapped clean off from the body and one wing shattered, its flying days over for good.

Maisie, you little bitch, she thought, tears swimming to her eyes.

'Everything all right?' asked Rick, chucking onions in the frying pan with a sizzle.

Jo held out the pieces of glass on her palm, not trusting herself to speak. She actually felt like crying for that eight-year-old girl who'd loved the little bird so much, who'd made a nest for it in her drawer out of tissue paper and glittery beads, who'd stroked its head sometimes and wondered where her dad was now, and if he ever thought about her still.

Wiping his hands on the tea-towel, Rick came over to see. 'Oh, shit! How did that happen?'

'At a wild guess, your daughter,' Jo said, the words bursting out of her. 'She was here earlier – you know how much she's got it in for me. And—'

'Maisie wouldn't do that!' he said in surprise. He actually took a step back, as if detaching himself from Jo. *You insult my daughter, you insult me.*

Jo narrowed her eyes. For real? 'Well, I didn't do it,' she replied. 'And I'm pretty sure you didn't.' Come *on*, Rick, she thought. You've got to take my side on this one. You surely can't defend your kid when she's just wantonly destroyed one of my favourite possessions?

'It must have been an accident,' he said, already turning back towards his dinner preparations. 'Like with that clay trophy that got broken. I'm sure I can glue it. No big deal.'

No big deal, Jo repeated to herself. But it *was* a big deal – it really was, to her. Did Rick genuinely not get that? Equating her mistakenly knocking that stupid trophy off the shelf with Maisie's deliberate spite was spectacularly unfair. And the bird *wouldn't* glue back together anyway, not without leaving ugly scars. All of a sudden, it felt like the last straw.

'Listen,' she said baldly, the broken pieces still in her hand. 'I'm not sure this is . . . working out. Me staying here, I mean.'

But he'd just chucked a couple of steaks into the pan and the sizzling was louder still. 'What?' he called, turning and seeing her stricken face. 'Oh, Jo. Come on. I'll fix it, don't be upset.'

'I know, but . . .' Had he even heard her? 'I *am* upset,' she said quietly. 'I know it's just a thing, but it was really special to me.' She swallowed. 'Look, this was only a temporary arrangement, wasn't it, me being here? And maybe it was too much, too soon. I'll . . . I'll start looking for some other place to rent. We both need some space.'

His mouth dropped open. 'Jo! Because your ornament got broken?'

'No, not just that . . .' She felt herself cringing at the hurt look on his face. 'You've been so generous. And I'm not ungrateful, but . . .'

'I don't understand,' he said, confused. 'I thought things were going well. Aren't they?' He put the spatula down and came over to her. 'Aren't they?'

'They are! They're going really well in terms of me and you, but I'm . . .' She didn't know how to articulate her feelings. She just wanted to go back to feeling like strong, independent Jo again, the Jo who had her own space, her own life – one that didn't include a malevolent teenager. It seemed as if she hadn't seen that version of herself for a while. 'Ignore me,' she mumbled, dropping her gaze. 'I'm not explaining myself very well.'

He put his arm round her, and she held herself awkwardly so that the broken glass wouldn't cut into her skin.

'Hey, don't worry about it,' he said. 'Let's just have dinner and a nice evening. See how you feel in the morning, yeah? We've got a whole weekend to ourselves, remember. Just the two of us.'

'Just the two of us,' she repeated, unsure what else to say. Maybe a break from Maisie would make her feel better, she thought, retreating to put the glass fragments somewhere safe. Maybe this was just a relationship wobble, now that the honeymoon period was wearing off. And Rick was a good bloke, she reminded herself. But was he good enough for her to keep putting up with his daughter's malice?

'You have reached your destination,' said the satnav the next morning.

'I certainly have,' agreed Jo, parking the car with an apprehensive glance at her surroundings. Because here she was in Ash Grove, Didsbury, the epicentre of Manchester's middle-class residents, with their gorgeous big houses and their Range Rover-filled driveways, and a genteel refined hush as the well-off went about their Saturday-morning business. With her car window down, she could hear the hum of a lawnmower, the faint scrape of cello scales floating on the breeze, and the low rumble of two Bugaboos being pushed by lithe, coiffed women across the street. Five minutes' walk away there were fancy bakeries, and nice gift shops with polka-dot curtains; there was a tapas bar, and a spa, and a moodily lit wine bar . . . What was more, Rick himself had told her that he'd once lived somewhere on this very street with Polly and Maisie; he'd been a part of this community, perhaps jogging along the tree-lined avenues on sunny weekend mornings, calling out pleasantries to the neighbours. She imagined him manhandling a huge Christmas tree through the front door in Decembers gone by, popping down to the organic butcher's for the Sunday joint, greeting the landlord by name every time he went into the local pub . . .

'We're in another world now, Toto,' Jo murmured to the satnav, which chose not to respond. A world, that was, where Polly and Maisie still lived, by the way. Christ, no wonder Maisie looked down on Jo at every opportunity, if she was used to this way of life. Thank goodness she'd never actually glimpsed just how shabby and dingy Jo's rented flat had been; she'd really have had something to be snooty about then.

Not that Jo had come here expressly to *stalk* Polly and Maisie, or anything. Tempting as it was to go peering through the windows and letterboxes along the street, hungrily seeking out evidence of How the Other Half Lived, she was a better person than that. Absolutely. Okay, so she *had* driven along the road very, very slowly, nosily drinking in the details, but that was because she was a responsible driver and this was a residential area with small children and cats and . . . oh, whatever. Yes, all right, she had been peering beadily in all directions in the hope of spotting Polly and Maisie in their natural habitat as well. Which was clearly ridiculous, because she was not about to get into some petty rivalry about who was winning at life, she reminded herself sternly, switching off the engine and clambering out of her old rust-bucket. Not least because there was no doubting who would emerge victorious.

Anyway, moving on! She had come to visit Bill and Miriam, not to get sucked into self-doubt again. It would be some breathing space from Rick's flat as well, a bit of time to herself to clear her head. They didn't have to be joined at the hip for the entire weekend, did they?

Reaching into the boot, she took out the bunch of flowers and the box of Roses she'd picked up en route, then locked the car and walked towards number forty-seven: the Kerwins' house. And what a beautiful house it was, too, with its veranda-style open stone porch, big enough to house a rustic iron swing-seat with bright scatter cushions, and a rack for wellingtons. Jo's heart clenched a little, remembering how Miriam had spoken of her love of horses, and wondered if she'd sat here to take off her boots after a visit to the stable yard, before the accident had robbed her of all that. Life could be so unkind, couldn't it? So brutal. Your whole future could turn like the spinning of a penny. *Heads, you lose.*

Jo had just pressed the old-fashioned doorbell – you

could actually hear a real bell jingling inside – when she became aware of raised voices from behind her, disturbing the otherwise tranquil stillness of the street. 'But you said I could go, Mum. You *said*!'

The second voice was less shrill, but the sound carried on the air nonetheless. 'I said no such thing, and we both know it. And that's the end of it.'

'But everyone else will be going! I'll literally be the only person in my class who isn't there. That is so *unfair*!'

Ears on stalks, Jo's adrenalin pumped hard as she realized she knew that voice, had heard its whining, argumentative tone oh-so-many times before. It was Maisie, she was sure of it, which meant, presumably, that the other voice, older and crosser-sounding, was Polly's. Oh my God. Talk about timing. They must be walking up the road right there behind her. Dare she turn round and risk being seen? She desperately wanted to get a look at her rival, that bloody nemesis of hers who'd lurked at the shadowy edges of her relationship this whole time. But what if she was spotted?

'For heaven's sake, I've said *no*. I don't care if you're the only person not going. It's too much, Maisie. The answer is no.'

The voices sounded nearer still and Jo froze, wondering if it was in her to drop noiselessly to the ground and carry out a stunt roll so that she was behind the stone ledge, avoiding detection. Styling it out like James Bond. Let's face it: no. Knowing her luck, she'd put her back out, or crush the massive bunch of flowers she was clutching. Ah, *flowers*, she thought in the next second. Maybe that was the solution. Lifting up the bouquet so as to disguise her face, she turned very slowly and peeped furtively out at the street through the blooms.

'Oh *Mum*! I can't believe you're *doing* this to me! I'm going to ask Dad. He'll let me go.'

Whoa. It really was them, in the flesh, and on the other side of the road just level with her now. Ducking into a crouch, Jo shielded her face with the flowers – please don't look this way, please don't see me – then scuttled to the side of the veranda, where she was able to peer over, with the subjects in her sights. Maisie was in a white vest top and black denim skirt with a big star-shaped necklace and sparkly flip-flops, her hair loose and wild about her shoulders, her hands flying up expressively as she railed at her mother. Meanwhile Polly was . . . Jo bit her lip. To be honest, Polly was quite a lot less chic in real life than she'd been expecting, in white chinos and a striped Breton top, her blonde hair up in a ponytail and big sunglasses on her nose. Actually quite . . . ordinary-looking. Frazzled, even. Trying to put an arm around her daughter, only for Maisie to fling it off, shout, 'I hate you!' and run headlong down the street. Gosh. This was a far cry from the smugly perfect relationship Jo had been envisaging, it had to be said.

'Hello? Can I help you?'

Shit! In all the drama, she'd completely forgotten that she'd ever rung the doorbell of the Kerwins' house – and there was Bill Kerwin now, standing in his doorway, wearing a mustard cardigan and corduroy trousers and catching Jo right out, crouched as she was on his veranda, spying blatantly on passers-by. This was not a good look, by anyone's measure.

Straightening up awkwardly, Jo brushed down her denim skirt, feeling like the most horrible, nosy person in the world. Real Didsburians probably never behaved this way; she bet they were all far too well mannered and respectable. 'Hello,' she said, blushing wildly. 'Bill? I'm Jo. We've spoken on the phone.' She held out the flowers and chocolates. 'I was just passing and thought I'd bring these for you and Miriam.'

His chin wobbled momentarily and his eyes went misty. 'That's very kind,' he said. 'Can you stay for a brew? Miriam's in the garden, she'd be very pleased to see you.'

'Thanks,' said Jo. 'That would be lovely.'

Jo hadn't expected to feel particularly emotional about coming here, but as she followed Bill through the (beautiful, elegant) house and out into the (gorgeous, flower-filled) garden, she could feel a lump swelling in her throat as she saw the wheelchair parked up beneath a cherry tree, with

Miriam sitting there, a pale-blue blanket draped across her legs. All of a sudden she found herself flashing back to the scene of the crash, kneeling amidst the broken glass on the pavement and holding Miriam's hand; trying to comfort her amidst the chaos and distress, the wail of sirens. Remembering how brave the older woman had been at the time, how incredibly stoic in the face of disaster. Remembering too just how upset, how shaken she'd felt herself in the aftermath. How she'd leaned against Rick, and still hadn't quite pulled herself upright again.

'Look who was knocking at our door, lovey!' said Bill in an artificially bright voice, but then he stopped dead almost immediately and put a finger to his lips. 'Ah. She's dozed off. Do you mind if we . . . ?' He wheeled about, indicating the door they'd just come through. 'Let's leave her be,' he said, heading inside again. 'She's still on all these painkillers and she had a bad night last night.' His lips twisted together apologetically. 'It's hard for her.'

'Of course, absolutely,' Jo replied, feeling wretched for both the Kerwins. Her eye was caught by the sight of the blanket as she turned away and she felt a pang, knowing that it covered what was left of Miriam's legs after the operations she'd endured. Poor Miriam. And poor Bill.

The kitchen was wide and airy, streaming with light from two huge skylights in the sloping ceiling, and there was a black cat snoozing in a sunny spot on the windowsill, its ears pricking up as they came in. Bill poured two glasses of elderflower cordial then set about putting the flowers in a vase of water, rather clumsily, as if this was women's work in his opinion, to which he was not accustomed. Jo's heart went out to him. 'How are you bearing up then?' she asked gently, just as he said, 'So you know them, do you, the Silvers?'

It took her a second to process his question and then her blush returned, deeper and hotter, as she realized he was asking about that cringe-worthy moment on his veranda, where he'd caught her spying on Polly and Maisie. 'Um . . . Well, sort of,' she said, hedging around the truth.

'Mmm,' he said, his tone non-committal. 'Friends of yours, are they?'

'Well . . . No,' she confessed, not sure how to explain without sounding like some paranoid stalker-ish weirdo. 'Er . . .'

But to her surprise, he looked her in the eye and nodded. 'Don't worry,' he said. 'I guess it's the same for nurses as doctors, isn't it, that patient-confidentiality thing. You're not allowed to tell me, officially. But it's okay, we know about the drinking.'

Jo blinked. Wait – he thought Polly was one of her patients? And did he just say . . . ? 'The drinking,' she echoed, her mind racing.

'It's not exactly a secret, is it? Not down this road,

anyway. I think everyone here has seen and heard— Anyway.' He stopped himself. 'I don't like to gossip, you know. Only I do worry about that kid. It can't be easy for her.'

Things were starting to piece together in Jo's head, a picture appearing on a jigsaw – a very different sort of picture from the one she'd imagined all this time. 'No,' she replied slowly, remembering how Maisie had turned up that first time at the restaurant because she'd been locked out of the house. Where had Polly been then – and how had it happened? she wondered now. It hadn't occurred to her at the time to think in depth about the situation, because she'd been so unnerved by the girl's unfriendliness. And then there was the fact that Rick was so protective of his daughter, so patient; the way he'd drop everything if Maisie asked him to. Jo had pegged her as some spoiled brat, but perhaps there was more to the situation than that. 'It can't be easy,' she added.

'No.' He had finished stuffing the flowers haphazardly into a vase – he was never going to be a contender for the nearest village show – and eyed them with a dubious air. 'No,' he repeated, wiping his hands on his trousers. 'After the police came out that time, I thought: eh up, social services will be next; but . . .' He shrugged. 'I guess they don't have the same resources these days, do they? You'll know all about that.'

'That's right,' Jo replied. The *police*, she was thinking,

trying to hide her alarm. What had been going on? And how much of this did Rick know about? He had always been so reticent about his ex-wife, so reluctant to divulge anything. 'Let's hope things pick up for her soon,' she added lamely, not sure what else to say. 'But how about you, anyway, Bill? How are you managing? I know it must be hard.'

His hands trembled on the vase. 'It is,' he agreed, not meeting her eye. 'It's really hard.' He sat down at the table across from her and stared into his drink. 'I thought, you know, when she came home from hospital, it would be better, but . . .' He shook his head slowly. 'It's not the same as it was. It's never going to be the same as it was. And that . . .' He broke off momentarily, battling with his emotions. 'That's pretty tough to get your head round. For her, too.'

'I'm sure it is,' Jo said gently. The car crash had lasted seconds but the repercussions rippled on and on, affecting so many people's futures. 'I can't imagine how difficult it must be.'

He wiped his eye with his knuckles. 'In sickness and in health, I said on our wedding day. In sickness and in health. And I meant it! I still mean it. I just never imagined that . . .' He shrugged, his hands falling palm up on the table. 'I never thought . . .'

'Of course you didn't,' Jo said. 'Nobody imagines that. You've been desperately unlucky. Terribly unlucky, the pair of you. I'm so sorry.' She sighed because every instinct in her wanted to find a silver lining, to make this whole situation better for him, but sometimes there really was no silver lining to be found. Sometimes you just needed to be there and listen, offer companionship and solidarity rather than solutions. 'Are you getting enough help?' she asked after a moment. 'Do you have family nearby who can take care of practical things – shopping and that – for the time being? The nurses are still coming round, I take it?'

He blew his nose in a crumpled white handkerchief and nodded. 'Oh aye, yeah, we've got the palliative nurses here every day,' he replied. 'And the neighbours have been smashing. Couldn't ask for better neighbours. They've brought round food, picked up shopping, helped me with laundry. One lady, Maureen, has even sorted out a cleaner for us, and she's been brilliant. I mean, I didn't even know how to work the Hoover.' He shrugged, his face rueful. 'Our son's down in London, he's a vet so it's hard for him to take time off, but he's been up when he can.' He blew his nose again. 'Everyone's been very kind. It's just . . .'

Jo reached over and took his hand. 'I know.'

'She's not going to get better, is she? She's never going to be my Miriam again.' His chest heaved as he battled with his distress; it was enough to break your heart.

'I know,' Jo said again, a huge lump in her throat. 'And there's just no quick fix for that, is there? Which must be . . .' she thought about saying 'challenging' but decided it sounded too patronizing, '. . . bloody awful,' she finished instead.

'It is. It really is. Because I've always been able to fix other things, you see. I was an engineer for forty years before I retired: good around the house. Never a squeaking door or a loose floorboard in this place, I can tell you. But now, when my wife needs help, I can't do anything, I can't mend her. Nobody can.' He shook his head, tears in his eyes. 'Anyway.' He swallowed hard, trying to smile. 'I love her, and I'm doing my best. And that's all any of us can do, right?'

Jo had tears in her own eyes now. She gripped his hand with both of hers. 'That's right. And you're doing a great job here, Bill. A really great job. She's lucky to have you.'

Chapter Twenty-Four

India was wearing her magic knickers and could hardly breathe as she sat down in the corner of the pub with a vodka tonic. 'Better make that a double,' she'd advised the barmaid. She was going to need all the help she could get tonight, let's face it.

'Meeting an old school friend in town,' she'd told Dan breezily, amidst the usual post-dinner chaos of herding soap-dodging children into the bathroom, listening to George explaining to her in great detail how a combustion engine worked, running the nit-comb through Esme's hair, trying to get to the bottom of why Kit had come home with somebody else's lunchbox, and disinfecting all her mini maracas following a puking incident at the final music session of the afternoon.

He'd barely glanced up from the *Star Wars* comic he was nobly looking at with Kit. Perhaps for the thousandth time. 'All right,' he'd said, as Kit gave him an indignant nudge and scolded, 'Dad, are you listening? I said, look, there's Darth Maul. See him spying on them there?'

'Oh yes, you're right, well spotted,' Dan had said, winking at India in a conspiratorial way.

She'd thought of that wink as she scrubbed at the maracas, rinsing them in water so hot her hands were bright red by the end. The wink that said, 'We're a team, me and you' and 'We love our boy, don't we?', not to mention 'Yeah, and we both know it's your turn to read this bloody comic with him next time, okay?' She and Dan might have their ups and downs, like any couple, but they *were* a good team, at the end of the day. So why had she never been able to tell him the truth about what had happened, with Robin and Alice? Why couldn't she be straight with him now about this 'old school friend' of hers? *Oh yeah, by the way, did I mention, he was my first love? The first love to end all first loves, and the one I've never really managed to achieve full closure on?*

To make her feel worse, Dan's mum had phoned just before India had left, enquiring solicitously, 'And how is his poor wee ear, now?', which made India feel like the worst wife ever, because she hadn't really thought to give a shit about her husband's poor wee ear. 'Um, fine, I think,' she'd mumbled. 'I'll just get him for you and he can tell you all about it.'

Sipping her vodka – super-pokey – she glanced up at the door as it opened, but it was only some twenty-something couple holding hands, her towing him to the bar and then beaming up adorably at him. Sweet. She bet they didn't have any dark secrets silted away out of sight.

Does your husband know about me? Robin had written in a second Facebook message, when she hadn't replied immediately to his first one asking her out for a drink. The question had left a bad taste in India's mouth. Was that supposed to be a threat? she wondered, staring worriedly at the screen. Was he holding their shared mistakes above her head, like a bomb that he could detonate whenever he felt so inclined? A shudder had run through her, followed swiftly by a twist of annoyance at his own self-aggrandisement. Get over yourself, love, she felt like replying. It was a long time ago. Don't you dare try and bully me now, when you didn't exactly cover yourself in glory, either.

Obviously she had voiced no such thing, though, merely typed a stilted reply saying that a drink would be very nice – how about at the Old Nag's Head?

And now here she was, in a really uncomfortable new dress that she'd spent far too much money on because she wanted to look fabulous tonight – not for his sake, but for hers, to remind her that she was doing fine without him, thanks for asking. The outfit had looked pretty good in the changing-room mirror, especially when she sucked in her stomach, but when she'd put it on tonight she couldn't help thinking: *Mutton*. The neckline was too low, the fit was horribly tight around the bum and she was no longer convinced that the colour – jade green – suited her. In fact, if anything it made her look peaky rather than dazzling.

She tugged at the skirt, feeling certain there was a metaphor somewhere in this: about trying on a new life and discovering that it didn't really fit or suit her after all. Oh, bloody hell, *shush*, India. It was just a *drink*. She'd be home again in a few hours and she could put tonight – and Robin – behind her once more.

'You're looking very stern there, if I may say so.'

She jumped because he'd suddenly materialized in front of her, looking amused and catching her quite unawares. Standing up, slightly uncomfortably in her flab-squeezing magic knickers, she did her best to hide her flustered panic and plastered on a bright smile instead. 'Hi! Good to see you.' Were they going to hug? Kiss each other on the cheek? Shake hands? Ah, an awkward hug: okay then. She hoped she hadn't left a sweaty hand print on the back of his leather jacket. Meanwhile, he smelled of cheap aftershave and whisky, and she felt her spirits sinking. How many drinks had he necked already?

'You all right?' he asked as they parted, and he put a pint on the table. He flashed her one of his wolfish grins. 'Not having second thoughts about meeting me, were you?'

'No!' she lied. 'Of course not. Always nice to catch up

with an old friend.' *You're not that special*, being the subtext. *I do this regularly, for all you know*.

'An old friend,' he repeated, catching her eye as he sat down, and she blushed as he surely knew she would. 'Well, here's to friendship.' He raised his glass and she clinked it against his. 'And catching up on . . . what, twenty-one years?'

'Twenty-one years,' she agreed. 'Time flies.' There was a short, polite pause then she ploughed on, determined to steer the conversation in his direction, seeing as he'd eluded her personal questions last time. 'Tell me about you. Are you married? Kids?'

'Was married. Didn't last. Two kids, although I don't see them these days.' He eyed her over the top of his pint. 'Three kids, I guess, if you include . . .' He indicated her, his face giving nothing away.

She met his gaze full on. Oh no you don't, she thought. Don't start. 'How about work? Had a good week?' she asked, trying to keep her voice level, although she could feel a slow simmer of anger taking hold. If he had come here looking for a fight, then he had picked the wrong woman.

He gave a snort. 'I could ask you the same thing. Baby music classes? What's that all about? Bit below you, isn't it?'

'Why do you say that?' she countered.

'You know why I'm saying it – because you were the big music star back then. All your performances and practice sessions and that. Those distinctions you got on your grades. Your dreams! That amazing music college you were so keen to go to. I thought you were going to be the next Nigel Kennedy. Nigella Kennedy – whatever.'

She sighed and the anger went out of her because he was right, and she still felt sad to think of that defeated teenage India, who'd once made such big, optimistic plans. 'Yeah, I know. I thought I was. too. Only . . .' She couldn't quite meet his eyes. 'Life gets in the way, right?' She swirled her drink around, the ice knocking against the side of the glass, remembering how she had given her violin to the charity shop at the end of that summer and had never lifted a bow since.

'But you still play, don't you? As well as your "baby classes"?' he persisted. You could practically hear his inverted commas.

She shook her head. 'Nope.' Sometimes she would hear a piece of music and imagine her own fingers on the strings; she would find herself disagreeing with the musician's interpretation, or she would appreciate the technique, the dynamics, the emotions conjured from the notes. Sometimes she even dreamed she was performing in a concert with an audience of hundreds, and she'd wake up in a sweat, panicking that she couldn't remember how to play.

'How about you?' she said, unable to bear the look of surprise on his face. 'Youth work, was it, you said you did?'

'Yeah.' He shrugged. 'Never made it as a professional

footballer. Never made it as anything, really. We're a right pair, aren't we?'

Speak for yourself, mate, she thought, her smile tightening, then she tugged at the neck of her dress where it had slipped down another centimetre. 'Ah, well, everyone has their teenage dreams,' she said. 'It's practically the law.' Time for another change of subject. 'Um . . . So are you still in touch with anyone from school?'

'Course I'm not,' he scoffed. 'Best thing I ever did, getting away from that place.'

Was that a veiled attack on her? Probably. She sighed. This was hard work, virtually impossible to get a conversation going, let alone draw anything out of him. 'How about your parents?' she tried. 'Are they okay?'

He shook his head, looking impatient. 'I don't give a shit about my parents and I'm pretty sure you don't, either,' he replied. 'Fuck's sake, Ind, I thought we were here to talk about us, not school or work or fucking parents.'

'What do you mean, "us"?' she asked warily.

'You know what I mean! Us – me and you: what happened.' His eyes narrowed and he knocked back the rest of his pint. 'How you killed our baby,' he went on and she gasped, winded by his cruelty. 'Bet he doesn't know that, eh, does he? That husband of yours. Dan, isn't it? Dan the plumber. Bet you never told him that little story, did you?'

So this was why he'd come: revenge. This was what he

wanted, to rail at her and punish her, to put her in her place. He must have been hanging on to his rage for all these years, letting it seethe away inside him, a foaming stew of bitterness.

'It wasn't like— Do you know what, I don't have to sit here and listen to this,' she said, half-rising in her seat. Fuck off, Robin, she thought. Just get stuffed. An image flashed into her head of Dan winking at her as she left, Dan with his arm around Kit, reading that God-awful *Star Wars* comic, and she felt like crying at her own lack of judgement in coming out at all.

'Yes, you do,' he replied, putting a hand on her arm to stop her. 'Because I know you've been thinking about it, too. About what would have happened if you'd had the guts to run away with me that night. About how—'

'Oh God, Robin, will you listen to yourself? We were *kids*,' she said, shaking his hand off her, still standing. 'We were barely eighteen, we didn't have a clue. We wouldn't have lasted five minutes out in the real world.' She glared at him, feeling nothing but contempt. 'You don't know what you're talking about.'

'Yeah, I do, because I *did* manage out there. I managed fine for years, while you took the coward's way out and did exactly what Mummy and D—'

She bristled all over. How *dare* he? 'I didn't take the coward's way out,' she hissed through gritted teeth, wishing she'd never come here, wishing she'd never bumped into him in the first place. Some things were best left sealed up and undisturbed. What good was it now, raking over all of this?

'. . . Daddy wanted you to do. What do you mean?' He leaned closer, his eyes fixed on hers. 'What are you saying?'

She sat down heavily. Sod it, she was going to have to tell him now. Just what she didn't want. 'I know you think I went along for an abortion there and then,' she said, every word feeling like an effort, 'but I didn't.'

There. That had shut him up. His whole body tautened in surprise, his head turned. 'You . . . didn't?'

'No. I didn't, Robin. So maybe, just maybe, it's time to rethink your assumptions about me and what actually happened.' Her voice rose with dislike, and the anger for him that she'd held in check for so long bubbled up inside. 'And maybe – here's a suggestion for you – if you'd bothered to stick around and help me, instead of flouncing off on your own, you could have found this out back then, too.'

She had completely taken the wind out of his sails with that little speech. For the first time since they'd been back in touch, he seemed unsure of himself, as if the world had just slipped a few degrees on its axis. *You don't know me*, she thought, watching the emotions flash across his face.

'I . . . Right,' he said after a moment's recalibration. 'So . . . you had the baby? What do you mean?'

She shut her eyes briefly, trying to find the strength she needed to tell him the story after so long. She owed him that much, she guessed.

'I changed my mind,' she began baldly. 'My parents were pushing me to have an abortion and, yes, I went along for the appointment, but I couldn't go through with it. I left messages for you with your parents, but they didn't know where you were or how to get hold of you. So I decided to go it alone. To do it all by myself.'

'Oh God.' Give him credit, he looked quite stricken. And damn right, too, she thought, remembering how frightened she had been, how conflicted. 'I'm sorry,' he stammered, the brittle facade no longer there. 'Shit. I just assumed . . .'

She let the silence hang for a moment, accusing and condemning. Yeah. You assumed. I had noticed. 'It was a pretty grim summer,' she went on, fiddling with her vodka glass, turning it in circles to give her hands something to do. 'I screwed up my A-levels. Didn't get into "that amazing music college" after all, funnily enough.'

Her pointed glance was sufficient to make Robin turn his eyes down to the table, his earlier jibe about her baby music classes resurfacing between them. Tosser.

'I had a scan when the baby was twenty weeks old and found out . . .' She swallowed. It was harder to say than she'd thought. 'Found out I was expecting a girl.' She couldn't bring herself to look at him. 'But I also found out that . . . the baby didn't look quite . . . right.'

It was never going to leave her, ever, that moment when she'd glanced across at the sonographer and seen the alarm on his face; how he'd hurried out of the room to find a doctor to confirm his suspicions. She'd lain there, cold gel slathered all over her belly, feeling numb with fear, an awful dread rising in her that perhaps she'd done something terrible to the baby when she'd chucked herself off the top step back at home, landing with a carpet-burning thump at the bottom.

Robin rubbed a hand over his face, looking agitated. 'What was wrong? Christ, I had no idea. What was wrong with the baby?'

'She wasn't developing properly.' A tear rolled down India's cheek, probably taking half of her carefully applied mascara with it, but she didn't care. She could still picture the screen on which the consultant had talked her through the image, gently pointing out the bell-shaped chest, the bowed and deformed legs, the disproportionately large head. The images haunted her at night sometimes, as they had haunted her through every one of her subsequent pregnancies. 'The doctors told me that her lungs would be too tiny to cope outside the womb, that I'd give birth to her and she would almost certainly die anyway.'

(*Was it my fault?* she had heard herself whispering, agonized, to the consultant.

No, absolutely not, he had replied firmly, looking her in the eye. It was perhaps the kindest thing anyone had ever said to her.)

Robin's face had twisted unhappily. 'Oh no.' He put his hand on hers again, but this time it was compassionate rather than preventative. 'Oh, India.'

'I didn't know what else to do.' Her voice had become a squeak, and she put her hands up to her face because she was terrified she was about to burst into sobs. 'I was a *teenager.*' She swallowed, trying to get a grip, because there was still the last and worst part of the story yet to come. 'The doctors said a termination might be for the best, and I . . .' She couldn't look at him. 'I was scared and alone, and so I . . . so I said yes. Yes to the termination.' And then some last vestige of defensiveness kicked in and she was rounding on him, daring him to take her to task for it. 'But if you want to go there – if you want to accuse me of "killing our baby", then you need to take a damn good look at yourself.' She jabbed her finger, rage rising again. 'And you need to ask yourself: where were you when I was having to go through this, the worst time of my life, the hardest decision I've ever had to make. Where were you? Bloody nowhere. Running away like a fucking *kid*. So don't you dare – don't you *dare* try and . . .' She banged a fist on the table, tears running openly down her face, her voice shaking. 'Don't even go there.'

He was silent for a moment, his expression anguished. His whole demeanour had changed. Now he was looking at her without his guard up, without that filter of resentment, and it was as if they could see each other's real selves for the first time. 'I'm sorry,' he said eventually. Sincerely, honestly. 'If I'd had any idea—'

She cut him off, not wanting to hear excuses. 'I still had to give birth to her, you know. Did I mention that bit? Yeah. It wasn't the easy option, by any means. Or – what was it you said? – the coward's way out. If only.'

'India, I am so truly—'

'I had to go through all that pain, knowing she was going to die anyway. Knowing that she couldn't survive more than a few breaths. Does that make me a bad person? Does that make me someone to judge and sneer at? Go ahead, if you want, but you couldn't make me feel any worse about it, believe me.' Her breath was coming in short ragged bursts, and she clenched and unclenched her fists, trying to regain some equilibrium. 'I called her Alice, if you were wondering. Alice May Burrell. We had a funeral for her and everything. And not a single day goes by without me thinking about her. Not a single bloody day, Robin. Thinking how old she would be now, what she might be doing, if she'd lived, if she'd been well.'

He was staring at her, as if a penny had just dropped. 'She'd have been twenty, just like . . .'

'Yeah. Got it. Just like Alice Goldsmith. Don't you love a coincidence?' She gave a mirthless laugh, wondering how on earth they'd got to this situation, where she was baring her soul to him, of all people, decades too late, in a crappy old boozer in town. But he'd pushed her to this. He'd backed her right into a corner. And if he didn't like what she was saying, then frankly he only had himself to blame.

'And that was why you were at the funeral . . .'

'That was why I was at the funeral.' The rage had gone out of her again, dropping away like a tide. 'Yeah. Because it brought everything back. Because I've not been able to think about anything else recently.' India clenched her fists under the table, deciding that she wouldn't bother telling him how desperate she'd been for this other Alice to make it, for her to be all right. How obsessive she'd been about the situation, how it had seemed – stupidly – that this young woman could offer some form of redemption for her. Or not, after all, as it had turned out. 'Anyway. There we are. All caught up. Feel free to sneer. I know you want to.'

'I don't. I'm not going to. I wouldn't *sneer* when you've just told me that.' He was silent for a few moments, staring down at the table. 'I did feel angry,' he confessed in a low voice eventually. 'When you didn't show up that night. I thought you didn't love me any more. That you didn't care.'

She shook her head slowly, remembering that he, too, had been so young. Eighteen and anguished, trying to do the right thing, driven by that wild passion of his. Of course he would have taken it as a personal rejection. 'I did care,' she told him, replaying how scared she'd been that night, how she hadn't slept at all, wondering if she was making a terrible mistake by not meeting him, not taking the chance. 'But I was freaking out, too. And trying to work out how I felt about being pregnant and what the hell I was going to do.' She finished her drink, feeling wrung out. Spent. 'But it wasn't that I had stopped loving you. Not at all.'

There was a moment's silence, then he tilted his head towards her empty glass. 'Can I buy you another?'

'No, thanks. I don't know if there's anything left to say.' She waited for him to make some barbed comment about her running off to her husband, but he didn't, mercifully. 'Well,' she went on, getting to her feet. 'I wish I could say it's been lovely, but . . .'

'India, wait. Don't go like this. Can't we just – remember the good stuff, first? With affection?' Robin's face was the most earnest she'd seen it. Was that a note of pleading in his voice even? 'Once upon a time, we meant everything to one another. This is probably the last time our paths will cross.

Can we at least try to end on a good note, so that it wasn't all . . . in vain?'

'Well,' she said again, then hesitated. Her overriding instinct was to go home, to throw her arms around her husband and count her blessings, but then again, maybe he had a point. 'Is that even possible?'

'Yes! Because we had good times, as well, didn't we? We had so many laughs. All those awful love-songs we wrote together . . .'

A long-distant memory surfaced in her head: the pair of them sitting on his bedroom floor, leaning against each other and hooting with mirth as they came up with filthy lyrics and put them to music. Despite herself, she felt a tiny smile twist her lips. 'I'd forgotten those,' she admitted.

'And the parties – Jesus! Remember the one at Craig's house where we accidentally set fire to his dad's shed?'

'*You* set fire to it, you mean – it wasn't me, mucking around with lighter fuel—'

'And that college trip to Scarborough, remember?' His face had become animated, his hands gesticulating. 'Those stupid dares we did: everyone drinking Thunderbird and going skinny-dipping. You getting in trouble with that policeman . . .'

'I so didn't!' she spluttered. 'What about you, getting us chucked out of that café when you decided to start an argument with those evangelicals?'

The mood had shifted somehow, and then, as memory after memory rose unbidden, the tone of their conversation became friendlier, softer, and it was as if the years seemed to roll back, magically, to a time when everything had been okay; when they had been young and in love and had whole worlds of opportunities stretching out before them. Was this what forgiveness felt like? she wondered. Was this finally closure? Whatever you called it, she was glad of this evening, all of a sudden. Glad that she had told her story at last, unpacked it before him and looked him, unblinking, in the eye. What was more, Robin understood and he was sorry, and now they had come out through the other side, just about in one piece.

'You were such a beautiful golden shining girl,' he said suddenly, eyes misty.

'Stop that,' she said, embarrassed. 'All teenagers are.'

'No, but you were different. You were special. And talented.' He took her hands. 'I'm sorry about . . . everything. I should have come back earlier, made sure you were okay. We could have made the decisions together, if I hadn't been so . . . so stupidly proud.' He fiddled with a set of keys, jingling them between his fingers. 'I thought you'd be wafting about at your fancy music college, though, falling in love with another musician and – I dunno – joining an orchestra and travelling all round the world.' He hung his head. 'I'm sorry if I . . . ruined that for you.'

'Oh, Robin,' she said, with a sigh. 'It's all water under the bridge. It doesn't matter now. I'm fine.'

'Are you? Really?'

'Yes,' she said firmly, looking him in the eye. 'Yes, I am.'

Chapter Twenty-Five

If Laura *was* coming down with something, as Jim had suggested after the washout that had been Gayle's birthday drinks, it was a very strange something that resisted all her attempts at self-diagnosis. A horrible dragging lethargy settled on her the whole weekend, as if she were battling a low-level virus, leaving her feeling washed out and weak.

'Heartbreak,' her mum diagnosed briskly when they spoke on the phone. 'That bloody Matt, I could kill him with my bare hands, I really could. Bloody men, honestly, they're all as bad. I'm waiting any day for Jo to tell me that her new fella has turned out to be some murderer or a paedophile or—'

'He's not a paedophile,' Laura groaned wearily. 'And I'm pretty sure he's not a murderer, either.'

'You keep telling yourself that,' Helen said, with a meaningful sniff. 'But they're all the same really. Bastards.' She made a huffing sound. 'And I still haven't met him yet, by the way. It's like your sister's ashamed of me or something.'

'I can't imagine why,' Laura replied. *Heartbreak, indeed*, she thought later, blinking awake after she'd dozed off on the sofa in front of some cheesy game-show. Her mum was so quick to blame men for everything that went wrong in the world. Car broken down? Bloody men. Council tax going up? Bloody men. Pouring with rain? Somehow this would be the fault of a brainless, useless man too, no doubt about it.

Deciding to ignore her mother's diagnosis, Laura turned to Dr Google instead, but scared herself so much by researching 'ME symptoms', and then 'brain tumour', that she ended up phoning her local surgery first thing on Monday morning to book an appointment. That would make Matt sorry, wouldn't it, if she was dying, when he'd been so cold with her on the phone, she found herself thinking. Imagine the guilt he'd feel then, for the rest of his life. And serve him right!

By a stroke of luck, the receptionist had just had a cancellation that very evening for a locum doctor, and so Laura was able to go there straight from work. Dr Munroe, the locum, turned out to be an avuncular sort of man with a craggy, serious face, who listened closely as she poured out every random symptom she could think of – the fainting and dizziness, the exhaustion, the general feeling of being unwell. Afterwards Laura found that she was holding her breath, dreading him giving a grim nod and booking her in for blood tests and a brain scan at the hospital. Instead he asked, 'Is there a chance that you might be pregnant?'

Ha. She almost laughed in his face. If she'd been seeing her usual doctor, Dr Daniels, who was Welsh and motherly, who knew all about the miscarriages and had the kindest, most sympathetic face, then such a stupid, cruel question would never have been asked, let alone with this mild banality. She pressed her lips together, trying to compose herself. 'No,' she replied flatly.

'And you're sure about that?'

Laura clenched her fists at the side of the chair. Was he deliberately trying to torture her, to rub her nose in her sad, single, childless situation? 'I'm sure,' she said through gritted teeth. 'I had a period last month as usual, so . . . So, no.' Let's move on.

He nodded. 'It is not impossible to have what looks like a period during the early months of pregnancy,' he replied. 'Are you currently using any form of contraception?'

Only my husband leaving me, she almost quipped, but managed to shake her head without any sarcastic remarks. This was ridiculous, though; a definite case of barking up the wrong tree. She knew she wasn't pregnant because . . . well, she didn't *feel* pregnant, for starters. And as an expert on the subject, who had thought about it fairly obsessively in recent months, it wasn't as if she wouldn't have noticed. *I think I know my own body*, she felt like telling him.

'Okay, well, let's just find out for definite – if only so that we can rule it out before going any further.' He went to a cupboard and produced a see-through plastic pot. 'If you wouldn't mind providing me with a urine sample, please? The Ladies is out in the corridor.'

She stared at the plastic pot in disbelief, then took it from his hand, her cheeks burning with a sudden rush of humiliation. For goodness' sake! Was he some kind of sadist? There was no *way* Dr Daniels would have been so insensitive as to put her through this, after everything that had happened, especially when Laura had just sat there and said point-blank that she wasn't pregnant.

'Is there a problem?' asked Dr Munroe, and she felt like throwing the pot in his stupid, craggy old face.

'No,' she mumbled, rising to her feet. What the hell, she thought in resignation, heading for the Ladies. She would get this over with, prove him wrong and then let him proceed with the job of telling her that actually she had a brain tumour – sorry about that.

Returning to the doctor's office a few minutes later, bearing a warm pot of her own pee, she was so certain of what the test would show that she didn't even bother getting her hopes up. Not so much as a flicker. She didn't even watch as he dipped the stick in to see the result. And there she'd been, worried that she might be wasting his time, she thought scathingly, when in fact he was the one who was wasting—

'Ah,' he said, nodding. 'So according to this, you are very much pregnant, as it happens. Which would explain the dizziness and tiredness and – well, all of your other symptoms, too, basically.'

Laura stared at him for a full five seconds, then shook her head. 'No,' she said firmly. 'I . . . There must be a mistake. I'm definitely not pregnant. I mean . . .' Her head moved again, side to side, no, no, no. 'I know I'm not.'

'These tests are highly accurate,' he told her in a gentler voice, as if he was dealing with a simpleton. 'And even though you might not feel pregnant, I can assure you that you are.'

It was as if the world had shrunk down to a very small space, just her and this man in his tweedy jacket, looking steadily and seriously back at her. 'If this is a joke . . .' she gasped, unable to comprehend.

'It's not a joke.' He steepled his fingers together and leaned forward a little. 'Am I to take it that this is . . . unwelcome news?'

She still couldn't take it in. There had to be a mistake. When had she conceived? Because she'd been having *periods*! Plus she'd been eating all the wrong things – chips and ice cream, and round after round of buttery toast. No folic acid. No supplements. And . . . Oh my God. She'd been drinking so much *wine*. Far too much wine! 'I'm . . .' She could hardly speak because her head was seething and swarming with questions. 'I'm just a bit shocked.' She blinked, but this wasn't even a strange too-much-cheese dream, it was actually happening. It was real. 'Are you *sure*?'

'I'm sure. We could do another test if you really wanted to, but after everything you told me, all the symptoms you described, it does seem pretty cut and dried.'

Laura put a hand up to her mouth, remembering with horror just how many bottles had gone clanking into her recycling box lately. 'I haven't been looking after myself, though,' she said anxiously. 'I would have stopped drinking if I'd known – and my husband has left me, so I've been . . .' The guilt was terrible. You heard such hideous things about Foetal Alcohol Syndrome. 'I didn't know,' she whispered, a tear rolling down her cheek. 'I mean, I'm not saying I'm an alcoholic, I don't have a *problem*, but I . . . I have been drinking more than usual. And eating Brie. *And* I had prawns last week and . . .'

'Okay, well, we are where we are, try not to—'

Her voice was rising. 'When I was pregnant before, I did everything right,' she gulped. She felt a desperate urgency to convince him of this, that she wasn't just some feckless headcase who didn't care about her own babies. 'I took folic acid, I ate really healthily, I didn't take any risks . . .' She dashed the tears away. Shock was still thumping through her. She was *pregnant*, she thought dazedly. When it had seemed impossible. When she'd been considering a sperm donor and going it alone. And now . . . A thought struck her belatedly. Oh Lord – *Matt*. This was how they would get back together! He would be so thrilled when she told him. And they would live happily ever after and . . .

She was dimly aware of the doctor speaking again. '. . . book you in for an antenatal appointment with our team of midwives, and perhaps a dating scan, so that you can find out how far along you might be . . .'

'Yes,' she managed to say. Midwives. A scan. The antenatal clinic. These were words she hadn't been expecting to hear so soon, perhaps not ever again. It was as if she'd been bestowed with the most precious and unexpected of gifts. One last chance. 'Wow. I mean – thank you.'

'And in the meantime, you could try eating more iron-rich foods or taking a supplement to combat the dizzy feelings . . .'

She couldn't quite comprehend the enormity of this conversation, hardly able to hear the advice the doctor was giving her. *I'm pregnant. This is happening. There is a tiny baby growing inside me right now.* She put her hands on her stomach in wonderment. *Hello, in there. I'm your mummy. I'm sorry about all the wine. That will be coming to a stop right now, don't you worry.* 'Thank you,' she said again, the words not intended solely for him, but to her own body as well, and to the world in general, to the glorious, crazy twist of Fate that had made this happen. Hope swelled inside her and it was the most joyful and wonderful sensation. *Hope* – oh, how she had missed it! Welcome back, old friend. Any minute now she would hug that doctor and – no. Calm down, Laura. No hugging.

The doctor was eyeing her beaming face with bemusement. He must think she was a complete lunatic, crying one minute and then exuberant to the point of near-derangement in the next. Hey, that was hormones for you, though, right? At least she had a good excuse for her mad behaviour. 'So if you've got any further questions?' he asked.

She shook her head because she had three different pregnancy books at home, plus the entire Internet at her disposal, and of course she had been here before. And then she sobered up almost completely, because yes, she *had* been here before, and it had gone wrong every time so far. Who was to say this wouldn't happen again? Who was to say there wouldn't be a further cruel twist yet to come, that her hope wouldn't be doused with another low, digging pain and blood in her knickers, that this wouldn't all end in further heartbreak? 'I think I've got everything I need,' she replied. 'Thanks. Very much.'

One last chance, she repeated to herself as she left the surgery in a daze, a hand stealing back to her stomach with that same startled awe. Whatever happened, she was going to cling on to that feeling of hope. Cling on and not let go. Because maybe this, right here, was the happy ending she'd been holding out for.

Chapter Twenty-Six

'And . . . run on the spot. Fast as you can. Really go for it, pump, pump, pump. Hard! Fast! Keep going. Keep going! Your body is an oiled *machine*. Your body is amazing. Feel those endorphins. Admire your own strength. You've got this. Hard! Fast! Run!'

In a quiet corner of Platt Fields Park, Eve was pounding up and down along with a motley group of Lycra-clad people, lungs heaving, fists like pistons, her mind empty of everything other than the dogged will to keep going, to resist being beaten by this or anything. Lewis was at the front of the group, his red hair like a flaming halo around his head as the sun lit him from behind.

'And . . . stop. Let your arms float down. Feel your body tingling. Feel your blood pounding. Look up at the sky and let your thoughts fall away, drifting far out into the distance. Focus only on your breath as it goes in . . . and out . . . In . . . and out . . .'

Eve's limbs throbbed as the class began winding down.

They had jogged for miles en masse, they had performed squat thrusts and push-ups, lunges and star jumps, and she had forced herself through all of it with unyielding determination. Rubbish, feeble body, she had raged throughout. How dare you fail me? How dare you go wrong on me? I'll show you. I'll beat you. Consider this your first warning.

'Are you on your own?' the nurse had said earlier when he saw her waiting there in the corridor, and she'd known immediately, from the way he'd asked the question with that air of concern, that the news she had come for could only be bad.

Yes, she was on her own, she had said, hackles rising in a bid to pre-empt any unwanted pity with defiance. Wasn't everyone on their own at the end of the day, anyway? Why would she need anyone else, when she had built up that careful barrier around herself, brick by brick, to form a miniature kingdom, which she had run with superb self-sufficiency for years and years? And wasn't that the wisest of precautions? (Okay, so she hadn't said *all* of that out loud, even though the words had drummed defensively around her head.)

'Grab your right ankle and pull the leg behind you, stretching out the quads. Deep, long breaths now as you feel the stretch . . .'

Eve obeyed, gripping her ankle, her hand slippery with sweat, the breath panting out of her. She'd come here on a whim, throwing on the gym kit she kept in the boot of her car, because . . . well, because she couldn't face going back to the office and tussling with her clients' paperwork after receiving the news. Also because she'd remembered, just by chance, Lewis talking about his afternoon classes in the park, and how he loved that it was this random mix of pensioners and students and new mums whose babies dozed in buggies beside them. But mostly she'd come because she wanted to do something physical, really push herself hard, in order to prove that she still could. Remind herself that she wasn't dead yet.

'You might not think so right now, but you're actually pretty lucky to have found a lump at all,' the doctor had said, once he'd dropped the cancer bombshell. He had a lilt to his voice, steady brown eyes, photographs of two beaming girls in school uniform and neatly plaited hair on his desk. 'Because at least that brought you in here to us. With DCIS cases there aren't always obvious symptoms; it can go undetected for a long time. The fact that you're here, and we've been able to make an early diagnosis, is a very good start.'

A good start? Lucky? Yeah, sure, she felt really lucky. Unbelievably lucky to have tested positive for DCIS – or rather, Ductal Carcinoma In Situ, to give it its full and terrifying name. Oh, she had learned all sorts of new terms and acronyms today. Lobules, for instance. The terminal duct lobular unit. There was an alarming-looking information leaflet stuffed in her handbag too, which she hadn't dared look at yet.

'Shake out the right leg and now swap sides, bringing the left leg up behind so that the thigh is stretched out. Really pull it back, that's it. And hold.'

He was good at this, Eve registered belatedly, as Lewis demonstrated at the front of the class. He had just the right amount of push and enthusiasm to drive the class through all the exercises, spotting any stragglers and cajoling them along. For her part, she'd turned up bristling with pent-up energy – rage and aggression, really, if she was honest – hoping to channel it into a hard, obliterating workout. Hoping to exhaust herself so that she didn't feel anything any more. Admittedly this course of action hadn't entirely worked. She still felt raw with the shock of the news, stunned that something had gone wrong in her own traitorous body, and so scared it was hard to breathe whenever she thought about what might become of her. But in a funny sort of way, coming here had definitely helped take the edge off things, numbing her in the way that a large gin and tonic could. She hadn't been expecting to experience the warm exuberant glow now coursing through her bloodstream as she stretched out her legs, either. So maybe her body was still good for something, at least.

'We will be looking at surgery, followed by radiotherapy,'

the doctor had informed her in his calm, kind way. 'In your case, as the DCIS does not affect a large area of the breast, it won't be necessary to carry out a mastectomy – that is to say, the removal of all the breast tissue.'

'I do know what a mastectomy is,' Eve had snapped, before putting a hand up to her mouth in the next moment, shocked by her own rudeness. 'Sorry. I didn't mean . . . I'm really sorry. It's a lot to take in.'

A lot to take in. God, even by her standards, that was pathetically restrained. Ridiculously understated. She'd found herself laughing in a mad sort of way, hysteria building. *A lot to take in! When he's just told me I've got cancer! How bloody British was that?* Then she had to battle really hard to pull herself together, before the doctor started questioning her sanity.

Oh shit, though. Shit shitting shitting shit. How was she going to get through this? How was she going to manage? The doctor had said that DCIS, as the earliest form of breast cancer, was eminently curable; he had given her all sorts of facts and statistics, which the accountant in her was trying to cling to, rationally. But the rest of her – the mum, the wife, the ordinary frightened woman – was struggling to come to terms with it all. So much for the nine in ten. Not so lucky after all, Eve.

'And . . . thank you. Great work, everyone. See you all next week. If you could hand over your money before you leave, that would be brilliant,' Lewis said, raising his hands above his head to applaud the group, before fishing in the pocket of his shorts and pulling out a small creased notebook with an elastic band around it.

Eve pushed her sweaty hair back off her face and gave her arms and legs a last shake as members of the group drifted over to him, handing over notes and coins, which he stuffed into a zipped pocket. So this was his accounts system, she thought, rolling her eyes, as she saw him scribble names haphazardly in his book. She might have guessed. Two or three people even seemed to be slinking away without making any kind of payment, she noticed, her gaze hardening, but Lewis appeared quite unaware. Did he actually know how many people he'd just had in his class? Even with her own head jumbled full of worrying thoughts, she couldn't help thinking how impossibly disorganized this all seemed. When the class he'd run had been well structured, well executed and perfectly timed, too. Why was he so bad at making sure he was paid for his efforts?

'Excuse me!' she found herself yelling after two of the men who were walking in the other direction. 'Haven't you forgotten something?'

They looked suitably sheepish as they turned around and she made the money sign at them, rubbing her fingers and thumb together in a pointed I-see-you sort of way. It was even better when they changed course and made the walk of shame towards Lewis, ferreting in their pockets for cash.

Tutting under her breath, she followed them over, waiting until everyone else had paid him before she opened her purse. 'So this is why your accounts are so bloody awful,' she said, only half-joking as she handed over a ten-pound note. 'I hope you'll be going straight home to input all of your takings onto a spreadsheet for me.'

'Eve! Good to see you. Did you enjoy the class?' he asked with a grin, completely ignoring her comments and stuffing the tenner into his pocket with all the other crumpled notes. 'You were really going for it. I'm impressed. How are you, anyway? Any news?'

Now it was her turn to assume temporary deafness. 'You know, you'd make life a lot easier for yourself if you got people to sign up at the start of a six-week block or whatever. Maybe even get some direct debits going, rather than this – randomly taking cash off people and hoping everyone coughs up,' she told him tartly. Most of the group had thinned away by now, people peeling off in pairs, all pink and shiny from exertion, a few blokes still in a cluster nearby. 'Next time you come into the office I could show you how to set up a new system, and it would really streamline your business model.'

'Sure, yeah.' He gave her an odd look. 'Eve. Are you okay?'

'Then you wouldn't have to worry about people not paying or not turning up, because they've already committed, they've bought into what you're doing – literally – so . . .'

'Eve.' He took her gently by the shoulders and she shut her mouth with a snap. 'Talk to me. And not about bloody business models or accounts. Are you all right?'

She drew breath, wanting to carry on with what she'd been saying, to tell him about the business software she'd recommend, which would really, really help him – but he was looking at her so intently, so firmly, that the words dried on her tongue. Instead she shook her head, her eyes sliding to the ground. 'Not exactly,' she admitted.

'What, you mean . . . ?' He couldn't say what he wanted to, either, all of a sudden.

'Yes.' Her exhalation was like a sigh of resignation as it left her body. 'Bad news.'

His cheeks had been flushed from the exercise, but now they paled with her words. 'Aw, shite, Eve. Bloody hell. I'm sorry.'

'It's fine. It's going to be fine. I just need to . . .' She shrugged miserably and then her next words came out in a whisper. 'I just need to get my head around it.'

'You going to be in the pub later, Lewis?' The men nearby were poised to leave, turning to look over at them.

'Not sure yet,' Lewis called back, a hand in the air. 'I'll

give you a ring.' He turned back to Eve. 'How long have you known?'

'Today. This afternoon. About two hours ago. It's fine,' she said once more, as if repeating herself might make the words come true. Then she looked at her watch: four-fifteen. 'In fact, I should go really, the girls will be wondering where I am. I'll have to start cooking dinner soon. Spaghetti bolognese tonight.'

She was babbling again, because she could tell he was shocked to see her here at all; shocked that she'd just charged around doing all that exercise when she was full to the brim with this unspoken, unshared bad news. 'Eve, no,' he said. 'I'm not sure that's such a good idea.'

'What, spaghetti bolognese?' she asked facetiously, trying to make a joke out of it. 'I've got a good recipe, with—'

'No, I mean, you pretending that everything's all right. You going home and making spaghetti bolognese like nothing's happened.' He looked wary, as if he knew he had to tread carefully. 'Because it *has* happened, Eve. And I know you're good at sorting things out and managing brilliantly, but . . . they need to know now. You've got to let them in.'

She was feeling light-headed suddenly and swayed on her feet. All that running and jumping, without drinking enough water, probably. *It's a lot to take in*, she heard her own voice bleating, high-pitched and tremulous. Yeah, you don't say.

'Look, I'm going to come with you,' he said. 'And we're going to sort out a friend who can mind your kids tonight while you and your husband have a proper talk – or I can look after them, if need be. I know you're going to say you don't need any help,' he added quickly, putting up his hand as she opened her mouth to argue, 'but I'm telling you – you do. Sure, you're the expert on business models and all that stuff, but take it from me, you're bloody rubbish at letting other people pick up the slack when it comes to you, Eve Taylor. Rubbish at it, do you hear?'

A weak sort of whimper came out of her, the faint sound of one final protest. 'I . . .'

'And this is where that all changes,' he went on, taking no notice. 'Now. Where's your car? Are you okay to drive, or do you want me to do it? I'll try not to knock over any cyclists, I promise. Come on – I mean it. I'm not taking no for an answer. Let's go.'

'Of *course* I'll have them!' India cried. 'No problem. Is everything all right?'

On reaching the car, Eve, in an uncharacteristic admission of weakness, had felt that she couldn't face the journey home after all and had slid into the passenger seat, while Lewis took the wheel and instructed her to start making calls. Asking friends for favours – even good friends like India – just did not come easily to her; it never had. Perhaps it was pig-headed, perhaps you could be *too* independent about such things, but she'd always been the type who preferred to do something herself rather than ask anyone else for assistance. Of all her children's early storybooks, Eve had identified most with Little Red Hen, whose catchphrase had been (in hindsight, the kind of martyrish) 'Then I shall do it myself'.

This passenger arrangement meant she had Lewis giving her a pointed side-eye as he steered deftly through the heinous school-run traffic, the phone like a lead weight in her hand. 'Go on,' he'd ordered her, and so she had taken a deep breath and reluctantly dialled. Sure enough, it had proved every bit as difficult and awkward as she'd anticipated, asking India if she'd mind picking up the girls and giving them dinner tonight, and she'd felt obliged to apologize, several times over, for the short notice and add, also several times over, that it really didn't matter if India couldn't do it.

It came as something of a shock, then, to have her friend exclaim in the next breath that it was fine, absolutely – she'd sling a couple more sausages in the pan, no trouble at all. In fact, India had said, given the thousand or so favours Eve had done for her, she couldn't be happier to pay one back. But . . . 'Eve?' she asked, following Eve's mumble of thanks. 'Are you all right?'

Eve wasn't sure how to answer that. She had never been a very convincing liar. 'I've just had one of those days,' she confessed, which was true at least. 'I'll tell you about it some other time.'

'Oh, love! Can I make you dinner as well? Is there anything else I can do?'

There was such warmth in India's voice, such straightforward kindness, that tears pricked Eve's eyes. 'Thank you,' she said, 'but I'm going to . . .' It was hard to get the words out. 'I'm going to have dinner with Neil. We need to talk.'

'Okay,' said India slowly, although you could almost hear the million questions that now buzzed, unasked, through the receiver. She was probably thinking Eve's marriage was going down the pan, just like Laura's had recently done. 'Okay, sure. But . . . well, I'm here, all right? If you need me. And if you want the girls to stay over, or . . . or anything else, just say. All right? Because you know I won't mind.'

'Thank you,' mumbled Eve again. And that was the daft thing, because she *did* know India wouldn't mind. She wouldn't mind any of this – the extra sausages in the pan, the extra settings at the table, even unfolding a couple of camp-beds and unrolling the sleeping bags . . . No, she'd just get on with it, in her usual cheerful muddling-along sort of way. It occurred to Eve, for the first time, that actually India was the sort of person who *liked* being able to help. Not in a pious Mother Teresa sort of way, but in a genuine, good-person, good-friend way. And by *not* letting her help for all those years, Eve had denied her that pleasure. She had effectively rejected her own friend. Why hadn't she worked that out before?

'Thank you so much,' she repeated, feeling emotional. And actually, now that she was in this position, it was remarkably comforting, knowing that there was a friend who had her back, a friend who said, 'I'm here if you need me.' Who would have thought? Who knew? 'You're a star. I owe you one.'

'No, you bloody don't,' India told her with a little laugh in her voice. 'You really don't, Eve. And you're welcome. I mean it. Any time at all.'

Eve let out a long, tired breath as she hung up. Then she rang the girls to tell them the plan and apologize for not being there, and even though Grace asked suspiciously, 'Are you okay? You sound a bit weird,' she was able to gloss over the question with enough breeziness to pass as convincing.

'Two down, one to go,' she told Lewis, who took a hand from the steering wheel to give her an encouraging thumbs up. 'Just the big one now.'

'You can do it,' he said.

Neil sounded quite surprised when Eve called and asked him to leave work as soon as possible and come home, because she had something to tell him. As with India, you could almost hear the possibilities whizzing around his brain as he took it in, calculations being made, conclusions jumped to. Her husband was not the sort of man to panic, but his voice sounded fearful with urgency as he asked, 'Has something happened to one of the girls?'

The girls were fine, she assured him. Look, she didn't want to talk about this on the phone. But please – and she wouldn't ask, unless it was important – please come home. Now.

By the time Lewis had dropped her off, Grace and Sophie had already been whisked away by India (for which Eve sent up a silent prayer of thanks). She then proceeded to have a minor flap about Lewis being stranded far from home – oh, she was so selfish, she hadn't been thinking! – before he calmly pointed out that there was a perfectly good bus stop down the road and he was a big boy, he could manage to get home all by himself.

Having said goodbye, Eve with fervent gratitude for everything Lewis had done, she let herself into the house and exhaled shakily into its expectant silence.

Okay. Now for the hardest part.

After showering and changing, she wandered through the quiet house, gazing at the family photos lovingly hung up around the walls. The girls as babies, toothy and cute. Her and Neil on their wedding day, wreathed in smiles. Holiday snaps and snowy-day pictures and her favourite, a Christmas Day photo from five years ago or so, with the girls holding up their presents, shiny-eyed with joy. So much happiness, she thought, reaching out a finger to touch their faces. So many good times. She wasn't ready for all that to be taken away from her yet. She couldn't bear the thought of future Christmases without her, future holiday photos with an empty space where she should have been.

She sank into a chair, still dwelling on her daughters' beautiful smiles. Had she been a good enough mother? Had she filled them with enough confidence, enough love? She had done her best, but sometimes she got the distinct feeling that her girls wished she was more like India, laid-back and quick to laugh when things went wrong, rather than uptight and naggy like her. Then she remembered what Lewis had said about spontaneity, about leaving room for it in life, and frowned to herself. Was that what was missing in her? The fun that came from the unexpected? The liberation of just . . . letting go? If she could have another chance at life, a second try, maybe she'd do it all differently, she thought with a sigh. She'd do it better, appreciate every moment with them.

Goodness knows how long she stayed sitting there in silence, but then the front door was opening and Neil's voice floated through, jerking her out of her thoughts. 'Eve? I'm back. Are you there? Eve?' He appeared in the doorway, looking pale and worried, his hair standing on end a little where she guessed he'd been raking through it anxiously whenever the traffic seized up. 'What is it, what's wrong?'

This was it: the moment of truth, as they liked to say on *The X Factor*. No going back now. She looked at his dear, troubled face and felt sick that she was about to change everything; shake the safe, careful structure of their marriage, with what she had to say. 'Why don't you sit down?' she suggested nervously. This was the kind of news that needed the support of a sofa before it could be released.

Once she started talking, she couldn't stop. She told him everything from start to finish, her fears, her hospital visits, the diagnosis . . . out it all came, her quiet words filling up the space between them, his expression changing from concern to alarm to shock, with each new turn in the tale. She could read the disquiet on his face every time Lewis's name came up, his evident confusion that his wife had chosen to confide in a stranger rather than him – her own husband – and guilt cut through her because he was right, of course, and she had no good way of explaining herself. 'So I should receive a date for surgery in the next few days, but the consultant thought they'd want me in pretty soon – a week or thereabouts,' she finished. 'And that's . . . that's my news.'

'Oh, Eve,' he said, and then he was hugging her, for a long time, tight and comforting, and he was promising that they would see this through together, that he'd be with her every step of the way. And then, because he was Neil and it was in his DNA to try to solve a problem, he started googling and researching, and telling her all the positive things he could find about her condition: that it was eminently curable. Very early cancer. Full recovery.

Yes, she said, feeling tired and tearful, and too wary to dare let herself believe any of it just yet.

It was only later on, when the girls were back home and in bed, and Neil had had time to digest what she'd told him, two glasses of whisky down, that he started to become – not angry, exactly, but noticeably hurt in regards to her previous silence. 'I wish you'd told me,' he blurted out. 'I can't believe you went through all of that, for weeks and weeks, without saying anything. I'm not having a go at you, but . . . You went to some *guy* you didn't even know, before you told *me*? I don't understand. Is something going on between you two?'

'No!' she cried. 'I promise. It's not like that.'

'So then . . . why? Why him and not me?'

She hung her head because there was no rational answer that would satisfy him, and because this, in one short question, was the nub of all that was wrong with her. She flashed back to the triumphant day of her GCSE results, when her dad had praised her – for the first time ever – and how it had meant precisely nothing. When she'd thought, actually: do you know what, Dad, you can't affect how I feel about myself any more. When she had begun bricking up the wall, thinking it was self-reliance and admirable independence, when instead . . .

A tear rolled down her cheek. When, instead, she had become the sort of woman who went to hospital appointments with random strangers because she was so damn afraid of appearing vulnerable to her loved ones. 'I'm sorry,' she said, twisting her fingers together, too ashamed to look at his face. 'I don't know why.'

He sighed, his confusion evident and then, perhaps heightened by the whisky, his emotions got the better of him. 'Look, you've got to let me in, Eve. You never let me in! What is the point of me being your husband if you never tell me how you're feeling? You never let anyone help you.'

'I know,' she said miserably. 'I'm sorry.'

'It makes me feel marginalized, you know. Like I'm not important. Like I don't matter!' His voice rose and then he broke off, looking uncomfortable, as if remembering why it was they were having this discussion in the first place. Oh yeah. Wife with cancer. Better rein it in. 'Sorry,' he mumbled. 'I'm not having a pop. Wrong time and place for this conversation, yeah? But . . .' He shrugged. 'That's just how I feel.'

She reached over and took his hand. This hand, which had held hers on their first dates, and as they stood there making their marriage vows in the registry office, and as she had laboured with both their girls. His strong steady hand that she knew so well. Yet lately she had ignored that hand and what it signified, even though it had been hers for the taking this whole time. 'It's okay,' she said quietly. 'You're right. And we do need to have this conversation properly some other time – I hear what you're saying.' Her voice rose in anguish. 'It wasn't because I didn't love you though that I didn't say anything. I just . . .'

'It's all right,' he said. 'You're used to being able to cope; I know that. But – please. Talk to me. I want you to be able to talk to me. To trust me with your doubts and worries. The whole world knows you're strong and capable, Eve. But sometimes . . .' He swirled his whisky around in his glass, struggling to find the words. 'Sometimes it takes the most strength to admit that you're a little bit scared. To say: I need help. To say: I can't manage on my own. And you can always lean on me, Eve. Please take that into consideration. You can always lean on me.'

She nodded, the words resonating with truth. Then she looked him in the eye and took a deep breath. 'I'm scared,' she told him. 'I . . . I need help. I can't manage on my own.'

And then he was hugging her again and they were both crying and he was saying, 'I'm here. I've got you. I'm here.'

Chapter Twenty-Seven

According to the dating scan, Laura was already fourteen weeks pregnant. *Fourteen weeks*, and she hadn't had the faintest clue! She still couldn't quite get her head around it, waking every morning and thrilling all over again to the news, when she remembered. Hey – I'm pregnant. I'm really, really pregnant!

You had to admit, it was as if Life was having a good old joke at her expense. Ladling on the irony for dramatic purposes. Because, as it now turned out, she'd already been pregnant when she and Matt had been arguing so passionately about whether or not to try for a baby. She'd been pregnant when their negotiations stalled and failed, when he had told her their marriage was breaking down, when he moved out. And she'd even been pregnant way back at India's birthday lunch too, when she'd assumed it was the crash that had propelled her into a renewed Must-Have-a-Baby mode. When, in fact, that little baby was already being formed, silently and secretly, cell by cell, and her hormones must have been going berserk all of their own accord. Meanwhile she hadn't even registered. So much for being one of those earth-mother types in tune with their own bodies, who simpered, hand on bump, *I just knew.*

Jo came to the scan with her and held her hand as the sonographer moved the device across her belly. Both sisters gasped as they saw the outlines of a tiny new human there on the screen. A baby. *Her* baby, floating in its dark watery world like a pale mystical sea creature. 'Hello, baby,' Laura whispered, eyes glued to its moving form. 'Hi there.'

'My first niece or nephew!' Jo cried, blowing her nose with uncharacteristic soppiness. 'I can't believe it, Laur.' And then they were both sniffling and damp-eyed at this miracle, this extraordinary feat of nature, this wonderful gift from nowhere.

Laura had sobered up in the very next moment, though. 'Does everything look . . . okay?' she asked, remembering with trepidation all those glasses of wine – bottles of wine, rather – that she'd drunk, in ignorance of the baby's presence. The dread she had felt ever since, the crippling fear that she might accidentally have caused some developmental damage to her own child – she'd had to ban herself from Google for a while because her hand kept typing 'Foetal Alcohol Syndrome' and clicking the results, in some horrific self-punishing way.

But 'Everything looks great,' the sonographer replied

with a smile, and it was, without question, quite the best sentence she'd ever heard.

'I've never got so far along in a pregnancy,' she said, her voice thick with emotion. She knew, from all her reading on the subject, that thirteen weeks was a sizeable milestone in pregnancy; that the risk of miscarriage dropped considerably once the baby had made it that far. And now it turned out that the two of them had already surpassed this mark, swept casually over the line together, as if it was the easiest thing ever. 'I never expected this to happen.'

Jo squeezed her fingers and Laura beamed at her, feeling dazed and blessed and oh, so happy. Wildly, deliriously happy. And hungry too actually, now that she thought about it. Insanely ravenous seemed to be her default setting these days.

'So, when are you going to tell him?' Jo asked later on, as Laura tucked into a round of ham sandwiches in the hospital coffee bar, followed by a banana, followed by – sod it, she wasn't *nearly* full yet – a damp and gooey chocolate brownie that she'd smuggled along in her handbag, in case of emergencies. They had both taken the morning off work to be here for Laura's ten-thirty appointment and it was now most definitely elevenses time. 'Matt, I mean. I take it he still doesn't know?'

Laura licked a chocolatey crumb from her finger. 'I was waiting to see if everything was okay first,' she admitted. 'I was so paranoid that I'd gone and ruined everything with all the booze, dreading them doing the scan and telling me that something was wrong. I thought: why tell him if – if, you know, there's bad news, or it all turned out to be a massive false alarm.' It was silly of her, especially when the doctor had assured her how accurate pregnancy tests were, but she'd been so convinced that she would show up for the scan, only to be told there had been a mistake and she wasn't really pregnant at all, that she had gone on to take three more tests in her own bathroom. Just to be certain. Even then, it wasn't until she saw the baby on the ultrasound screen that she was able to feel convinced. Okay, you *are* there. Good. Message from your mother: please stay right where you are, make yourself comfortable and let's see this through together. Got it?

'So now you know it's not a false alarm and everything *is* okay . . . ?' prompted Jo.

Laura bit her lip, not wanting to tempt Fate. Having miscarried in the past and experienced all the anguish that came with it, she knew she wouldn't feel completely relaxed that the baby was okay until he or she had actually been born and was in her arms, breathing and perfect. 'I'm not counting any chickens,' she told her sister. 'Things could still go wrong. We're not out of the woods yet.'

Jo gave her a suspicious look. 'What, so you're going to wait until you're huge and waddling, and practically in the delivery room, before you give poor Matt – the baby's *father* – the wink, are you? And what if he's back in Manchester and you bump into him? You'll have a job talking your way out of that one.'

She had a point. Annoyingly. 'Yeah, all right. I will *tell* him,' Laura said defensively. 'Obviously. I feel a bit weird about it, though. I mean, after all the things he said at the end, how certain he was that he wanted us to split up. He thinks he's made this clean break, and I'm going to be running after him, tapping him on the shoulder, saying, Guess what? Me again. I have news!' She rolled her eyes. 'It's been something of a roller coaster lately, as they say.'

'Luckily, you love roller coasters,' Jo reminded her drily. (This was true. Laura was one of those people who tried to sit right at the front of the ride and spent the whole time with their hands in the air, screaming breathlessly, before getting off, jelly-legged, and queuing up to go straight back round.) 'Anyway, he'll be over the moon. Proud as punch. And then you two can have a big romantic reunion and it'll be like it never happened. Happy families.'

'Do you think?' Jo seemed very certain about Matt's reaction; more certain, in fact, than Laura herself was.

'Of course! That's what you want, isn't it?' Jo eyed her over her mug of tea and there was just a second too long of silence. 'Laur?'

'Yeah. Yeah! Definitely. You know me, always love a

happy ending.' She licked her lips and patted her stomach, which was definitely starting to take on a more rounded shape. Although that could be all the baked goods she'd been scoffing, mind. 'I'll ring him later.'

'You're going to tell him on the *phone*?' Jo frowned. 'Isn't it kind of gigantic news to say on the phone, when you're miles away?'

'I guess so. But . . .' Laura scrunched up her face. 'I'm not sure he really wants to see me right now,' she confessed in a small voice. 'Last time we spoke he sounded fed up with me, as if I was getting on his nerves. Anyway, as you pointed out, he's miles away. He might not be back here for weeks on end.'

Jo looked unimpressed by her cowardice. 'Then you're just going to have to go up there and find him, aren't you?' she said. 'Come on. Matt loved you, for years and years and years. Nobody can switch that off overnight.' She poured herself more tea and pointed the teaspoon at Laura. 'Besides, he'd want to know. It's his child. So stop being such a wuss and do the right thing.'

As was so often the case, Laura had the nagging feeling that Jo might just be right. The problem buzzed insistently in her head over the next few days as she told her colleagues the news and then her mum. ('I'm going to be a grandma!' Helen had cried, sounding surprisingly choked up and maternal, for once. Then she'd spoiled the soppy moment by adding, 'Well, bugger me sideways', which was a lot less motherly, let alone grandmotherly.) Not-telling-Matt had seemed much easier when it had just been Laura herself in the know, but now that the secretary in the finance office at work knew, and Matt still didn't, she was becoming increasingly twitchy about this state of affairs.

Yes, okay, so she did really owe it to her ex to give him the news face-to-face, rather than for him to hear it down the end of a phone, all alone in his no-doubt-soulless rented place, she concluded, walking through town the following Saturday. Not least so that she could work out, from his expression, exactly how he felt about the situation. And about her, too. But not this weekend, though, not today, because Eve had suggested getting together for brunch at Rico's, an Aussie-style café in the Northern Quarter, and Laura was not about to pass up the opportunity of telling the other two her big news in person. Matt would just have to wait a bit longer.

She put a hand on her belly as she walked up through town, still delighted by the novelty of the small hard bump that was taking shape there beneath her pink T-shirt. The thought of saying the words, 'I'm going to have a baby' out loud to her favourite women when they, of all people, would know just what a massive deal that was, made her smile to herself at her sheer good fortune. Earlier in the week she'd met India for Pilates as usual and she'd felt so keyed up during the class that she'd hardly been able to concentrate. *I'm going to tell her in the pub*, she kept thinking. *I'm going to sit her down and tell her, and then, knowing India, she'll probably scream out loud with excitement and everyone will turn round and stare at us hugging, and I won't care a bit, because I'm pregnant and don't care about things like that any more.*

Except then the class had ended and, instead of raising an eyebrow and saying 'Pub?' like she normally did, India had been in an odd sort of mood, saying she was knackered and going home for an early night. So that had put the kybosh on that little announcement. Which was a double shame, actually, because Laura had been dying to know how India had got on with her old flame.

Still, maybe it was for the best, she thought, enjoying the feeling of her newly washed hair bouncing lightly on her shoulders as she turned off the High Street. (Her hair had never felt so great! She might still be tired and prone to dizzy spells, but her hair felt amazingly thick and lustrous and swingy, which was a source of huge joy.) Telling India *and* Eve both together today would be nicer anyway. Imagine their faces! They would, to a woman, be over the moon for her.

I know! she pictured herself saying, beaming. *I was surprised, too. Mother Nature, eh, what a teaser!*

The other three were already there when she arrived, on

one of the corner tables, with menus and coffee cups. Eve looked stunning as usual, in a fitted, flattering navy dress with a chunky silver necklace and ballet pumps, while India was wearing a wide-necked sage-coloured jersey top and black trousers, her hair spilling out of a messy bun. Jo, leaning forward, mid-discussion, her coppery hair falling around her face, was the first to notice Laura's arrival. 'Ah – here she is!' she cried as Laura approached.

'Hi, everyone, sorry I'm a bit late,' cried Laura, hugging them each in turn and beaming around the table. 'This was a good idea, Eve – nice one. Although you were all looking very serious when I came in, especially you, Jo,' she commented. 'Everything okay?'

Jo wrinkled her nose. 'Just asking these two for some parenting advice. Step-parenting advice, whatever. Because I am out of my depth with Maisie. I keep getting everything wrong. And I'm kind of at my wits' end.'

'To which I said, join the club,' India added, rolling her eyes comically. 'Because take it from me, every parent thinks like that. It's part of the job description, unfortunately.'

There was a time when Laura might have felt a tiny bit irritated by India's parenting pronouncements and her 'Take it from me' style, as if she was the expert on the subject and Laura knew nothing. Now it didn't seem to matter quite so much any more. 'Well,' she said, aware that she was about to hijack her sister's conversation, but unable to stop the words bubbling up inside her anyway. 'I'm going to be joining your club myself in the new year, as it happens. Because I am fourteen weeks pregnant. Yes! I just found out last week!'

India jumped up immediately, grabbing her with a squeal – 'Oh my GOD!' – exactly as Laura had known she would, followed by Eve too, who gave her a massive tight hug. But then something a bit weird happened. Eve didn't let go. In fact, she clung on to Laura and a second passed, then another, and she was still there, her face pressed into Laura's shoulder. 'Oh, Eve,' Laura said, laughing as she patted her friend's back, but also a tiny bit taken aback. Eve wasn't usually quite so demonstrative or touchy-feely. 'I know, right? We all thought it was never going to happen. But now . . .' She felt wetness through her T-shirt. 'Eve! You're not crying, are you?'

Eve finally lifted her head and her eyes were bloodshot. 'I'm sorry, I'm just . . .'

'You nana,' Laura scoffed, feeling touched by her friend's emotional response. 'And there was me thinking *I* was the hormonal one. I was crying at a Lloyds Bank advert the other day – how lame is that?'

Eve dabbed at her eyes with a napkin. Her mouth had gone a bit funny, as if she was on the verge of really crying, Laura thought, puzzled. 'Congratulations,' she said after a moment, lip still wobbling. 'That's such amazing news.'

'So what did Matt—?' India asked, just as the waitress appeared at the table.

'Can I take your orders, ladies?'

The topic was put momentarily on hold as they consulted the menus and there was some enjoyable deliberation over what everyone fancied most. 'God, I love eating for two,' Laura said cheerfully, deciding that yes, she certainly *could* manage the bacon and avocado house-special as well as a side order of banana bread with vanilla mascarpone. 'And a massive pot of tea,' she added for good measure.

No sooner had the waitress departed again than Laura opened her mouth, ready to answer India's question about Matt and prattle on happily about the baby and the visit to the doctor and the scan. Oh, it was so good to have great news to share, after all the doom and gloom of recent weeks! But Eve got there first, still with that same odd look on her face.

'Listen, guys, I've got something to say, and now everyone's here I just want to get it over with,' she began, twisting her hands together as if she was anxious. Laura frowned at the sight. This was out of the ordinary for cool, collected Eve, who usually sailed through life with such enviable ease. Oh no. Was there some problem with her and Neil? Her job? Don't say one of the girls was having a rough time at school?

'What is it?' Jo asked in surprise.

Eve swallowed and tried to smile, but she seemed highly agitated. 'It's . . . God. This isn't easy for me to say. Give me a minute.'

Laura was starting to feel worried. She took Eve's hand. 'What's wrong?'

'Pot of tea – was this for you?' The waitress was back, dumping a huge white teapot on the table in front of Laura. 'And an espresso?' India raised her hand mutely, her eyes still on Eve's pallid face. 'There we are. Enjoy.'

'Is this about the other night, when you wanted me to have the girls?' India asked and Eve nodded. 'Please, just tell us. Whatever it is, we're here for you, love. We're listening.'

'Well,' said Eve, and gave a strange, nervous sort of laugh. 'I'm going to ruin our lovely brunch now, I'm afraid, but I have to tell you. The thing is . . . I've had some bad news.'

Chapter Twenty-Eight

Jo felt utterly winded by shock, desperately upset for her friend. Poor brave secretive Eve. To think she had carried that burden of stress around by herself for all this time, for weeks and weeks, without telling any of her family and friends – it broke Jo's heart that she'd been too proud to do so. Not even Neil had known until the other night! But now at last super-capable, self-possessed Eve had met her match, realizing belatedly that even she might struggle to manage single-handedly from here on in. 'I've never been very good at asking for help,' she had said, eyes watery, 'but I might need some in the next few months. Would you . . . ? Do you think you might . . . ?'

God love her, she couldn't even get the questions out. 'Of *course* we'll help,' Jo assured her at once. 'You don't need to ask. Whatever it is, we'll help.'

'I've got to have surgery first, and then six weeks of radiotherapy every day,' Eve said, looking genuinely afraid.

Her mouth buckled. 'It's going to be a massive upheaval. It's going to take over my life.'

'Well, I can look after the girls, any time,' India offered immediately. 'You know I will.'

'And I can come to hospital appointments with you,' Jo said. 'Just say where and when – I've got tons of holiday left over and I can rearrange my shifts.'

'And I'll cook you loads of dinners to stock up your freezer, and do your washing – and I'll steal you lots of nice goodies from work . . .' Laura put in. 'Please let us help. We want to. We love you. And we know you'd do the same for us.'

Eve had become quite tearful with gratitude, thanking them all profusely. Then she went on to confess how upset Neil had been on hearing the news. Upset for her, but also because of how she'd held back on him. 'We've done a lot of soul-searching since then,' she admitted. 'Because we were both at fault. We had drifted apart, we had stopped talking properly. I found it hard to tell him something was wrong.' She pulled a face at her own black humour. 'In a mad sort of way, this has brought us back together, though. Cancer saved my marriage! That's not warped at all, is it?'

Oh, Eve. Jo couldn't remember seeing her friend cry, not since they'd been at school when Eve had fractured her elbow in a netball match. But today the tears had come rolling down her face over their huge plates of eggs and bacon and buttered sourdough toast, before she was all cried out, emotions spent. Then, when her face was blotchy and her shoulders had finally ceased heaving, she'd vanished to the loo with her hairbrush and lipstick and emerged looking a bit more like the old Eve, ready to face the world once more. 'Okay, I'm all right now. Time to talk about something else,' she'd insisted, and turned the conversation neatly back round to Laura's big news, demanding to hear all about it: how was she feeling, any thoughts about names, had she tried antenatal yoga? It was where all the best people went, after all – this with a sideways wink at India, because that was where the two of them had met.

'As soon as we both got the giggles about that woman who kept farting every time she moved into a new position, I thought: I like you,' India reminisced, twinkling her eyes over at Eve.

Eve smiled. 'I remember coming out of that class with you, and some bloke wolf-whistling us, and you – do you remember this? – you were seven months pregnant and yet you still chased him down the street, shouting that he was a sexist pig and should be ashamed of himself. And I thought: this woman is nuts and fearless, and I most definitely want to be her friend.'

They all laughed and India went a bit red. 'So much for the good old fearless days,' she groaned, looking up at the clock. 'I've got to meet Dan and the kids to go bowling in twenty minutes – yes, on the sunniest day of the year so far. This is what my life has become. And George will no doubt delight in telling me that I'm doing everything wrong, as usual.' She rolled her eyes. 'That boy, honestly, is going to end up one of those really annoying patronizing blokes, if I'm not careful. He's pegged me as this total incompetent who can do nothing right, whereas Dan is the ultimate parent who knows everything. Just once I'd like to impress my son, just once.' Another eye-roll. 'Something tells me it won't be at bowling, knowing my coordination, though.'

Eve nudged her. 'If it makes you feel any better, my girls think you're great. They had a brilliant time at yours the other night. Something about a wild game of Sardines, where everyone leapt out at Dan and scared the life out of him? They were very keen to re-enact it with Neil.'

India looked delighted. 'Really?' She laughed. 'That's funny, because my ingrates are always whinging about how useless I am, compared to you. Maybe we should swap.'

'Give me a few years and I'll be taking tips from both of you,' Laura declared, stretching sleepily. 'But in the meantime I'm going to waddle home and have a nap, for the baby's sake.'

'Something tells me this is going to be a new catchphrase of yours,' Jo said, groaning at the smug look on her sister's face. 'Eve, how about you? Please tell me you're not rushing off to do endless household chores, today of all days.'

Eve flushed, then gave a shy smile. 'Believe it or not, Neil and the girls have taken it upon themselves to clean the house and get on top of the laundry in my absence,' she said, before looking twitchy and adding, 'They're probably breaking things and shrinking all the woollens as we speak. I'm finding it quite hard to relax and let them get on with it, to be honest.'

'Oh, who cares about a few breakages, as long as the hoovering's done by someone else,' India said as the waitress brought over their bill. 'Lucky you! Make the most of it – have another coffee, I would.'

'Actually . . .' Eve looked a bit embarrassed. 'Neil's booked me in for a manicure at Preened and Polished. He's determined that I'm to chill out all day and not do anything.'

'Good,' said Jo. 'Quite right, too.'

'Bloody hell,' said India, impressed. 'Neil is setting the bar *high*. Wait till I tell Dan about this!'

Once the bill was paid, they said goodbye, with Eve promising to tell them when she got her surgery date, and the others repeating their promises of help. Feeling pensive, Jo made her way down towards Piccadilly Gardens, swerving through all the shoppers. It was half-past two in the afternoon now and the city was bathed in golden sunshine; crowds of people were pouring down from the station, the free buses sailing past were packed full of passengers and there was music spilling out of shopfronts and cafés. Despite the happy summery vibe, Jo found her thoughts sliding towards Rick, wishing that she could feel quite as confident in their relationship as Eve and Neil now seemed to have become. Was it deceitful of her that she hadn't told him about seeing Polly and Maisie arguing in the street the other week, or mentioned Bill's comment about the police having to be called in recently? Probably, but then Maisie was already such a stumbling block between them, such a sticking point, that Jo had not been able to find the words. She'd bitten her lip so many times about Rick's daughter that she would chew her own mouth off one of these days.

'Standard teenage fodder,' Eve had reassured her earlier when she'd poured out her grievances. 'Completely textbook behaviour.'

'Don't take it personally,' India had advised. 'It's all posturing, by the sound of it, and deep down I bet she's just terrified her dad's going to like you better than her.'

Good advice, sure, but it was hard not to take Maisie's behaviour personally when Jo's tentative attempts at bonding had been universally met with a wall of naked contempt. And sometimes, even though Jo was an adult and supposedly above teenage catcalling and bitchery, Maisie's comments hurt. They got to her, digging into all her old insecurities, reminding her of the mean girls she'd faced at school who'd teased her about her badly fitting uniform, her charity-shop winter coat, her hair – anything, really, given half a chance. It didn't feel like much fun, having to go through this all over again, twenty-five or so years later.

With nothing in particular planned for the rest of the afternoon, Jo found herself weaving towards Primark in order to pick up some summery tops and perhaps a floaty skirt or two. The warm weather was meant to last the whole week, according to the local forecast, and although her complexion was so pale she never really got a proper tan, she did love the feeling of sunshine on her skin: a proper tonic. But she was barely through the front doors of the shop when she noticed an altercation taking place right there in front of her: a burly security guard and a teenage girl with long tawny hair . . . Oh, crap. It was Maisie.

'Get off me! I didn't do anything!' Maisie was shrieking, trying to wrestle his meaty hand off her arm, while he did his best to steer her further back into the store. She had on a black skater skirt and a pink vest top with a denim jacket and black ballet pumps, a string of beads swinging from her neck as the two of them tussled.

A complicated mix of feelings surged inside Jo – surprise, concern and, although she was ashamed to admit it, definitely a tinge of Schadenfreude too. *Not so perfect now, are we?*

She hurried over to investigate. 'What's going on?'

Maisie looked positively mortified at Jo's arrival, her face flaring bright red, as if this was the worst of all possible outcomes. The security guard clung on to her, his expression stern, his voice loud enough to carry to all the shoppers in the vicinity. 'This here young lady and a couple of her mates have been caught trying to shoplift some sunglasses—'

'We didn't! I never!'

'And so I'm asking this young lady to prove it, by taking off her jacket and emptying her pockets.'

'I didn't take anything,' cried the young lady herself, this time to Jo, eyes hooded and sullen. 'I swear. It was the others.'

The security guard looked at Jo. 'You two know each other, do you?' he asked.

'Yes,' replied Jo, as Maisie's expression changed to the inevitable scowl. 'We do.' She hesitated, not sure what to say next, wishing she had India or Eve there for guidance. 'So where are the others then?' she asked, looking around. 'Your friends?'

'Legged it out the door, didn't they?' the man said crossly. He had damp patches under his arms and there was a sheen of sweat on his top lip; perhaps he wasn't in peak condition when it came to chasing after athletic teenage shoplifters. 'Unfortunately for this one, she wasn't so fast. Now then, jacket. Take it off. I don't have all day.'

Jo sighed, wishing she hadn't walked in on this. Having

heard Eve's terrible news, she was absolutely not in the mood for dealing with Maisie's latest drama. 'Look, she's told you she didn't take anything, I'm sure she's telling the truth,' she said to the guard, trying to reason with him, adult to adult.

'In which case, she won't mind removing her jacket and emptying her pockets, will she?' he replied, not budging an inch, one hand still circling Maisie's arm. He had a round, baby sort of face, slightly pocked skin; he couldn't have been older than twenty, Jo reckoned. Just trying to do his job. Fair enough. Wasn't everybody?

'Take your jacket off,' she ordered the girl wearily. 'Just do it, then you can go off and find these delightful friends of yours. Go on.'

Despite all the make-up, Maisie suddenly looked a lot younger than her thirteen years. Her lip gloss was coming off where she kept licking it nervously and this close up, you could see that her eye make-up had been amateurishly applied; her mascara clumpy, her eyebrows over-pencilled, her flicky eyeliner uneven. Not quite the ice princess after all. Just a scared kid whose bluff had been called.

'We were only mucking about,' said Maisie in a meek, not-at-all Maisie-ish voice, at which point Jo knew, immediately, that there definitely *was* something inside her jacket. Oh, great. 'I wasn't going to really *nick* anything . . .'

'Look, could we maybe go to an office somewhere?' Jo

asked the guard, conscious of the shoppers nearby, some of whom were stopping, quite blatantly, to watch, as if the three of them were an in-store theatre performance. 'Do this privately, without an audience gawping at us?'

He hesitated and she could see him weighing it up, whether to make a public spectacle of the girl or not.

'Please,' said Jo quietly. 'Look, she's only got a vest top on, she doesn't want the whole shop seeing her,' she improvised. 'I'll come too, obviously. I'll take responsibility for her.'

That seemed to swing it at least, and he led them through a door at the back of the shop, still holding Maisie's arm as if he fully expected her to dodge away from him at any moment. Down they went along a corridor to a quiet office, where he shut the door, let go of Maisie and folded his arms across his chest. 'Right, let's have it then,' he said.

Without looking at Jo, Maisie slid her thin arms from the jacket and handed it over to the beefy guard, her head down in guilty anticipation. In the next second, the man had dug a paw into one of the inner pockets and retrieved a pair of aviator sunglasses with the tag still attached. 'I thought as much,' he said, light glinting from the lenses as he held the glasses aloft, in the manner of an archaeologist having unearthed a priceless treasure from one of the great pyramids. 'What have you got to say for yourself now then, eh?'

Maisie, as it turned out, didn't have anything much to say

for herself, other than a muffled 'I'm really sorry', before crumpling into penitent tears.

'Oh dear,' Jo said grimly, catching the eye of the security guard. He appeared completely unmoved by the tears, as if he'd seen all this before. Every single Saturday, probably. 'So what happens now?' Would he call the police? she wondered, shooting a glance at Maisie, who was still weeping, clutching a small scraggly tissue that she'd retrieved from her bag.

The security guard scratched at his stubble for a moment, considering. Then he turned the sunglasses over, peering at them. 'Those girls I saw you with, they're in here all the time, trying to nick stuff,' he said, with a hard stare at Maisie. 'And one of these days I'm going to catch them, and they're going to be very sorry. But I haven't seen you here before, I'm glad to say. So that's something. And there's no damage done to the goods.'

Jo held her breath. 'So . . . ?'

He cleared his throat. 'So this time I'm going to let you off with a warning,' he said gruffly. 'But let me make this clear: if I catch you in here again, mucking about and trying to nick stuff, I'm going to be straight on the phone to the police and, take it from me, they will not be so nice to you. You'd get a criminal record, you know. A criminal record! If you want to go to college one day, or university, or when you come to get a job, that criminal record will be there, remember, and it doesn't look good, believe me. Not good at all.' His voice was getting louder and more severe, and Maisie seemed to be shrinking on the spot.

'No,' she mumbled. 'Thank you.'

'We appreciate that,' Jo felt obliged to say.

'I mean it, though,' he said. 'And tell those mates of yours, and all. In fact, word of advice.' He turned to Jo. 'You might want to suggest your daughter finds some new friends to hang around with. The two she was with today . . .' He shook his head. 'Heading down the slippery slope any day now, put it like that. And you don't want them dragging your girl with them.'

Jo couldn't quite look at Maisie, who was probably pulling an about-to-vomit face that this man could be so idiotic as to assume someone like *Jo* could possibly be her mother. Although if Jo put him straight, he might insist on ringing Maisie's real parents, she figured. Perhaps it was better to let that one go uncontested. 'Thank you,' was all she said. 'We'll certainly have a chat about it.' And with that, the ordeal seemed to be over.

Maisie shrugged on her jacket again, not saying a word as the two of them made their way back across the busy shop floor. Once outside the store, she hesitated, blinking in the bright sunshine. (Should have bought those sunglasses, shouldn't you? Jo thought, rather heartlessly.)

'Are you going to tell Dad?' the girl asked in a low voice.

And just like that, the power dynamic had shifted. Again Jo hesitated, wondering how best to reply. If she kept quiet about this, then Maisie would be in her debt, she realized – although that would mean keeping a secret from Rick, which wasn't ideal. But if Maisie was genuinely sorry and, more to the point, suitably shaken up to think twice about pulling such a stunt again, maybe she had been punished enough. Oh God. This was *hard*. Jo felt completely unqualified to make decisions about somebody else's child. 'I'm not sure,' she replied honestly. 'Look, there's a Caffè Nero round the corner, why don't we go and have a milkshake or something? Talk it through.'

Maisie flushed, looking very much as if 'talking it through' was the last thing she felt like doing, but to Jo's surprise – and no doubt with an eye on any repercussions, if she rudely refused – the girl nodded reluctantly and they trailed along there together.

It was only as they were waiting to be served that Jo remembered seeing all those clothes in Maisie's bedroom the other day, tags still attached, and all those expensive toiletries to boot. She'd thought at the time there was something odd about so much brand-new stuff being at Rick's place, rather than at Polly's – especially when she'd never heard anything about Rick taking his daughter on shopping trips. She could make a pretty good guess at where it had all come from now, though. 'You've done that before, haven't you?' she asked in a low voice, pretending to be browsing the menu above their heads. 'Nicking stuff, I mean. I've seen it in your room.'

Maisie picked at her nails, glaring and shrugging. Jo would take that as a yes, then, she decided, raising her eyes heavenwards. God. Worse than she'd thought. How the hell was she meant to deal with this sort of thing? Why wasn't there a manual?

Once they'd been served and were sitting at a table with a drink each, Jo decided to spare the lectures. Maisie wasn't an idiot, she didn't need Jo banging on about shoplifting or choosing her friends more carefully. Besides, she could tell the girl felt uneasy there with her and was itching to get away again. Bugger it, Jo thought, she might as well seize the moment and go straight in for the big stuff while she could, just get it out there. 'Do you know, a couple of months ago I was here in town when that car crashed near Peter Street,' she began conversationally. 'Do you remember hearing about it? It was a sunny day like this, really busy – people everywhere.'

There was suspicion in Maisie's expression as she eyed her over the straw in her drink, as if wondering where this might be leading. 'Yeah,' she said guardedly.

'And I rushed over to help some of the people who'd been injured, and this one woman, Miriam, she was called, gave me a card and asked me to ring her husband.'

'Right,' said Maisie, still with that 'So what?' look about her.

'So I did and – well, long story, but we stayed in touch. They're a really nice couple who live out in Didsbury. Ash Grove, funnily enough.'

Maisie's shoulders stiffened as she sucked her drink. Oh yeah. Here it comes.

'I went there the other week, because Miriam's out of hospital at last, and I was just knocking on their door when you and your mum went by,' Jo went on.

Cringe. That had got her. 'Oh,' said Maisie uncomfortably, her expression hard to read.

'Small world, right? I was surprised, too. Even more so when Bill said a few things about you and your mum. How you've not been getting on. How things have been difficult. And I just wondered—'

Maisie's hackles shot up; sensing sympathy – or, worse, pity – she bristled with defiance. 'I get it. You think that because I've had an argument with my mum it's made me go out trying to nick some sunglasses.' She held her hands up sarcastically, her top lip curling. 'Whoa. You got me there, Sherlock.'

'No,' said Jo, trying to keep her patience. 'I was going to say, I wondered how much your dad knew about all that. About what's been happening at home.' She could see mutiny setting in on the girl's face, so she wheeled out the big guns, quick. 'What with the police getting called out, that sort of thing.' Boom.

Maisie's eyes flashed with anger. 'Fuck's sake,' she growled. 'Who *is* this nosy old git anyway? Why is it any of his business?'

'He said the whole street knew about it,' Jo said mildly. 'I got the feeling he didn't *want* to make it his business, but . . .'

Maisie glowered. 'Yeah, right. Sounds like it.'

There was a moment of silence, then Jo tried again. 'Look, I didn't say anything to your dad, but maybe you should. If you're not happy, tell him. Because if the police have got involved, it's only a matter of time before word gets to social services and –'

'Don't. You don't . . . You don't understand,' Maisie said, but the fight seemed to have deserted her all of a sudden, her voice low, shoulders slumping.

'I might, you know,' said Jo in her gentlest voice. 'Try me.' A few seconds passed when she could sense Maisie struggling with her own emotions and then, at last, the girl seemed to unbend.

'She's just finding it hard,' she began, so quietly Jo had to strain to hear. 'Without Dad. And then she split up with Mike, her boyfriend.'

'Ah,' said Jo, and waited.

A whole minute passed without either of them speaking

and then Maisie went on, as if she couldn't hold it in any longer. 'She gets drunk sometimes,' she mumbled, speaking more to the table than to Jo. 'And she keeps . . . forgetting things.'

'What sort of things?'

'Like school things. Dinner money. Sometimes she forgets to pick me up from places and I can't get home. It's not on purpose or anything,' she added defensively, then shrugged. 'She's always really sorry.'

'Have you tried saying any of this to your dad?'

'Well, I can't, can I, cos you're always there,' Maisie snapped.

Touché. 'I guess I have been lately,' Jo realized, remembering what India had said about Maisie probably fearing that her dad would love his girlfriend more than her. Perhaps this was really what it boiled down to. 'And you need your space with him.'

'Well, duh,' said Maisie, but it was said without her usual level of waspishness at least.

'Don't you *duh* me!' cried Jo, pantomiming crossness, hands on her hips. Was it her imagination or did Maisie's lips twitch, ever so slightly, as if she might be on the verge of a smile? And then she was remembering too late how, with the mean girls at school that Maisie had reminded her of, there had so often been some unpleasant story or other in the background. An abusive uncle. A bitter parental divorce. A sibling in and out of prison. Nobody's life was black and white. 'Look, I'm sorry,' she went on. 'We've not got off to a great start, me and you, but I'm not trying to take your dad away from you at all. I swear. I'm going to get on the case and find a new flat to rent soon; me moving in was only ever a temporary arrangement.'

Maisie sucked up more of her shake and then muttered, to Jo's surprise, 'I'm sorry I broke your bird. I was just feeling mad with everything.'

Oh my goodness. Talk about a breakthrough. Jo had to stop herself from checking out of the window for a flying pig flapping by. 'It's okay,' she replied quietly. 'We've all been there. And I appreciate the apology.'

Silence fell again, apart from the slurping of Maisie's shake as she pushed the straw around for the last few mouthfuls. Any minute now, she'd be up from her seat and this moment would be over. Jo thought hard about what she wanted to say before that happened. 'You know . . . I had a difficult relationship with my mum, growing up. I still do, actually. She drives me and my sister completely mad, even now. I'm not saying your mum's like that,' she went on hurriedly. 'But I do know that, unlike me, you've got a great dad who absolutely adores you. He'd hate to think you were unhappy and didn't want him to know about it. Plus . . .' She poked her straw around in her own shake, bracing herself for rejection. 'Plus you've got me to talk to as well, remember.

If you want.' She kept going before Maisie could shoot her down. 'And I'm a nurse and, believe me, I've heard *everything* by now. I am one hundred per cent unshockable. We nurses are good listeners and we can keep secrets, too.'

Maisie tipped her head on one side. 'Does that mean you won't tell Dad about what happened in Primark?'

Jo smiled at her. She'd walked right into that one, hadn't she? 'As long as you talk to him about how you feel – properly, I mean – then I'm going to be, like, Primark? What the hell happened in Primark? I don't remember anything happening in Primark.'

And then the tension left Maisie's face and she was smiling, too. Just a small, shy smile – grudging almost, as if she'd rather not be doing it, but a genuine one nonetheless. 'All right,' she said. 'Deal.'

Jo finished her drink. 'Tell you what,' she said. 'I'm going to ring your dad right now and say to him that I'm going to spend the rest of the day with my sister. Tonight as well, actually. And I'll probably take her out for Sunday lunch tomorrow, seeing as she's pregnant and hungry all the time. So why don't you go round there this afternoon and hang out with him for a bit? Without me cramping your style?'

She got a proper smile for that. A real shiny-eyed grateful smile, and a nod of the head. 'Thanks,' said Maisie. Was that a bridge being built between them? wondered Jo, daring to hope. The weapons-down ending of a bitter civil war? It was a step forward, anyway; a moment of mutual understanding. A nudge, too, for her to crack on with flat-hunting sooner rather than later.

A burst of optimism flared inside Jo as she fished in her bag for her phone and dialled Rick's number; with Maisie peering into a pocket mirror and cack-handedly applying more eyeliner while she waited. Goodness, was that even a prickle of *affection* for the girl that Jo was experiencing all of a sudden? Whatever the case, this was, most definitely, a start.

Chapter Twenty-Nine

Eve had spent so long feeling as if Death was one step behind her that as she was wheeled towards the operating theatre, she half-expected the Grim Reaper himself to come trotting along too, scythe slung over a shoulder, that ghastly skeletal smirk. *We meet at last*; one bony finger crooked and beckoning. *Your time is up.*

'You're not going to die,' Neil had told her categorically, as had all the doctors and nurses she had spoken to. 'The odds are in your favour, love. We're going to beat this.'

'Yes, but . . .' She managed to stop herself from pointing out that this wasn't necessarily the end of it. From what she had dared read, there was a chance that, when the pathologist analysed the breast tissue that had been removed from her, he or she might find an area of invasive cancer cells lurking there, as well as the DCIS. For all she knew, the cancer might already have snaked insidiously into her lymph nodes, which would mean . . .

No. Stop, Eve. She really did have to call time on these

Internet searches. As important as it was to be well informed about your own body, you could know too much sometimes. You could scare yourself to death.

She had tried not to make too big a deal of the operation to the girls, first thing that morning. The school holidays had just begun and India had arrived in order to pick them up for the day. 'I'm going to be *fine*, don't worry. I'll almost certainly be back here for tea, and it'll all be over,' she told them in the most bright and cheerful voice she could manage. 'Now you just have a lovely day and don't even *think* about me, okay? Dad will keep you posted. Are your phones charged? Well done. Anyone need the loo before you go?'

'Mum, don't fuss,' said Sophie, squirming out of her embrace. She'd requested a serious haircut recently to mark the end of primary school, and all her lovely locks were now gone, reduced to a cute, quirky elfin haircut that made her cheekbones stand out and her eyes look huge and fawn-like. No more plaits, no more bunches, no more winding long strands of it around her thumb to suck. Eve couldn't quite come to terms with this new grown-up version of her daughter, more spiky, less cuddly. Every day it was as if the invisible threads between them tautened a little tighter as Sophie tried to yank herself away.

'I'm not fussing, I'm—'

'You *are* fussing, actually, but it's okay,' Grace said, her head almost reaching Eve's shoulder as she at least gave her a goodbye hug, her cloud of long dark hair so similar to Eve's, falling down her back. 'Don't worry, Mum, we'll be all right. Don't *you* even think about *us*, okay?'

'That told you,' India said as Eve blinked away the sudden dampness in her eyes that had appeared. (Since when did her eldest girl become so mature and empathetic anyway?)

'We'll neither of us think of the other,' Eve promised jokily, giving Grace a last grateful squeeze, knowing already this wouldn't be possible. 'See you later. Be good. Text Dad, won't you, if you—'

'Muuum!' Sophie cried, throwing up her hands with flamboyant melodrama. And then they'd gone, and Neil was checking that the back door was locked and telling her it was their turn, they'd better get a move on, and was she ready?

She hesitated in the hall, wanting to put her hands over her breasts protectively, suddenly scared of the knife that awaited her. 'I hope I don't end up looking too . . . butchered,' she said in a low voice, as he stood, one hand on the handle of the front door. 'I hope I still feel like me, at the end. Like a woman.'

'I'm sure you will,' he told her. 'Feel like you, I mean. They said they would only need to take out a small amount, didn't they?'

'I know, but there's not that much there to spare in the

first place,' she replied, grimacing. She took another step forward, then stopped again. 'I just keep thinking I might never wear a bikini again. I might not even want to look at myself in the mirror again. And you might not fancy me, either. How shallow is that?'

He walked back and put his arms around her and she held herself very still and tight because she knew, if he started being kind, that she was probably going to end up crying again. 'It's not shallow,' he said. 'I'm sure everyone in your position feels like that. It's scary. It's the unknown. But we can't do anything about it now, it's out of our control.'

She leaned against him, grateful for his solidity. 'That's the bit I like least of all,' she said, her voice small.

'I know it is. So let's just get through the op and see where we are, yeah? One step at a time.' He dropped a kiss on her head. 'Tell you what, when you feel like wearing a bikini again, I'll wear one too, and then nobody will even glance your way. Okay? But come on, we need to go. Are you ready?'

She gave a snuffling little laugh at the image of him trying to squeeze into one of her bikinis and felt a tiny bit better. 'I'm ready,' she said. And in a funny sort of way, once she was in the car and they were heading towards the hospital, once she was changing into a hospital gown and the doctors were preparing to begin the localization procedure that preceded the surgery, she did actually *feel* ready. It was a cliché, sure, when people talked about battling cancer as if engaging in some kind of war, but as she was wheeled down the corridor towards the operating theatre, she felt, for the first time, that she understood why this metaphor was used. Because she *wanted* to fight. She wanted it out of her, stopped in its tracks, and she had this whole battalion of skilled, experienced doctors and nurses on her side. You think you can take me on, cancer? You think can mess me up? Well, screw you, she thought defiantly. You are not welcome in my body. So you can bugger right off.

'You okay, love?' the nurse asked, as they waited for the lift, and for an awful moment Eve thought she might have said all of that out loud.

She managed a small, polite smile. 'I'm okay,' she confirmed.

The surgery, while not exactly a pleasant experience, was over fairly swiftly at least, and Eve and Neil were back home that same evening, tired but relieved that it was behind them. It was the next part of the process, the recovery, that was to prove more tiresome. Having always been a very healthy sort of person, only ever going into hospital twice before, to have the girls, and then bouncing back quickly each time, Eve had assumed she'd return to her usual busy, efficient lifestyle as soon as possible when it came to dealing with this, too.

'You'll hardly notice I'm gone,' she had assured her boss, Frances, outlining her plans to fit in radiotherapy sessions around her work, and catching up later in the evenings if necessary. Frances seemed less convinced, urging Eve to take at least a week off following her op, and refusing to be drawn on the radiotherapy issue, maintaining a 'Let's play it by ear' approach. 'The most important thing is that you have enough time to recuperate and heal,' she had said. 'In this instance, clients come second. We can rearrange your workload, it's not a problem.'

Recognizing the glint in her boss's eyes that said she was absolutely not about to budge, Eve had agreed eventually, not wanting to argue, although privately she had scoffed at Frances for being so uncharacteristically soft. When, knowing her, she'd be back in the office a day after the op – you just wait. That would show Frances that she was no lightweight.

Her own flesh and blood had other ideas, however. Eve had not expected to feel so utterly drained of energy, both physically and emotionally, while she waited for the results to be returned from the pathologist's lab. She was tender and sore, she couldn't sleep well because her poor left breast throbbed like a hot pulse if she accidentally rolled over onto it, and it was a huge effort simply to drag herself out of bed.

'So don't,' Jo told her firmly, one afternoon when she'd popped round to visit. '*Don't* drag yourself out of bed. Your body is telling you it needs to rest. You've been through a lot, Eve. Go back to bed.'

Eve had never liked being told what to do, not even by a best friend. 'But—' she protested, on the verge of listing that she had the girls to think about, the house was a mess, she needed to order an online supermarket shop . . .

'No buts,' Jo interrupted, holding a finger up before Eve could voice any of this. 'You're not so important that the world's about to stop spinning just because you stay in bed. Off you go. I'll run the Hoover round and the girls can sort the laundry out. Do you want me to bring you up a cup of tea?'

There was no arguing with Jo, when she was in full nursing mode. There was no arguing with India, either, who had wangled a spare key from Neil and came and went, bringing bags of groceries and whisking the girls away on day-trips like a small bossy domestic angel. Laura, too, batch-cooked lasagnes and soups and crumbles, filling the freezer with neatly labelled foil dishes and dropping off baskets of luxury moisturizers and bath cremes that she'd smuggled from work. Eve could have wept with gratitude, she really could, except she was so wrung out with tiredness that even weeping seemed like an effort. But she was thankful for it all. Humbled, too, by their visible and continuing displays of friendship. They were the best, no doubt about it.

As for Neil and the girls, it was fair to say that they were totally rising to the challenge of her being out of action, dealing with the day-to-day running of the house far more competently than she had ever given them credit for. Okay, so Grace's idea of how to make up the beds was still quite a distance from the crisp hospital corners that Eve had perfected over the years, and she had to bite her tongue practically every night when Neil stacked up the dishwasher in a less effective way than her preferred method, but . . . Well. Perhaps it didn't really matter all that much, at the end of the day. Not as much as she'd once thought.

Besides, was it her imagination or did the girls seem to be . . . well, growing up pretty brilliantly, actually, with their new responsibilities and independence? Sophie had discovered a new talent when it came to cooking and was busily working her way through Eve's *Nigella Express* book. 'Seared Salmon and Singapore Noodles tonight, Mum!' she could be heard to say, shaking the sizzling contents of a pan like a pro. Did Neil, too, seem glad of the chance to be looking after her for once, to find new gentle ways to show that he cared, with a hot-water bottle here, and a downloaded podcast there? Plus, without Eve in the background tsk-ing and saying 'Oh, let *me* do it', when he fumbled around the washing-machine controls, he had mastered its temperamental nature now, all by himself. In fact he had even taken to the black mildewy marks around the rubber seal of the door with white vinegar over the weekend, having read a useful tip on the side of the detergent packet.

Maybe, just maybe, Jo had a point. The world *was* still turning and the house hadn't fallen down without her there at the helm. Had Eve grossly underestimated her family? Had they been complicit in allowing her to?

Oh, this was a brave new world all right. A changed new world, which was scary and uncertain, with the possibility of darker clouds yet to come on the horizon – but a world, nonetheless, where she had been shown that she was loved and cared for. Where the laundry still got done and the dinner was still put on the table, albeit with just about every single utensil and pan needing to be washed afterwards. But, really, you couldn't ask for more than that, could you?

Chapter Thirty

'This train will shortly be arriving in Newcastle. All passengers for Newcastle, please alight here. Newcastle, your next station stop, in approximately two minutes.'

Yes, love, we get it, Newcastle – no need to bang on, Laura thought, heaving herself up from her seat with a little *Oof* noise. She was coming up to seventeen weeks pregnant now and still only had a modest bump, but she was really enjoying playing up to the novelty of carrying her own tiny passenger, putting a hand in the small of her back whenever she had to stand up for any length of time, and updating everyone in her office on just how hungry, tired, sweaty or flatulent she happened to be feeling at random moments. ('Too much information,' Jim kept telling her unhappily, but she honestly didn't care.)

The train doors swished open and she stepped onto the platform. Just before five o'clock: perfect timing, she thought, seeing the large digital clocks overhead. It was the last Friday in July, rather chilly and grey for the time of year, and she had taken the afternoon off work in order to catch the train north to see Matt. Jo had made no bones about what a badly thought-through idea this was, in her eyes – 'What if he's got plans?' – but Laura had decided not to phone ahead to arrange anything. She wanted to surprise him, to see the look on his face, when he saw her waddling towards him, bump first.

'Of course he won't have plans, he doesn't have any mates up there,' she'd scoffed in reply. 'Look, let me do it my way, all right? Don't argue with a pregnant woman.' (She loved saying that. In fact, Jo was threatening to get a T-shirt made up with those very words emblazoned across the front, because according to her, Laura had been saying it quite a lot. Whatever. There were worse catchphrases, right? Besides, it was extremely good advice.)

'Make sure you get an open return ticket, that's all, in case you end up staying over,' Jo had said, tapping her nose annoyingly, unable to resist the last word. 'If you know what I mean.'

In truth, the main reason Laura hadn't phoned Matt in advance was because, right up until the last minute, she thought she might change her mind and bottle out. Not because she didn't want to tell him her news – of course she did – but because she was scared that he might not smile when he saw her. Or, worse, that he would see her bump and his face would be like, *Oh, shit*. Jo might seem convinced that Laura and Matt were going to have this amazing joyful reunion, running towards each other in slow motion like in some cheesy romcom, but Laura felt too apprehensive to start counting any chickens. After all, he'd said to her face that he had fallen out of love with her, hadn't he? He'd said he thought they were done. And a baby was definitely not some form of magic glue that could stick together broken bridges and create a perfectly restored marriage – ta-dah! No cracks!

I think we've reached the end of the road, Laura, he'd said. *Don't you? Deep down?* There was no baby in the world that could miraculously delete words like that from a woman's brain.

Oh God. Please let this be all right. Please let him be happy about the news. She couldn't bear the thought of him turning her away in dismissal: *I don't want you OR your baby, all right?* Especially not after a two-and-a-half-hour train journey, when she was dying for a wee and some proper food.

Exiting the station, she took a few deep breaths, then headed for the taxi rank. Come *on*, she ordered herself. Positive thoughts. This was *Matt*. He was a thoroughly decent person. Just because they had split up did not mean he would have turned into an unfeeling monster. He would know just how much a healthy pregnancy meant to her.

A short while later, the taxi driver had taken her through

the magnificent Victorian streets of the city centre and out to the Quayside where the Millennium Bridge curved like a white harp across the Tyne a short distance away. 'Here y'are, pet,' said the driver, pulling on the handbrake.

Here she was indeed, she thought, paying his fare and then perching purposefully on a cold stone wall outside Matt's office building, a breeze buffeting its way up the street from the grey river. Here she was in Newcastle, waiting for her ex-husband to walk out through that very door so that she could tell him he was going to be a father. It all felt very dramatic, like something from a soap opera. She was half-expecting to hear a crescendo of music building around her as she waited for the moment, the *duff-duff* of an *EastEnders* cliffhanger as she dropped the bombshell. Then she found herself distractedly hoping she wasn't going to get piles from sitting here on this freezing wall for too much longer, which rather took away something from the whole scene. (Piles! That was one pregnancy side-effect she was most definitely hoping to avoid.)

Five minutes dragged breathlessly by. Then another five. Laura's self-willed positive thoughts began to slide slowly into doubt. What if, she thought despondently, she was too late because the company let their staff go early on a Friday afternoon? What if she was sitting here and Matt had already gone, off to some bar, celebrating the start of the weekend with colleagues, or back to his miserable bedsit on his own? (She couldn't know for sure it *was* a miserable bedsit, obviously, but she had been picturing it that way. With damp in the back wall and the smell of mildew and mothballs, and tobacco stains on the ceilings.) *I told you so!* Jo sighed in her ear. *Didn't I say you should have phoned him?*

But wait – here was someone leaving now, she noticed, brightening as the door of the building opened at last. The office block was set twenty metres or so back from the road, and Laura heaved herself off the wall and skulked on the pavement, trying to look unobtrusive as two suited women carrying laptop bags emerged down the path, their cheerful voices carrying on the breeze. Ah – and another man behind them, too, talking into a mobile phone and striding onto the pavement with swift Friday-night steps. Perhaps there was still hope for Matt's appearance, after all.

The trickle of people soon became a gush. Clusters of employees poured out, many of them discussing which pubs they were heading to, while Laura loitered faux-casually, scanning face after face. No, no, no. No. Still no. And then, finally, the door opened again and her heart gave a jump because there he was: Matt, just as she'd seen him so many times before in his grey Marks & Spencer suit and favourite red tie. His Friday tie, as she'd teased him in the past, and her face softened, remembering. It was so strange to see him here, out of context, in this new city for which he'd left her behind.

She took a step forward, a hesitant smile on her face, one hand ready to wave . . . but then froze as he stepped out of the building and she realized he was turning to look affectionately down at a woman beside him. A beautiful woman, moreover, with black ringletty curls and cherry-red lipstick, way bolder than any shade Laura would dare wear. She gulped, her breath catching as she saw that they were laughing together, walking very close to one another as they came down the front two steps and . . . Oh God. And his hand had shyly found hers. They were *holding hands*.

No, she thought, staring, hardly able to breathe. He'd met someone else already? The thought had not even occurred to her. Was she really so forgettable that after mere weeks Matt had put her, his *wife*, out of his mind?

Every instinct was screaming at her to just turn and go, to put her head down and get out of there fast, before he saw her. But she couldn't move because she kept thinking: no. Wait. There must be a mistake. She must have got this wrong. And then it was too late to turn and go, because his eyes suddenly widened in surprise, he dropped the ringletty woman's hand, and his mouth was forming the shape of her name. '*Laura?*'

She folded her arms across her chest, smarting with dismay. Here she was in a new teal-coloured wrap dress that everyone at work had said really brought out the colour of her eyes, and she had curled her hair especially, and bothered with some fancy strappy sandals even though they made her feet hurt after ten minutes, but all of a sudden she felt like a fat old frump compared to Matt's new friend, in her red lipstick and stylish pale-grey shift dress.

'Someone you know?' the woman said, her gaze lighting on Laura with interest as they drew level. She was nearly as tall as Matt and had long shapely legs, worst luck, and Laura felt her face burn under the scrutiny.

'Um,' said Matt, his face turning red, too, as he looked from one woman to the other. 'This is Laura,' he said. 'Um. Laura, Elaine. El, do you want to go ahead with the others?' He gave an awkward shrug. 'I'll give you a ring.'

El? thought Laura, her mind freefalling. *This* was Elaine, his new boss? She gulped, trying to digest this development. From what Matt had said, she'd always imagined the mysterious Elaine as being in her fifties, a matronly, overbearing sort of woman. Not this . . . this toned, glamorous *fox*.

Elaine shrugged coolly, then touched her fingertips first to her own lips and then to Matt's cheek in an annoying coquettish manner, before leaving. Presumably her not-so-subtle means of staking a claim, Laura thought, stunned. *He's mine now, bitch. Hands off.*

'Oh my God,' she croaked, trying to take it in, shock still reverberating through her as Elaine walked away without looking back. Matt and Elaine, eh? It all made sense now.

How could she have been so stupid, so blind? How could she not have guessed?

Matt was looking simultaneously confused and guilty. 'What are you doing here, Laura?'

'How long has that been going on?' she countered, miserably. Because how could he be happy about the news she had for him now, when he was seeing someone else? How was this ever going to work out? 'Is that why you left?'

'Laura—' He broke off, crestfallen. 'It's not like that.' He sighed, his eyes drifting after Elaine, who had caught up with some of the other staff members, linking arms with two blokes so that they proceeded along in a chain. Matt wanted to be there with them too, she could tell, not here on a pavement with his angry ex-wife.

Oh hell, she thought, watching his face. Arriving unannounced like this *had* been a mistake. A fool's errand. And the sooner she was back on the train home again, with a consolatory chicken pasty and a muffin, the better. 'I won't keep you,' she said frostily. 'I just thought it would be courteous of me to let you know in person that I'm expecting our child in January.' She waited a beat for his reaction, but his face was completely blank. 'Yes, it was a surprise to me, too,' she went on. 'And yes, it *is* yours and is very healthy, by the way – if you care, that is. But I'll let you get on with your new mates now, anyway. See you around.'

She made as if to turn – *Don't mess with a pregnant*

woman! – but he had taken her arm and was steering her gently back. 'Laura . . . wait,' he said. His gaze dipped to her belly as if seeking proof, and then back up to her face. 'I can't believe – God! January, did you say? *Whoa.*' He blinked, emotions flickering across his face. She could see panic there, and questions. Doubts. Bewilderment. But was he pleased, too?

'I know it's a lot to take in, out of thc blue,' she said, relenting a touch. 'I couldn't believe it, either, at first. I'd fainted a couple of times and went to the doctor, assuming I had some virus. Never dreaming for a minute that . . .'

'Do you want to keep it?' he blurted out, and her jaw nearly hit the floor.

'Do I want to *keep* it?' she echoed, aghast that he even had to ask. Was this the same man who'd held her hand in the hospital after the miscarriages? Who'd seen her at her lowest and most despairing? 'Keep our baby, after all those years of wanting one, and all the traumas we went through?'

'All right, all right.' He put his hand up. 'I was only asking.' He shifted from foot to foot. 'I suppose you want some money.'

Again, shock floored her. Why was he saying these things? 'Matt . . . this is your *child*,' she reminded him, dumbfounded. 'Your son or daughter. *Our* son or daughter. Do you not care? Are you saying you don't want to be involved – you just want to fob me off with some *cash*?' It hurt, actually. It really hurt. She took a step back from him, reeling. 'I can't believe you even—'

'I *do* care!' he blustered. 'Of course I care.' He broke off, scratching his head and looking so awkward and weak – and *useless*, quite frankly – that it was all Laura could do not to thump him one. Come *on*, Matt. Get a grip, will you?

'Look. Let's not do this in the middle of the street,' he went on after a moment, reaching out to touch her arm again. 'I'm sorry. I'm saying all the wrong things, but it's only because this is so unexpected. Like a dream.'

'It's not a dream,' Laura said fiercely.

'I know, I know! It's real – and you're . . . you're *pregnant*, God, and I'm . . .' He shook his head as if trying to rattle the reality down into his brain. Then he seemed to pull himself together. 'Let's go and have a drink and something to eat. Talk about this. Are you hungry?'

It was pretty much the first thoughtful and vaguely nice thing he'd said to her in this whole exchange. 'Yes,' she mumbled. 'I'm always hungry.'

'Right. Well, let's go to Malmaison then,' he said. 'It's just a few minutes away, and everyone from work's headed on into town, so we won't be disturbed. My treat.' The news was sinking in now, she could tell, and a dazed sort of smile broke onto his face at last, like the sun straggling through after a thunderstorm. 'Do you mind if I . . . ?' he said, one hand hovering tentatively above her belly.

She shook her head, feeling weirdly shy, as if this was a complete stranger asking, rather than her actual husband. 'Be my guest,' she said, enjoying his expression of marvel as he put a hand on her bump and gently pressed. 'Harder than you expect, isn't it?' she commented after a moment. 'Like a drum.'

'Yeah,' he said, their eyes meeting. 'Wow, Laura. And everything's . . . all right? You've been feeling okay?' he asked as he took his hand away and they started walking down the road together.

Ah, *there* he was, she thought in sudden relief: the man she'd been married to, the one who'd always looked out for her. He had shrugged off his new Newcastle self like a jacket that didn't suit him, and was back. 'I'm really okay,' she assured him. 'I think I even felt a kick the other day, although Jo said it could just be wind. But yeah. Everything's fine. I had a scan and he or she is looking good. I'll show you a picture, once we're inside.'

Perhaps it was the breeze gusting in his eyes making them water, but there was definitely a glistening there as they waited to cross the road. 'I'm going to be a dad,' he said, still in that shocked sort of wonder, and he gave a little laugh. 'I'm actually going to be a dad.'

She smiled up at him. 'You're actually going to be a dad,' she agreed.

Chapter Thirty-One

Dear Mr and Mrs Goldsmith

I hope you don't mind me writing to you. My name is India Westwood, and I just wanted to say how sorry I was to hear about your daughter. She sounded such a vibrant, loving person; you must have been so very proud of her.

I feel I also owe you an explanation. I am the person who came to the hospital with all those random gifts for Alice back in May. You probably wondered why someone would turn up with bag-loads of things for her when they didn't even know her. At the time I knew I was behaving oddly, but I felt compelled to do it. I hope you will understand why.

The thing was, years ago, I had a daughter called Alice, too. She would have been almost exactly the same age as your Alice. My Alice died when she was very, very tiny and I thought I had dealt with her loss at the time, but really I just buried all my pain somewhere deep down and out of sight, and kept it hidden this whole while. But when I heard about your Alice, it brought everything back to me – all the sadness and anguish and guilt. I felt overwhelmed. I stopped thinking straight. I am a thirty-nine-year-old woman with three lovely children and a great husband, but all of a sudden I was eighteen and obliterated by hurt again.

I've never stopped thinking about my Alice. I've often wondered what sort of a person she would be, what she would be doing, if she'd have fallen in love, whether she'd have travelled, if she was musical or athletic or a clown or . . . You get the gist. And so I bought all those things for your daughter because I couldn't buy them for my own girl. I know this probably sounds stupid, but it did bring me some comfort. And I hoped desperately that your Alice would pull through, and I just wanted to do something positive, I suppose.

By all accounts, your Alice was a remarkable young woman: the sort of person any parent would love to have as a daughter. I'm just so sorry that you have lost her, and sincerely hope my actions have not caused you any further distress.

Very best wishes

India Westwood

This whole business of coming clean, of lifting the lid and shining a light into the darkest corners of your soul, was cathartic, but also exhausting, India thought, folding the letter neatly in thirds and then stuffing it into an envelope. Would she post it? Perhaps not. She'd written it more for herself than for the poor grieving Goldsmiths; they had other things on their minds right now, after all. But in a strange sort of way, the act of sitting there, trying to find the words and expressing herself in writing, was soothing in itself. Bit by bit, she was doing her best to make sense of the world.

Since her evening with Robin, it was as if a giant hand had taken hold of her life and shaken it so thoroughly that nothing looked quite as it used to do. Her long-held feelings of regret about Alice seemed a shade less dark and all-encompassing than they had before, now that she'd voiced them, setting them free into the pub with him that night. Conversely, the way she felt about Dan and the children suddenly seemed much clearer and easier: she loved them, simple as that. For all her what-ifs and doubts, she realized now that they were the very centre of her world, contributing so much to who she was as a person. She had been hugging them all a lot recently, feeling renewed gratitude for them and their adorable, funny, maddening, messy and frequently disgusting ways.

Something had shifted in terms of her attitude towards

work, too, because she realized with a sharp certainty that she had fallen out of love with Mini Music classes quite some time ago and that, goodness, it had been the most tremendous relief to be packing everything away at the end of the summer term, ready for a lovely long break. Into the box went the tambourines and the maracas and drums, and she wondered if this might be a good time to move on, make a change. Would it be the end of the world if she sold the franchise to another person and took her career in a different direction? Probably not. She was only thirty-nine after all. Still young!

She and Robin had agreed that it was best not to keep in touch, and she was confident this was the right decision. He vanished from her Facebook contacts overnight, and she found that she wasn't too sorry. Of course she would always have a soft spot for him, first love and all that, but after the tumult of angst and emotion they'd been through, she wasn't sure they'd ever be able to enjoy an easy friendship now. 'No hard feelings,' they'd said as they hugged goodbye one last time. It was a good way to part, as if they'd made their peace and were at last ready to move forward, without the other's shadow dogging their respective paths.

Now the only thing left to do was to bare her soul to Dan, to pluck up the courage and share the whole story with him at last. Which was easier said than done, having kept the secret folded up inside herself for the fifteen whole years they'd been together. It wasn't exactly a nice story to tell.

She had bided her time, dealing with all the mayhem that the end of term inevitably brought: sports days, summer fairs, school trips and what-have-you, as well as organizing a rota with some other mums to help out with Grace and Sophie while Eve recovered from surgery. India was going to make this a good summer, she had vowed, full of fun stuff: long afternoons in the park, home-made ice lollies in the freezer, a trip to the trampoline centre, baking sessions . . . She'd never be grumpy, she'd always be cheerful, she would count her blessings and enjoy her own children, and definitely not be one of those mums who had a permanent countdown going for when school would reopen again. Well, perhaps that was a bit optimistic. She would try, though, at least.

Anyway, they were off for a fortnight's holiday in the Lake District first, which was pretty much her favourite place in the whole world. It always marked a hiatus, this two-week break every year in the same rented cottage, where the rest of their lives receded and it was just the five of them, on the boat across Windermere, throwing themselves into Coniston Water and shrieking with the cold, wandering into Ambleside to stock up with paper bags of flavoured fudge, a new book from Fred's or hot pasties for lunch. It was where they seemed to laugh most as a family, even if it rained; it was where she felt fondest of them all.

And so one night, once the children were spark out in their beds after a long looping walk around Loughrigg Fell, India set up two deckchairs in the sleepy quiet of the back garden for herself and Dan and poured them each a beer. It felt like the right time to tell him, beneath the big wide skies, so far from the bustle and noise of home.

'Listen, Dan, I know I've been a bit of a maniac lately,' she began with a nervous laugh, 'but there's a reason for that. And it's something I probably should have told you about years ago, but I've never quite had the guts.' Deep breath. Here we go. And then, before he could make a quip or interrupt, she launched into the story, head-first, and told him everything. Robin. The pregnancy. His disappearance. Her terrible, heart-breaking decision. And how tiny Alice had been born and then died, with barely a whisper of breath in between.

'Oh, love,' he said to her with such kindness, she could feel herself begin to break a little inside, and she had to hurry on with the tale before she lost her thread, to see it all the way through to the epilogue. The epilogue, that was, concerning the other Alice, and how desperately India had wanted her to live. How, for a crazy few weeks, she'd been caught up in the Goldsmith family's story, as if it was hers, too; how hard she had taken the loss when this other Alice had eventually slipped away. 'So . . . yeah. That's it,' she finished lamely, not daring to look at him.

He didn't reply for a moment, just put his hand on hers and gave her fingers a squeeze. 'You know . . . I kind of knew all along there was something,' he said slowly. 'Your mum made this off-guard comment when George was born – a *Thank God this one's all right* sort of thing, and I always wondered. It's not something you can really ask, though. I thought: if she wants to tell me, she will.'

'Eventually,' India agreed, poking the tufty grass with her bare foot. 'Eleven years later, after a weird summer meltdown. But I got there in the end.'

He squeezed her hand again. 'I'm glad you told me,' he said.

'And you don't . . . hate me?' she asked in a small voice.

'Oh God, love, of course I don't. How could I hate you? Come here,' he said, shuffling his deckchair right over beside hers, so that he could put his arms properly around her and hold her. He smelled clean and good and faintly beery – her husband, in four words, she thought to herself in amused affection. 'I feel sad for you, that's all. That you had to go through that on your own, when you were so young. It must have been bloody awful. Do you feel better for talking about it?'

She leaned against him, her clean, good, faintly beery man, and felt comforted by his proximity, his steadiness.

'Much better. Thanks. And being here is great, too. Puts stuff in perspective.'

'Being here is always great,' he agreed, his arms still tight around her.

They sipped their beers and she let her breath whistle out, feeling her shoulders sink, the tension departing. 'I feel like I've taken my eye off the ball a bit lately,' she confessed, 'and I'm sorry. I've been so tangled up with what might have been, all those parallel lives I kept obsessing over . . . I forgot to pay attention to my real life, to all of you. But that's going to change, okay? I've got my head straight about it again now.'

'Oh, Ind,' he said affectionately. 'Don't be daft. We're all still here, aren't we? Maybe that was just you getting your midlife crisis over early, that's all. Me, on the other hand – I'm planning to get one of them red sports cars and be done with it, for mine. None of this hand-wringing and "what-iffing" for me, I can tell you that much.' He nudged her and she smiled. He always knew how to lift a moment out of the emotional depths. Then he cleared his throat. 'Sounds a bit of a plonker, if you ask me, that Robin bloke,' he went on. 'Bit of a drama queen.'

'Yeah, he was,' she said, because obviously this was the only possible reply. He wasn't the jealous type, Dan, but all the same, it didn't hurt to make clear to one's other half the absolute snuffing-out of an old flame. 'It never would have worked, the two of us.'

'Especially when you went on to meet me, and realized what you'd been missing all that time,' he added, just for good measure, preening himself comically.

'Well, yeah, *exactly*,' she assured him.

He grinned at her and she knew it was going to be all right, that they would be okay. 'Talking of midlife crises, I've been thinking. I'm not sure I want to carry on doing Mini Music any more,' she went on. 'I think I'm done with "The Wheels on the Bus" and Miss Fucking Polly and her sodding dolly.'

'That's her full name, is it? The X-rated version?' He swigged his beer. 'Well, it's probably time you got a proper job anyway,' he said and she gave a snort. 'Try plumbing – get your hands dirty for a change. Earn a real living, one that doesn't involve nursery rhymes.'

She poked his ankle with her bare toe, knowing he was only teasing. 'That's what I love about you: you're so supportive of my career. Aren't I the lucky one?'

'I do my best,' he said. 'Seriously, though. Whatever makes you happy. Go back to college. Do something new. Run for prime minister. Whatever you fancy, love. I'll be right behind you.' He nudged his leg against hers and the innuendo in his words didn't elude her.

'Right behind me, eh?' She raised an eyebrow.

'If that's where you want me, yeah. Any time, babe.'

Maybe the beer had gone to her head or maybe it was the sheer relief of having told Dan her secret after so long, but India suddenly felt light-headed with love for him, for her good, kind husband. What was more, she could sense that reckless type of holiday lust bubbling up inside her, the sort that came from being far from home with your nearest and dearest, when there was evening sunshine gilding the world, and the certain knowledge that your children were all flat out asleep. When the night was still young.

She stood up and grabbed his hand. 'How about now?' she said.

'Stab it, Mum, just stab into it with the scissors. Harder than that! Why don't you let Dad do it?'

'What IS it?'

'Kit, stop pushing, you're standing on my foot.'

'I hope it's a ray-gun. Do you think it's a ray-gun, Mum?'

India was on her knees in the living room, slicing painstakingly through the thick layers of packing tape that sealed every edge of the long, rectangular package. Meanwhile her children were practically hopping up and down around her with impatience, jostling to see. 'It's probably not a ray-gun, Kit,' she said, pushing the hair out of her eyes. 'And thanks for the suggestion, George, but I think I can manage.'

'What if it's a droid? Our own droid! I hope it's like BB-8, a mini one, a really cute mini – ow! Don't hit me!'

'Guys!' India cried, rolling her eyes at Dan, who'd just come in with a coffee for her.

'Let your mother open her droid in peace,' he warned them.

They had been on the way back home from the holiday earlier that day, all freckled and sun-dusted, with whole bin bags of muddy laundry in the boot, when her mum had texted India to say that a large mysterious parcel had arrived for her, and did they want to stop off and pick it up en route? Needless to say, there had been only one answer to *that*.

The parcel had 'FRAGILE' stickers all over it, and India had absolutely no idea what it might be, or why it had been sent to her mum's house over in Cheetham Hill, where she'd grown up all those years ago. Then she cut through the last piece of tape and pulled back the lid and . . . Oh. Her eyes misted suddenly. Oh, he hadn't, had he?

There inside was what looked suspiciously like a violin case and a letter with her name on it. Robin's handwriting. Of course – he *would* send it to her old house, as he didn't know her current address. 'It's a violin,' she said stupidly.

Kit made a huffing sound. 'Boring!' he moaned, throwing himself onto the sofa.

'Why have you got a violin?' Esme asked, leaning forward and stroking the case. 'Can I open it, Mum?'

Dan was scratching his neck in a casual, I'm-not-bothered sort of way. Perhaps too casual, now that India looked more closely. 'I take it this is from old Lover-boy?' he asked, and India flushed.

'I think so,' she said guardedly. 'Yes, Es, you can unzip it. Very carefully now.' Her fingers felt clammy as she picked up the envelope and she wished she could scurry away somewhere private to read the contents, but knew that would only arouse Dan's suspicions. So she ran a finger under the flap to open it, pulled out a handwritten letter and read:

> *Dear India*
>
> *I know we said goodbye and that we wouldn't see each other again, but I've been feeling sad about you giving up your music. You were so brilliant, Ind. You had a real gift. I bet it's still there somewhere beneath all the layers, you know. So here – have a violin from me. It won't be as good as your old one but it's all I could afford, so I hope you can overlook any flaws.*
>
> *Until we met again, I had wasted so many years thinking myself hard done by, feeling bitter and angry, making wrong assumptions about you and what had happened. Without wanting to sound melodramatic, it coloured the way I treated my ex-wife and my kids, too, for which I feel ashamed.*

I'm going to sort it out, put things right with them, try again. So thanks for setting me straight. For the first time in ages, I feel optimistic. That things might be okay.

I'm glad everything worked out well for you anyway. You were always this golden, shining light of a girl, India. The sort of person everyone wanted to be with, who everyone loved. I wish you all the best, the happiest of lives. You deserve it. I'm sorry I let you down back in the day.

Do an old friend a favour, though, and give the violin another go, yeah? For me, but also for you.

All the best

Robin

She blinked and handed the letter wordlessly to Dan, because she knew he was dying to know what it said. And then she bent down to where Esme had unzipped the case to reveal a glossy, amber-coloured violin and pulled it out, the wood cool and smooth to the touch.

'Mum, can you *play* it?' George asked, fascinated. 'Can *you* play the *violin*?'

'I've probably forgotten everything,' she said, plucking the strings gently. 'And it's horrendously out of tune.' But then she lifted it to her shoulder and, without even having to think, her fingers were forming note positions on the instrument's slender neck, the muscle memory guiding them effortlessly into place as if they'd never been away. For a moment it was as if she was back in the small dusty practice room of her old school, just her and the music, hours lost amidst soaring, spiralling melodies. She'd have to get some decent rosin, she found herself thinking, see if she could download some kind of tuning app, order a load of sheet music . . .

George was still looking at her in astonishment. 'Yes,' she told him, feeling an unexpected little frisson of pleasure. Pride, too, that she might actually be able to confound her eldest son's low expectations of her, just this once. 'I can play the violin, George. And do you know what? I used to be pretty good at it, too.'

Chapter Thirty-Two

When her phone buzzed with an incoming text on Saturday morning, waking her up, Jo wasn't sure where she was at first. The filmy pink light was unfamiliar; not the usual dense darkness of Rick's bedroom with its thick blackout curtains, and the pillow smelled different. Blinking, her mind foggy, she peered short-sightedly at the looming shadowy shape over on the far wall, before the penny dropped. Of course – they were boxes of her possessions, yet to be unpacked, and she was in her new flat, having spent her very first night there. *Home*, as she had to start thinking of it.

'Hello,' she whispered into the room, hoping Rick wouldn't wake up and tease her for being sentimental about bricks and mortar. In truth, she had never been so happy to pick up a set of new keys in her life. Much as she'd enjoyed staying with him for so many weeks, it was only as she'd stepped across the threshold yesterday afternoon, with the 'Essentials' box in her arms (kettle, mugs, tea, coffee, biscuits), that she breathed in the scent of independence once more and realized how much she'd missed it. It had all been too much, too soon, the two of them, and now they could take a small step back, still dating and together, but each with their own precious space again.

Her eyes adjusted to the half-darkness and she smiled to herself as she gazed around at the tiny cast-iron fireplace, the beautiful old ceiling rose from which hung a bare light bulb (she'd get round to sorting out a lampshade soon), the vase of flowers on the mantelpiece, courtesy of India, who'd popped round with them, plus a bottle of Prosecco and a sheaf of leaflets for all the best takeaways in the area ('You'll thank me for this tonight – don't say I'm not good to you,' she'd said). The flat was on the second floor of a gorgeous old Victorian house just off Cross Street: handy for work, near all her friends, and only half an hour into the city to see Rick. She'd taken on a twelve-month rental and the landlord was the brother of her colleague, Alison, 'And he's totally not dodgy,' she had vowed. It was shaping up to be a pretty good move, in all.

Later that weekend she would pick up some paint samples and daub possible shades on these walls, she thought happily. Perhaps a nice soft blue or a sea green. She'd unpack all her kitchen bits and bobs, hang her clothes up in the wardrobe, rearrange the furniture in the living room, tune in the TV . . . oh, and just as soon as she got her Internet up and running, she would be downloading all her favourite cheesy TV programmes to watch in blissful peace, too. Face-pack on. Naffest pyjamas. Definitely ice cream.

Then she remembered her buzzing phone and groped around on the floor for it. Ah! A message from Laura: *Well, it's a beautiful morning here in Newcastle . . . ;-)*

'Oh my *God*,' said Jo, sitting bolt upright in bed as the implications of this filtered through. 'Yes. YES!'

Rick rolled over sleepily, opening one eye a crack. He'd helped her cart all her boxes in the day before, then they'd ordered in pizza (thanks, India) and he'd produced a bottle of champagne, which they'd had to drink out of mugs, because she hadn't been able to find the box with her wine glasses. Then they'd christened her new bath together, along with the Prosecco; a happy time, in short. 'Are you practising some weird *Harry Met Sally* thing there?' he murmured now, draping a hand over her thigh. 'Or are you just pleased to see me?'

'It's Laura,' Jo replied, glued to her phone as she opened the picture her sister had sent, which showed blue skies above a glittering river – the Tyne, presumably. 'She must have stayed over with Matt. Oh, this is the best news. I'm so happy!'

Ignoring her boyfriend's wandering hands, she typed a quick reply: *YESSSS! I knew it! Are you two back together?*

She beamed across at Rick, whose eyes were shut again, although by the way his fingers were stealthily inching their way up her body, she guessed that he wasn't *completely* asleep. 'That is so brilliant,' she sighed, snuggling further back into bed with him. 'Don't you just love a happy ending?'

'I'll tell you what would be the best kind of happy ending right now,' he mumbled, rolling on top of her.

Jo gave a muffled laugh from beneath the hot weight of him and then her phone buzzed again with a new text. She just had time to read the words *It's complicated* . . . onscreen, along with a load of seemingly random emojis – a baby, a house, a red lipstick? – before Rick had grabbed the phone from her hand and thrown it across the room.

'Hey!' she cried indignantly, but then his mouth was on hers and they were exchanging disgusting morning-breath tastes and laughing at how gross the other one was, and what complete and utter perverts they must be to find this remotely horny . . . and by then it somehow didn't seem to matter any more.

'That is the second time we've had sex in my flat,' she said breathlessly a while later, 'and I haven't even been in here a full day.'

'I know,' he said, lying flat on his back with his eyes shut once more. 'Good, isn't it? I think I might move in with you, if this is the standard rate around here.'

She laughed at the smirk on his face. They had reached a good place, the two of them, in the last week or so. Following her breakthrough with Maisie, Jo had given Rick and his daughter more space, choosing to absent herself tactfully by spending nights and weekend time with her sister and friends, so that nobody was cramping anybody else's style. Meanwhile, true to her promise, Maisie had confessed to Rick how difficult things had become living at home with Polly, telling him that the two of them had been arguing a lot, that Polly had maybe been drinking too much, and that there'd been 'a bit of trouble' when the police came out, following complaints from the neighbours about loud music and shouting. As a result, emergency talks had been held between Rick and Polly, involving heated words and recriminations apparently, before they'd calmed down, remembering that they both loved their daughter. After that, relations had become slightly more conciliatory.

A new arrangement had been drawn up so that everyone knew where Maisie was supposed to be on any given day; Rick would do more to help, Polly was going to ease up on the drinking and get herself organized. That was the plan, anyway, and who knew how things would pan out in reality – but at least they both cared enough to give it a try.

As for Jo and Maisie . . . the two of them were still a work in progress. Jo had kept to her side of the deal, conveniently 'forgetting' that the Primark incident had ever taken place, and, on the few occasions they'd seen each other since, they had been polite and civil to one another. No more name-calling. No more rudeness or answering back. No more resentment towards the other for merely existing, at least not outwardly anyway. A small step forward, in other words.

'Fancy a coffee?' she asked, standing up and then remembering her phone, tossed away onto the carpet, and that last mysterious text that had come in.

'Please,' Rick said, and Jo padded through to the kitchen, glancing down at the screen. In truth, she wasn't really au fait with emojis – smiley face, sad face, that was about her limit – but apparently her sister was more clued up, judging by the string of mini-pictures she'd included in her message.

A man, a woman, a cocktail glass – well, that seemed straightforward; Laura and Matt having a drink together, Jo supposed. Next was a suitcase, a baby, a red lipstick, a confused face, question marks . . .

Jo's own face twisted in confusion. Were they going away together? A holiday with the baby? You'd have thought there would be at least *one* smiling face if so, not to mention love-hearts galore. *It's complicated*, Laura had written gnomically, and although Jo typed back *Complicated how?*, no further explanation came. Hmm. *Ring me if you want to chat*, she typed, just as Rick appeared in the kitchen doorway, fully dressed.

'While you're making coffee, I'll nip out and scavenge the streets for breakfast ingredients,' he said cheerfully. 'Bread, eggs, beans, bacon, butter . . . anything else beginning with "b" while I'm there?'

'Um . . . beers? Joking. How about sausages? Sausages with a silent "b", that is?'

He grinned. 'Sausages with a silent "b" coming up,' he said, then vanished, only for his head to reappear around the door a second later. 'By the way,' he said, 'just so you know, this is totally me buttering you up, getting in your good books, because I forgot to tell you: I've promised to take Maisie out tonight. To some God-awful teen band or other, where I'm going to be the oldest person there by, like, several decades.' He looked so glum that she couldn't help laughing.

'Sounds fun.'

'Are you saying you want to go, too?' he asked hopefully. 'Because it can be arranged. You can totally come, too.'

'What, and spoil your dad-and-daughter evening? I wouldn't dream of it!' she cried, thinking happily of trashy catch-up TV and Häagen-Dazs. *Come to Mama . . .*

His face fell. 'I thought you might say that. Ah well. Tomorrow we'll do something, yeah? Just me and you. We could go to Blackpool or somewhere, be cheesy day-trippers.'

'Cool,' she said, spooning coffee granules into the mugs and smiling at the way his hair was cowlicking up from his head where he'd slept on it funny. God, he was adorable, he really was. If it wasn't for the fact that he was about to go and buy all sorts of lovely things for breakfast, she would totally be pouncing on him now and snogging that gorgeous face of his again.

Then an idea struck her. 'You know . . . you could ask Maisie if she fancies a cheesy day-trip, too, if you want. Maybe with a friend, so they can go off together on the scary rides while we try on Kiss Me Quick hats and buy lollipops shaped like penises.'

'Speak for yourself,' he told her, mock-indignantly, but then hesitated. 'Are you sure? About Maisie?'

'Yeah, why not?' she replied, feeling magnanimous. 'If she wants to, that is. Just a thought.' Then she bustled over to the stack of unopened boxes marked 'Kitchen Stuff' so that he couldn't see the goofy smile on her face, the pleasure she was experiencing from holding out that olive branch. It felt surprisingly great. 'Right, now to see if I can track down a frying pan before you come back with the provisions,' she said, changing the subject.

He was still there, head hanging around the door, watching her rip through the packing tape. 'I love you,' he said, and she looked up and beamed at him.

'I love you, too,' she said. 'And I'll love you even more when you bring home the bacon.'

And then he was gone, laughing, and she stood there, peering into her box of saucepans and mixing bowls and utensils, feeling as if this weekend was going to be very enjoyable indeed.

Chapter Thirty-Three

A week after her surgery, Eve and Neil were called back to the hospital in order for her to be given the pathologist's report. To say that she was a mess of nerves was a huge understatement. She'd barely slept the night before, dreading being told the worst. Without fail, the news had been bad each time so far. Would her luck have changed at last?

But this time the doctor had smiled as they sat down in his office. And this time it *was* good news: the pathologist was confident that the cancer was non-invasive, and that all the DCIS had been safely removed. 'The prognosis is positive,' the doctor told them, as Eve and Neil sat there holding hands in shocked, happy relief. Was that the old Grim Reaper melting away into the background, defeated this time? It did feel as if she'd been given a stay of execution, a second chance. 'Thank you,' whispered Eve gratefully, vowing there and then that she would appreciate and celebrate every hour, every day, from here on in.

Now there was the radiotherapy to get through and

although it wasn't exactly something to look forward to, it didn't hurt at least, she discovered, and was over quickly each time, the nursing staff being as kind and competent as you could wish for. It sounded churlish to complain that the biggest inconvenience was the getting to and from hospital every weekday. Her wounds were healing without infection, there was still some pain and discomfort, but really, in the grand scheme of things, these all seemed like small prices to pay. She was one of the lucky ones, after all.

Of course, nobody was given a free pass forever. Eve knew full well there was no guarantee she wouldn't get full-blown cancer eventually, especially as she'd learned that there was a 10 per cent chance of recurrence in the treated breast in years to come. If the last few months had taught her anything, though, it was that sometimes life was simply beyond your control. Sometimes you just had to roll with the punches. It had also shown her that she had people around her who would support her through anything – her own personal team of cheerleaders. And this had turned out to be immensely comforting.

Back she went to the office and, because she was still fundamentally Eve and was never going to stop loving having a good system in place, she drew up a comprehensive chart on which she factored in all her hospital appointments and engineered her workload accordingly.

'Listen, don't worry about organizing the team-building

away-day by the way, somebody else can sort that out,' Frances told her, but Eve shook her head and smiled.

'It's all right, I've actually had a bit of a brainwave about that,' she replied. 'Leave it to me.'

The next day at work Eve had just finished wrangling with a set of VAT returns, when the receptionist rang to tell her that a certain Lewis Mulligan had arrived for his appointment and was waiting downstairs. On time and everything, Eve noted, raising an eyebrow as she grabbed her notes and went to meet him.

She felt quite emotional as she saw him sitting there in one of his obscure-band T-shirts and jeans, a trainer-clad foot keeping time to whatever music he was listening to through his earbuds. He unhooked them when he saw her, got up and grinned. 'Hey. How are you?'

Her throat was tight suddenly as she smiled back, because it was the first time she'd seen him since that crazy dream-like day when she'd been given her shattering diagnosis; the day he'd practically scooped her up off the floor after his boot-camp session and sorted her life out for her, pretty much. 'I'm doing okay,' she said, and then, before she could start stressing out about the etiquette of public displays of affection with clients, she hugged him, albeit in a careful, still-sore-breast kind of way. 'So far, so good. How about you?'

'All the better for seeing you,' he said. 'I'm really glad you're all right.' They smiled at one another, then he cleared his throat. Down to business. 'So I got your message . . . ?'

'Yes. Thanks for coming in. Shall we go upstairs? I've booked one of our meeting rooms so that we can chat in private.'

He stuffed his music player in his back pocket, raising an eyebrow. 'Sounds posh.'

'Only the best for you, Lewis,' she told him. 'I've ordered us some coffee as well. There might even be biscuits, if we're lucky.'

'Now you're talking,' he said, following her up the stairs.

It felt slightly odd, meeting him on her turf like this again, as Eve the professional, when the last few times they'd seen each other the dynamics had been completely different. Understandably, she found it impossible to start off without acknowledging that fact. 'First of all,' she said, when they were both seated with their posh coffees and – yes! – very nice shortbread biscuits, 'I just want to say thank you. For everything. Honestly, Lewis, that day I'd found out the news and you were just so brilliant and capable and kind . . . I can't thank you enough.'

He was busy brushing crumbs off his T-shirt, but paused to shrug. 'You can,' he told her. 'You just did. It's fine, Eve. Really.'

'Well, anyway. You were a real friend when I needed one. I appreciate it.' She smiled self-consciously. 'You know, I don't want to sound like a cliché, but this whole experience has been one life-lesson after another. I've had to change my mind about quite a few things, namely that we're all good at different aspects of life. Me – I'm great at organizing. Less great on the old emotional-intelligence front.' She felt shy all of a sudden, to be getting so personal. 'You – you're the other way round.'

Now Lewis looked self-conscious, too. 'Aww, away with you. Anyone would have done the same.'

'They wouldn't,' she told him, ignoring his embarrassed expression. Life-lesson number 375: there was more to her clients than simply their accounts. Lewis, for example, was a complete pain in the neck when it came to his haphazard ideas of paperwork, but he was kind and sincere and hard-working. Maggie Doherty, her make-up-artist client, needed reminding at least three times before she might pay her bills, but it transpired that her sister had undergone similar treatment to Eve, and she'd sent a bunch of the most gorgeous white roses and a very expensive-looking lipstick to the office when she'd heard Eve's news. As for Enzo Fantini, who wrote a series of highly successful thrillers and was the most aggravating and unreliable client of the lot ('Bloody authors are the worst,' her boss Frances was fond of sighing in disapproval) . . . well, he had turned out to be incredibly generous, too, insisting on taking her for a very nice lunch when he found out she was ill.

'*Anyway*,' she went on, 'I've been trying to think how I can pay you back, after everything you've done. And to start with, I've drawn up a proper business plan for you, with a much better accounting system.'

He groaned and then laughed, splaying one hand across his face. 'Of course you have. I should have guessed. And here I was, thinking you might shout me a pint or something.'

'A pint?' she chided. 'This is way more useful than a pint. This is going to completely transform your business. It's the answer to all your prayers, I promise.'

'My prayers tend to be about winning the lottery, but . . .' He laughed again. 'Thanks for the thought. I appreciate it. Very generous.'

'So if you look here,' she pointed at her printout, 'I'm suggesting a new payment system; the software is very straightforward and will save you so much time. I've given you a sample balance sheet, so you can start recording your income and outgoings. You should look at creating your own website, maybe building social-media presence – oh, and my friend Laura, she's got good marketing and design contacts. I've put her details down here . . .'

'Thank you,' he said. 'That's fantastic, Eve. Really useful.'

'That's not all,' she went on. 'I loved your boot-camp session the other week, you know. Even though I was going a bit mad that day, I thought it was great. And that you were, too.'

'*Were?*' he repeated, raising a gingery eyebrow.

'Are, then. Whatever. I'll definitely be back, dragging some mates along too, just as soon as I can run without worrying that my boob is going to fall apart.' They both winced at the image and she hurried on. 'So my big question is: how do you feel about doing some similar sessions for a company team-building day? Like . . . *this* company?'

That was more like it: a proper pleased and surprised reaction this time, rather than groaning and teasing. 'Seriously?' Lewis asked. 'I mean – yeah! Absolutely. That would be really cool. That would be brilliant!'

She beamed back at him. 'Great. Well, maybe you could have a think about ideas and come back to me in a few days? My boss wants it all organized for the first week in September.' She handed him a piece of paper that she'd typed up earlier, 'I've put down the details here.' (Of course she had.) 'Numbers. Timings. Ideas for locations. Oh, and our budget, too.' She watched him reading the information, his face lighting up, and couldn't resist giving him a nudge. 'You know, all sorts of other companies do this sort of thing – there's probably hundreds of people like me across Manchester, looking out for activities that their office can take part in. I don't want to get ahead of myself but, you know, if we *do* go ahead and you enjoy running sessions for our team-building day, you could certainly look at branching out into this area.'

'Yeah!' He was wholly animated with enthusiasm now. 'Such a great idea. Aye, I'm definitely up for that.' He winked. 'I might even draw up a plan. Make some calculations. Write a *proposal*.'

She pantomimed shock and they both laughed. 'Better than a pint now, eh?' she couldn't resist asking.

He was grinning from ear to ear. 'Way better than a pint,' he agreed.

Chapter Thirty-Four

'Oh my God, you went to *Newcastle*! And what did he say? Was there a magical reunion?' India's eyes were bright with excitement but then she hesitated, the glass of wine halfway up to her mouth, as she struggled to decipher her friend's expression. 'Or . . . not?'

Laura fidgeted on the sofa. She had never done so much soul-searching since coming back to Manchester on Saturday afternoon. Even now, three days later, in their usual post-Pilates pub catch-up, her brain still felt exhausted. 'Well, we went and had dinner together,' she began, 'and that was really nice . . .'

It had felt cosy and intimate in the hotel restaurant; they'd been seated at a table beside a wide arched window that looked out over the river, and the staff were just the right mixture of friendliness and discretion. After a large glass of red wine, Matt started to relax and told her more about his new job, and how much he was enjoying the challenge, and what a great city he was finding this to be. Laura too chatted about office gossip, and how lovely her boss, Deborah, had been about the pregnancy, and how surprisingly generous the maternity package there was ('Why do you think I keep having more babies? It's not for my own sanity, believe me,' Gayle had quipped when Laura brought up the subject). And yet for all their pleasantries, neither of them could quite bring themselves to tackle the elephant in the room.

So what happens now?

What about us?

Is *there even an 'us' any more, or did we get past that?*

Matt's phone buzzed intermittently during the main course and he would check the screen each time, but ignored whoever was trying to reach him. The interruptions were starting to set Laura's teeth on edge – was it colleagues down the pub, that ravishing Elaine woman? Since when did Matt become so in-demand, anyway? Then, on her way back from the loo, she saw him speaking to someone in a low voice, the phone against his ear, his features creased in a frown. Uh-oh.

'Well, I can't really – I'll explain when I see you . . . No, because it's a bit more complicated than that. No! Look, I—'

Oh dear. Trouble in paradise. Then he glanced up and saw her hovering there, at which point his expression changed.

'I've got to go. I'll talk to you later. I'm not sure, but – okay. Bye.'

Laura decided to bite the bullet. What the hell. 'Was that Elaine?' she asked, sitting down and pretending to be interested in the dessert menu so that she didn't have to watch his face.

('Wait a minute. You were *pretending* to be interested in the dessert menu? You?' India asked sceptically at this point.

'Oh, all right, I *was* interested, but I couldn't concentrate because I was wondering what he was going to say,' Laura replied, pulling a face. 'May I continue?'

'Please do. What *did* he say?')

He said, 'Um. Yeah.'

There was a long silence. Matt wasn't exactly giving anything away. 'Are you and Elaine . . . serious?' she asked next, risking a glance over at him. His expression was one of agony.

'Well . . .' he began, then stopped.

'It's all right, you can tell me. I'd rather know.' Her hand stole down to her belly as if, ridiculously, she could cover the baby's ears, prevent him or her from hearing. *Don't listen to this bit, okay? I'm pretty sure your dad's about to tell me he's in love with someone else. Things could get tricky.*

'Well . . .' he said again and she felt her spirits sink. This hesitation of his in replying *had* to mean yes. Surely if it was a mere random fling, he'd have been talking the relationship down by now? He sighed. 'I do like her,' he admitted mournfully.

Bang. There went the door, slamming shut on her reunion hopes. 'She's very pretty,' Laura said, forcing herself to speak the words, her fingernails digging into her own palm. He was choosing Elaine, she could tell. The baby hadn't changed anything. *Sorry, kid. I appreciate this is not great for you. I'm trying my best here.*

'Yes, but . . .' he said wretchedly, and she knew that the 'but' in the rest of his sentence was her, his pregnant ex-wife. The flesh-and-blood problem. *Yes, but you're having our baby now, aren't you? Which kind of puts a spanner in the works.*

'You don't have to say it,' she told him, before he could elaborate. Mouth suddenly dry, she picked up the water jug to refill her glass, but her hand must have been shaking because she spilled it on the table, and then the waitress was back over there, fussing about with napkins, and the moment slipped away from them.

They ordered dessert and another glass of red wine for Matt, and then neither of them knew what else to say.

'I think we need to sleep on this,' Laura suggested eventually. 'There's a lot to mull over.' *Mull over*, like they were deciding which kind of dishwasher to buy. Meanwhile their baby was floating unwittingly inside her, tiny pale hands opening and closing like starfish in the darkness.

'Yes,' he agreed. 'You're right.' He'd never been one to relish a big emotional conversation, after all; give him a decision on white goods any day.

'We need to think about what we both want,' she went on, 'and try to work out how we're going to . . .' She gestured down at her belly. 'How we do this.'

'Yes,' he said again.

('Oh love,' India said, reaching over and patting Laura's hand as this was all recounted. 'Sounds kind of stressful.'

'Well . . .' Laura wrinkled her nose. 'It was and it wasn't. I mean, yes, unfortunately, there was no straightforward: "Hooray, let's get back together" situation. But I felt as if we were equal partners in the decision, like we both reached the same conclusion.'

'Which was?'

'So after dinner, I ended up going back to his place . . .' Laura went on.)

And far from it being the dank, mildewy hovel she had envisaged, 'his place' turned out to be a smart, clean apartment in a brand-new block ten minutes' walk away. 'Sorry about the mess,' he'd said, as he pushed open the front door and led her into the spotless, rectangular living room, but in Laura's eyes, there really *was* no mess, because there was hardly anything in there, bar a few pieces of furniture.

'It's so . . . minimalist!' she blurted out after a moment, because the walls were so bare, the room so devoid of any personality whatsoever, it might as well have been a hotel room. She thought of home – the house they'd shared for so long – with its cluttered shelves, the photos all over the fridge door, the jumble of vases and clocks and books that had always felt so homely, in her eyes. Had he actually hankered after this kind of sleek, pared-back space all along? A blank canvas, to match this new life of his?

Remembering her manners, she quickly added, 'It's lovely', because he now looked defensive, and she made a point of strolling over to the back window and praising the view.

('*Was* there even a good view, or were you just trying to bullshit your way out of hurting his feelings?' India asked.

The view was of some shop buildings and a car park, with the merest hint of river if you squinted, Laura told her, pulling a face. Guilty as charged.)

Matt went into the kitchen (small, plain, bland; as if he spent very little time there) in order to get them each a drink, while Laura headed for the bathroom. Her pregnancy bladder was calling, but as well as that, her feelings were see-sawing all over the place and she needed to sit down for a moment on her own and gather herself, even if just on the loo. What to do, what to feel, how to try and make sense of all this? she wondered, locking the door behind her and exhaling heavily. Back in the restaurant, things had been fairly amicable as long as they'd kept to safe subjects like work. For a short while, she'd almost been able to pretend they'd never split up in the first place – barring the few times when Elaine had made her presence felt, that was. But now she was here, in his flat – this place he'd moved into without her – everything felt different again. She was a guest in his new home, and this was proof, if she needed it, that he'd started another life that didn't include her.

She stared at his toothbrush by the sink and at the dark-blue towel on the rail, recognizing it as one from the set they'd received as a wedding present. (She'd kept the hand towel and the bath sheet; he'd taken the others.) His old maroon dressing gown hung from the back of the door, his favourite shower gel was on a shelf in the cubicle. Then she looked up at her own flushed face in the mirrored cabinet on the wall, feeling confused. Here were all his familiar things in an unfamiliar context. He really had left her. So what happened now? What did you do when your greatest wish came true, after your marriage had broken down?

('Please tell me you opened the bathroom cabinet,' India put in, leaning forward in anticipation.)

Laura *did* open the bathroom cabinet, obviously, because that was the done thing when you were shamelessly snooping round your ex-husband's new house. And there inside was . . .

('Oh no,' India groaned, when Laura paused. 'I wish I hadn't asked now. What?')

There inside was a MAC Ruby Woo lipstick, some facial cleansing wipes, a contact-lens case and fluid ('Matt has perfect eyesight, by the way,' Laura told India) and a second toothbrush. Right, thought Laura in dismay, quickly shutting the door again. Okay. So whatever was going on with Elaine, it was clearly serious enough that she was moving spare toiletries into his bathroom for all those nights she stayed over.

I do like her, he'd said guardedly, but they had clearly gone beyond holding hands and first dates. You didn't go leaving a fifteen-quid lipstick at someone else's house unless you were pretty sure you'd be back to collect it again.

Once she'd finished in the bathroom, Laura walked out in a daze. Sod it, in for a penny, in for a pound, she told herself and so, instead of returning to find Matt in the kitchen, she headed in the opposite direction in search of his bedroom. Let's have you, she thought. Let's just see.

The first door along the corridor led to a dinky white-painted spare bedroom with a single made-up bed against the wall and a proper view of the Tyne from the window, but very little else. Moving along, she opened a second door to find a larger bedroom, and her gaze swung around forensically, searching for further evidence of his relationship.

Item one: a baby-pink kimono hanging up on the back of the door.

Item two: the bed had been made up with a new duvet cover she didn't recognize – cream with sprigs of red flowers spangled across it. And a big scarlet heart-shaped cushion amidst the pillows. (Oh God. Sappy or what? Had *she* bought it for him?)

Item three: a box of condoms on one of the bedside tables.

Item four: a framed selfie of Matt with Elaine on a beach together, hanging above the bed.

Item five—

'There you are!' said Matt uneasily, appearing behind her. 'Got lost, did you?'

She jumped. 'I was just . . .' Busted. *I was just poking around behind your back.* 'Sorry,' she mumbled.

'It's cool,' he said, even though they both knew it wasn't. Not really. 'Shall we go back in the living room?' he suggested. 'I didn't have any peppermint tea, but there's blackcurrant, is that all right?'

She smiled at him sadly and he had the grace to turn red. Matt hated fruity teas. Tea was supposed to taste like *tea*, he always grumbled whenever Laura came back from the supermarket with anything other than Tetley. Was this blackcurrant tea further evidence of Elaine making herself at home? Undoubtedly. Had she infiltrated *all* the cupboards in this place? It was certainly starting to look that way.

'Brilliant,' she said, following him back down the corridor, then she couldn't resist adding a dig, just to remind him how well she knew him. 'You're having one yourself, are you, or . . . ?'

'I'm having a beer,' he told her. She wasn't going to catch him out that easily.

They sat down, perching uncomfortably on the slippery imitation-leather sofa, and she found herself cursing her own impulsive nature for coming here on a whim like this. If she'd listened to Jo, if she'd thought it through properly, she'd have done the sensible thing, which was to find out when he was next in Manchester and have the conversation on home ground. Now look at her, stranded in his quiet soulless living room, sipping her too-hot, not-strong-enough blackcurrant tea – *Elaine's* tea – and assuring him it was 'Perfect'. Was he sitting there thinking how much of a contrast this was, having Laura here instead of his new girlfriend? She bet the two of them had much cosier evenings together, feet up with a takeaway or watching some box-set on Netflix. Snogging on this very sofa. And the rest. It was enough to make her inch forward even further.

('But what about you?' India put in. 'How did you feel – were you still attracted to him? Did you still feel in love with him?'

Well, that was the odd thing, really. Because Laura did still have this reservoir of love for Matt deep down, as she suspected he did for her, after all their years together, so many shared experiences and good times. 'But did I feel like throwing myself at him and kissing him passionately?' she asked aloud, then shook her head. 'No. I didn't. I looked at him and it was more like looking at a brother. An old beloved friend.'

'You didn't want to rip your brother's clothes off?' India confirmed. 'Glad to hear it. Because there's a name for that. It's actually kind of frowned upon.')

India could try to make a joke of it, lift the mood, but it had been a sombre moment when Laura realized that the spark between her and Matt had quietly dampened and gone out. That she had moved on, too – not with another lover, but emotionally. Mentally. Maybe, she'd concluded, there was no point 'sleeping on it' as they'd previously agreed. The signs were all pointing in only one direction.

'Listen . . .' She took a deep breath, knowing that once she'd said this, there might not be a way back again. 'I kind of get the feeling that you and Elaine are making a go of things here, and that you're not really in a position to come back to Manchester just because I'm pregnant with our baby. That we've split up now and – well . . . that's not going to change.' She caught his eye and he looked down at his lap, twisting the bottle of beer around between his fingers. 'And do you know what? That's okay, Matt. It's really okay.'

'I feel so torn,' he confessed. 'The minute it sank in that you were pregnant, that I was going to be a dad, my instinct was to go straight home – Manchester home, I mean. To try again. And we still could, you know. If you really want that.

If you think that's the right thing, then maybe we should try. For the sake of our baby. Our child.'

Oh God, look at him, he was being so earnest and kind and lovely, it was sending her emotions into complete overdrive. But she had to be realistic here. They both had to face up to the truth. She swallowed hard. 'Part of me would love that too, you know,' she confessed in a low voice, because who *wouldn't* want their child to grow up with two parents, at the end of the day? It would have been the neat, perfect ending to the whole story.

But then she had to look away because she knew the next bit was going to take real guts to say. 'At the same time though . . . there's got to be more to it than that, hasn't there?' she ventured. 'We can't just get back together because of the baby. Would we be doing so otherwise, if I wasn't pregnant?' As their gazes locked, she shook her head, slowly and miserably, and knew that he agreed. And this was what it came down to: their sad bittersweet ending, which was messy and complex, which refused to be tied up neatly like a parcel. A tear rolled down her cheek suddenly. Even though she knew that they were being honest and true, that this was the right way forward for them, she wished it didn't have to feel like such an utter tragedy.

'Damn it,' he said, and she understood exactly how he felt, nodding wordlessly for fear that she might release an inadvertent sob.

(India's eyes were sparkling with unshed tears as Laura reached this part of the story, and she let out an unhappy sigh. 'Oh . . . *bums*,' she said sympathetically. 'Bugger and balls. Although bless him for being willing to give it a try,' she added after a moment. 'The fact that he still loved you enough that he would give up Newcastle and Elaine and his job to make a go of it, if you wanted – it's actually really romantic. In a platonic, brotherly, we're-over sort of way.'

'I know,' Laura agreed. 'He's a good person. We just got our timing wrong.' She remembered the look of relief that had flashed across Matt's face when she'd let him off the hook; proof that they had made the correct decision, but sobering nonetheless. 'I think we could have tried again, for the sake of it, and ended up resenting each other, and arguing, and both feeling that we'd made a mistake. So we've avoided that, at least.')

All the same, there was a genuine sadness between them, the recognition that they really had reached the end of the road as a couple. That wasn't easy to come to terms with. But eventually the conversation moved round to the baby, and what names they both liked, and what sort of grandparents their own parents would be (his: brilliant, hers: quite possibly dreadful) and then, by the end of the evening, he was saying that his job here was only for a year initially, he could easily transfer back to Manchester afterwards in order to be more of a hands-on dad. How he'd make sure that their child was a United fan, and that in time he'd take him or her to however many home games he could afford; and then they actually ended up having quite a laugh about which of their characteristics they hoped the baby might inherit.

('He'll be a great dad, I know it,' she told India. 'Kind and funny and dependable, exactly how a dad should be. Only . . . living somewhere else.')

Later on, Laura was just about to ask if she could crash out for the night on that single bed in his spare room, when she felt a ripple inside, a definite proper kick. 'Quick! Come here! The baby's moving,' she cried and, after a moment's hesitation, he shuffled along the sofa and put his hand on her belly to feel.

Thump. Thump. Boof.

'Did you feel it?' she gasped, eyes shining.

He nodded, his face full of wonder. 'Whoa,' he said, eyes wide and delighted. Then he grinned proudly. 'Proper good kick, that. Definitely going to be a goal-scorer, this kid.'

And then they were both smiling goofily at each other, and the baby was kicking again too, as if determined to join in the moment. Maybe, thought Laura with a sudden rush of hope, this could still be okay, they could make it work out after all. Couldn't they?

Chapter Thirty-Five

It was a Saturday six weeks later and one of those warm, golden early-autumn days where the sun fell like syrup across the city centre and you could still get away without wearing tights. Just about. If you walked quickly, anyway, thought Jo, picking up her pace as a cool breeze whipped around her bare legs.

'Table for four? This way. You're the first one here,' the waiter said, when she arrived at San Carlo a few minutes later. It had been her birthday two days earlier and she was meeting the girls for lunch in her favourite Italian restaurant, a new silver bangle gleaming around her wrist. The bangle was from Rick, as had been the breakfast in bed, and then, later, the bunch of flowers that arrived for her at the surgery, to a chorus of approving 'Ooh's from all the patients in reception. She'd been whisked out that night, too, for cocktails and tapas at La Bandera . . . God, he was good to her, that man of hers. She had felt special and loved the entire day.

'Can I get you a drink while you are waiting?' the waiter asked, as Jo sat down at the table.

'A glass of Prosecco would be lovely, please,' she replied. 'Actually . . . could you make that a bottle, with four glasses? Thanks.'

She smiled to herself as he bustled away again, returning with an ice bucket and a fat, misted bottle soon afterwards. Forty-three wasn't a particularly momentous kind of birthday, but Jo had been feeling recently as if maybe this was *her* decade. As a teenager and in her twenties, she'd often felt an outsider – too sensible to be debauched and outrageous at parties, never smoking or drinking much. By her thirties, she was settled down, playing house when others were going off travelling or throwing themselves into exciting careers, and she'd always seen herself as something of a misfit, never quite fitting in to large social groups.

Nowadays, she no longer cared so much about these things. Nowadays, it didn't seem to matter – she was just herself, Jo, and that was fine, actually. Perhaps deep down, she'd been in her forties all along, and her real age had only just caught up with her. Whatever the case, this was turning out to be a good decade so far: a decade when she was starting to feel, at last, as if she was in the right place at the right time; as if she had got to grips with who she was as a person, and what made her happy. Friends, laughter, sunny days, waking up with Rick, Prosecco at lunchtime – yes, all of those for starters today, and why not, now and then? Getting older was about recognizing such moments and enjoying them. Feeling comfortable in your own skin and making the most of life.

Blimey, hark at her, getting all philosophical and worldly-wise, she thought as she sipped her drink, bubbles fizzing in her nose. *Jo's Guide to Life: The Contented Decade. Chapter One: You're Fine, Don't Worry About It.*

'Hey! You're looking very far away there. Setting the world to rights?'

Here was Eve, punctual as ever, looking tired but smiling in a silky cerise blouse, a denim skirt and gorgeous knee-high brown boots. 'Something like that,' Jo admitted, standing up to hug her. 'How are you, love? How did you get on this week?'

'Good,' said Eve, slipping off her jacket and sitting down. Her radiotherapy sessions had finally come to an end and she'd just had her first normal week back at work. 'Do you know what, it actually felt blissfully relaxing to have full days in the office again, rather than chopping up the time with hospital appointments. I kept checking my watch, thinking I'd have to dash over there, before remembering I didn't have to any more.' She gave a rather self-conscious fist-pump. 'Yay.'

'Yay,' Jo echoed, pouring her a drink and passing it across

the table. 'And they've signed you off, it's all clear and looking good?'

'The treatment worked, yes,' Eve said. 'I mean, obviously I'll have to be super-vigilant for evermore now, and there will be loads of check-ups to come. But for the time being, it's over. Job done. It's still there in the back of my mind – and it's still scary as hell, but the stats are positive. And we all know how much I love stats.'

'Like you love life itself,' Jo agreed drily. 'I'm so pleased for you. What a relief.'

'It feels bloody brilliant, I can tell you. Like a millstone's been lifted from around my neck. Like the Grim Reaper has finally shuffled away to pick on someone else, and I'm no longer in his shadow.'

'Well, good riddance to him, and the millstone, and the whole wretched disease. Cheers to reaching the end and coming out the other side,' Jo said, lifting her glass in the air. They clinked them together and smiled. 'And Wednesday? How was that?'

The question made Eve look even happier. Since she'd gone in for surgery, Neil had apparently taken over a sizeable chunk of the chores around the house and been more engaged with the rest of the family. More to the point, Eve had relaxed about trying to do everything herself, and actually let him. From what she'd said to Jo, the cancer diagnosis had been a wake-up call to him, the realization of how precious his family were and, as a result, he'd renegotiated his workload, so that he could take every other Wednesday off, in order to spend it with his wife who just so happened to have Wednesdays off, too. 'It was blissful,' she replied. 'We went and had lunch in a pub, and then a lovely long walk together . . . It was such a treat, having a date on a weekday like that.'

'A fortnightly day off, just the two of you – it's a great idea,' Jo said.

'I know! Actual time to do stuff as a couple again . . . It's going to really change our relationship, I think,' Eve agreed, smiling. 'Even if we end up hoovering or sorting out the linen cupboard together, I don't mind. And he's starting to see the sense in my laundry system now anyway, so – what? What's so funny?'

Jo laughed because however relaxed and laid-back this new Eve claimed to be, she was never going to be *that* laid-back when it came to certain things. 'You know how to live, you guys. *Now* I'm jealous.'

To her credit, Eve was able to laugh at herself. 'I know. I'm a nightmare,' she agreed. 'But less of a nightmare these days, honestly. I've come to terms with the fact that life does have a habit of surprising you, however carefully you think you've got it all nailed down. Although my household systems *are* better: fact.'

'Eve!'

'I'm joking. Kind of. And anyway, our days are not all going to be about hoovering and laundry,' she added quickly. 'We're going to take it in turns to suggest days out, too. Be culture vultures at the Whitworth, or catch a matinee at the cinema – how utterly brilliant and outrageous does that sound, for a wet Wednesday afternoon?'

'I'm outraged,' Jo confirmed. 'Not to mention wildly envious. And seriously tempted to start bunking off on wet Wednesday afternoons myself, and all. But I'm glad for you. That definitely deserves celebrating.'

'There you are!' came a voice as they were clinking glasses for the second time, and along came India in a charcoal-coloured wrap dress with a chunky silver necklace, her long chestnut hair up in a soft, loose chignon. 'Hello, gorgeous ones,' she cried, arriving at the table in a waft of perfume. 'Happy birthday, Jo! You look fab. New haircut?'

They hugged one another, then Jo touched her hair self-consciously. 'New shampoo,' she admitted. 'This amazing frizz-free stuff, recommended to me by – wait for it – Maisie.'

India raised both eyebrows and her mouth fell open for good measure. Never one to use a single facial expression when there was scope for two. 'What, she suggested you try a frizz-free shampoo? Cheeky little so-and-so! God! I thought you two were okay these days?'

'It wasn't really like that,' Jo said. 'We were – well, I think you'd call it "bonding". We were bonding over shampoo ads on telly: you know, how cringey and awful they were, and actually having a bit of a laugh together.'

'This is Rick's daughter?' put in Eve, sounding surprised.

'Yeah! Turns out we have the same terrible taste in trashy TV programmes and everything,' Jo said, smirking as she thought of Rick throwing up his hands in exasperation when it turned out that both Jo and Maisie wanted to watch *Project Runway* on his flat-screen TV when some Champions League match was on at the same time. ('Outvoted!' Maisie had cried triumphantly, winking at Jo. That wink! That shared little victory! It had given Jo a genuine shot of hope for the future.) 'And anyway we were watching – oh, here's Laura. Over here!'

The story was lost and forgotten as Laura appeared, bump first, all rosy cheeks and swishy blonde hair, but the details weren't really important. The main thing was that a new truce had been forged between Jo and Maisie, a shift in the dynamic that meant they were no longer in direct competition with Rick for his attention. At first they had been polite to each other, rather formal, as if – for Maisie, at least – it was an effort to force civilities, but over the weeks they had begun to relax in each other's company. Maisie had dropped all references and comparisons to Polly, thank goodness. Jo was being sensitive about Maisie and her dad having time together without her in the room. What was more, Maisie had even come and confided in her on a few occasions, particularly when it came to bodily facts versus myths.

'I can't ask my mum this, right, because she'll totally think it's me; and I can't ask my dad, either, because he'll go ballistic and be straight into school, wanting to talk to the teachers,' she'd begun awkwardly the other day, turning pink around the ears. It had been just the two of them in the flat, Rick having gone out to pick up a Chinese takeaway for dinner. 'And what with you being a nurse and that . . . Well, basically, my friend had sex with her boyfriend when she was on her period and now she's worried she might be pregnant, but I said she can't be. Can she?'

God, who would be a teenager again, thought Jo as she picked her way carefully through the minefield each time, being honest and upfront, trying not to patronize or judge, not batting an eyelid even though, when she'd been Maisie's age, she'd still worn knee-socks and spent her spare time squeezing blackheads and reading pony stories rather than anything more risqué. All the same, she was happy to be there to answer any questions. Flattered, too, to be asked in the first place, taking it as a sign that Maisie respected her opinion on such matters and had deemed her somebody worth confiding in, these days. With that and their new-found shared love of tacky TV programmes . . . well. Empires had been built on less, Jo figured.

Laura was resplendent in a stretchy turquoise top that

showed off her burgeoning belly. 'Birthday girl! Did you have a lovely day?' she cried, putting a beautifully wrapped present on the table and taking a chair. 'You all look fabulous by the way. Have we got menus yet? Thanks. I'm starving.'

She looked so happy, Jo thought fondly, taking in her shining eyes as she let the others feel her bump and chattered on with her news. Matt had been down a week ago, turning up with a pushchair ('a travel system', Laura called it) plus a cot, and his dad had helped them paint the spare room a sunshiny yellow for the baby's nursery, too. Laura's in-laws were proving to be brilliant all round, as it happened – thrilled about their new grandchild-to-be and already offering to help out with childcare for when Laura decided to go back to work. More surprisingly, Helen had come over unexpectedly clucky too, a softer side of her emerging as she went with Laura to her midwife appointments, already petitioning to be there for the birth. ('Helen's a very nice name for a girl,' she'd remarked innocently. 'Just saying.')

Elsewhere, Laura's colleague Gayle had dropped off huge bin bags full of tiny baby clothes for her, claiming that her ovaries were spent, after four of her own children, and that Laura was welcome to the rest of her baby paraphernalia whenever she wanted it. And Jo, too, along with India and Eve, had made it clear that they were on hand and would be the most devoted of aunties. ('Honestly!' Laura had laughed. 'Everyone's making such a fuss – and I *am* grateful, truly – but it's only a *baby*, at the end of the day. I mean, how hard can it be?' Judging from the look that India and Eve had exchanged, Jo had the feeling her sister might be in for a small shock, come January.)

They ordered some food and then Eve entertained them with stories about the company away-day she'd recently organized, which had gone really well, with Lewis, her friend, turning out to be an absolute star performer. 'So much so that my boss, Frances, wants him to come in and do some regular sessions with us all,' she said. 'She's pimping him out to her other boss-friends, too, so he's got these hordes of middle-aged women panting after him right now. Cougar alert!' she giggled, making sexy growling noises.

'Hooray for all of that,' Laura said, hand hovering over the cheesy bruschetta. 'Anyone mind if I have the last bit? Thanks. Yum. This is *good*.'

'So Eve's out of the woods, and making dreams come true for hot young Scottish men – hmm, that sounds wrong, but you know what I mean,' Jo summed up. 'Meanwhile, I've negotiated a historic peace treaty with Rick's daughter; and Laura is . . . permanently hungry and going to get heartburn any minute, if I know her as well as I think I do.'

Laura made an indignant noise through her mouthful, then clutched at her heart dramatically, which made them all laugh.

'That leaves you, India. How are things? Laura said you've taken up the violin or something?' Jo finished.

India's lips gave a funny little twist. 'Well . . .' she began.

It had been the happiest of discoveries for India, having her own violin again and realizing that, after a somewhat rusty start, she could still play and that it made her feel wonderfully . . . well, *alive*, if that wasn't too melodramatic a word to use. She'd had a couple of lessons with a local teacher, just to remind herself of the basics, and then George had found some app on the iPad, which proved to be a treasure trove of sheet music, and she'd plunged back in, picking her way through some easy waltzes and minuets at first, before gradually moving on to harder pieces that took greater concentration and practice. She would pick up her bow, meaning just to have a quick ten-minute play, but somehow an hour would slip by; a heavenly hour when she lost herself utterly in the music, working on the dynamics and rhythms of a piece, marvelling repeatedly that she was playing again, that she had retained so much musical knowledge up there in her brain, as if it had been waiting patiently for her return all along.

Even better was the fact that, along with the music, came forgiveness – forgiveness of her own self. Because that was why she'd stopped playing in the first place: out of self-punishment, desolation at Alice's death, the conviction that she didn't deserve to be happy any more. But now those feelings had finally evaporated, leaving a space inside her to be filled with more uplifting things: listening to Tchaikovsky's heavenly violin concerto at top volume in the car and letting the emotions wash over her; plucking up the courage to join a local string group, as suggested by her teacher, and absolutely loving every rehearsal session; even thinking ahead to taking a teaching diploma of her own one day and moving into that field. It would be a damn sight more interesting than Mini Music, that was for sure, and, with that end in sight, she'd taken a deep breath and agreed to sell on the franchise at the end of the year.

'You dark horse, you!' Jo cried as India told her friends this. Well, most of it, anyway. They still didn't know about Alice, and all the complicated feelings she had tied up in that story, yet to be fully untangled. Perhaps that was a tale for another day, when she had dealt with it properly herself. She was getting there, though. Maybe in a few months' time, when there was enough distance between now and the events of the summer, she might be ready to bare her soul to them.

India smiled and wrinkled her nose as they started teasing her, trying to guess what other obscure hidden talents she might have kept quiet about ('British Scrabble champion?' 'Expert bonsai-grower?' 'Snake-charmer?'). Even if she had the odd secret from her friends, at least she had been honest with Dan now, and since her mega-confessional over the summer, they'd felt closer than ever: a good solid relationship cemented with trust. Determined to carve out some proper time together, the two of them had recently started a salsa class once a week – 'No arguing!' she'd cried, booking them in online. Despite his initial protests, he'd proved surprisingly adept at the old salsa moves, sure-footed and actually quite . . . well, seductive, to be honest. Was there anything sexier than being swung around the dance floor by your loved one, hips swinging suggestively, a twinkle in the eye? She could even forgive him for being better at it than she was. 'Still got it,' he'd say, winking, whenever the teacher singled him out for praise.

Robin hadn't been in touch again, which was a good thing; old hurts laid to rest. But she had received a letter from Mr and Mrs Goldsmith in reply to her own agonized-over missive, which had both comforted her and made her cry. *We understand*, Mrs Goldsmith had written in rounded black letters. *Thank you for explaining. We're sorry you lost your Alice, too.*

Goodness, why was she thinking such maudlin thoughts today, when it was Jo's special lunch, and there was so much water under the bridge since her own birthday celebrations? It was partly having recognized lately that this was life – this random collection of moments and experiences strung together like beads on a string: pain, happiness, doubt and wonder, accumulating to make one beautiful, messy, glorious necklace. Why had it taken her so long to realize that the dark and difficult times had their place there too, and actually served to accentuate the sheen of the more joyful ones? Living through pain and coming out the other side, braver and more resilient, was what being human was all about. Not that she was about to start pontificating on such deep and philosophical matters to her friends right now, especially when they'd probably all wised up to such things long ago anyway. Look at them today, enjoying and celebrating the good times! She was glad for them, so glad.

'Hey, do you know what I've just realized?' she said, a new thought striking her as the waiter appeared to take their starter plates away. 'Next time we have one of these lunches, for Eve's birthday, it'll be January – and there might be five of us here, if Laura's baby is the punctual sort.'

They all made excited squealing noises, and Laura instinctively put her hand on her belly, beaming. 'Oh my God, yes,' she said. 'How terrifying and brilliant. We'll probably both be crying, knowing my luck.'

'You won't be,' Jo said kindly.

'You'd better not be,' Eve put in warningly, which made them laugh again.

'Do you know, I've thought a lot about what happened when we were at Jean-Paul's for my lunch back in May,' India said suddenly. 'The crash and everything, that crazy slow-motion scene, how dramatic and scary and horrible it all was.' The others fell silent, their faces sobering. 'And do you remember, the head waiter came over to us and gave us brandy and he was like: You're the lucky ones, or something.'

'That's right,' Laura said. 'Which was a bit naff, I remember thinking – like, I actually felt guilty for being "lucky" when those other people . . . weren't.'

'Yes, and it was almost like a curse because, having been told we were lucky, I then seemed to have one piece of bad luck after another,' Eve put in. 'I totally went spinning off afterwards. I didn't feel normal again for ages.'

'Oh God, me too,' India said. 'I definitely lost the plot.'

'It was the shock,' Jo agreed. 'It affected all of us. How could it not?'

'Exactly,' India said. 'But looking on the bright side, I feel as if things have turned round for all of us again now. I *do* feel lucky. I've got you guys and Dan, and I'm starting to feel as if I might know what I want to do with my life at long last.'

'And I'm having a baby, when I thought I never would, and Jo's madly loved up with Mr Wonderful,' Laura added. 'We're just owning that bright side these days, basically.'

'And I must be the luckiest one of all, because I cheated Death,' Eve said, rolling her eyes, 'or at least, that's what it feels like. *Plus* I've got the best friends ever.'

India found herself sniffling just a tiny bit, to hear Eve being so uncharacteristically soppy. Today was going to be notched up as a happy memory, she knew it already, with each of them in a good place, equilibrium restored. And hadn't she just been thinking it was important to celebrate the best moments in life, when you didn't know what might be coming next? 'I think that deserves a toast,' she declared, filling their glasses, 'and definitely another bottle, too. To us – all four of us – and our good friendship, good health and good fortune. To being lucky ones!'

'To being lucky ones,' they chorused, clinking their glasses together across the table.

Their food arrived in the next moment and then the four of them were digging hungrily into bowls of steaming pasta and enormous pizzas and salad. The conversation turned to Eve's plans for a massive Up-Yours-Cancer dinner party, and how Rick was taking Jo off to Paris the following weekend as a birthday treat, and how excited Laura was for the baby, and then India was on her feet, with an impression of Dan doing a salsa move, apparently called 'Chica Brutal', which had them all in stitches.

A random stranger walking by just then and glancing through the window might have observed them there, faces flushed, all talking at once, and made a snap judgement, as we all do – that the four women looked happy, that they clearly enjoyed life. The passer-by might even have smiled a bit at India's unflattering impression of her husband sticking his bum out and gyrating, although it would have been understandable if they didn't immediately identify this as the Chica Brutal move.

And then, if this same stranger happened to walk a few streets further along, they might have gone on to glimpse Grace Taylor, too: lip-glossed and hair curled, waiting nervously on the corner for a first date with a boy from school, a boy about whom she'd gigglingly confide, 'He's so lush, Mum' to Eve a fortnight later; a boy she'd go on to date for two whole years, in fact right until she made the startling discovery that actually, do you know what, she preferred girls after all. Meanwhile, out towards Rochdale, Robin Fielding was parking outside a terraced house and plucking up the courage to see his long-estranged daughter, Chloe, for the first time in twelve years. Apparently she was six months pregnant and he was going to be a grandad before he was even forty years old, which had come as something of a shock. Still, he thought, turning off the engine and grabbing the bunch of white carnations he'd tucked in the passenger footwell, maybe he'd turn out to be a better grandad than he'd been a father so far. Second chances, and all that. And people could change, couldn't they?

Across the city, Lewis Mulligan and his girlfriend Katie were walking into the animal shelter, Lewis having decided to take the plunge and adopt Huxley, the rescue dog, as his official 'man's best friend'. Later that day, out on a long rambling hike together, Lewis would reach for Katie's hand and suggest, rather shyly, that maybe they could look at renting some new wee house together, make a real go of things, what did she think? And then they would both start laughing, because Huxley would choose that very moment to come bounding back up to them, tail wagging, eyes bright, as if he wanted to hear Katie's answer too, and then Katie would turn, smiling, to Lewis and say yes. *Yes!*

Over in Didsbury, Bill Kerwin was opening the door to his handsome son, Andrew, who'd decided he was tired of London and wanted to move back up north to be nearer his beloved parents. Miriam would cry with happiness, relieved that life could still offer up good surprises to her after all, while Bill would be so overcome with emotion that he'd have to blow his nose at least three times. And in a year or so, Andrew would be at work in his new veterinary surgery when a woman called Polly would come in for an appointment with her poorly cat. Andrew and Polly would both be surprised to experience a little frisson as their eyes met, and he would think, *That is a very attractive woman.*

Elsewhere, Helen Nicholls was patting her hair in front of her hall mirror, before grabbing her purse to go to the shops, little knowing that she was about to clatter her trolley into a man in Tesco, and that they'd laugh and get chatting and he would turn out to be the absolute love of her life. For real, this time. And she'd never have to say the words 'Bloody men' again, for as long as she lived. Well. Perhaps very occasionally, when he forgot to put the bins out, but she'd say it affectionately and forgive him straight afterwards, because that was what you did, when it was the absolute love of your life, right?

Further away still – miles away, in fact, in a semi-detached house in Nottingham – a woman was opening a letter and clapping her hand to her mouth in joy because she'd been offered her dream job, working as a senior consultant in Wythenshawe Hospital, Manchester. And in years to come she would be sitting down in a small, hushed room at her clinic, opposite Eve and Neil Taylor, and she would clear her throat and say . . .

But these are all other stories, of course – and there are many different endings to a story. Besides which, our random stranger, walking past the San Carlo restaurant on this particular lunchtime in September, wouldn't have been aware of any of those other possibilities. They'd simply have glanced through the window, seen Jo, Eve, Laura and India together and thought: *Those women look happy.*

And they were.

Afterword

Whenever I start a new book, one of the most enjoyable decisions I get to make is where the action will take place. The backdrop can be every bit as important as the characters in terms of establishing a tone, and I always love spending time in the area, so as to find the locations for scenes and soak up the atmosphere.

For a novel that is so much about friendship, Manchester felt like the perfect choice of setting, as it is one of the friendliest cities I've ever been to. I stayed for a few days in early 2017, pounding the streets and looking at everything through my characters' eyes – where would they live? Work? Drink cocktails? – and everyone I spoke to was unfailingly helpful and full of suggestions. (Thank you, if you were one of those people!) It had been some years since I'd visited, and I found myself appreciating anew the handsome old buildings, the bustling streets, the rich sense of history and of course that excellent Manc humour. I did end up fictionalizing some places within the novel, but I hope the city is still recognizable to those in the know.

Since I finished the first draft of this book, Manchester has suffered heartbreak and horror in the form of a despicable act of terror. Like many others, I was sickened when I saw the news, and can only imagine the shock and pain that the victims and their families have suffered. But what a tribute to the city's spirit and character, that there were so many resulting acts of kindness and compassion, and that people came together in solidarity, refusing to be cowed.

Thanks for having me, Manchester. You're fabulous. I can't wait to come back.

Acknowledgements

Thanks to the wonderful team at Pan Macmillan – Caroline, Anna, Sarah, Katie, Jez, Stuart, Alex, Kate, Charlotte, Jess and all the fabulous sales reps. It's a great pleasure to work with such a creative, dynamic and frankly lovely bunch of people.

Thanks to Lizzy Kremer, my agent, for support, advice, laughs and some fantastically posh cakes. Thanks also to her hard-working colleagues at David Higham.

Thanks to Caroline Styles who patiently answered all my medical questions. Any mistakes are definitely mine.

Thanks to my family for the cups of tea, encouragement and love, and for reminding me that there are often more important things in life than chapter-wrangling.

Finally, thanks to my readers, who have been so funny, friendly, supportive and kind over the years. I really appreciate all your nice messages and comments. Hope you enjoyed this book!

Find out more
about Lucy and her books at
www.lucydiamond.co.uk

Or say hello at her Facebook page
www.facebook.com/LucyDiamondAuthor